# THE PRISONER OF PARADISE

BY THE SAME AUTHOR

*Reef*
*The Sandglass*
*Heaven's Edge*
*The Match*

STORIES

*Monkfish Moon*
*O Colleccionador de Especiarias*

# THE PRISONER OF PARADISE

## ROMESH GUNESEKERA

B L O O M S B U R Y

LONDON · BERLIN · NEW YORK · SYDNEY

First published in Great Britain 2012

Copyright © 2012 by Romesh Gunesekera

The moral right of the author has been asserted

Bloomsbury Publishing, London, Berlin, New York and Sydney
50 Bedford Square, London WC1B 3DP

A CIP catalogue record for this book is available from the British Library

ISBN 978 1 4088 0426 1
10 9 8 7 6 5 4 3 2 1

Typeset by Hewer Text UK Ltd, Edinburgh
Printed in the UK by Clays Ltd, St Ives plc

www.bloomsbury.com/romeshgunesekera

Helen

*A hope beyond the shadow of a dream.*

John Keats

# 1825

# MAURITIUS

# PART I

# Chapter 1

THE BAY was bright and blue. On the edge, the small island port lay basking in the sun. Only in her dreams had Lucy Gladwell seen such dazzling light spilling from the sky. The anchor dropped to a rousing cheer: the drumming of fists and feet, firkins and kilderkins, kegs and clogs and pails and mops rolled around the ship. After five months at sea, at last the *Liberty* had arrived.

'Take hold of your hat, my dear,' Betty Huyton warned her niece, as Lucy was lowered over the side in her chair. 'You would not want that in the water now, would you?'

Never mind the hat: there are gurnards, dragonfish and sharks lurking beneath the surface, Lucy thought, and here I am dangling in mid-air, close to tipping into the sea.

Before the apparatus had come to a rest, Lucy jumped on to the narrow skiff waiting to ferry them to the pier. Mrs Huyton pinned her from the top deck with a sharp grey eye. 'Over to the left, Lucy, if you would?'

A pale, clean-shaven stray moon bobbed up next to her aunt. 'Steady, Miss Gladwell,' the Revd Archibald Constantine beamed. 'Be careful.'

Lucy rolled her eyes and blew out a silent riposte. Would the two of them never stop?

She wiggled towards the stern and lodged her case against the side; on top she balanced a small gift box neatly tied with a red ribbon. Hat clamped tight, she sat feeling raggedy, coars-ened by salt but stuffed full of sea dreams, excited to be on the brink of a new life. There was never a landfall as sweet as this.

Under her feet she could feel the squelch of fresh algae. Slipping off her shoe, she dug a toe in and prodded a damp strand shaped like a pod of peas. A bubble burst. Delighted she popped another and another, until the boatman behind her hooted, 'Fou, fou.'

Lucy spun round, unnerved.

'Watch out,' her aunt called out. Too late: the small ribboned box flew overboard.

The boy at the other end of the boat, young and jaunty, blacker than any of the lascars on board the *Liberty*, laughed and hooked the package with his long sharp crook. Little jewelled fish jumped over the breaking white caps and loose spray. She wished she could too, and swim carefree slipping the straps and strings of silly custom and fusty decorum. One day, she thought. But not yet. Instead she wiped the box with the hem of her skirt and wedged it more securely by her side. Why was it, she wanted to know, even in this new age, so much harder for a girl to go to sea than a boy?

A moment later the chair was hauled back up and Mrs Huyton seated herself, wrapping the folds of her pelisse robe in a prayer; her brittle elegant face stiff against the sea's nips.

While everyone else fussed over her aunt's regal descent, chintz unfurled, parasol in tow, Lucy trailed her innocent hand over the side and touched the sparkling water; she wanted to tickle open the sea and taste its soul. She wanted much more from the world than could be found within England's pebbly shores. When she put her fingers to her lips, she nearly swooned. Here at last was the true nectar of the south she had so longed for: strong and sweet, amniotic and electric, laced with a hint of the immortal.

Then the oars dipped in and they scudded landward. The dark blue seas she had conjured out of the verses of Byron, turned with each scoop into gorgeous China jade. Lucy felt she was on the crest of a wave.

'Look, Lucy, there he is. Your Uncle George.' Betty Huyton lifted her hand.

On the quayside, between a pile of hemp sacks and several tufty coops of floundering chickens, Lucy spotted an Englishman flicking his cane at a small dumpy supplicant. A goat nibbled at his feet. George Huyton tossed some coins into the man's straw hat and came forward: a squarer, heftier figure than Lucy remembered from his hasty visits to her grandfather's house. He had been a busy, secretive man who carried boiled sweets in his pocket. She had been twelve years old, the last occasion, and the plum-coloured bonnet that she had to wear, much to her disgust, flared again – inside her head this time. Uncle George had whistled low and chided her mother for hiding Lucy's lovely brown hair from the autumn light. As he stopped in front of her now – a shadow from the past – she thought there still was an odour of singed wool about him from the night he burnt his coat, reaching across the Danish candelabra to fondle a ringlet. She met his eyes bravely. Her mother's death, and her father's two years before, she had borne as though she alone must spin the earth and renew the day. Her slim frame, like her buoyant face, gave no hint of grief or trouble.

'My dears, how marvellous to see you. Lucy, welcome to your new home in our Mauritius. I must say I had no idea you would have grown to be so delightful a young lady.' He tucked the baton under an arm and held out his large hands. Lucy stepped forward and curtsied, uncertain how to react now that she was, as she understood, a young woman in her prime. She held out her dry hand. A flurry of wings scumbled the air behind her; loud tipsy seabirds wheeled about. He had her mother's sharp blue eyes. Imperial, she thought, and impervious even to this southern sun. 'Well, my dear. Most pleasing, is she not?' He winked at his wife.

Betty Huyton looked at him in surprise. 'She is indeed most delightful company, George. We have had a very good voyage and are quite ready to be settled at home. I trust my Ambleside is in good order?'

'Of course, my dear. Not only the house, but the whole of the island awaits you in splendid order.' He chuckled, pleased with his expansive declaration. 'And you too, young Miss Lucy Gladwell,' he added, giving Lucy's warm hand, which he still clasped lightly, a little shake.

Flustered, she offered him the damp parcel steaming as it swung on its limp ribbon. Her tongue finally slipped a knot. 'I am sorry, sir,' she said awkwardly, suddenly hotter inside than out. 'It fell in the water.'

'What is it?'

'Cuban cigars, sir. Purchased from the Strand.' She glanced at her aunt anxiously.

8

George Huyton broke into a laugh. 'Salted now, are they? Never mind, dear Lucy, they will soon dry out here.' He shook the box. 'I must thank you. I hear these have become quite the thing in London.'

A cow ambled past, udders flapping in the muggy air. The jetty rocked. A troupe of stevedores began to unload a barge full of grain, chanting something that was incomprehensible to Lucy as they threw the sacks from one to another. The goat, now tethered short, bleated as a couple of mangy mongrels closed in, sniffing at the sea-rot oozing out of the nearby carts. A bunch of men in rags shouted and hustled the sailors. One brawny lascar, tattooed with serpents, flung a rope across. His mate, already ashore, quickly fastened it to a bollard while others clamoured for the packets and trunks. Lucy shrank back, amazed at the abundance of bare limbs. Black and brown. The sun lit Mrs Huyton's face as she struggled with her parasol. 'You too, Lucy. You must take cover. The sun in the tropics is really quite fierce.'

Further along, down on the beach, a gang of dark men chained to each other hummed and droned, breaking rocks; their picks and hammers swung and clanged, crumbling the edge of the island, eroding its contours.

Lucy stayed close to her aunt, clinging to her arm. Her quick eyes counted them. 'Why are those men in chains?'

George Huyton cocked his head. 'Convicts, my dear. Shipped over from India. We have rather a lot of them here. They can be worked in the sun, you see.'

'Are Indians dangerous, to be chained so?' Lucy asked. Aunt Betty had not mentioned any such threat; nor had any of the officers in her conversations at sea. To her thinking, there was no purpose in punishment, nor profit in restraint. At nineteen, her keen young mind was charged by her heart.

'Criminals, Lucy. Robbers and suchlike. I dare say a few have attempted murder, but we have them under complete control here. Nothing to worry about.' He smiled unctuously. 'How do you find our climate, Lucy?'

'Balmy, Mr Huyton.' She tried not to choke. 'Warm and pleasant,' she added. In her uncle's smooth, smiling presence Lucy steadied herself and quickly began to see again some charm in the scene, both in rhythm and colour, despite the desperadoes and the abomination of their labour.

'Good breeze out here but the town, I am afraid, can be rather clammy. Ladies of a delicate nature prefer not to linger, especially in the midday. Therefore direct to your aunt's little haven we shall proceed. Ambleside forthwith.' He offered them each an arm and steered a path through the tangle of bleached lobster pots and fishing nets. 'And, Lucy, do call me uncle. We are very easy-going out here in our sunny little colony.'

Stepping between sacks of rice and corn and stacks of seaworn crates reeking of fish and seaweed, between carts drawn by ponies and men with glistening shoulders and shanks and shaved heads, the trio at last reached the gates where a crowd of hawkers thronged around, ululating, spitting and crying out. '*Voulez-vous baguette?*' shouted a man with a handkerchief knotted over his head, looking directly at Lucy. Another taller man with a pitted face barked out, '*Ananas, ananas,*' and tipped forward a basin of jagged sweet-smelling yellow fruit. George Huyton wielded his cane with both hands. 'Get away with you. Out. Out.' Two young brown boys dodged him and brandished bundles of green twigs. Mr Huyton hissed at them and turned to Lucy. 'Every time a ship sails in, the lads go mad.'

A few yards away a machete flashed down and cracked open a nut the size of a child's skull.

Lucy felt something lurch inside as though she was still on a rolling deck, mid-sea. Her senses crashed into each other, pitched from the unfamiliar to the unimagined. Her aunt had told her the island would be like nothing she had ever read about: that the noise, the heat, the brightness was beyond the grasp of pretty English poesy. Lucy had laughed at her aunt's untutored warnings: beyond Thomas Moore? John Keats? But now, jostled from eye to ear, she was awestruck.

'What is it they want?' she asked her uncle. One of the boys pressed closer and she attempted a smile, captivated by the youngster's beaming brown face.

'Money, my dear. They would like to sell you sugar cane.'

The boy pulled a rough, round, stubby stem of about eight inches out of his bundle.

'Is that what it is? What does one do with it?'

Her aunt's face twisted in distaste. 'The locals chew the little stump for a sweet, but there is nothing a lady could make of it before it reaches the mill.'

Mr Huyton chuckled. 'I have seen some young damsels here stir their tea with a strip.'

'Creoles, perhaps. But not a proper English lady.'

Another young lad thrust a wild hairy fruit up in the air. Mr Huyton pushed him back with his cane. 'Scat, you little rascal. Out of the way.' He swung the cane back and forth severely.

'Uncle, be careful.' Lucy grabbed his arm. 'You might hurt him.'

He laughed again. 'Not to worry, my dear. These little fellars are quite used to canes.'

'You cannot beat them, Uncle George?' She pulled at his stick.

He held fast, grinning at her determination. 'Not without reason, my dear. Of course not. We are proud to run a very enlightened administration here, as you will see. They are a happy enough bunch, even though the young scallywags are sometimes a little wayward.'

'But they mean no harm, surely. Look how they smile.' She tried again, wanting to draw them close. Life for a barefoot boy, whether here or on the banks of the Thames, could not be easy. She knew, despite her recent misfortune, that she was by virtue of her upbringing a creature from a world beyond their imaginings. She wanted to change that and mingle with them all.

She was about to open her purse, but the boys suddenly left and crowded around the shiny Revd Constantine who was bouncing behind with two fellow passengers, a proud Company man of considerable appetite, and a permanently crumpled clerk from Calcutta, neither of whom had had very much to say out at sea.

Beyond the black iron gates, tipped with what looked to Lucy like barbed arrowheads, an avenue of enormous muscular trees stretched out into the swirling heart of the town. The dark rippled trunks billowed into a canopy of mossy foliage and an unexpected display of delicate, effeminate red flowers. Everything was so jumbled, she thought, as though some primitive painter's palette had been cut to pieces.

'Is it not flamboyant, Lucy?' her aunt exclaimed. 'It does revive me to see such lively colour again.'

'Was it gloomy at Cape Town, my dear? Did you not visit the Company gardens you so admired last time?' Her husband kicked a spidery creature out of his way. A tarantula, Lucy shuddered. Or a giant spider crab?

Her aunt squinted down at it. 'I am afraid we were both a little indisposed at the Cape and did not venture out of our room very much.' Unperturbed, she sighed. 'But the view was magnificent from our window.'

A vivid green streak split the sky. Startled, Lucy asked, 'Is that a parrot?' She could not believe so much could flit so swiftly from imagination into actuality.

George Huyton's leathery lids drooped at the corners. 'Although we have no vast hinterland, we do have flowers and birds galore, dear Lucy. You will find a profusion of them at Ambleside.'

When her aunt had recommended, six months earlier, that Lucy travel with her to Mauritius, Lucy had imagined a journey into Eden. She had often dreamed of places woven out of popular tales and romantic verse; she longed to cross the deserts of Arabia, enter the palaces of India, the ports of the world from Turkey to Malaya where her father had sailed. The hints of those naval expeditions in his clipped sentences, the smell of foreign spice that seeped out of his sea clothes, mixed with the exotic stories in her grandfather's library, made the prospect of a voyage to the latitudes of the south impossible to refuse. Not that she felt she had much choice: the loss of both parents, and the family house to creditors from Maidstone, had left her hollow and homeless. She had lived all her life in the same house – converted by her grandfather into a paper mill and printing shop – which she had peopled with figures from her books more real than all her neighbours. She had no young friends – her schooling was by her mother – but she had never been lonely; not until the house was stripped of all its familiarity that last awful week before her aunt arrived to rescue her. She was not a girl who cried much, but she did not know where to go. 'Although there is no immediate inheritance, my dear, your Uncle George had been entrusted by your grandfather with sufficient capital – insulated from the business – for you to receive a decent annuity at your coming of age in two years' time,' her aunt had explained. 'Until then it is only right that you should be in the care of your nearest kin, even if in the further reaches of our new empire.'

Lucy had pinched the skin between her fingers, as she had as a child, to feel the tiny sensation grow and draw her into the real world. 'I am not afraid, Aunt Betty. I want to see foreign lands. My father chased the corsairs into the Mascarenes. I'd like to see something of what he saw.' She had blinked, suddenly conscious of how little he had left for her, how thin a membrane of memories she had of a father in her childhood.

Her aunt had smoothed the lace around her neck. 'That would have been when the Navy was after Robert Surcouf, my dear. It is a much happier place now.'

They had boarded the *Liberty* soon after and Lucy had watched England's shoreline recede; within weeks Africa reeled into view. Now, on this breezy tropical island, far from the grime of metropolitan chimneys and the flurry of battered Thames ferries, she found a fresh crisp world rejuvenating her senses.

Mr Huyton beckoned his coachman and one of the

carriages resting under the trees jerked into life; a pair of pretty bays with braided manes whinnied and started towards them.

'Is this a new vehicle, George?' his wife asked. Her thin lips curled in, determined to control any hint of further surprise.

'Only on loan, alas. I asked Denis to get it from the official depot for today. I thought we should welcome Lucy with appropriate fanfare. Poor old Bonnie is lame and would not do.'

The carriage came to a halt and the coachman climbed down. '*Bonjour, madame.*' He touched his hat.

'Good morning, Denis,' Mrs Huyton replied in English. 'I am glad to see you in good health.'

Lucy took the seat facing forward so that she could observe the island unfold before her.

'We shall ride through the town, Lucy, and you can see what a splendid place it is.' Her uncle patted her knee as though she was still his twelve-year-old niece.

Lucy flinched and swallowed hard.

'Very oppressive,' Mrs Huyton warned. 'The heat can be most intense. We spent our first four months in this town, Lucy, and I was constantly suffering from headaches. I thought it might be the cholera that had been rampant before we arrived, but it was apparently the sea breeze that was damaging.'

'Is the sea breeze not cooling and a welcome palliative, Aunt Betty?'

'Not in Port Louis, my dear. Here it is regarded much like the *mal'aria* of Italy. Poor Denis, for example, who you would think from his complexion alone to be thoroughly habituated to the climate, is, on the contrary, often quite dizzy with it.'

A gust of warm air blew a trail of spent pink blossom across the road like tumbling butterflies.

Mr Huyton laughed. 'Betty, you must not prejudice her so. Port Louis is a fine town, Lucy. You will enjoy it. We have a colourful market, excellent establishments, a theatre, a race-course, and many splendid gardens.' He cast his hand outside the confines of the carriage like a lord outlining his grounds. 'There are some very eligible colonists on the island, you know, and they keep the place in excellent order.' The dimple in his prow-like chin deepened as he smiled. 'I think you will find we have quite a lot to offer, provided you avoid the sun at its peak and are not averse to French.'

The carriage turned off the fine, straight, tree-lined avenue and started up a winding irregular road where row upon row of jalousied shops teemed with people of many shapes and hues – a variety not to be found in Lucy's native Bridleton or even, she thought, the heart of multifarious London. From head to toe, a display of diversity she had not imagined avail-able outside the realm of fantasy. She sat forward, peering at every new thing. They passed a palanquin with veiled windows, carried by two glistening men dressed as if in an illustration from some penny romance: maroon headbands, open vests – no other upper garments – and pleated cloths wound around their lower extremities approximating to pantaloons. 'They run barefoot,' Lucy exclaimed, admiring their manly grace.

'Only the French would wish to be joggled so,' Betty Huyton sniffed. A quick rummage in her silvery green reti-cule produced a small fan which she used to clear the air of the earthy odour from the perspiring trotters.

16

George Huyton diverted their attention by pointing out the commercial buildings pressed against the hill. Many had been built in stops and starts by the haphazard smiles of mercantile fortune: crooked lines jammed together, stone steps stumbling out of kilter; ramshackle shops and erratic emporiums competing colourfully against each other, cutting margins and shaving corners. 'A thriving sector.'

'Where are the residences?' Lucy asked mystified.

'The English quarter is higher up. Some fine houses there, but your aunt was very keen for us to reside out of town. You see, Lucy, she requires a garden big enough for a lake even though she hardly even paddles.'

'A pond, George. Please, only a pond. And to be a little distant from the prying eyes of this enclave of cast-offs. One needs good, clean air, my dear. One really does. You will see when you reach Ambleside why I was adamant we should move out into the country.'

Lucy hid a smile. All through their voyage her aunt had invoked the house as her remedy for any adversity; a refuge without parallel. A place of great spiritual and material safety.

Leaving town, the carriage began the climb into the surrounding hills with small bumps of increasing intensity. Once it had attained a good height, Mr Huyton commanded the coachman to stop for Lucy to enjoy the view. A groggy cock crowed in the calm, hazy air. The leaves of the acacia and sour fruit trees on the hillside stirred lazily and the long yellow grass below them lay low in a daze.

George Huyton stood up and drew in a loud lungful of air. 'Look at that, my dear. Is it not as pretty as any rosy Canaletto in the galleries of London?' He seemed to Lucy like the

Colossus of Rhodes that her grandfather liked to toast. A man feeding the torch of liberty kindled within.

The town did look picturesque with its fretwork of gardens and frothy green boulevards, the neat white squares of porticoed buildings facing the wide blue satin sea, its population mere dots and barely distinguishable.

'It is as pretty as a summer's day.' A fair match, she thought, gamely, to any *vedutista*'s attempt to depict the beauty of human endeavour on nature's intractable canvas, or something like that.

'This is truly an isle of opportunity,' her uncle declared. 'You must remember that, Lucy. We are lucky to have wrested it from the French.'

'Not luck, Uncle. Surely not?' Lucy's eyes darted back to him. 'I have heard my father say the battles were hard and without valour all would have been lost.'

'Quite right, my dear. Pluck, not luck, was indeed our advantage. Your father was a most valiant man.'

He launched into a disquisition on how the British victory in 1810 ended ninety years of French vacillation; and how the subsequent Treaty of Paris marked the start of a great enterprise where control of the Cape, Ceylon and Mauritius, would ensure that trade with India would be for ever British and noble. All the while, Lucy was tussling with the misery of her father's last months.

For a girl who had believed her father to be a commodore, his creeping disintegration had been difficult to bear. One strut after another seemed to give way in the slow collapse of a man's frame. It was the force of an argument written by Major John Cartwright calling rightly for a union between moderates and radicals for the purpose of reforming Parliament, that drove Lucy's father to Manchester one fateful summer's day. Lucy remembered the frown on his face as he left the house so disturbed he even forgot his hat. He returned from Peterloo – where the Manchester Yeomanry and the cavalry had unleashed unprecedented violence against the protesters – injured beyond repair in eye, chest and knee. Thereafter, only stirring to warn her, 'Life, my child, is full of bloody traps.'

On board the ship, two degrees south of Madeira, on the other side of Africa, Lucy had asked her aunt why she had left her native West Indies. 'Was it misfortune, or love, or marriage?'

'They are not incompatible,' her aunt had smiled. 'I wanted something more than a life on a plantation. But England was too cold for a colonial like me.'

The sky had been grey like the wing of a giant seagull at Lucy's own departure. And then, as they cast off, gulls were suddenly everywhere, crying. The Thames was so wide, she could barely see the shaved empty slopes of Kent as they sailed. 'I also am glad to have left England. I do not want to go back to the cold. To ice in my bones. To winter. No more chilly winds for me, or snow-sifted hedgerows. I want to be warm for ever too, Aunt Betty.'

The first time she had read in Mr Moore's golden book of *Lalla Rookh* the bold assertion that 'nothing could be more beautiful than the leaves of mango-trees and acacias . . .' she had believed it, and now, within hours of landing, she discovered she was right to have done so.

# Chapter 2

L UCY CAUGHT a glimpse of a white house through the trees; then the carriage turned into a wide gate flanked by two sleepy stone lions and Ambleside came enchantingly into full view: a grand house with a sweeping grey roof and graceful white pillars reposing in sunshine, dimpled with gabled windows and elegant shutters on the upper and the lower floors. 'It's like a poem,' she whispered to her aunt. Appearing, she thought, like an image rising up from a page. A large shade tree protected the front verandah and the gardens spread beyond it in a carnival of colour. The shrubs newly trimmed; the grass verge fanned by the slow wide murmurs of a well-oiled scythe.

The carriage came to a stop; the horses jangled their steely bridles almost out of time. A young boy, dressed in white, appeared from around the side of the house. He wiped his hands on a cloth, which he slung over his shoulder, and kept his head bent low but his eyes were eager as he came forward. He held open the door for Mrs Huyton.

'Thank you, Muru. I am glad to see you in your smart new uniform. Very good.'

'Welcome home, ma'am,' he replied in a sweet, soft, airy warble, hiding his teeth with his fingers.

'Lucy, this is Muru, the boy I told you about.' Mrs Huyton turned back to him. 'Miss Lucy will be the lady who will instruct you in your daily duties, Muru, once she has settled in.'

On board the ship, when her aunt had spoken to her about servants and duties, Lucy had imagined a swarm of industrious, efficient, faceless workers ministering to the needs of a queen, and even now, floating in the casual grandeur of Ambleside with the scent of honey in the air, the full impact of her aunt's words did not immediately sink in.

'Welcome, missie,' the boy beamed.

Lucy smiled uncertainly. A boy? Instruct, her aunt had said. How, in this land where even the flowers run riot?

Mr Huyton followed Lucy out of the carriage. 'I asked the boy to arrange the ivory room for Lucy, as you suggested in your letter, my dear.'

'Ivory?' Lucy felt she was ascending a throne.

'Our landlord is a Hindoo, you understand. A man from India, and in your room he has had a small ivory frieze done of a parade of elephants, I suppose to remind him of his homeland. Rather handsome, I must say. The inlay, I mean, Lucy.'

'Your aunt was not very taken with the idea of it being called the elephant room, so ivory room it is.'

The boy, Muru, followed the conversation with great intensity, as though each word he heard needed to be placed in a mental dictionary and treasured.

'I look forward to it. I think I should very much like an

elephant parade in my room.' Lucy whirled around a host of imaginary beasts and husky handsome mahouts.

'I trust you will find much to content you, Lucy, at Ambleside.' Her aunt held out her parasol. Ivory-handled, Lucy noted.

The boy collected it as though even his smallest movement had been carefully drafted from a manual at Hampton Court.

Inside the house, Lucy found a spaciousness unusual in English houses of her acquaintance and an abundance of bare polished surfaces: floorboards, sideboards, uncovered chairs, naked tables of various sizes and shapes, an impressive gleaming wooden staircase. Before the stairs, on a heavy carved central table, stood a large brass urn with an extraordinary display. Tall ferns, clusters of vegetative spears, broad leafy blades, and a carefully arranged girdle of green, yellow and pink succulent lanterns shaped like claws and beaks. The presentation had the appearance of solidity and permanence: Lucy could not imagine any component wilting. It was completely at odds with the frail temporality that would typify an English bouquet of spring blossom.

'Splendid,' Mrs Huyton breathed from behind. 'Muru, you have surpassed yourself. I think this arrangement is positively the best you have ever done.'

Muru lowered his head bashfully. 'For your homecoming, ma'am.'

Mrs Huyton stroked one of the hanging succulents. 'Touch them, Lucy. You will find these flowers quite unlike anything you would have come across before. Heliconias. My favourites for indoors. They last for simply ages. I love the rose, of course, but the rose in my view is a flower best kept uncut to enliven the garden.'

The cold, waxy, hard outline of the beaky blossom felt inorganic to Lucy and yet seemed to assert a hold on life far more tenacious than that of any ordinary sentient creature. Sharp-edged, with angles and corners – nothing delicate – but exuding a disturbing sensuality. The tip pricked her finger.

'It's like a flower in armour.' Lucy pulled back, leaving a speck of red to bloom like a fairy queen before a florid knight.

'For the eye to love, not the nose. A very refined line, and a gorgeous colour, don't you think? Barely any scent at all. Now let us get you settled, Lucy. When you are refreshed you can come down for some juice and I will introduce you to the household. There is much for you to learn here, Lucy. You will find there is rather more to be done at Ambleside than at any house or cottage factory in Bridleton.'

'I am sure, Aunt Betty. Ambleside is a palace.'

The ivory room was peaceful: white walls, white linen, a line of miniature elephants with mirrors on their ears; two large windows open to a vast lawn. Lucy could make out a wooden rooftop on one side, beyond a boundary parapet, and then a swirl of jealous treetops circling a gem of still water. Further on she could see fields ready for planting and cropped by jungle. The browns and greens darker and brighter, more dramatic than she had ever seen in England. Everything poised: the air heavy with warm scent, light crackling in burnt yellows. Salt and sugar swelling every bud; birdsong and whistles whirling.

Looking at it all, she felt overwhelmed.

Her hands trembled a little as she unpacked her books and put them out on the shelf next to the writing table: *Endymion*, *Rasselas*, *Oroonoko* and, especially, Thomas Moore's *Lalla Rookh* – a delectable romance of a princess on an Eastern journey, in love with Feramorz the poet, a prince in disguise. A heroine who vicariously experiences adventures in verse and finally finds happiness in a royal Cashmeer garden. Her balm. These, and one Mary Wollstonecraft, were the precious few possessions she had been able to hide before the bailiffs had arrived; familiar cloth-bound printed worlds where her imagination could soar, but remain always within grammatical safety.

Facing the window, she took a moment to open one; she wanted to read a few lines aloud and let the syllables seep into the floorboards and make the place her own. " 'In some melodious plot of beechen green and shadows number-less . . .' " She recited the lines while small red ants danced lightly on the windowsill.

At the edge of the lawn below, a boy, skinnier and blacker than the one whom she had met on arrival, crouched cutting a trench with a small hand spade. He moved sideways on his haunches, like a man-sized stick insect, a few inches at a time scraping at the ground. A dark skin, she was beginning to understand, was in this land always yoked to servitude. She could hear the boy's blade strike the earth, crunching and slicing the soil in a metre of its own. The sound of a grave being dug. But it wasn't, she corrected herself. This was a garden being prepared to renew itself under the instruction of a cultivated lady. A fly buzzed and bumped against the window frame chasing the vapour of warm paint.

In this sunny southern island bursting with colour and full of the sounds of singing and buzzing, gurgling and rustling, whistling and whispering, Lucy felt undeservedly lucky. She had opened a new page and discovered the romance of her most treasured poems igniting directly the fuses of her imagination. Surely it was a place of deliverance?

A faint tread outside the door interrupted her thoughts. Muru entered barefoot, with a flask of water and a glass on a wooden tray.

'Missie, this to keep in the room. Madam says you find it very thirsty here, not like Inglan.'

She smiled and reached to collect the tray. 'Thank you.'

'No, missie. I arrange.' He swung it away from her and went over to the side table. 'Also, madam says I must show this.' He drew back a curtain at the far end of the room to reveal an elegantly shaped tub. 'For bath. You call, missie, and I bring hot water. Towels here.' He patted a fresh white pile on a small cane chair next to it. 'You like it now, missie?'

'Now?'

'Nice and warmy like madam likes?'

He looked eager. But could she give him such an onerous task? A gangly boy with skinny fingers and a dark bursting mouth? Suppressing her disquiet, she nodded. 'I should like that, Muru.' She leaned towards him, keen to find some midway bond. 'I should like that very much. Warmy, like madam.'

He was a good boy, she thought to herself. Gentle and lovely. I cannot ever be severe with him. Although they were of a similar age, she wondered if the disparity of circumstance between them was perhaps insurmountable. They must inhabit such different worlds: she carrying an England of the mind, he an India of his ancestors – an enormous jungle of elephants and tigers. Could they have anything in common, other than the plain fact that on this island they both breathed the same natural air? It was a question she would leave for another day.

When Muru had gone, she unpacked more of her things. She did not want him, or anyone else, going through her clothes, any more than she wanted them leafing through her books. She liked her room. She realised she liked all she could see of Ambleside. She wanted to capture every fleeting thought and sensation evoked by her ivory room, the house, the garden. Would pen and journal be enough? So much teemed around her. She could not keep still. She wanted to be everywhere. Her garden in Bridleton had been less than a tenth of the size of this nabob's lawn: in summer full of foxgloves and dog roses that ran wild and then, for the rest of the year, offering nothing but tiny red hips and sprays of dead wood until the snowdrops appeared. Mother had been the only gardener and that too only in fits and starts when spring goaded her with yellow buds, or a windfall of bruised apples made it imperative to prepare for a change of season. Here it seemed growth was perpetual.

She went downstairs and made her way to an entrancing pergola of scarlet pendants. She found a stone bench hidden in the shade. The boy who had been working outside had disappeared; probably dragooned into heating the water, she thought. To her surprise, it pleased her that so much effort might be expended simply to satisfy a girl's whim; perhaps that was as it should be. Part of the requirement of attaining womanhood in a foreign climate. She sat down and opened her journal, pencil poised, barely able to contain her excitement. This air, this sense of promise was something she had once thought she would never feel. It had always seemed to her to be in a place beyond her physical reach, hovering at the edge of a dream.

Hardly ten minutes had passed when she heard footsteps crunching the pink gravel of the drive like clamshells. She peeped out of a gap in her bower and saw a tall bold man striding up to the house as though he owned it.

He wore a tasselled shawl, stippled with gold, over a blue silk jacket, and a sash around his middle as if he were Surcouf himself, king of the corsairs, sailing into his Mauritian lair with his ruffles all puffed, having plundered the seas of legitimate colonial trade. He cast a dark eye over the Arabian jessamine and the pots of spotted maidenhair wavering on the front step. 'Ahoy!' he called out, and followed it with an odd guttural foreign sound that she immediately imagined might be heard in the ports of Taprobane, or some such improbable place. The leather creaked as he swayed in his tall black boots, craning his neck and sniffing at the damp air as though he were testing it for a hint of spice, or the oils of Oudh, or had caught the perfume of Pandora hidden in the sandalwood box next to her bed upstairs.

Mesmerised, she closed her journal and sank deeper behind the tinsel leaves, safely out of reach, while yet keeping him in sight and within earshot.

Plucky Muru put down his pail of steaming water and hopped out to meet the visitor. 'Sir?' He chewed his thumbnail.

The visitor studied the boy and then said, 'I must see Mr Huyton. I have a let-*tar*.'

He broke the last word and stretched out his dark neck as if he wanted to retrieve the final syllable even as he spoke it.

Muru told him that the master had gone to Port Louis on business.

'Mr Huyton is gone?' The visitor sucked in his upper lip. He rocked his head as though his thoughts needed rearranging and crossed his fine arms. 'In that case, make sure he receives it immediately upon his return.' His English was spoken in the manner of a schoolmaster translating a foreign idiom; as if he must twitch all the muscles around his mouth to get the right word in the right place.

Muru held out both hands. 'I give it, sir. Thank you, sir.'

To Lucy it was as though they were in a fandango. Muru, small and eager like a wren, taking the female part; the iridescent visitor, a peacock fanning his tail.

'Be sure Mr Huyton receives it immediately upon his return.' The intriguing visitor raised his little finger, adorned with a ruby set in Indian gold. Why his little finger like that? she wondered. Perhaps it indicates a warning in his country, or is a symbol of a secret pact between persons of a common Asiatic heritage.

He tipped forward and cupping a hand around his mouth, whispered into Muru's ear.

A moment later, Muru scampered up the steps and placed the letter on the brass table. A light breeze blew a few leaves across the verandah. The visitor turned, crunching more innocent gravel under his heel, and contemplated his footprints pressed in the fragrant ground. He cast another pensive look at the house, and then set off as if back towards the ocean.

Lucy emerged and called Muru over. 'Was that our Hindoo landlord?'

'Not Mr Badani, missie,' he grinned. 'No, that is a new gentleman from the bad land of Ravana. Not the king, but like him.'

'What did he want?'

'The *masta*. He left a letter.'

'I saw him whisper.'

'Wanted to know, who in the house. I say, "Only madam *inside*." True no, missie?'

'Yes,' she said. 'But please, Muru, you must not bite your fingernails when you are greeting visitors.' Aunt Betty, she knew from her acidity at the Captain's table on the *Liberty*, was very particular about such things.

He looked dismayed. 'Sorry, missie.' He picked a small white flower and put it in his pail. 'Bath ready soon, missie.' He hurried back into the house.

Lucy stopped on the verandah and examined the envelope. It was addressed in the most exquisite writing: the flourishes in perfect balance. A small work of art. The letter was sealed and there was no prospect of an accidental glimpse of more penmanship: the vellum heavy and of good quality and the dollop of crimson wax as handsome as a king's.

Later, steeped in a warm aromatic bath, strewn with rose petals and perfumed with drops of lemon grass, gazing out through the open window at the high blue sky, Lucy began to sense just how different her life in the colony might turn out to be. Not only for the fragrance in every breath of air, the brightness in every colour, but because the acoustics of life itself seemed different: sounds of fluttering everywhere, the pounding of the sea a dozen miles away. Her heart like a drum in a symphony of sensualities.

Could he really be royalty?

On the long voyage over, Lucy's aunt used to say to her that maintaining a house in the tropics was harder than running an empire. 'You will have a troop of helpers, my dear, but they need serious management. I have a bible of housekeeping, from my mother's dear friend Mrs Anscombe, that will become your bedside reading, but nothing compares to learning by experience.' She had found it amusing when Lucy had said in the dining cabin that her ambition was not to be a housekeeper of any sort. Not for her a life of neatly folded towels and cedar-scented cupboards, of regimented cutlery cabinets and sentinel measuring jugs, of household efficiency and laundry management. 'I will not be bound by dusters and rosters. I have my books and my poetry, Aunt Betty.' She had crumpled her napkin defiantly. 'I want to live the life of a free mind.'

'Would you prefer to be a governess than a wife then, Lucy?' her aunt had asked, puzzled.

'No,' she had said then as now, half woman, half girl, sinking down in the warm scented water, playing at Princess Lalla slipping through the pages of a dream. 'No, I want to break out of purdah and dance with dolphins and peacocks in a world of my making.'

The long table on the verandah facing the lawn was laden with a medley of squashed pastries and wayward biscuits. Sunlight spread like thin butter along the edge of a lemon cake. Mrs Huyton sat at the far end. To Lucy she looked like a great egret come home, her weary wings folded, surveying a land she had made her own.

'Do sit down, Lucy, and have a nibble. Are you happily settled in your room?'

'It is a lovely room. I had a warm bath with flowers floating in it.' Even in her most extravagant fantasies, she had never imagined anything like it.

'Very good, my dear. It is necessary in this climate to bathe frequently. You will find there is no harm in it whatsoever. And dear Muru is very efficient, and quite a sensitive little artist. Now, how about some juice? You could try the very sweet sugar water that will be offered to you everywhere on the island, or some lime juice which I much prefer and is rather healthier, in my opinion, for an Englishwoman's complexion.'

'As you recommend, Aunt Betty.'

Her aunt picked up a large shrouded glass jug and poured out a small cloud. 'You may like to add one or two lumps of sugar to it, which is permissible.'

'Do you grow it in the garden?'

'Good heavens, no. But we do purchase it directly from Monsieur Champney's mill once a fortnight. You should see the block, my dear. We will do a little tour of the kitchen, and indeed the house, in a moment. You must meet all the staff before we draw up your responsibilities. There is much to learn here, Lucy.'

'Is Uncle George not joining us?'

'Your uncle is an inordinately busy man. He takes his office most seriously.'

'Is it secret missionary work?' Lucy asked excitedly.

'Why on earth would you think that?'

'Something you said to the Reverend on the ship.'

'I was teasing the old cabbage. No, it is as I have told you. Your uncle is part of the colonial administration here. No secret mission. His responsibilities are to do with the roads. Therefore he is constantly out inspecting this or that culvert in the country. But you will find, my dear, that our life in this colony is different in almost every aspect from what you might be used to in England.'

'We did not set much store by convention in our house,' Lucy retorted. The freedom her grandfather had given her, growing up in his house with her mother, was her most formative experience. He had been convinced that only custom and tyranny diminished men and women; not the lack of intelligence. 'We are all born equal but are made unequal by the design of scoundrels,' he had often warned her, and had urged her to be independent of mind and circumstance.

'I understand, my dear. Your grandfather was rather unconventional. But in this house we try to make a marriage of different conventions to suit, as I say, the climate. Your uncle has an English breakfast but dines late in the evening, after dark, as is the custom here. He is rarely at home for luncheon.'

'I am not fussy about meals, Aunt Betty,' Lucy said lightly. 'I'd be happy with an apple. I can fish, you know? And I have roasted a trout on a spit like an American Indian.'

'Well, Miss Pocahontas, why not make a start with some banana cake. I don't think you would ever have had that in England, my dear.'

'Never.' Lucy grinned. 'There is enough for an army here, Aunt Betty. Are you expecting the cavalry?'

Her aunt laughed and explained that one always had to make provisions for the household. One did not merely feed oneself and one's husband – there were the houseboys, the gardener, the coachman, the cook and unexpected guests to cater for. 'It requires more than mere aptitude, my dear. One must apply intellect and foresight to ensure efficiency in a proper house.'

'There was a vi;itor here earlier,' Lucy said, inexplicably flustered at the thought. She quickly piled her plate and started to eat.

'I expect that was Henri Benoît, our little French friend with his pot of honey.'

'More Indian – I mean Eastern Indian. He brought a letter for Uncle George.'

'Oh, yes. We do have Indians, too, to cater for. Was it Mr Badani, then?'

'Muru said it was not the landlord.'

'Not another Malabar merchant. Never mind. Come, Lucy, have something to eat. After that I shall show you around.'

Lucy picked out a tiny striated seed from her piece of cake. 'I have to say I did not anticipate so very grand a house, Aunt Betty. Or such fancy neighbours.'

'At this latitude, my dear, everything becomes somewhat magnified. I do love the house. Although now owned by a Hindoo, it was built by a Frenchman and greatly improved by an Englishman. It is a very special place, don't you agree? And the grounds give one so much scope.' Mrs Huyton took Lucy by the hand and they descended on to the lawn. 'The African violets are exceptional, don't you think? Mr Pottinger, at the nursery, keeps a good stock of both local and imported species but I do take some satisfaction in ordering seeds from England before he does.' Her face bunched naughtily. 'That *Eugenia uniflora*, for example. Or pitanga, as they say. From Brazil, would you believe, via Brompton Park, of course.'

They crossed the lawn. 'The gazebo over there is very pleasant for enjoying the garden, but if you would like to dream of larger vistas, we have a hut down on the terrace at the bottom that is utterly charming.'

Lucy could sense again the great chaos of vegetation pressing in from the periphery: tall palms and busy trees surging in all directions, a jumble barely held at bay by the garden's line of pert cannas and ornate arches. She went to the terrace steps. She could feel the sap bubble at the edges. Her aunt was close behind. 'Even your uncle admits this is most uplifting. When you find the management of the house is too much on top of you, I recommend you come here, my dear, and revive your faith in nature, if not, alas, human nature.'

As imperiously as rounding the Horn, they slowly made their way to the back of the house. 'We have, as you can see, a number of outhouses. In most Creole residences you will find the entire house arranged thus, in pieces as it were. At Ambleside we have a compromise or perhaps, you might say, a conjunction of the English and the Creole. Over there is the cookhouse, although you will find that Josephine does most of her cooking out in the yard at the back. Then, on that side, you have the servants' quarters, partitioned to separate the functions of sleeping and washing. There is room for rather a lot of them. More than we can afford to keep right now.' She removed a small lace handkerchief from under her sleeve and patted her forehead. 'Good English-speaking ones are a rare commodity at any rate.'

'Commodity?'

'It is only a manner of speaking, my dear. You will find that Josephine and the boys are very close to me, but out here, in the East, there is a certain brutality to our language that is difficult to prevent.'

'I noticed, even on board the ship.' Lucy paused.

A short, round black woman came to the doorway of the cookhouse. '*Madame, non zonion, non ziromon.*' She struck the side of her head and expostulated a string of other slippery sounds. Words Lucy could not decipher, let alone understand.

'This is Josephine, our cook, who is forever out of onions. I asked her to make some soup for you but she says there is not a single onion left, which I am afraid I find difficult to believe.'

'Good afternoon,' Lucy said with a shy smile, hoping to catch more of the warmth she had seen in Muru. The black woman responded with a shrug and a *bonjour* rather more sibilant than the French Lucy was familiar with, but the curl around her lips ran rapidly across her face.

Mrs Huyton spoke with deliberate precision describing Lucy as her niece from England.

'Inglan?' Josephine's face dropped in dismay.

'Is something wrong?' Lucy asked, worried at her reaction.

'*Française, mademoiselle?*'

Her aunt intervened. 'Lucy, my dear, do not give in. Keep to the English. She must learn to speak properly.'

Lucy felt confused by the competition. 'Is Josephine French?'

'That is neither here nor there, my dear. We are English.' She turned to the cook. 'Only English, please, Josephine.'

'No onions, no cook, madame.'

'There is a delivery due this afternoon. Mr Huyton has bought a goat and a great many provisions. You ask Denis about it.'

'Tcha, madame.' Josephine's cheeks flapped. 'I donno what you do.' Lucy thought the cook's whole flabby body rippled like a sea.

That evening her aunt provided Lucy with her initial commission. 'I am going to start you off, Lucy, with full responsibility for all the indoor plants, including those on the verandah, the flower arrangements and the room cleaning. Muru, of course, will do what is required, but you must oversee it.'

'You mean watch?'

'No, my dear. Remember what I said about an officer at sea? You make periodic checks and ensure the crew work to standard.'

'But Muru will know what to do better than I do.'

'He is a clever boy, no doubt, but you are the mistress of the house.'

'Mistress?'

'Well, I am. But you are the one I will put in charge. In due course all the housework the boys do – Muru and Jacob – will be your responsibility. The supervision of the kitchen

36

– with that battleaxe Josephine – and the garden, with my Tusa, I shall retain.'

On the voyage Lucy had tried to imagine this graduated society where a man's life was circumscribed by his superior's desires, and a woman's by the remit of her allowance. She had sat on the poop deck and tried to steer her thoughts towards a colonial life, but instead of the faded threads of naval splendour, her thoughts had always flown to bazaars and baksheesh, sultans and sheikhs, kings and camels. Fate and romance.

The birdsong next morning laced the sky in a tapestry of sound; melodies that burst the octaves she had always thought were the limits of harmony. Cocoroos punctuated by coos and tweets; a chorus of pips and purls and curls and caws. Sunlight streamed in through the slats of the shutters. Lucy flung them open. The sun reached deep below her skin like the tongue of an inner flame. The air uncoiled. She wanted to shed her nightclothes and fly out of the window.

Instead she slipped into her lightest summer dress and went downstairs to the morning room. A glass glistened on the table. She sat and sipped the bitter-sweet juice. In the mirror opposite, Muru bobbed up and down, skating as it were, from side to side in the hall. She turned around and knelt on the sofa to watch: he was indeed skating on a peculiar husk-like semi-sphere tethered to his foot.

'Polishing, missie,' he replied when she asked him what he was doing. 'Every day must do this floor, or that, or that. You like?'

'Very good,' she nodded. 'You do a good job with that contraption.'

'Coconut, missie. Not contraption. You have not it in Inglan?'

'England. Quite so, Muru. We do not have such things in England.'

'Not in Le France, also, I think.'

'I don't know, Muru. I imagine not. In any case we would generally use a brush, or a cloth, for this task.'

He grinned. 'You, missie? Do polishing? Not the servant?'

Lucy explained that at her house in England they had not always had servants. Her grandfather hired help on a different basis. The floors were not polished every day – he would have seen no sense in it. Her father, however, did bring something of his naval roster to the house when he took over, requiring the treatment of wood once every season. A decrepit old sailor would turn up and wax the place as though it were a yacht. A sailing boat, Lucy explained to Muru.

His eyes, full of rushed hopes, were quite beautiful, she thought.

'A sailing boat, missie? I like a sailing boat.'

'You like to sail in a boat, Muru?'

He shrugged. 'If I get the chance, missie. I only see them in the harbour. Never from inside.'

'But you must have come on one from India.'

'No, missie. No sailing boat.'

'Really?'

'I come from here, missie.'

It had not occurred to her that he might have been native to the island. She had assumed everyone on the island was a migrant. 'Where were you born, Muru?'

'Inside town, missie. East side.'

'What about your parents? Are they still in town? Do you have brothers and sisters? I would love to meet your family.'

He shrugged again and smiled. 'Must finish floor, missie.'


'I left a card at the Willcox house and at Champney's to inform them of your return, my dear,' George Huyton said to his wife over his evening tipple.

'Did you remember to turn down the corner?'

'Of course I did, but I don't quite see the point. Everyone in the district must be aware by now that we have a young lady in the house.'

'Madame Benoît did drop in with Henri this morning.'

'In that case, I expect the whole island would be informed by now. You will have quite a stream of callers.' He rubbed his hands noisily and whistled. 'I shall make myself scarce and leave you, my dear wife, to contend with the panting hordes you have set haring.'

'No, George, we will not have callers until next week, after May Day. Only then will it begin in earnest.'

'Is there a May ball?' Lucy looked up.

'We have a fair on Saturday,' her uncle replied. 'The season begins after that. Balls, races, parties. There is a surprising variety, I am told.'

'If you can bear the bustle of the town.'

'Do you not like the season, Aunt Betty?'

'At my age, I am happier in my garden. But at your age, my dear, regular social intercourse is something of a necessity. This year, we have the honour of the Prince of Ceylon and his retinue attending, which will be an improvement on Henri and company.'

'A prince?' The visitor she had seen, vivid as ever, sprang into her mind. He was a prince.

George Huyton snorted. 'He is a villain to be exiled here, Betty, with his co-conspirator and an interpreter. You must not mistake his incarceration for a royal visit.' He patted his niece lightly on her arm. 'Nevertheless, my dear Lucy, you will find May Day in Port Louis quite an entertainment.'

# Chapter 3

IN THE two years since her father died, Lucy had found that her life was a constant flux of unsatisfactory emotion. One moment she was no more than a child full of uncertain promise being prodded and pulled by fancy and fear; the next, a creature brimming with will and determination with nowhere to go. A young woman for whom the world's mystery lay only in her own heart, and for whom the truth of human travail deferentially gathered its cloak and hid.

Her mother, wrapped in despondency, had been of no help; Lucy had no bearings with which to navigate the confusing reactions of the world outside to her intrusion. When strangers turned their heads towards her, she knew it had something to do with her looks, but could only respond with indifference.

Now, at Ambleside, she found a welcome order: everything and everyone had an allotted place and the trick of adult helmsmanship seemed to lie in latching on to the pattern. Her aunt's coaching throughout the long voyage, and the Reverend's sermons on the morality of civilised man, gave her, she felt, a good chance of gaining some solid ground.

George Huyton unfolded the letter and looked at it yet again. He had been carrying it in his pocket for two days not knowing quite what to do with it. 'An infernal nuisance, these bloody chaps from Ceylon.'

'The Prince?' Mrs Huyton raised her eyes from the hoop of cloth on which she was working. Lamplight spun off the curved shiny wood and was swallowed by the ring of darkness around the house.

'Not him. The other fellow. Don what's-his-name.'

'I thought it was the Prince who came with the letter.' Lucy tried to sound calm.

'He has no English. It would have been the interpreter. But I don't understand why on earth that ass wants to get involved in piffling little petitions now.'

'If he is a scrivener, it must come naturally to him,' Mrs Huyton suggested.

'Nothing is natural with donkeys like him except discontent.' The harshness with which he spoke frightened Lucy. Mr Huyton took a sip of wine and sloshed it around his mouth, staring out at the garden. She followed his gaze. The rain had stopped but had left a sheen on every leaf that caught bits of moonlight like shards of broken glass; the lawn was a carpet of crumbled stars. She turned to her uncle. What was out there that so inflamed him? She watched him rub his right temple with two stubby fingers as though he was shooting himself in the head with a pistol. A small red patch spread across his forehead under the pressure. The

42

whole of his face seemed hewn out of solid planks of flesh, square-cut at every level with the nose jointed in, the chin dovetailed. The sawn-off brow suggested that even his eyes might be in square sockets and it always came as a surprise to her to discover his irises were round shots, bright and blue like her mother's. 'He does no good meddling with the labourers,' he added. 'And what interest does the fellow have in a temple? I am sure he subscribes to no religion whatsoever.'

'Are they not spiritual?' Lucy asked, surprised.

'This Don fellow knows nothing. The troublemaker is that dark little rascal on Champney's estate. Always agitating. Should have been chucked off the boat with a cannonball between his legs.'

'A cane cutter?' Mrs Huyton was unruffled.

'Used to be. Then he got himself a foothold at the mill. That young fool Champney – the son, Antoine – thought the bugger was good at whipping the others into line. He does not understand how diabolic these scoundrels are.'

'I quite like that young Antoine.' Mrs Huyton glanced wickedly at Lucy. 'Among the French he is by far the most advanced, don't you think? He helped the Hindoos organise a festival, did he not?'

'He had no choice. They are yet unconverted. The mill would have been sabotaged otherwise. Our man, Badani, showed him how to buy them off. The boy has no grip on the place, but old Patrice "Champs" is desperate to make a bloody planter out of him.' George Huyton continued to catalogue the injustice of Bourbon wealth in the age of Britannia, while his wife quietly filled the gaps in her embroidery.

She was making the outline of an orchid in purple thread. It was not an activity Lucy could ever indulge in, although her aunt had tried to convince her of its virtues many times. 'Out of nothing, my dear, you will find you have made something quite pleasing. There is no harm in that, and perhaps even some modest good.' A very pretty image for sure, Lucy thought, but to no particular purpose. Although she had to acknowledge the imitation had a permanence that a natural flower which blooms and wilts did not.

'If you were to speak to him, George,' Mrs Huyton suggested, after a lull, 'perhaps it could be resolved quite easily?'

'Speak to whom? Champney?'

'Don Lambodar, my dear. Your petitioner, the interpreter. We should invite him to tea.'

'Have you gone completely mad, Betty? What a preposterous idea.' He smoothed down the edge of his lapel as if to curb the vagaries of his heart.

The following morning, Aunt Betty returned to the subject. She said she had heard that the Prince's cousin, Mr Asoka, apparently accompanied by Don Lambodar, had entertained the Lawson family with Ceylonese verse and song.

'The two of them are nothing but charlatans,' Mr Huyton declared.

Muru brought in the eggs and bacon just then and Mrs Huyton allowed a light smile to hover about her lips. 'I must say Don Lambodar certainly dresses very handsomely as he goes about.'

'A dandy, if you ask me. A buffoon and a dandy, those two.'

'Quite.' Mrs Huyton inspected the bacon on her plate. 'Muru, is this from the new parcel I ordered?'

'Yes, ma'am.'

'It looks a little thin, don't you think?'

George Huyton stuffed a whole rasher into his mouth and champed at it like an angry horse. 'It has been cut for Continentals, my dear. You should have a word with Baxter. You must not let things slip.'

Lucy, who had no interest in Baxter the butcher, tried to imagine the royal interpreter at his breakfast instead. Being tropical, would he eat fruit rather than meat? Or perhaps, like Muru, a spiced fish stew with that pungent green herb and black pepper she had noticed bubbling in a pot yesterday?

'What about this Prince?' Lucy asked, moving on to imagine an even grander figure than the visitor she had seen.

'What about him?' He spread an enormous dollop of the new guava compote, made by his wife, across a thick piece of charred bread.

'He is not a buffoon, is he?'

George Huyton choked back a laugh. 'Good heavens, no, Lucy. He is as wily as they come. Ran rings around our chaps in Colombo, they say. Cunning old fox, that fellow. Could not have the crown in his own country, but this exile has made the scoundrel almost a king in a much pleasanter land. I rather think he must be glad to be here.'

'Surely not, my dear. It must be very hard for him to be removed and kept apart from his people.'

'But it is a jolly good life, Betty. A jolly good life for a turn-coat. The chap could not be trusted, you know. They say he was ready to lead a rebellion against us just because he was not given the title he wanted. The title, mind you. A mere word on a piece of paper, or papyrus, or ola or whatever the hell it is they use out there. They lack loyalty, these blackguards. You cannot depend on them, however obsequious they may appear to be. No sense of honour, you see.'

Lucy could not restrain herself. 'Why should the Prince not fight for his rightful place?' she blurted out. 'After all, what were we doing there, crusading in his Ceylon? Or here for that matter? He is the Prince of his people, so why should he not have his title?'

Mrs Huyton, unlike her niece, thought for a good long while before speaking. 'I remember you did quite a song and dance yourself about Percy's knighthood, when you were in London. Rather piqued you, *Mister* George, if I am not mistaken. For at least six weeks you were –'

'Don't be ridiculous. Not the same thing at all, Betty. Not at all. Moreover, Lucy my dear, you should understand that every ruddy Harry in India claims to be a bubble-headed prince. It means absolutely nothing. This fellow has no people, Lucy. Just rabble that can be divided anyway you like.' He pushed aside his breakfast plate and gulped down his grapefruit juice. 'Anyway, no time for this idle chatter. I must be off. Clarke is building a new bridge with his sepoys and the damn fool has done it all wrong. Alignment is not one of his strengths. What is the point of him speaking Hindoostani, if he can't even hold a ruler straight? His tomfoolery means I have to ask a damn French Company man to assist and be obliged to them again.'

After he left, Lucy asked her aunt when she thought they might meet the Ceylonese.

'I expect we should invite them over some time quite soon. Perhaps when your uncle is in a more convivial mood.' She straightened the butter knife she had inadvertently bent with the pressure of her right hand. 'If he does not reply to this letter of Mr Don, then I will.'

After breakfast, she asked Lucy to accompany her to the nursery at Miramont. 'I hear they have a new Chinese rose apparently in bloom. I should very much like to see it.'

The road to Miramont passed the north end of Monsieur Champney's cane fields. The earth was dark and rich. Every inch of this lush island seemed to Lucy primed to burst. Off the high road, between Ambleside and the nursery, there were three other houses. Only the nearest, a frumpy French villa in distempered yellow belonging to Monsieur Dupont, struck a sour note; next to it a mansion of a family that had gone to Pondicherry four years ago, and had not yet returned, revelled in wild flowers; and the last, although a modest plain bungalow in white, set back from the road, flaunted a flourishing garden of colourful hibiscus.

'In there is a man who really should be a king.' Mrs Huyton nodded at the bungalow.

'Is that where the Ceylonese reside?'

'No. It belongs to Mr Amos. The finest example of the thrift and conscientiousness available to the enslaved of this island. A former slave who bought his freedom and educated himself.'

'How could he *buy* freedom?'

'He was lucky enough to be taken by a Syrian who was willing to sell him his liberty, day by day, over the years. Mr

Amos kept up his remittances unfailingly so that in time he bought a free Monday, then a free Tuesday, and so on until eventually he had purchased each day of the week and his complete emancipation. Even so, he continued to work until he could finally acquire not only his manumission but also his own property.'

'So, he is in society now?'

Betty Huyton made a small grimace. 'Not quite, my dear. But he is very civilised.'

The nursery, situated on a hill, boasted a small stream by its side from which spiral ferns and arum leaves sprang. The mossy slopes were overrun with peri ferns, hydrangea and wild rhubarb. Mr Pottinger, the nurseryman, had constructed several glasshouses and a number of small model gardens. Mrs Huyton was especially drawn to his more formal ones with box hedges in mathematical patterns and controlled beds where every flowering appeared like passion loosened within a bond of fidelity. 'I do adore the way he gets the red and orange to be like so many candles en masse,' she said. Lucy much preferred to see nature untrammelled; she liked to think that there was more in this world than man could constrain with a spade and a trellis.

As they alighted, Lucy suggested they look for something lively to decorate the corner post of the front verandah, in addition to the rose that was their main object. 'A bright clematis, perhaps?'

'Are we too reserved, Lucy? Is that what you think?'

'Your garden, Aunt Betty, is so lovely. It is everything you said it would be, but I feel it should come rushing into the house.' The bevelled edges of the white timber column, the

48

ornamental wooden railings on either side, needed some entanglement with the teeming life outside, in her opinion.

'I must say you have done very well with those colourful pots at the front, my dear. Very quick and most pleasing.'

To her surprise, Lucy felt proud to have made such a mark with her first domestic endeavour. 'I am sorry the big one broke in the transfer.'

'No matter. We can get another.' Mrs Huyton hitched her skirt to clear a patch of mud. Grey stepping stones bound by saxifrage led them up to the top where they found, to Lucy's surprise, that they were not alone.

'Good morning, Mr Amos,' Mrs Huyton called out. 'This is my niece, Miss Lucy Gladwell, from England.'

'Good morning, ma'am, and to you, Miss.' Mr Amos bowed his head, lowering a perfectly round bush of pure white hair, first to Mrs Huyton and then to Lucy. 'I heard you were back, ma'am.' His dark pantaloons were frayed, Lucy noted. The coat worn to a faded sheen. His shrunken left thumb had no nail; Lucy inwardly recoiled, straining to keep her eyes on his weathered face and not notice any other deformity from his early life.

'The new oriental rose, ma'am, if that be what you are here for, is in flower at the end of the terrace, just past the water trough.'

'Thank you, Mr Amos.' Mrs Huyton turned her head graciously to a side. 'The Chinese rose is indeed why we have come.'

The two ladies walked along one path, and he on the other, separated by a line of pink shrubs.

'I read in the journal of our Society of Arts and Sciences

that although its origins are in China, Mr Pottinger has obtained this particular consignment from a garden in India. It is a hybrid. A very exciting development whereby two varieties are cross-bred so as to strengthen the stem without diminishing the flower.'

'Is that so?' Mrs Huyton raised a finely plucked eyebrow.

'Yes. I understand even Mr Telfair is much excited by the prospect.'

'Mr Telfair is quite an enthusiast for the novel. But I imagine he sees Mr Pottinger's nursery as something of a distraction.'

'How is that, ma'am?'

'The Botanic Gardens he is so keen to supervise are a more sombre affair. Roses, flowers of any kind, cross-bred or pure, are not in abundance there, Mr Amos, except at the very entrance. Strong wood and serious foliage are his abiding interest, I believe.'

Mr Amos nodded slowly. 'I know what you mean. The dearth of delicacy in his schemes is to be lamented, although many of the trees do have blossom. The *bois de chèvre*, in particular, is very handsome at this time of year.'

'You are quite right, Mr Amos.'

He smiled. 'However I must admit I am more fond of good strong wood myself. We need strength more than finery.'

'But there is strength in beauty, as indeed beauty in strength, is there not, Mr Amos?' Lucy interjected, intrigued by the depth of his conversation and relishing the prospect of a serious argument.

Mr Amos looked at her in some surprise. 'That is true, Miss Lucy. But perhaps more in an abstract sense. I was refer-ring to the physical strength of hardwood trees.'

'A flower can be firm and strong,' Lucy insisted.

Mrs Huyton placed a hand on her niece, but Mr Amos encouraged the debate by brushing his fingers against a rose. 'These petals?'

'No, Mr Amos. But what about the heliconias? Durable *and* beautiful.' She turned to her aunt. 'We should invite Mr Amos to Ambleside and show him our Muru's floral arrangement, Aunt Betty.'

Mrs Huyton sniffed lightly. 'I am sure Mr Amos is well acquainted with the heliconia.'

'Indeed, ma'am, I am.' He bowed understandingly, the faint flicker of doubt and confusion swiftly extinguished. 'I congratulate you, Miss Gladwell. A most effective argument, excellently supported. I am persuaded.'

Although pleased to have succeeded, she felt undermined by his restraint. He had been a slave. Why was he not more enraged?

They reached the new display: a three-tiered stand. The shrubs had fresh glossy foliage and teemed with yellow-tipped buds. A few had burst open into frilly gowns.

Mrs Huyton bent over a bloom. 'Delightful.'

Lucy too put her nose to one and breathed in the rich, heady musk.

Mr Amos lifted one of the pots, freeing the stems that had become entangled. The roots protruding from the drainage hole on the bottom scrabbled in the air. 'These are ready to go into the ground,' he intoned low and priestlike. 'But they will need a great deal of care.'

'The scent reminds me of my grandfather's garden,' Mrs Huyton sighed. 'The roses were in such profusion there that the fragrance was noticeable from the roadside.'

'And where might that be, ma'am? This garden of your grandpapa?'

'Warwickshire, Mr Amos. I have been to the house only once, this last year, when I was visiting England. He is long dead of course and the house now belongs to a retired manufacturer from Birmingham, but I wanted to know something of my ancestors, you know, and I took a coach to see it for myself.'

'I understand. It is important to know of one's antecedents when one can.'

'Such a beautiful English village. The rose is its very soul.'

Mr Amos stared sadly at the flower in the pot. 'A very stirring thing.'

'And you, Mr Amos?' Lucy asked, keen to learn more about him. 'Are your people from Malagasy?' She knew many of the slaves on the island were brought from there.

'Africa, Miss Lucy. Africa.' He made a gesture that seemed to encompass both east and west. She thought she could see the whole mighty continent settle in his grave face.

From the road, a hundred yards below them, a loud clanking of chains disrupted their conversation. A troop of about a dozen Hindoo convicts shuffled into view, their dark bare bodies streaked with ash. An officer on horseback accompanied them, smacking his whip from time to time to punctuate the sound of the irons being dragged between their wretched manacled feet. The cloud of dust stained the air, sucking even the scent of the roses down and deadening it.

'They are brought from Bombay and Bengal now,' Mr Amos said quietly, running his finger inside the damp edge of his fuzzy collar. Then he excused himself.

The ladies watched him slowly descend. By the time he reached the road, the prisoners had gone. Mrs Huyton turned to Lucy, her eyes dim and pensive. 'You know, Lucy, if my friends in Jamaica had seen us chatting so amiably with a man as black as Mr Amos they would have been horrified. It could never happen in the West Indies that I was brought up in. Quite unthinkable.' She frowned at the flowers. 'How absurd! It is very wrong, is it not, Lucy, to treat a person as an inferior because of his complexion? His hue?'

'Then why are the convicts here always darker than us? And why is marriage between the races forbidden by the law? Isn't that what you said to the Reverend on the ship?'

Mrs Huyton glanced at her, and then down at the road where the pale reddish pall had clotted. 'Yes, Lucy, but that is not quite the point. In any case, liaisons across the great divide are much practised even if not condoned legally, as you will see from the abundance of piccaninnies in this district. Men in this environment find it difficult to control themselves. But no good ever comes of it. Such entanglements can only end in tears. If you look, you will see all around you, Lucy, the tragic consequences of miscegenation.'

'But that makes no sense at all, Aunt Betty. You said they are not inferior as some stupid people think. In fact, do we not adorn their lands, their history, their bodies with romance, like in Arabia or India? Yet the individual, like these men in chains, or Mr Amos, we treat with such violence.' She paused to catch her breath but then, before she could say anything more, there was the rustle of a stiffened skirt. Jeanette, Mr Pottinger's daughter, appeared from behind the rose stand.

'Do you like our new Silk Tea rose, Mrs Huyton? The colour is so . . .' Hot spots danced from cheek to cheek of her pretty, plump face.

'Yellow?'

'Buttery. Like heavenly butter. The Meka Ladies Group last week adored it.'

Lucy, exasperated by the abrupt return to the domestic world, muttered to herself a lament for toast and jam.

'Should I call a boy, Mrs Huyton? Would you like to choose a plant?'

'What do you think, Lucy? Shall I get two for the western parterre?'

Jeanette smiled coyly at Lucy. 'You must be the new lady from London?'

'I am Lucy.'

'Do you like plays, Lucy? I hear the London stage is amazing. We have a new play opening here next month.'

'The Garrison Players again?' Mrs Huyton put a hand to her ear.

'Yes, Mrs Huyton. They are doing Shakespeare. Captain Finders, you know, is a virtuoso.'

'It will be very good then, I am sure. Is that handsome Sergeant Murray in it? A wonder he is still single with all these French girls exercising their English with such ardour.'

A surge of crimson rushed from Jeanette's bosom up her neck, ring by ring. Her blood had a remarkable propensity to ebb and flow under her skin for all to see, as though every thought that rose in her was ensconced in a visceral sensation. The pressure, accentuated by her high-boned bodice, was close to bursting. 'I do not know.' Her mouth slackened as though the puppeteer's strings had been cut; she looked at Lucy helplessly.

'Well, I am sure it will be a very fine evening. Now, Lucy, would you say these two specimens at the end would be best for us? Silk Tea is a very odd name, don't you think?'

'What's in a name?' Lucy's mouth wavered. 'They are handsome enough.'

'In that case, Jeanette, if you would be so good as to have them put in our carriage, I shall go and settle the account with your father.'

Lucy, conscious that she ought to show some horticultural zest, asked, 'What about the clematis?'

'Yes, my dear, do go with Jeanette and choose a good strong climber.' She let a small gleam escape.

Jeanette led the way. The sun caught her hair, trailing out of her bonnet, and turned the curls a darker shade of auburn; her shoulders were hunched and from behind she looked as though she was struggling to keep something in.

'What is it?' Lucy asked, racing to catch up with her.

She looked blank. 'I am sorry?'

'What is it that Mr Pottinger is doing with the glasshouses?' They were all empty except for piles of manure.

'It is an experiment. My father intends to cross-breed various plants to better suit the climate here. This is a very special climate and he says the flora needs to be special too. Like us.'

'I am sure he is correct.'

Jeanette's head bobbed. 'Lucy, will you come to the play? Could we go together? It would be so nice. I should like it very much.' She spoke quickly as though the words had to be got out all at once, if at all. 'You must have seen so many wonderful plays in London.'

Lucy stumbled as the path turned rocky. 'Well, I am sure I would like to, but –'

'Please, do come. I should like so very much to sit with you and hear all about England.'

'That is charming of you.' Lucy wondered if she should confess how little she knew beyond what she had read.

'I would like to tell my father that we are going together. He is not one for entertainment.'

Lucy imagined Mr Pottinger with a pair of secateurs in his hand, nipping a bud here, a tendril there, moving swiftly to keep nature's tendencies in constant check. 'Is that so?'

'You will come then?' She lifted her face up in the air, undoing the knot that had contorted her frame and bound her shoulders.

'I will ask my aunt,' Lucy promised. 'I will ask if I could go with you. When is it?'

'After May Day we have the races, a fortnight later the play.' Her face grew more animated. 'Then the first ball. You have arrived just in time for our season, Lucy. You will love it here.'

# Chapter 4

A T THE end of the week, small fires and torches spluttered around the field behind the Presbytery causing havoc at the fringes.

Sergeant Murray fanned the acrid air. 'You see that, Mr Don? Fire-eaters, our very own blackamoor May Day dragons.' He nudged the tall civilian in his charge. 'Have you ever seen anything like it?'

Don Lambodar replied, as politely as an interpreter of royalty should. 'We have fire-eaters on our island of Lanka too.' Burnt and crusty fire-dancers also; fire-walkers, fire-breathers, fire-worshippers, the whole flaming fireworks, he wanted to add. 'The god of fire himself lives in a temple in Ceylon, daubed in molten wax with flickering tongues of flames painted on his torrid torso.'

'Fantastic.' Sergeant Murray's big bony face cracked open. 'Fantastic, Mr Don. I like it. I like your talk, Mr Don. You are a real talker.'

The Prince, resplendent in his royal gown, frowned at the young soldier. 'What is wrong with the fellow?' he asked Don Lambodar in Sinhala.

'We are being initiated into an English festival to celebrate fertility and rebirth. It fires him up.'

'Rebirth?' The Prince inclined his head thoughtfully. 'Is it time to be reborn?'

Sergeant Murray led them to the main avenue of battered stalls. 'Mr Don, would you and His Highness care for some beer?'

The Prince abstained. Asoka, the Prince's cousin, was the one for beer, but he had wandered off on his own. 'Thank you, but no.'

'If you don't mind then, Mr Don, I shall get a pint for myself and be back in a jiffy.'

Two clowns tottered across their path, juggling skittles and pulling faces. A horse-headed man on stilts stooped over them, cackling and making lewd signs. The sweet smell of burnt flesh, incense and fermented yeast filled the air; smoke gargled out of thick-lipped braziers.

The Prince covered his nose and mouth with his hand and made towards a garlanded enclosure near one of the pavilions. 'This is like our Kataragama without the benefit of divinity,' he muttered. 'All the pain of penance with no redemption.'

Rubbish. Kataragama, in Don's view, was a place where believers of every faith punished their bodies for hard cash and temporal gain. The citadel of a jealous, cruel god who promised vulgar rewards for crude self-flagellation: hanging by flesh-barbs, tongue-piercing, fire-walking. Spiritual redemption and divinity did not come into it. The issue was pure materiality. Corporality at best.

'Have you ever been to the temple of Kataragama?' he asked, masking his scepticism with the lightest of queries.

The Prince did not reply immediately. He liked to invite silence around his words so that the wings of a quotation might flutter over each and every utterance he made.

'Once,' he eventually said.

'For penance or assistance?'

'When mortals grow truly monstrous, the gods lose all hold.'

The crowd thickened. Men with red caps, women with white bonnets, swirled around, crying and shrieking. The Prince, butted from behind, struggled to keep his balance. Don Lambodar grasped him by the arm and slipped him out of the flow.

A grinning giant in a striped coat and top hat beckoned them through a gate. Bending low, he swept out a long arm. 'This way, mister. This way. Right this way.'

Sweeter music played inside; flags flew high as men and women, girls and boys, skipped and danced around a tall drunken flagpole, winding ribbons around it one way and then the other.

'Come, sir,' one called, waving. 'Join us.'

The Prince nodded politely.

When Sergeant Murray returned, he found the two of them pinned like giant moths against the rails. 'Are you not able to dance, gentlemen?'

Don said they were intrigued but not moved.

'Come, sir. Come. It is only a wee hop and a skip. Even I can do it. It is not an English dance here. It is a jollification for all, a spree for free.'

Someone banged a drum and the Sergeant joined with a whoop, swinging from ribbon to ribbon.

It was then that Don noticed the slim young woman on the

periphery, braced, as it were, against the spectacle. Her hair down on her shoulders – no hat, no bonnet – Lucy Gladwell seemed poised like a young deer to flee from the hunters on the carousel. She had a basket on her arm whose contents were discreetly covered by a white napkin. As he watched, a young ragamuffin came up to her with his hand out. Rather than shooing him away, she lowered herself down to his height. After listening to him, she delved into her basket and produced an orange. He grabbed at it but she did not let go. She said something to him and he nodded; only then did she release her hold. As the boy started to make off with the fruit, she straightened up. 'Wait,' she cried. The boy stopped. 'Come to the house and I will give you some work,' she called out in French. Then she recklessly threw him another fruit which went wide and struck the Navy's model pontoon. A piece of rigging fell. Alarmed, she turned. Don quickly looked away, their eyes tangling only for the briefest of moments.

'Our guests from Ceylon, Miss Gladwell, here at the pleasure of His Majesty,' Sergeant Murray smirked, introducing his two charges to the orange-chucker. 'The Prince of Ceylon and his most excellent interpreter, Mr Don. Presenting Miss Lucy Gladwell of Ambleside.'

The Prince was a gracious man of noble distinguished looks – silver hair in a topknot, a firm wise face of serious experience, a beard that became him like precious metal on a granite hillside – but even so, Don thought, she seemed to study the older man for an absurd length of time. Don pulled at the cuffs of his blue coat, and offered a greeting.

'The famous interpreter?' She acknowledged him with a

cautious smile. 'Your Ceylon, I have read, is the island of the fabled lotus.'

Don Lambodar looked at her smooth hands, held in a diviner's pose. 'It is indeed the island of the lotus with a thousand petals. A blossom that can brush away all the tribulations of the mortal world from Dutch cannons to stray oranges.'

Her eyes widened in surprise as if she were taken aback that he spoke her English so easily. But why should the language not be mine too? he thought. Mine surely is every word I utter? I own my tongue, my lips and my mouth, so why not the syllables I pronounce? Why famous anyway?

'Is it then Homer's land of the lotus-eaters?' she asked, bemused. 'Do you eat the flower to forget and sleep?'

'Fire-eaters, Miss.' Sergeant Murray shook his head and swatted at a cloud of dusk gnats hovering between them. 'According to our Mr Don, his is an island of fire-eaters. He has never mentioned any dozy lotus.'

'It is our visitors, your compatriots, dear lady, who mistake the lotus for the poppy and desire to ingest it.' The blood flowed thick through his body, ripening his mellow voice. 'We see it as a thing more sacred. A beautiful manifestation of the spirit of life, imbued with the colour of heaven, rather than a remedy for insomnia.'

She listened intently as though he were probing a poem. A very tiny tremor crept over her lips. 'Very finely put, Mr Don.' She pulled her shawl close around her, feeling unexpectedly womanly.

'Given the right circumstances, the words form themselves, Miss Gladwell.' Don Lambodar preened, pleased at her attention.

Her head dipped as she raised her shoulders innocently. 'That sounds more like a hymn to inspiration than the practice of someone obliged to express the opinions of others.' She glanced at the Prince for confirmation. He gave a rare smile and ambled towards a nearby nut seller. Sergeant Murray followed him.

Don Lambodar hesitated. 'I am not solely a mouthpiece. I am at liberty to speak my mind, Miss Gladwell.'

She touched the base of her throat lightly as if to free a word. 'You must be very fortunate, Mr Don.' Then, with sudden candour, she added, 'I wish I were able to do so too.'

'What could possibly prevent you from doing exactly as you wish?'

Despite her tone, her eyes glowed. 'In our position, we do as we are obliged, Mr Don, not simply as we wish.'

'Are you speaking of constraints peculiar to this country?'

'I refer to the nature of an orderly society in general, as well as the situation for a woman here.' Her quick young face grew animated. 'Our actions are hemmed in, our capabilities shrunk to purpose. More so when we are newly arrived, as indeed I am as well as you. But then perhaps this island is not as astonishing to you as it is to me.'

He had never conversed with a young woman like this before; so seriously and yet so intoxicatingly. The urgency of her expression, like her swerving grace, was disquieting. 'Our circumstances, since our arrival, have been very agreeable. Here the climate is indeed temperate. In general it is certainly cooler, and milder, albeit somewhat wetter, than anywhere on our coast between Puttalam and Beruwela. Much more like in our hills, even though we are never as high here as we would be at the Prince's old court. The mountains are small and, to my eyes at least, grossly deformed, but the vegetation is very familiar; the flora is much like our own, with the additional benefit of a vibrant African bloom. Only the fauna is somewhat poor ...'

She was squinting at the ground; her mouth tightened as she tried to smother a smile. He realised he was blathering and stopped. Bird cries around them rose to a crescendo, drowning out the sounds of revelry, much as darkness did against the last flares of daylight. Her shadow merged tantalisingly with his in the wake of the slipping sun. Then she glanced back up.

'I find it quite wonderful. The colours, the birds, the flowers, even the tiny insects.' She paused, her face radiant. 'And that gorgeous blue coat of yours,' she added with an impulsive grin.

'I suppose Ambleside is very different from what you would have imagined from your parlour in England.' He was chuffed it had created an impression.

She drew in a large breath quite uninhibitedly. 'On the contrary, it is very much as I imagined it, only magnified a hundredfold from the very first day.'

Don Lambodar compared her enthusiasm to his feelings on arrival, when they had been escorted off the ship by torchlight. 'Our landfall was at night. More forbidding than magical.'

'But is not the sea very beautiful and full of poetry under the stars?'

'You mean the fish twinkle in stanzas?' He permitted himself a small smile.

'It is in the sound, Mr Don. Here, on this island, you can hear the surf break upon the beach to an iambic beat. Each

wave like a drumbeat calling us to an epic as old as the ocean.'
She softened her expression as though she might fall into a
trance. 'Every night I listen to it before I sleep. I love it.'

'Can you hear it at Ambleside?'

'You can hear everything at Ambleside, Mr Don.'

'I have been there, but only seen the very grand entrance.
Those lazy lions guarding pots of maidenhair.'

'I know.' She smiled, remembering her first glimpse of him.

Before he could ask with sufficient delicacy how she knew
what he had seen, Asoka, the Prince's cousin, strutted in and
usurped his place with a lavish bow. A small round man, he
made up for size with exuberance. Don froze as the brass bun
introduced himself, wittering on about the joys of English
dance and merrymaking.

A few minutes later a cannon boomed to signal the beginning
of the evening ritual with the flag. Sergeant Murray returned
with a paper cone of peanuts. 'Excuse me, Miss Gladwell,
although the festivities will continue, the gentlemen are required
back at their lodgings and I must escort them directly.'

Don bade farewell on behalf of the Prince and himself and
thanked her for her acquaintance, while Asoka kissed her
hand, unashamedly, and made her laugh rather more gaily
than Don had thought possible.

'A very astute young woman,' the Prince remarked as they
walked towards their carriage, 'even if a little excitable.'

'You understood her?' Don glanced back. Asoka had
dropped behind and was now pressing his lips to a tankard.

'I could tell from her expression, and the brightness in her
eyes. She has much to say, I have no doubt, if only our randy
*redhi-hora* gives her a chance.'

'She is certainly not one for reticence.' Her impatient face brimming with the insouciance of youth and her sex thrilled him, floating in and out of his mind.

The Prince stared at him and then added, 'I expect she is here to be married.'

'Why do you say that?'

'Is it not obvious? Youth and beauty unbridled here on this colony? Why else would she have come? You ask our guard, or Captain Gates. He seems to know what is going on here.' He stifled a laugh. 'But don't get ideas above your station, my young Don. The English do not like that.'

Captain Gates, their thin-nosed superintendent, was a stickler for status. He had wanted to know, on the very first day, whether Don was related to the Prince.

We are not even of the same tribe, let alone clan, Don had replied. Only since landing on Mauritius had he begun to understand the advantage a modest drop or two of royal blood had on the quality of everyday life. He discovered a surprising empathy among the islanders for the Ancien Régime; it seemed Voltaire and Montesquieu had not travelled this far south, although Don had found their ideas easily enough in the back alleys of Colombo. The Captain explained that the island had been a French royal possession and although at the time of the Revolution there may well have been some sympathy for Jacobin notions, the prospect of the abolition of slavery was too much for the French planters. They declared independence from France and relied on the corsairs for protection. The island returned to French rule only with Napoleon, and common sense only after his defeat.

When Don Lambodar conveyed this account to the Prince, later on, the royal throat made a raspy hissing sound in response. 'It is a matter of colonial pride for the Captain. You see, the British, having lost America, like to practise their colonial experiments on small islands. Only once they have built up enough steam will they will make their bid for something big, like India.'

'What about the war with France?'

'Wars in Europe are matters of sibling rivalry. Not about establishing colonies. This is a new thing. In our countries, as in America, their ambition and their desires are different.'

Don was not convinced. 'The Romans and the Greeks, the Muslims and the Christians, were all on missions to establish colonies and converts. The British are only obsessed with trade.'

'Nonsense. What they want is a place to inhabit. Physical space and mental space. They have taken my land and your mind, Don Lambodar. Make no mistake about it. And a colony established upon the mind is perhaps the more serious deformation.' The Prince's eyes clouded as though they had been made redundant by the press of memory and now saw more of what he remembered than what surrounded him.

According to Mr Amos, whom Don had befriended soon after he arrived, exile was more than geographical displacement: it was a disconnection from reality.

The two had first met outside the gates of the Botanic Gardens where Mr Amos had helped Don decipher an abstruse proclamation of local regulations. They immediately recognised in each other a fondness for grammar and intellectual exercise. Since then they would seek each other out, usually in the Gardens, for a regular bout of strenuous conversation.

The last time they had spoken, Mr Amos had urged Don to study his situation more closely and work harder to realise his full potential whatever the constraints put upon him.

'Is that how you freed yourself from the bonds you were born into?' Don knew Mr Amos had been a slave in the south of the island.

A thin furrow wrecked Mr Amos's shining forehead. 'I studied the strictures and then worked to remove them. I refused to be incarcerated in my mind as well as my body.'

'Did you have a mentor?' Don asked, trying to imagine the undertaking.

'I have my faith, my friend, and He has given us the example of Mr Jean Baptiste Lislet Geoffroy.' He rubbed his temple thoughtfully. 'A free black man. A geographer, an engineer and a meteorologist. He made maps of our Mascarene Islands and is responsible for the proper functioning of Port Louis: the water supply, sanitation and suchlike.'

'Clearly a man of many talents.'

'I have heard him speak most inspiringly at the Assembly of People of Colour. A wonderful exposition of the theory of electromagnetism.' Mr Amos pressed his elbows excitedly into his knees as though he wanted to launch into the air like a crow. 'Do you realise electricity has a magnetic effect, attracting two things together? It is a most amazing discovery made by the Danish scientist Ørsted. It is so inspiring to see the world through the eyes of a genius. Mr Geoffroy believes fervently in the power of education. He was the first of us to be elected to the Academy of Sciences in Paris before the Revolution.'

'I should like to hear this marvel whose imprint extends from the heavens to the sewers.'

'I have suggested to the Reverend Constantine that he is invited to speak at the church when he returns from his current expedition. You must come to the church, my boy. It is a very good place and open to men of all persuasions.'

'The Church has shaped my life already.' Don plucked a dead leaf and lowered his voice. 'The truth is that if not for a certain Mr Henderson, an American of serious Christian persuasion, I would still be languishing in a Colombo poppy parlour.'

'Poppy? You mean like the business of that English lackey, Mr Badani?'

Don stifled a laugh. 'Badani is no lackey. Is he not the linch-pin, even the mainstay, of the community here? But you are right, my undoing was indeed an Englishman. Colin Taylor, to be precise, Mr Henderson's English cousin and my supervisor in Colombo.' The chubby hedonist in his tight breeches flickered in Don's mind, grasping after a marooned lascar's ripened tip and kneeling for purposes too carnal for his cousin, and indeed the high-minded Mr Amos, ever to imagine.

'These young supervisors from Europe grow very wild in their appetites abroad, I know,' Mr Amos clucked. The furrow on his forehead grew deeper, crumpling the offensive thought.

Don nodded. 'Provided I could find him a few grains of opium and a night-ship with a tight enough porthole, he would be happily sated and very generous.' Taylor had bought him silk shirts, jewels, peacock cravats and coloured shoes, giving him a taste for luxury, urging him to suck the glowing bowl of a Persian pipe, or the musky crotch of a nautch star, and laugh at the problems of the poor. He had coddled him like a pet on an invisible leash, throttling Don, bit by bit, with excess.

'A ship?' Mr Amos cocked his head. 'Was it he who sent you sailing to our Mauritius?'

'No, Mr Henderson was the one who delivered me. One day, he said he had found a possible fresh start for me. The British were sending the Prince – who had been imprisoned without charge for several years – into exile, for his greater liberty, and needed an interpreter. He told me to apply for the position.'

'Greater liberty?' Mr Amos scoffed.

'The British had no evidence against him, but were afraid to set him free in case he started a rebellion. I believe Mr Henderson was the one who suggested they might clothe exile in the guise of liberty.'

'Very astute, your American.'

'He had influence by virtue of his work in Vaddukoddai, where he had founded a school to preach the Gospel. He was a Protestant and this was much in his favour, given the hold the Catholics had gained in the North.'

'One has to be very particular about such things.' Mr Amos uncurled a questioning finger. 'But your Prince then, you only met through this American?'

'He arranged the interview.' Don recalled that pivotal day. The Prince was standing by a window, twirling the tip of a pigeon feather in his ear. When Don entered the room, he stopped cleaning and waved the feather about like a sword.

Questions flew regarding Don's home town, his family, his education. 'When the Prince discovered I was outside his clan – all of them being too devious by half – he pronounced himself satisfied to the British aides in charge of his deportation.'

'Did you not have questions of your own?'

'I was to act as interpreter and scribe for the Prince. My salary was specified as twice what I was receiving from Taylor and, in addition, I would be given free board and lodging. The contract was almost too good to be true.'

Mr Amos screwed up his eyes until the pupils were barely visible, his lids hung like grey parchment scrolls. 'A proper letter of employment between employee and employer should be a mark of a civilisation that truly understands freedom.'

It was only on the voyage, aboard the *Melbourne*, that Don had begun to appreciate his good fortune. He had not only escaped from Taylor, but now saw the world with a clarity he had never believed possible. He thought the sea itself did that for him. Despite his ancestors' predilection for the dhow, he had no idea what an island was before they set sail. His whole previous world – the Colombo fort, the clerk's office, Lady Teresa's boudoir, the poppy parlour, the house his mother had worked in, the entire town – then shrank to a place the size of his hand. It had no reach once the line of beach palms slipped below the horizon. Three weeks later, when they rounded the outcrop of Tonneliers and he saw the fort on the welted edge of Port Louis, wreathed in the rags of dusk, he felt a sadness that was not to do with the landing they would soon make and the new home he would have to find, but entirely to do with the smallness of their lives. A settlement seen from the sea is a very curious thing, he realised: who are these people who have come together to live in one place? And why? He had the frightening thought that it was not his will that had brought him but some greater force working out its own design; a pattern that he was too small to see but could only feel through its effect, like the current of an ocean manifested in its waves.

Don pulled in his shoulders and tightened up. 'But there is a peculiar discrepancy in the British mind that I cannot understand. A contradiction in purpose.'

'The British are mercantile in character, so I suppose you mean something of an economic confusion rather than a spiritual one?'

'I have read their books, you know, Mr Amos. Many of them. On the one hand, their much esteemed Adam Smith says very plainly that slavery can only be detrimental to the wealth of a society as it removes the motor of profit from the hand of the labourer and relies only on violence to gain efficiency, and yet the business of slavery is buttressed by beef and beer at every opportunity. It makes so little sense in logic.'

Mr Amos lowered his head and slowly stroked the thin ridges on the side of his face. 'Luck not logic dictates our lives, my young friend. But there is merit in looking beyond one's own good fortune and putting one's learning into action. Service to God is what we are here for, not servitude to man.'

# Chapter 5

T HE ACCOMMODATION the Prince had been allocated was plain and simple: a cottage with three austere bedrooms and a dining parlour of thrifty proportions. To his credit the Prince had not complained, despite Asoka's gibes, and was content that it was separate and distant from the other prisoners – commoners from their homeland, except for the two convicts assigned to serve him: Khola a slow, sulky servant, and Surangani, a cook-woman of considerable woe but who offered the solace of a familiar, even if monotonous, diet of rice and curry.

The front verandah was a disaster: cracked and broken with sticks poking out of the daub and both front pillars out of joint. The one rattan armchair was a wreck. The initial task the Prince had set Don Lambodar was to write a letter to Captain Gates requesting a number of critical repairs.

'Put it in your best English that this is a matter of urgency,' the Prince had instructed. 'Make it clear that we must be in a position to receive visitors immediately.'

'Should we not tell him that when we see him?'

'A formal letter is more expedient. It is the most effective means of precipitating action: this much I have learned from the British administration in Ceylon. In fact, can you also add to this letter a list of our other requirements in enumerated order?'

'Each room has a bed, a table and a chest of drawers,' Don had pointed out. 'What is to be enumerated?'

'Think of our potential visitors. We need a divan and a chair for the verandah. We need wine and champagne – you know how the English and the French find alcohol essential for the comfort of their backsides.' He glanced around to see if Asoka was in hearing. 'But locked. We must have a lockable cabinet for the drink. Also ensure there is coffee and foreign biscuits. One cannot serve only vegetable patties to guests. We may not be here out of our own volition, but we must endeavour to show ourselves as ambassadors and act with propriety. Please write politely but firmly. It is the most effective course of action with these people. As a young scrivener you will do well to remember that.'

'I will, sire, I will.' The Prince was a man from whom Don was determined to learn.


After the Sergeant had returned them to their wattly cottage that fateful May Day, Don tried to distract himself with Dr Johnson's dictionary, but Lucy Gladwell's words, her quick lips and bright eyes kept bringing him back to their encounter. All his thoughts and actions seemed to be drawn by her – even his visit to Ambleside. He told the Prince about it.

'You know I have been to her house.'

'Already?'

'So alluring.'

'A colonial house? Or do you mean the girl?'

'Ambleside is a mansion unlike anything I have seen.'

'We, in Lanka, have not had the pleasure of entertaining the French on the rampage. Perhaps that is the difference. Some confusion in the architecture, an extra roll and curlicue here and there.'

'I would not say it is confused. It is actually beautiful.'

The Prince winced at his interpreter's occidental bent. 'You have been inside?'

Don lowered his head. 'Not yet.'

'Could it be, then, that it has the charm of the forbidden? You – the young – are often attracted to what is prohibited.'

'I would not say that the house is forbidden. No one was there, except the servant boy, when I visited.'

'What business did you have?' The Prince raised a circum-flex above his right eye. 'You are not reaching for something you ought not to, are you?'

'It is a serious matter of natural rights. I am negotiating with the authorities, following your example.'

'Not too closely, I hope, for your sake.' His eyes narrowed. 'What is at stake?'

'The rights of Narayena – a Hindoo slave.'

Don's mission had started a fortnight earlier, before Lucy Gladwell had set foot on the island.

The Prince had been at cards with Asoka the evening it began. Don Lambodar, settled in the disastrous armchair, had lit his pipe. He had only taken a puff or two, when Narayena pushed open the gate – a small pointy man with hard black eyes and claw-like hands; a gambler whose luck had mostly served to stiffen him against unfavourable odds. Don had first met him at the rum tavern, attracted by his weird imprecations in archaic Tamil and his colourful pink shirt. Narayena had enthusiastically befriended him and divulged a tip about the midnight wrestling match; Don had wagered a packet – and lost it. Later he had learned that Narayena had been brought to the island some twenty years earlier and put to work in the nearby plantation along with a dozen other slave boys caught on the Coromandel Coast of India. They lived severed from homeland and history, separated even from the community of free Malabar merchants and Madras artisans, reliant upon brittle splinters of random memories and a mishmash of rituals to maintain their slowly fading identity. Narayena, determined to fight against the force that seemed set upon his gradual annihilation – whether at a gambler's den or a miller's stone – had an admirable fervour to him that could fan flames out of cinders, hope out of despair, but rarely a winning streak.

'Sir, you must help us,' he implored, cracking his knuckles one after another.

Don sucked his pipe harder; his face kippered in the slow glow. The interruption was not welcome. He had heard that there had been trouble at Narayena's workplace; no doubt, he thought, a result of another futile long shot. 'I have no power to alleviate your situation.' Be sonorous and peaceful, he told himself, be like a properly educated man.

'But, sir, you do.' With his bare foot Narayena marked a line in the moon dust. 'You have the power to talk to the English lords in their own manner.'

'Have you not spoken to anyone?'

Narayena's tongue clicked rapidly. He had picked up Kreol early and become the spokesman for his group, but after the British took over the island, although he learned some plantation English, he was not able to gain direct access to the new rulers.

'You must tell them Monsieur Patrice Champney gives us nothing. Now, when we have done our *kovil*, by ourselves, in our own Sunday time, with our labour, he wants to steal the stone. Is not right.' He paused, letting his words gather the strands of collective injury. 'We been pulled across the Black Water – *kala pani*, Mr Don – and we must do *puja* to compensate. For leaving our motherland. For new vows. Must make this place our own. We need a *kovil* to worship. You understand, no?' His disjointed hands twisted together. 'Sorry you lost money on my advice, but we are in a big darkness. You, sir, can help us. Justice must prevail, no, even for poor muckers?'

Don Lambodar could not disagree. It was unjust to deprive a man of his spiritual moorings, but not unexpected from a plantation man whose whole way of life was steeped in the business of injustice, whose profits all depended upon acquisition and appropriation. Nevertheless, Don had heard Captain Gates describe Patrice Champney as a cultured man. 'Very well. I shall speak to Monsieur Champney.'

'That is no good. He is not a man who can listen. He and his tadpole have no humanity. You must go higher. The big *masta*. The English Governor.'

'No, we cannot go straight to him.' Don tapped his pipe thoughtfully. 'The alternative is to approach Mr Huyton instead. As a superintendent, he is the Governor's representative for the area.'

Narayena looked doubtful. 'Your Captain Gates is a kinder man.'

Don shook his head. 'Captain Gates is in hospital at Grand River, suffering from influenza. If one cannot get satisfaction from Monsieur Champney, then Huyton is the proper person to go to. He has to do what is right.'

'Why?'

'He is an official. A superintendent.'

Narayena rubbed the knuckles of his hooked hand until they shone. 'Because otherwise we make too much trouble? Nothing to do with what is right, is it?'

'I will write him a letter. That is what this situation requires.' As he had learned from the Prince, the spoken word evaporates too soon; it survives only in the form that suits the hearer; it is too susceptible to amendment and cannot be trusted in memory. Whereas inked words survive both the originator and the recipient, enduring as an indictment of the moment for as long as literacy remains, carrying their own weight rather than the pomp of their originator.

He was not a royal scribe for nothing.

'Give me the facts,' Don added gruffly.

'Sir, I married three year ago. Good woman, plain but clean – you saw her passing by last week – but for all this time we are not blessed. We work hard. Cut cane, bundle cane, plant cane. Too hard to reproduce anything but cane. I tell her she needs strengthening. I do this and that so she can eat better. My wife, soon she is eating curd and honey all the time. Nuts and bananas. Getting fat everywhere but there.' He spread out his hands around his belly. 'Then, in a dream, I see a white girl flat on the beach. I see a big goat sitting like a king with a pipe in his mouth, watching. Eating *paan*. He is very big, sir, and he tells me I must make a vow and then will I have progeny. He says from my loins can spout progeny stronger than the white people sinking in sand. So I make the vow, sir, to build a lingam of thanks if we are given a son.'

'Is it so good a life here that you wish it replicated?'

'Sir, when we die we must be reborn. I want a son to make sure this will be a better place for me to come back to one day. To clear the place of cane, of French pride, of Britishers. Clear it and make it a place for us to play cards and carom, *chaturanga* and dice, and dream the dreams of our ancestors.'

'And now you have this son.'

'Three month ago my wife gives birth. Healthy brat. Loud voice, ten fingers and ten toes and all his other vital parts. My wife is so happy now she cries with delight every night when I perform the conjugal act. I ask Sri Badani for guidance and he asks the holy man who says by the pond on Alderman road is the place for a temple of thanks.' He gestured in the direction of the rising moon. 'All us plantation Hindoo boys got together to build it: from the mill and neighbouring fields. Merit for all, no? And all want sons. This place is warm like holy ground. Have you not felt it, Mr Don? When a place belongs not to us but to that which is greater than us, we feel it in the soles of our feet. You feel that, Mr Don, do you not?'

Don Lambodar could not tell if the land belonged to the god of the hills, or the god up in heaven. He was not at all sure. Religion, be it of his ancestors' sacred fire, his grandfather's Holy Book, his father's elephant-headed patron of letters, or that of his mother's Awakened One, meant little to him. Too much of religion was bound to property – spiritual and temporal – for his liking. Perhaps the land belongs only to the trees and plants that grow on it, he sometimes thought, whereas we and our gods are to it only as birds are to the air.

'This is not an inhospitable land,' he said to Narayena. 'Many would like to lay claim to it, however small the patch. Monsieur Champney's Belvédère plantation runs to the north, the south and the east of this spot, am I right? Your temple is to the west?'

'The road forks. We make a square of ten lengths each side, and put up a mud wall to keep the pigs out. Inside we plant flowers to harvest for offerings. Small temple but room for three shrines. Already Ganesh is there, you will be pleased to know, sir, and brother Rahul is making the other two. Not enough tiles to roof the whole thing, so only the alcoves are covered. But you walk across the threshold, man, you feel protected.'

'Not, it seems, from the disapproval of Monsieur Champney?' The situation, Don could see, was not good. The British had ruled Mauritius for fifteen years or so, but the French had laid the ground rules. 'The road itself then belongs to the plantation? Or does it mark a border?'

'The road is ours. We make it.'

'You?'

'The labourers are from my homeland. Sir, you see them. Indian convicts. All on our side.'

'Not even the spades and shovels belong to the prisoners,'

Don retorted. Yet, there seemed a challenge here worth making. In service – however dissimilar – perhaps we do have a bond, he thought. He told Narayena that he would construct a case. Narayena and his lot may be enslaved but their labour on Sundays was deemed their own, and their customs and practices were not outlawed. They were indeed encouraged to fend for themselves: grow beans, trap fish, regenerate and worship. The matter, he reckoned, hinged on a modern understanding of the nature and dignity of manual work and the fundamental rights expressed in the French Declaration: liberty and equality.

Narayena, bent and squinting, stirred in Don a memory of his boyhood friend Akmal. They used to spend hours together, day after day, knee-deep in the small stream that ran below Don's uncle's paddy field, catching small brown fish with ekel traps. They never spoke much; Akmal was a thin lanky boy with undeveloped testicles and a modest vocabulary. His squeaky voice so knotted to be hardly worth the effort of loosening, but he offered companionship: faithful, unobtrusive, constant. He had one eye awkwardly angled, as though on a different plane, which gave him the capacity to see through the water's surface with remarkable precision. Or was it luck that enabled him to catch fish so well?

Narayena was no fisherman, and clearly not much luck had ever come his impoverished way. The birth of a son might have heralded a change of fortune but, with Monsieur Champney's actions now, it looked as though this was not to be. Was it Narayena's eye, the slight roll his left one did as it tried to focus, that linked the two – Narayena and Akmal – in his mind?

'Does he who labours not own at least some proportion of the fruits of his labour?'

Thus he put it in his letter to Mr Huyton: an urgent plea for justice in a virgin land where, if not for the curse of cane and a certain ignobility among the first settlers, equity and equality might have been its *raison d'être*. In an ideal world, as he understood from the famous Second Treatise by the anonymous English philosopher, all inhabitants of a civilised country should enjoy the same benefits of living without want or distress in a state of perfect freedom; each would endeavour to meet his own needs rather than that of a minority who exploit the advantage they have gained through violence or the accidents of history. It seemed to him an ideal worth striving for, despite the gross indecencies of the real world.

'Who else should own the fruits of his labour?' he added.

There, that is it. He pressed the nib in on the final dot. If this were one of their famous plays, he fancied now might be the moment for a theatrical flourish and a speech for posterity: 'A plain question, sir, but one whose answer, I believe, may have considerable consequences and in many different dimensions, from that of the slave to that of the scribe, and unravel and unshackle much within and without the empires of modern commerce. This I believe to be the case not only here in this island of captives, but in any society of unequal parts where men live without compact or consent but in a state of war against their loss of liberty.'

He intended to hand the letter to Huyton personally and thus establish a channel between imperial authority and the labourers – Messrs Narayena and company – he had agreed to represent. To get the Superintendent to read the argument having had sight of the scribe's importunate eyes, as it were, was his goal.

And so, armed with his petition, he had gone the next day to the lion's den: intersecting his first sight of Ambleside with Lucy's arrival and her first secret glimpse of him.

'I am surprised at you, Don Lambodar, risking our good standing in this way, and for the sake of a little shrine. I did not think you supported idolatry. You struck me as a rationalist.' The Prince tapped his forehead gently.

'I am not a believer, but these men need a voice. I used the voice of reason, tempered by the arguments of modern philosophers, in English.'

'The English voice of the Hindoos? Is that what you are now? An Englishman in a brown skin?' He smirked with a nutcracker's childish delight.

'Were you not impressed when your English friend in Colombo – the Agent – turned native? Did you not think that was the epitome of civilisation? To be able to cross the boundary and become another?'

The Prince's face turned sour. 'But in the end, he reverted. Despite his sarong and his *sereppu*, inside his head, I am afraid, he remained a Briton. He sacrificed friendship for the sake of an English baronetcy. Appearances are always merely appearances, my boy. Do not be so easily fooled.'

# PART II

# Chapter 6

'OF COURSE you must go to the club tomorrow. The races are quite a different matter from yokels cavorting around a maypole. You cannot predict what you will find, my dear. Much changes, within and without, in the period of a month.'

'Some things may, Aunt Betty, but our society here seems not to, much as you may wish it.' Henri Benoît was one she had in mind who always popped up like an unwelcome growth in an awkward place, first at the house with a pot of honey – and his mother – then at the May fête, munching his monkey nuts, and then just two days later inspecting hair oil at the general store. His family had been on the island for a hundred years and originally came with the French East India Company. Henri, encouraged by his mother, had developed a fascination for the English, which rather set them apart from the Creoles, like the Duponts, and even the newer planters such as the Champneys. 'I really have no interest in a wild goose chase.' Lucy threw her pompom into Muru's new flower arrangement and flounced out to her refuge: the garden hut on the lower terrace.

In the hut she could be alone without fear of consequence; warm her bare feet on the apron of old stones laid
out in front, unseen by the world of custom and convention.
Even her legs right up to her knees could be bared, for no
one would disturb her. No marauders, no pirates, no roving
strangers. If Muru needed to call her, he would sing from
the birdbath on the lawn, high and plaintive, leaden-eyed, a
song forlorn. She had been on the island only a matter of
weeks; already she felt the place was as much hers as anybody
else's. But it was not enough.

Thick clouds had boiled over the treetops and threatened
to blot out all light. She could smell rain in the air – dark and
big, not the passing noiseless noontide rain of a romantic
poem. The rain would comfort her, she knew. Unsalted tears,
unadulterated by the despair of the old.

With the first silvery drops, she stepped out and held open
her hands. English rain had never felt like this; it always
brought some chill with it and was never as life-giving as the
sun when it shone. Here it was the opposite: the sun was to be
avoided lest it burn white skin to brown, or even black,
whereas the rain brought life. The trees, the bushes, the flowers, even the cane called out for the warm wet freckles to
bubble. She wanted to be like the Indian boys she had seen
down by the river. Somehow free to shed their rags and dive
with the rain into the water. She too wanted to swim free
with the coloured fish, feel them dart around her naked limbs
nibbling at the crescent rims hardening her young heels.

The rain turned heavy, splattering the roof noisily; quickly
becoming a downpour, flattening the grass and digging up the
flower beds. The gutter collapsed, adding another cascade: the

roar of rain drowned out the voice in her head so that she could no longer hear herself, but she could not stop thinking. She wanted the rain to reach inside and rinse all her thoughts; to unmuddy the veins that were confused by her heart. This little room was her island. Isolated. In this deluge she would not hear Muru even if he sang his highest aria, with a banana leaf held up for shelter. She knew he would not come. No one would come. Not even by pirogue or schooner. Not until the sun's yellow fingers began to part the clouds and make of the moist, glittery air a soft rainbow necklace for the earth and for her.

At the racecourse, as she had feared, Henri Benoît was waiting, eager as a hare. He sprang out from behind the very first striped marquee.

'Ha,' he burst out with that forced gaiety he used to cover his ineptitude. His manners she could not fault, but he had little sense of his limitations, or the picture he presented when he bared his teeth. 'Ha, mademoiselle, can I offer you some refreshment?'

Lucy bit her lip. 'Good morning, Henri.'

'Some coffee? Champagne?'

'I would like some lime juice.'

'*Limonade?*'

'Lime or lemon, whichever, Henri. If it is no trouble to you.'

His eyes fluttered like wild bunting. 'Oh, yes, of course. I mean, it is trouble not at all.' He fumbled around his pockets as though he carried a siphon hidden within. 'Have the seat? Over there. Please do. I go immediately . . .'

'Thank you.' Lucy accepted, if only to speed him on his way, and sat on a white wooden bench by the giant fan of a traveller's palm. The day was exceedingly hot. Observing a trickle of sap, she felt an affinity to the leaky plant. Behind her, in the marquee, voices – planters, she presumed – discussed the efficiency of Mr Telfair's model estate. A dispute rose over the virtues of the new machinery and the task-work regime recently introduced at his famous sugar mill. 'Too good to be true, if you ask me,' someone grunted. She was about to turn her attention to the more pressing issue of humidity and moisture control when she heard the mellifluous voice of Don Lambodar. His jet-black hair, his large, long eyes and his curiously delicate features, close to curling at the edges, swirled in her mind merging that first sight of him at Ambleside to the meeting at the fête.

She heard him say, 'In our country we much prefer the ardour of a working hand to the dull thump of machinery.' His lips, she recalled, were the colour of mulled wine.

'Not possible today, Mr Don. Here our English abolitionists would have us completely untie ourselves from the business of slavery,' someone replied with apparent regret.

'I do not mean physical labour out of duress, sir. I mean obligation and custom. Take flour, for example. In our country a woman pounds rice in a mortar to make flour for the breakfast of her husband, well before the sun is up, as a matter of duty. No man would dream of eating crumpets made out of flour ground mechanically at a stranger's mill. Flour that might be a day old. Why, that would be unthinkable. Unnatural.'

'The females in your country are perhaps more pliable than here, my dear fellow.'

Don Lambodar's voice rose, as did Lucy's fury on the other side of the canvas. 'Not at all. I see no difference. An English muffin may be a little paler, but it crumbles much the same, I have no doubt.'

Much laughter erupted inside. 'You would have them for breakfast, would you? Have their delicate hands at the pestle, would you, Mr Don.'

'I have noticed their hands, delicate as they are, seem indeed stronger than ...' What? What would he dare say? Lucy seethed. Their minds?

Lucy's blood ran high in her cheeks; hot rivulets gushed between whalebone and cross-cotton. The man should be shamed – if not hanged, drawn and quartered – and the company he kept put in stocks and pelted with cabbages, tomatoes and alligator eggs. They must be the scum of Port Louis tipplers: redundant slave traders, vagrants and dregs, abusing worse than they had been abused themselves. Fortunately, some applause from the racing enclosure distracted the discussion in the marquee and then Henri returned.

'*Limonade.*' He raised two cloudy glasses triumphantly.

'Henri, what tent is that?'

'I am very sorry. The crowd is rowdy in there. I should have escorted you to the other side.'

'What is Mr Don doing in there?'

'The fellow from Ceylon? Would you like to meet him?'

'Most certainly not.' She told Henri that Don Lambodar was a man of such ill manners that he did not deserve the attention of a dormouse.

'Oh? I thought he was of some nobility.'

'I have heard him speak and I do not think much of his opinions.'

'In that case, I shall avoid him henceforth.'

'I would like to see the horses, Henri. Shall we go?'

'But your drink?'

'I can walk with a glass in my hand just as well as you can, dear Henri.'

He looked down and pawed at the ground with his neat little shoes. 'Yes, of course.'

Lucy was not fond of racing, which most of the ladies of Port Louis – especially the French mesdames – seemed to enjoy. They would sit in their chairs, row upon row, like bundles of cloth at a market stall and flutter madly when the horses sped by, as if enlivened only by those thundering hooves shaking the earth beneath them. To be whipped so vehemently simply to run around a silly ring was a monstrously unjust thing, in her opinion. The creatures spurred to the course rarely looked magnificent; browbeaten and broken in spirit, they were forced to subjugate their own passions for the infinitely more prosaic ambitions of their heartless owners and stunted jockeys. A rosette in blue, or yellow, or red was not sufficient compensation, she thought; nothing could be. She much preferred to see them in the field where they would be their own masters and enjoy something of their native spirit, grazing and swishing their tails, snorting the melancholy wind as it blew through the Madagascar firs to sting their nostrils with the fine salt of a wild African sea. At the stands, she would rather watch the glossy-haired coloured ladies lift their skirts and play with their wits – swaying and swinging with no concern other than their own pleasure, or so it seemed to her. She wished she could be as gay. Full-grown and womanly. Although her toes twitched just to see them, she could not lose herself so easily. To be English in Port Louis was to be bridled by the greater mission of the mother country and her destiny; she felt she had to conform to special standards and show a British indifference and a deeper titanic worth. Her Aunt Betty subscribed to the notion admirably: her head was always protected by a hat abroad; she would drink tea rather than *eau sucrée* whenever possible; she never spoke French, if it could be avoided, and her English, in public, was as neatly clipped as a court wig.

Should I be clipped too, Lucy wondered, lest I fly, incensed as I am by the tongue of a charlatan? A true poet is a creature of the finest sensibilities, not the coarsest. So, what is he?

'Is there a horse you favour?' Henri asked, eager as ever to break into her thoughts.

'The palomino, if she were free.'

'Free?'

'I would like to set her free, Henri. Let her roam down in the Savanne, out on the beach. Free to do as she pleases.' She saw beauty unleashed: splashing through the sea froth as the waves laced her hooves, galloping, ears back, her mane up like a sail, her muscles locking and clicking, her eyes unfettered as the ocean.

As she spoke, a shadow loomed, engulfing the line she cast in the sun.

'A fine sentiment, my lady.' The timbre of Don Lambodar's voice was like a gong behind her. Lucy quickened against it.

'But to do what one is trained to do is not a restraint. It is a proper freedom. The horse I am sure is freest on the course, running as it should. It has been bred for that purpose. I do believe it is happier racing on the turf than chewing grass like a cow.'

She turned, determined to keep her movement slow against this barrage of conservative nonsense. 'Mr Don?'

Their eyes briefly clashed before he glanced down.

'Forgive me, but we have been introduced, at that curious ceremony with the ribbons and the pole, the other day. Don Lambodar, at your service.'

'You would have the horse race and, no doubt, the slave for ever enslaved?'

'Only if it is their proper place.'

'I understand. Yes.' Lucy tried to control her voice as it slid between temper and tempo, heart and heat. 'We are all in our proper place, when restrained, but you? Is that so?'

His mouth curled. 'Quite possibly.'

'Quite wrong,' she retorted. 'Our proper place is to be unshackled. Freedom is not apportionable. Only a criminal should be confined.'

'Ah, yes, Miss Gladwell.' His chest puffed out in goosey pride. 'I remember you feel somewhat hemmed in.'

She detected a note of contempt, as though he thought confinement was the natural lot of a creature in skirts. She would have spoken more, of women and mills, his pestle and mortar, the pounding preferably of dandy impostors of proper gentlemen and true poets, but she felt something slip inside her. Or was it under her feet? The humidity was intolerable. The wooden platform creaked. She did not wish him to think she had stooped so low as to catch his vulgarity as he revelled with his uncouth company drinking gin in a pyjama tent of slothy buffoons.

Henri cleared his throat. 'Well, Monsieur Don, that is most interesting. Now, if you will excuse us, we were just going over to the –'

'Of course. Pardon my intrusion.' He retracted his head, very slightly, and waited as though the ground was his and the other two the foreign trespassers.

Henri gathered Lucy's arm and attempted to steer her around Don's firmly planted heels, but became hopelessly muddled.

Once they reached the promenade, Henri looked back and hissed, 'A highly disagreeable fellow, as you say. Yes, indeed. He could have moved at least an inch. So rude.'

The encounter unsettled Lucy. Don Lambodar, she estimated, must be twenty-five or twenty-six years old, although from his swagger he probably liked to think himself older. Despite her abhorrence of his opinions, she found something compelling about him. His face was steep; his cheeks rushed down to a sharp chin dominated by such large, dark, confusing lips; his eyes so different from Muru's – disturbing – although their complexions were very similar.

I know it is impossible, she thought, but I would dearly like to know something of my destiny. I do not need to know every detail of what will become of me, not the name or face of every man I should meet, not the weather (be it rain or shine) of each day, not even the sum totals of blessings and curses that seem to dot our daily lives, but simply the broad outline of how it will be. The future. Will it be happy?

Will I find satisfaction? At least for some small portion of my allotted time? Is that too much to ask?

She could sense there, at the racecourse, a huge desire around her, among the island's gamblers, for just such a glimpse of the future. A premonition, a vision, a momentary flash of the finishing post and the colour of the jockey's blouse as the winning horse streaks past. She could see men wincing and mincing, twisting screws of paper, their brows furrowed with racing thoughts, predicting everything and nothing. Grappling with futility. *If only, if only,* their expressions seemed to say as their fingers turned this way and that. But all she wanted to know was whether tomorrow would lead her closer to something she could believe was the purpose of her life. And, what could *he* be in her world?

Henri was so oblivious of her thoughts that for a moment she felt a tenderness for him as for some helpless beached porpoise. She could see he was controlled by small desires. Perhaps that was better than to be driven constantly by larger ones that one had no hope of understanding, let alone satisfying?

A bugle sounded; the palomino pricked up her ears.

'Now, Henri.' Lucy leaned on his arm. 'Now let us go up to our places.'

The pavilion had been repainted for the season in the colour of daffodils; all the hardwood had been varnished; the brass polished to perfection. At the entrance, a thickset Indian gentleman dressed in grey linen greeted them confidently. 'This way, mademoiselle, the race is about to begin.' He quickly introduced himself as Mr Badani. Henri explained to Lucy that Mr Badani had been the moving force behind the organising of the race. 'Just a touch of paint here and there, don't you know. Nothing too strenuous.' Badani modestly spun an expert hand and flashed a sharp, easy smile.

'Mr Badani, the landlord?' Her eyes widened. 'I am Mrs Huyton's niece.'

'How very good to meet you. I hope you are enjoying Ambleside.'

'It is enchanting. The most wonderful place I have ever seen.'

'You are very kind. Now you must hurry for the race. Please, up the stairs.'

They found their seats just in time. The horses, milling about the starting rope, stomped and snorted and jostled each other. The palomino was particularly edgy and shied away every time the jockey tried to get her in position. Two or three of the other horses pushed ahead, raising their heads and champing at their bits; then the starter made his signal and the rope was raised. Immediately all the animals swung into line and set off like leaves before a gush of water. All except the palomino who reared up and unseated her jockey. Henri leapt to his feet. A grey had shot ahead and led the field around the first bend. Henri whooped in delight. 'That's my girl.' Lucy, relieved to see the palomino run free, along the track but out of the race, turned her attention to the spectators.

She spotted Don Lambodar on the stand above the coloured ladies. She could not help wondering where the balance of his face would lie if the coils of his hair were cut into the shape of an English, or French, head? She watched him pull

out a piece of paper from one of the many pockets that decorated his blue Byzantine coat. He studied it, apparently less
caught up in the excitement of the moment. Elephants, she
imagined, was what he would prefer to see thundering past
on some rajah's beach. Cotton enveloped her ears, deafening
them to the tumult around. Her eyes clouded except for the
small circle upon which she was focused. Don Lambodar
searched another pocket and found a pencil. He glanced in
her direction. Then, leaning against the rail, ignoring the
hubbub around him and acting for all the world as though he
were in his own study, he set about scribbling.

# Chapter 7

THE PRINCE had put on his English clothes for his constitutional, and a hat to hide his topknot.

'How was your race meet yesterday?' he asked Don, taking his stick and testing it with a couple of sharp taps on the floor.

Don looked up from his papers. 'A very social occasion, but financially unprofitable.'

The Prince clucked disapprovingly. 'Gambling on ignorance is very unwise. You should be more careful.'

Don tried to make light of it with a smile. 'I was poorly advised.'

A small brown spice finch landed on the windowsill and looked about expectantly before pecking at the paltry offering sprinkled on it.

'A common complaint these days, but it is no excuse,' the Prince replied, inspecting the bird. 'Much better you leave that Narayena to his own pot and stick to exercising your legs in the Gardens with me.'

The Botanic Gardens had been nurtured as a haven – an island within an island. Foreign plants from all over the world

– Ceylon, Polynesia, the Ivory Coast – had been imported, much as the people of Mauritius had been, but to a condition of care largely absent outside its walls and railings. The bushes that lined the entrance to the Gardens danced, fresh and lucent; the cannas proudly flapped their red and yellow speckled coxcombs in the breeze.

The Prince carried a small hemp sack in which he had collected bird feed. Every time bread was broken he would scoop up the crumbs into it; stale pieces of baguette were always put in there to be crushed underarm, along with biscuits and flakes of roti. Into the mixture he would add wild berries, seeds, ears of grain. Then, on his stately peram- bulations, he would cast handfuls of floury potpourri like coins to the poor. Within moments, pigeons and shrikes, the bulbul and the fody would be nibbling at his feet as though he were the Emperor of ornithologists.

On this occasion, the Prince waved his companion away with an impatient hand. 'Let me be on my own for a while.'

Don Lambodar left him on his bench and wandered over to the lotus pond. Several of the big water lilies had flowered. Sitting down on the low wall around the pond, Don mused on the good fortune that had brought him to such a place and the mystery of Lucy Gladwell's erratic charm.

On the other side of the water, he saw the dignified Mr Amos. As he drew near Don could see that his friend was puffing and short of breath. 'The fellow is mad,' Mr Amos muttered. He tugged at his collar, loosening it. 'Utterly mad.'

'Has the Prince misbehaved towards you?' Don asked, worried that their paths might have crossed. The Prince was not well disposed towards Africans, enslaved or free. The kaffir soldiers from Mozambique who had supplanted the more amenable Malay troops in the initial British invasion of Ceylon had left an unhappy impression on him, and only the other day he had scolded the black watchman at the Governor's residence – albeit in Sinhala – for merely failing to lower his head as he passed.

'No, my young friend, no. I have not seen your Prince. I refer to the Intendant – the Frenchman in charge of the Gardens. He has taken leave of his senses.' Mr Amos brushed aside a couple of bulbous red ants and sat down beside Don. 'He thinks the Gardens should be a cemetery. It is quite improper, in my view, and practically sacrilegious.'

Don smiled, relieved it was nothing more serious. 'It might enrich the soil. In time, perhaps the plants and trees here will serve as a very fitting memorial,' he joked.

Mr Amos looked at him with a painfully benign expression as though he must indulge naivety because it is inherent in youth. 'That clearly is not the case here.'

'Why do you think not?'

He sighed. 'My dear young man, I fear you do not understand the nature of his debased imagination. You have seen, no doubt, the glaring monument by the ostrich grass?'

'I see visitors – females – perusing it.'

'That is the legendary tomb of Virginie. You know the story of Paul and Virginie? Our most famous tragedy, the novel of Monsieur Bernadine de Saint-Pierre?'

'A book?'

'You are a literate young man. You should read it. An instructive tale, in its way, despite its many distortions.'

'About the Gardens?'

'No, our island. Paul and Virginie are brought up on an idyllic island. This one, apparently. Two white children who grow into a love of the purest kind, according to the author, unblemished by sin or their enslaving civilisation.' He rolled back his head so that his face was turned to the sky. 'They were in a paradise.'

'I can see how some parts might be described in heavenly terms.'

'But then, sadly, Virginie is sent to France for her education.'

'Was it such a tragedy to be educated?'

'Paul is left all alone here, longing for her return.' He paused and closed his eyes for a moment. Then he added, in a much lower voice, 'To be separated, my dear boy, is far worse than never to have met your mate. Ignorance, I am afraid, is preferable to loss.'

Don looked at the older man, puzzled. 'What? Does she never return?'

The dark creased eyelids flicked open. He carried on with the story. 'Paul learns to write, he studies. He finds a mentor. He reads and discovers the friendship of books. But his books never match the companionship of his love.'

'They never could,' Don said knowingly.

Mr Amos hummed. 'If there is the Gospel in the pages, one of course finds all the solace one needs, but this Paul only wants to read about France and to read Virginie's letters.'

'I see. He is not a Christian.'

'On her return journey, just off the coast and within Paul's sight, the ship is wrecked. Virginie, too modest to free herself of her Parisian apparel, is dragged into a whirlpool and drowns.' Mr Amos raised his eyebrows. 'He cannot live without her and he, poor boy, has insufficient faith in God's will. He suffers terribly until he dies of a broken heart. The point being that they can only be united in a true heaven.'

'And they are buried here.'

'Now do you see the madness of it?'

'I cannot say I do.'

'There is *no* Paul, *no* Virginie,' Mr Amos groaned in exasperation. 'They are a figment of a wandering imagination. The tomb is an illusion. And now the Intendant has decided that one false tomb – for Virginie – is not enough, but a second – to Paul – should be erected. Purely for the delectation of visiting European fancies. It is a waste of sympathy on a colossal scale.' Mr Amos banged his fists together.

'I don't understand why that is so upsetting.'

Mr Amos stared at Don. 'It is an affront, young man: an affront to the true suffering of which there is a surplus here in the cane fields and the factories throughout the land. Can you not see?' He bent over, breathing hard, buckling under the injustice. His head sank into his hands.

At that moment, Don Lambodar, enthralled by the idea of the two ill-fated lovers, did not fully appreciate the intensity of Mr Amos's feelings, nor see the justification for his indignation. 'Surely, Mr Amos, you will grant the art of tragedy – a tale of doomed love – the power to evince sympathies that may otherwise lie for ever dormant? To awaken us this way must be to our eventual benefit.'

Mr Amos glanced up, his eyes split in a flash of anger. 'Perhaps, if it is so designed. These tombs, however, are built to delude and gratify a baser instinct of sentimentality. They are likely to supplant the tale itself, in my opinion, and bind the mind to false contingencies. We are not talking poetry, man. This is vulgar mawkishness.'

In Mr Amos, Don had thought he had found a communicant, but now they seemed to be in separate spheres. 'Is it not natural to wish to bend fiction towards fact and vice versa?' The image of Lucy Gladwell, up in the pavilion at the racecourse, came back to him. He was sure she had been watching him.

'You must not confuse matters. Imagination has been given to us, as wings have been given to angels, to bring us closer to Him. We live on such wings for a purpose. God makes the world as it is for a purpose.'

'Including the suffering you spoke of, and the cruelty?'

Mr Amos rinsed his hand in the pond and shook the water off like a minister at a difficult baptism. When he spoke again, he spoke slowly. 'Life is a trial, my son, but we have the means to endure it.' His voice had a note of bitterness that Don had not heard before.

He drew back. 'And what would that be?'

Mr Amos's face lengthened. 'As I said, the gift that allows us to conceive a world beyond our own. One without the floggings, the amputations and the burnings that have plagued us. Without the malice that clots the hearts of small-minded men. The cruelty that hungers for a crust of blood on a man's back and human pain as the price of pleasure. A gift that should not be wasted on trivialities.'

Don put his hands together, as if he were moulding a new globe, and pressed them to his chest.

# Chapter 8

GEORGE HUYTON picked his way through several mounds of soiled linen on the back verandah, whistling Mozart and plucking at the occasional spider's lyre that hung behind the jalousies.

As the Governor's representative in Pamplemousses and the Superintendent of Transport for the island – a position that required him to inspect the roads and bridges built by the convict department – George Huyton was rarely to be found at his office in Port Louis for more than a couple of hours at a time. He had a wide area under his responsibility. 'It compares very favourably with the acreage of Belvédère,' he would quip, pitting his territory against that of the biggest estate on the island.

Lucy, curled up in a wicker chair sorting her aunt's sewing box, looked up. 'Where are you going today, Uncle George?'

'To the big house in Belvédère. I have to see that damn chap Champney again.' He adjusted his cravat to give his chin some florid support.

'May I come?'

'But today is dhobi day, Lucy, is it not?' His eyes crinkled as he strained at a smile. 'Your domestic duties must take precedence.'

George Huyton contemplated the large dark shade tree steaming in the morning sun and added his own coda. He was a man who knew his place well; who drew strength from the earth he stood upon and found the echoes of his deepest wishes resound from his adopted environment: from the trees, the rocks, the ravines, the hills, the heavy drifts of the ocean furled around the island, the reams of the sky.

A door opened and his wife came out with a pair of scissors in her hand. 'Will you be back this evening?'

Mr Huyton lightly smacked his ridingcrop against his leg. 'I have a mind to inspect the coast road after my meeting with the Frenchman.'

'On circuit overnight?'

'Perhaps.' He looked defiantly at her. 'Is there any reason not to?'

'I thought we might introduce Lucy to some of Josephine's native food tonight.'

'I doubt Creole bouillabaisse is to her taste, my dear.' He buttoned his coat briskly and started towards the coach house. 'Now, where the devil is that horse?'

At nine o'clock precisely Adonis, the dhobi, arrived with a pannier of pristine linen and garments, all washed and dried and ironed to perfection in some backwater that none of his customers had ever seen. A small wiry Indian with pale wrinkled hands, he had been washing clothes in Pamplemousses all his life and serviced most of the houses nearby.

'Good morning, Adonis.' Lucy flopped on the floor of the

verandah; her skirt spread like a puddle around her. Sewing and laundry could never be her favourite occupations, but she had liked Adonis from his very first visit. 'How is your family today?' she asked.

He swung the pannier down off his head with an indistinct grumble. 'Boy no good, missie. Girls only chit-chat.'

Muru peered around the corner and then hurried indoors to call Mrs Huyton.

'I hope you do not scold them, Adonis,' Lucy laughed.

'They never listen, missie, even if I shout my head off.' He slowly redid the flat-topped turban that protected his skull.

'There you are,' Mrs Huyton exclaimed, advancing to her pulpit.

Adonis started to unpack; he counted out the linen, the towels, the shirts and placed them in small piles on the bench while Muru called out the number in each category. Mrs Huyton marked the list. Once all the clean items were fully accounted for, the dirty washing was recorded. Occasionally there were moments of indecision – is it a sheet or an under sheet? Betty Huyton would have to adjudicate. 'That is an Egyptian cotton sheet. You must know it by now, Muru, surely? Lucy, please note.'

Muru beamed, scoring a point. 'Yes, ma'am. I know Egyptian, but this dhobi, he is saying it is ordinary. Change it to cheap Bombay, any damn chance.'

Adonis gasped and banged his forehead with the heel of his palm. 'Madam, this boy wicked. How he can say such things, I do not know. Your bad talk will be punished one day, boy.' He switched languages and added, 'You will be reborn a toad and croak until your tongue splits.'

'What about last time, dhobi man?' Muru wagged his head, dislodging specks of dry oil in the flatulent air of another domestic squabble and veering back into English.

'That was mistake. Madam, you know that was honest mistake.'

'Never mind, get on with it now. Miss Lucy will preside next time and she will not tolerate any such confusions.'

Adonis bundled up the washing and stuffed it all into his squeaky pannier. Lucy paid him his dues, trying in vain to hide a playful smile.

'Goodbye,' she said, 'be good to the little ones.'

'Right, Muru, all this can now be put away. That table-cloth we will need for tea, and the embroidered napkins too.' Mrs Huyton was quick to issue her commands before Lucy could even gather her thoughts. 'And, Muru, you must watch your language.'

'Yes, ma'am. Sorry, ma'am.' He disappeared into the house with an armful of crisp damask.

Betty Huyton fingered her rings and sighed. 'That dhobi can be very trying.'

'But he is honest, is he not?'

'My dear, if he could put this whole house on his head and carry it away, you can be sure he would.'

Lucy held back, dismissing her aunt's remarks as a slip of island slander insinuating itself into a temporary crack.

'I am almost done with the sewing box, but we have no black thread.'

'Really? Where does it all go?' Her aunt traced the line of her fine jawbone, bemused. 'Personally, I am not very fond of black. Far too mournful, don't you think?'

'Yes, Aunt Betty, but we do need some.'

'You must watch the new boy, Jacob. You know, Lucy, pilfering comes very naturally to some of these folk and must be firmly discouraged.'

'It is only thread,' Lucy exploded.

Her aunt surrendered. 'Indeed. I may well have put it somewhere out of sight. Such a gloomy colour anyway.' Her face relaxed. 'Tell me, did you meet young Henri Benoît yesterday? He was here with his usual tot of honey, but I think he was rather hoping to see you.'

'No, I didn't, Aunt Betty.'

'What do you think of him?'

Lucy cooled a little. 'Sweet enough but he has too keen a desire for a wife, which he mistakes for something greater.' She shut the box firmly and fastened the catch.

'What do you mean by greater, my dear?'

The question released a knot; she felt herself float up and gain a perspective she had not had before. 'He thinks he is in pursuit of love, when he is not. He wants comfort and, at best, *to* comfort.'

'I see.'

'He should turn his attention to the apothecary's daughter.'

'Dorothy? How very clever of you to think of her.' Mrs Huyton looked approvingly at Lucy. 'You are absolutely right. He clearly needs a wife like Dorothy to take the place of his mama.'

'Or a pet.'

'He and his mother, I find, are quite companionable, but I agree, only in small doses. If he is not to your taste, Lucy,

107

perhaps Antoine Champney would be the better mark. He is by far the more eligible.'

'I did not think you were so fond of the French, Aunt Betty.'

'Unfortunately, other than for soldiers, most of the available young men here are Gaulish. But despite that impediment, he is one well worth your attention, Lucy. Very well worth your attention. I rather wish your uncle had taken you over.' She pulled out one of the threads and examined it.

'We have been introduced.'

Her aunt started. 'Is that so?'

'At the apothecary's, as it happened. The Reverend introduced us. Mr Champney was in need of some medication.'

'No doubt he felt much better to have made your acquaintance. I hope our Dorothy was not there. We must engineer another meeting between the two of you soon.'

'I met the Ceylonese gentleman the other day too.' Lucy tried to steer her aunt away.

'The Prince?'

'No. Well, yes, him too. That was before. On May Day. But at the races, when I was with Henri, we came upon the one who speaks English.' She became uncertain now whether she should have mentioned the encounter at all. Her own feelings seemed to behave so unpredictably.

'I thought there are two of them that speak English.'

'It was the interpreter. Don Lambodar.'

'And?'

'He was on his own. And most ungracious.'

'Oh dear. I had heard they were quite refined in their manners.'

'It is his opinions that are objectionable.'

'I see. Then perhaps you should challenge them, don't you think? Opinions can change, unlike character, or indeed the physical attributes of a man. His nose, his brow, his eye. What do you make of them?'

'I had not noticed.' Lucy could see it was a mistake to have brought him into the conversation; a diversion that threatened a greater discomfort than the previous Gallic track her aunt had been negotiating. It was so difficult to know what to do. Every turn, at nineteen, was fraught with danger.

Fortunately, at that moment, George Huyton came stomping up to the house, waving his hat about. 'A productive morning, I hope? Clean sheets and towels?'

His wife, a little flustered to see him returned so soon, very nearly yelped. 'Good heavens. What happened, George?'

'Ran into a spot of bother. Some rowdy agitation at Belvédère. Those bloody French have no idea how to deal with coolies.'

'Did you have to intervene?' she asked, swiftly balancing concern, curiosity and discomfiture into expert wifely composure.

'I decided not to carry on. Champney should get an officer in before any nonsense spreads. You know how it is with them. Bush fire. Buggers understand only brute force and the more quickly it is applied the better.' He laughed and ruffled Lucy's sleeves. 'Do not be alarmed, my dear. We'll soon have it sorted.'

Lucy knew he did not really mean brute force. Her uncle liked to provoke her with exaggerations. The island was not about to be engulfed in flames. She understood that slavery, like its trade, must be abolished, but the difficulty she had in this world of coolies, slaves and servants was finding the line between service and servitude. When does one become the other? And does the distinction matter?

'Well, we cannot afford to lose any more time on ridiculous disputes, Lucy.' Her aunt clapped her hands. 'We have china to attend to, and the glasses.'

'My mother married too young, Lucy. It is a most vexed business to ascertain the correct age at which one might marry with success.' Mrs Huyton collected a brass key from a small lacquer box and opened the cabinet. She picked up a beautiful wine glass: a delicate round funnel, engraved with a six-petal rose in perpetual bloom, and balanced on a twisted spiral stem that linked two turban-like knots. 'She had a pair of these, from her wedding. Only one remains. Everything was a bit like that for her. One half of a marriage, one child out of two. Half a life.' She wiped the glass and put it back, carefully, to the side of a finely cut decanter. 'The boys know not to touch this shelf. I am the only one who can dust these.'

'Was your mother so very unhappy in her life?'

'No more than most of us, I suppose, dear child. But in her case perhaps the moments of joy that provide a married woman with some alleviation were very rare.'

'And you? Does Uncle George provide sufficient alleviation?'

'Of course, my dear. My mother was very glad to see me happily betrothed. As indeed I will be when it is your time.' She paused. A small mischievous smile crept over her face. Betty Huyton looked as though she believed she needed only to snap her fingers for the golden hoop of matrimonial fortune to girdle her niece.

Lucy laughed a little nervously and dodged its descent. 'My mother said I will never find a man with enough words to match the number I pour into my head from my books.'

'Marriage, my dear, is more than a conversation.' She handed Lucy a cloth. 'Perhaps you can do the decanter.'

'Surely, Aunt Betty, I must be able to converse with a man who would be my husband?' For a moment she looked distraught, trapped in the amber shafts of the sun with a flat sail. 'Why disrupt the pleasure of one's own company, if not for the exchange of thoughts? How else could we express our true feelings?'

'It does not always require one to exercise one's vocal cords.'

'I understand that, Aunt Betty. We can enjoy the companionship of a dog, or a bird, or a horse. But what is the point of a man if he cannot speak to you?' She picked up the decanter and absently dangled it by her side. 'The gift of language is surely to give us the finest means of expression: tender, strong, delicate, beautiful, firm, powerful, exquisite, magnificent —'

Her aunt steadied Lucy's hand. 'Quite, my dear. The English language is a very fine thing, and perhaps you will find a word-smith who will enthral you, but I hope he will not be a poet of penury, as I understand is so often the case. One needs more for one's comfort in this world than a rich vocabulary.' She quickly moved a couple of glasses out of the way.

'I am sorry.' Lucy dropped her voice, suddenly chastened for inadvertently belittling her uncle. Guilt warmed her face and drew beads of moisture to its edges. She cradled the decanter and ran the cloth down the spiralling grooves.

'Your uncle provides a very solid frame, my dear. We do enjoy our own preferences, as you will have noticed, but there is a great freedom in knowing where we each stand, and in reliability. And you must admit,' she added, the muscles of her face loosening, 'it is often an improvement to have him silent – even if brooding – than spouting the nonsense that sometimes issues out when he opens his mouth. Far, far better that it is kept shut.'

On her own Lucy could console herself. She understood her circumstances were not unfavourable: within two years she could expect to have an independent income from the money put aside, and out of reach of creditors, by her grandfather. Her uncle, she knew, would have ensured the money was wisely invested for her benefit. It was not necessary for her to marry, nor to follow the dictates of her aunt. She had no desire to be the property of any planter on the island, and no requirement. She found the rigidity of plantations abhorrent. The people – not only the slaves, but also the sirdars, the owners, everyone – seemed like the cane itself: regimented, narrow, controlled. Destined to be cut down. It was not right. A small cottage of her own was all she needed – whitewashed with blue shutters and bright red geraniums in pots. A garden where things would be left alone as much as possible. Where trees and plants would gain their natural shape; where the land and earth would breathe at their own pace. A garden where any kind of plant could find a place to grow. It would become an asylum for endangered beauty. The leaves around her cottage should unfurl for the sun rather than for her, the flowers blossom for the bees and the Olive White-eye to suck rather than for her to pluck. And if her womb should swell from a man's prick one day, and her breasts grow heavy in consequence, it would be for the sake of the child to come – not for a husband's craving for posterity within the rules of primitive primogeniture. She dreamed of a library of her own; a sunny room where a bowl of lavender would still the air while she turned a page and found another magical world. She wondered if it would be here on the isle of Mauritius? The good folk of Bridleton would never have imagined her living in a place such as this. They knew, of course, of her father's seafaring life, his campaigns and his expeditions; and there would have been others of their acquaintance who had ventured to India and further. But they never would have envisaged Lucy travelling beyond Bath or London – two places she could no longer imagine ever returning to. 'Didst thou not after other climates call?' was a line she loved for the world it opened in her mind. She had quoted it in her journal and had replied in firm ink: Yes, dear John Keats, yes, even in my dreams.

After the sun had set, she found Muru sitting on the front steps with his hands cupped around his ears. She asked him what he was doing.

'Listening, missie.'

There was a faint rhythmic thud from far away. 'The sea?'

'Hold breath, missie. Then you hear the boom-boom of the sea and drumming from the village beat together. Listen, missie.' He had a strange, almost inebriated smile on his face. 'The heartbeat of our island.'

# Chapter 9

MARKET DAY in Port Louis is a cacophony of colour: a pulsating jamboree of indigo, turmeric, lemon and jade. A hotchpotch where the produce of Batavia and Bombay, carpenters and potters, fishmongers and bean punters are jumbled up. Lucy picked her way past the basket weavers towards the pinkish curio stalls.

Asoka, sparring with a nervous porcelain pedlar, spotted her and swiftly recruited her to his side. 'Do you not agree that the asymmetry of the handles, the low curvature on this side against that, is a defect in this Chinese vase, Miss Gladwell?'

'It is not a perfection,' she said, drawn by the ease with which he engaged her.

'So there, my dear man!' He threw up a podgy little hand at the merchant. 'You see, it is indeed a defect. The lady agrees and you cannot fault her. It so happens I am prepared to be charitable.' He glanced at Lucy. 'I have to be, given our present state of affairs, as you must understand, Miss Gladwell.' He stared back at his timid adversary and slapped his chest, pretending to give his honest best. 'If it pleases you then, how about we agree midway between your price and my offer?'

The meek young Malabar smoothed his thin moustaches, spreading his thumb and forefinger down the sides of his mouth to ease his answer. 'You go below cost, sir. Too far. My margin so thin. How to feed my two-year-old daughter, my four-year-old son, my poor wife, my hungry mother, my widowed auntie? How, sir?'

'Hai! Hang it then. I'll meet your last price, man, but give the lady the silk rose then, at the very least.' He laughed loudly to prevent any protestation from the merchant, or Lucy, and presented the flower with a great flourish.

'Thank you, Mr Asoka. How perfect.' She saw no good reason to refuse and spoil the moment.

The business done, he tucked the vase under his arm and offered to accompany her. 'Let me be of service, Miss Gladwell. I can drive a hard bargain. The market, you see, is my natural playing field.'

'I am sure, Mr Asoka. No doubt you can. Although on this occasion I thought you met his price, rather than he yours?'

'But for more to the bargain. My eye was on the flower, you might say. Of course it helps, as you just saw, to have a trump to play.'

'It is not so flattering, Mr Asoka, for a lady to be considered merely a trump. In fact, it has a distinctly unpleasant ring to it.'

'Triumph, I think, is the sound one should associate. Triumph with trumpets to the back and to the fore. *Ta-ra-ra!*'

'So, you collect porcelain, Mr Asoka, do you? Vases and figurines?'

He bubbled again. 'It was merely an excuse to obtain the flower for you, Miss Gladwell. Otherwise I am sure you would have thought me too bold.'

'I do. I most certainly do. You are undoubtedly too bold, Mr Asoka.'

'Which is precisely why I am kept so under restraint by that eminent killjoy, your most boring Governor Cole, if I may dare say so?'

They walked on past the millinery stalls to the fruit vendors: the only orderly section of the market where pineapples, peaches and litchis flourished in carefully arranged abundance. Lucy could not but compare the decoration, with some considerable shame, to the hasty heaps in the barrows back in Bridleton, or in the calamities that passed for modern markets in England. 'Which would you recommend, Mr Asoka?'

'The pineapple, without a doubt.' He shut his eyes; his pert nose quivered as he breathed in the fruity air. 'The pineapple is at its very best.' He picked one from the middle of a parade of a dozen or so and sniffed the short, dry, woody stem. He put that one down, picked another and did the same. Then yet another, making a great show of it. The fourth he held up like a prize piglet at a country fair. 'This is the one. You can smell the sweetness, can you not? Here, hold it close and breathe in.'

Lucy took it from him and paid for it, before he had a chance to turn it into another sly gift.

'Have you a palanquin or a carriage, Miss Gladwell, to take you and your purchases home?' A bright smile played around his mouth.

'We do not travel by palanquin, Mr Asoka. Unlike the French, we have horses, not chairs, to carry us. The British purpose here is to build roads and provide carriages, as I am sure you appreciate.' She hesitated. 'And you? Are you with satisfactory transportation?'

'We have been provided with a carriage – for the Prince that is. Yes, indeed. And I have my shoes. As a rule, we do not travel about much, although I do admit we have been given very considerable freedom, even if not complete emancipation.'

'You mean, you have no transport today? In that case, would you like a ride back in our carriage? You are not far from Ambleside, I believe.' He was grinning so broadly now, Lucy suspected that this was a design he had been weaving from the very first moment he had seen her in the market.

'It would be my pleasure to keep your company a little longer, Miss Gladwell, that is if it is not unseemly for an English lady to be seen riding in coloured company without a chaperone.'

'It is an open carriage and there is no opprobrium in being charitable. Is the vase you bought very heavy, Mr Asoka?'

'As a matter of fact, it is much less delicate than I thought.' He helped her up the market steps and out of the gates. The vehicle was on the other side of the road; they crossed over, to save a turn, and climbed in.

As they went up Rue Marengo, they saw young Antoine Champney standing forlorn next to a collapsed gig.

Unmistakable for his blond hair and tall somewhat hunched frame, he presented a very different figure from Henri Benoît – the young Frenchman Lucy usually saw on her excursions.

She smiled to herself thinking of Aunt Betty's partiality towards Antoine, or at least his eligibility. At that moment, however, the Magnate Minor, marooned on the high road with a broken wheel, looked utterly lost. Lucy asked Denis, the coachman, to stop the carriage.

'Can we be of some assistance, Monsieur Champney?'

'No ... no, no,' Antoine stammered. 'It is only a wheel.'

'Perhaps we can take you somewhere? We are going to Pamplemousses.'

Her French was only passable but his, despite it being his native tongue, was not much more fluent.

'Well, perhaps, if I could ... I am due to meet my father and Mr Telfair at the Gardens. I fear we will not be repaired in time.'

'Of course,' Lucy said. 'Do join us. I was going there myself. My aunt wants me to consult one of the assistants. The carriage will drop us there and take Mr Asoka to his house.'

'Are you sure?'

'Quite sure.' She turned to Asoka and translated into English what she had proposed.

'Yes, of course, Miss Gladwell.' Then Asoka added, a little more curtly than normal, 'The more the merrier.'

Antoine Champney peered nervously at the carriage. He seemed burdened by promises and was clearly worried about getting to his father on time. The old man was by all accounts bilious by nature, but Lucy could not understand why Antoine should be so intimidated. He must surely understand that his father *needed* him to carry on the Champney enterprise, otherwise the dynast's efforts – a lifetime of connivance

– would have been entirely in vain. There must be some equality in their enterprise. She wondered, was the father as fearful of his son's flimsy resolve?

Antoine fumbled with the door and climbed in. He squeezed himself into a corner and seemed to be more preoccupied by Asoka's footwear than anything else. True, they were unusual shoes: the reddish leather soles curled up at the toes and were linked to thick bauble-strung straps tooled with elaborate arabesques. A treat for a tale of the most fabulous oriental splendour. She had not seen anything quite so fancy on a male foot before, and she supposed neither had Antoine – but his gauche behaviour did not promise much for the future of the Champney estate.

Asoka noticed their interest and turned his foot sideways to give a more complete view of the design. 'Moorish.' He tapped his nose.

'Is it Arabic?' Lucy leaned forward. 'The marks are very similar to those on my aunt's brass tray. All curlicues, dots and slashes.'

Antoine looked from one to the other, confused.

'From Egypt,' she explained as though she might have been Cleopatra once.

'Hai,' said Asoka who, unlike Antoine, was rarely at a loss for words however meaningless they might be. One of the horses shook its caged head and whinnied which, under the circumstances, seemed to Lucy a far more articulate response than either of her companions was capable of making.

'Moorish?' Antoine echoed at last, catching up with the drift of the conversation. His skin was extraordinarily pale, especially next to Asoka's, and his hair quite like frayed rope, but he did have, Lucy had to admit, a mouth of a very exquisite shape. Perhaps that was why, she thought, he might have such trouble speaking out. The wrong word might tear it, she imagined. How would anyone then repair that without love?

She had hoped that Asoka's natural gaiety might help during the course of their journey, but the reverse happened and Antoine Champney's disposition took its toll on Asoka.

When they reached the Botanic Gardens, Antoine mumbled his thanks and hurried to the Intendant's house; Lucy bade goodbye to Asoka and stepped down.

'Shall I stay with you, Miss Gladwell?'

'No, thank you, Mr Asoka. I am very content on my own,' she replied sweetly and instructed the coachman to carry on.

'*Lassanai, ney?*' Asoka asked Don in Sinhala, shaping a female figure in the air with his hands. Don, immersed in a copy of the *Edinburgh Review*, did not answer. Asoka asked again, 'Pretty, no? That Ambleside girl? What do you think?'

'Mr Huyton's niece?'

'Is that who she is? I thought she must be his daughter.'

'Mr Huyton has no children.'

'That is a little difficult to believe. A man in his position? Do you not think there would be a few of his bulbs and features scattered about his little kingdom?'

'Monsieur Dupont said she was Mr Huyton's niece when we met the other day.'

'Dupont is a mongrel himself who has no doubt populated the island in his own way.' Asoka unbuttoned his shirt and removed it. 'Anyway, she gave me a ride back from town. Very *charmante*, as they say here.'

'She brought you here?'

'Not quite. She is in the Gardens. Dropped herself off to talk to the trees.'

He made his way through to the back verandah where, two steps down, in the sandy yard, a stone pedestal stood with a basin of rainwater. He splashed his face and chest with several handfuls, exhaling loudly. Afterwards, he dried himself and settled down on the rattan recliner with a glass of Madeira to hand. He lay like a beetle on its back, his skinny arms and legs sticking out of his big round body uselessly. A Sinhala nobleman related to the Prince, he was the very opposite in habit and comportment. Born with a silver spoon, he liked to help himself first, before others, and believed quite happily that it was always right to do so. He raised his drink. 'Tell me, my Don, what would you do to entice an English girl?'

'An English girl?'

'Yes. You know. Lucy.'

'Entice?'

'Seduce, tempt . . . Choose your own word, but you know what I mean. How would you entrance a nubile young virgin's third eye? Kindle a flicker of ardour in her soul?'

'I think it might be a mistake. That young woman is not amenable to your crude pranks.'

'You think we are not equal to them, do you? Or is it that you have your own amatory designs, my Don Cupido? How do you plan to tickle her, *machang*? A little French buttery pastry with a squirt of your Dravidian charm?'

'Dravidian?' Don snapped back. 'You are quite off the mark on that. Anyway, she is a brash touchy girl.'

'Indeed. Attractively so, you must admit, my dear twinkle tongue. I see I shall have to engineer a little something before you do.' He closed his eyes and drew in a heavy, lubricious breath. 'Anyway, what are you then, if you are not Dravidian?'

Then, as though to illuminate their darker cells, the sun edged down and flattened against the gathering afternoon clouds. Asoka, muffled in dreams, started to snore.

Don readily admitted that he did not understand the female mind to any serious degree. It seemed to him unfair to characterise it as capricious, but he could think of no other explanation. What else could account for the discrepancy between her warm, if reckless, engagement at their first meeting and the sharp antagonism of the second at the Turf Club pavilion? It had been and continued to be incomprehensible. He had thought he was conducting a conversation, but discovered it had turned into a quarrel of silence with pauses and peripeteia of peculiar proportions. He had not intended to mock her in pronouncing the need for proper places, but she seemed to be absurdly affronted by the notion that the world had a natural order. Surely nature cannot be disrupted? Water flows, the wind blows, we grow old. She must understand that? He had only wished to compliment her by engaging in intelligent discourse rather than indulging in trifles and twaddle, but he worried now that perhaps he had said too little rather than too much.

He imagined her pacing the Gardens, marking his performance: as a linguist his shortcomings would be deemed serious, and as a man his defects irreparable. Perhaps she was the reason Mr Huyton had not responded yet to his letter. He thought he should go to the Gardens and see if she was still there. Repair or redeem.

He slipped in through the side entrance by the fish ponds and did a quick circuit of the outer circle, but saw no sign of his quarry. He noticed the coach house was empty. Clearly the supervisors had left, and it seemed unlikely that Lucy Gladwell would be roaming around alone. He decided to go back via the 'Avenue Erotique' where he could not but marvel again at the audacity of the French gardener who had placed a sausage tree on one side and the voluptuous coco de mer on the other. About twenty yards in, he stopped to pick up one of the rump-shaped double-coconuts that had fallen on the ground. A fine specimen to take back to the cottage as a tease for Asoka, agitating him no end with its replica of a naked unyielding pubis beneath the husk.

He was examining the smooth curve and cleft of it when her voice reprimanded him, somewhat breathlessly, from behind. 'Is it your habit to pick the fruit of these protected trees, Mr Lambodar?'

He wheeled around, trying to keep his embarrassment hidden, and bowed as far as it was possible. Her face was somewhat flushed as though some labour in her heart had burst the bounds of her English propriety. Her lips opened a little, playing mischievously at the corners of her mouth. She seemed unaware that she had strayed into such a salacious section of the Gardens.

'No, Miss Gladwell. It had fallen and was obstructing the path. I walk here every day and feel it is my duty to keep the path clear.' He tried to be unmoved, to keep calm and speak as fully and as transparently as possible.

'A coconut, is it not?' She inclined her head innocently and let a curl of dark hair slip about her eyes and catch with its tip a slice of sun.

'Of a kind, but rather large and unseemly,' he explained, ignoring the idea that the seed famously depicted Eve's own unadorned secret smile in its replica lips.

'How unkind of you, Mr Lambodar, to reprove nature for her generosity.' She extended her hands. 'May I?'

They were quite astonishing: smooth, supple, lily white with the faintest of lines on her palms as though her destiny was entirely her own and the gods of providence utterly benign or unable to draw the contours of her life, her heart and her mind.

Don manoeuvred the thing so that she could only glimpse its profile, rather than the pair of obscene spheres. 'It is very heavy.'

'Too heavy for our delicate hands?' She kept hers open, unnervingly outstretched. She was examining him with not the slightest reserve.

He placed the nut on the ground at a decent angle against the trunk of the tree and lodged his foot, toe down, in front. 'It is indeed perhaps an indelicate object to dwell on any further.' He moved his hands and felt a frisson in the air between them. The lemon grass behind her rasped; involuntarily his tongue followed suit.

Her hands receded; she folded her arms below her bosom. 'Indeed?'

He felt the sun burn the back of his neck. A pale creamy butterfly prayed on a leaf behind her. He wondered if her skin too glistened with the same brief silk powder. He leaned towards her as if to catch any loose drifting dust tinged with her alluring scent. His foot slipped. She peered down and coloured again from the sight of female anatomy so flagrantly delineated. He moved a little to one side; she did the same.

A merle whistled from somewhere between the lime bushes and she looked around in relief.

'Over there,' he pointed, glad of the distraction.

She has a strong firm jaw, he observed, holding in line an eager, energetic face whose muscles at that moment are clearly too tense. Her cheeks are taut, her lips tight and ready to burst, her tongue to dart.

'A dryad,' she announced, as though it mattered what it was, or what indeed she and he might be to a creature free of true emotion. Human emotion. His emotion.

He noticed a couple of saffron strands in her hair, or perhaps that was the effect of sunlight bouncing between the trees. Should not young Englishwomen always wear bonnets? he wondered, but thankfully did not ask. Instead he heard her whistle back to the bird, practically on tiptoe, with manifest disregard to any modesty. The merle took no notice of her antics and flew away towards the araucaria grove, seeking whatever comforts winged dryads desire in their incogitant lives.

She started after it.

'You enjoy birdsong, Miss Gladwell?' Don asked tentatively, a step behind her.

She stopped by an overgrown laurel arch and turned to look at him as though these were the first fair words he had spoken. Her eyes softened and sank. The light in them dimmed, as she searched within herself rather than without. When she replied, her voice was unexpectedly wistful. 'It is an anthem I wish would not ever fade.'

The tips of the green leaves brushed against her sleeve. Don reached out and pressed the eager sprigs back to clear the way. 'There is little in this world that does not wane, Miss Gladwell, however much we may wish it otherwise.'

It was a sentiment perhaps he should not have expressed to a young woman in bloom, even if it was a natural law; her retort was swift. The words locked to each other like a line of poetry.

'Undoubtedly so, Mr Lambodar, but surely that does not mean we should renounce beauty for truth?' She ducked through to the other side.

He followed, conceding the point with a slight smile, pleased at any rate that they had moved on to a plateau of serious philosophical engagement. She too seemed momentarily elated.

'May I perhaps escort you to the lily pond? There is a new lotus that is marvellous to behold.' He offered his arm, hoping they might bask in nature's more neutral glow and find common ground in a display of glorious colour and safer geometric patterns.

She glanced at his arm and froze instead.

'Thank you, but I am afraid I have no time just now.' She quickly distanced her thoughts from his, crushing the sail that had lifted him.

'No time for the flower of eternal beauty, a poem of a thousand petals?' He did not mean to deride her, but could not help the note of scorn sliding in. The wrong words again.

'Are you still attempting poetry, Mr Lambodar?' The yellow bubbles of a late laburnum spun in the slow breeze above her.

He shrank, temporarily bereft of any words. His eyes lingered, but she did not.


'Have you seen anything more of our visitors recently, Lucy? The Ceylonese?' Mrs Huyton asked, catching Lucy quite by surprise that evening as she inspected the linen cupboard, seeking some diversion. 'They were introduced to me the other day outside Mr Baxter's.'

Prickles Lucy did not know she had, flared up. 'They seem to be just about everywhere.'

She was cross that she had given Don Lambodar a glimpse of her inner thoughts in the Gardens; it seemed every time they had met, she had revealed more than she had intended.

'Are you complaining?' Her aunt folded a napkin over and pulled the corners to form a flower. 'There we are. Is that not like what we had at the purser's table on board the ship? Perhaps you could show Muru how to do them tonight.'

Embarrassment and his mockery, rather than any complaint, is what fuelled her indignation. 'I am not complaining at all. Mr Asoka can be very charming and appreciative.'

'Would you not say Don Lambodar has the finer appreciation of our customs?' Mrs Huyton posed the question with a sly glance.

'He is too vain, Aunt Betty, to appreciate anything but his own swagger.' She hoped her aunt would not notice the heat she felt in her cheeks.

'As it happens, I have sent an invitation to Mr Don Lambodar. He will come to tea tomorrow.'

'How could you?' Lucy cried, toppling a column of neatly piled cloths in her panic. 'Uncle George will be furious. He will not entertain him here.' Another encounter did not bear thinking about.

'In my view, your uncle is obliged to meet him. It is a matter of courtesy. He has neglected to answer the man's letter. In any case, did you not ask if we should have the Ceylonese over one day?'

'We were talking about the Prince.'

'We cannot have the Prince to tea while this unsavoury business of temples hangs in the air. No, my dear, we must clear things with Mr Lambodar first.'

'But he is intolerable.'

'Oh, don't be so silly, Lucy. We need to do it soon before your uncle bolts across to Pointe du Bambou again, or wherever in the bush it is he so likes to pot his holes.' She fanned herself briskly and settled back in her seat.

'Can we not invite Mr Asoka, at least, to leaven the deadly presence?'

'No, Lucy. Don Lambodar is coming to discuss a serious matter of correspondence.'

'Well, in that case, I don't see why I need to be here.'

'I think you should, my dear. It is only polite. And he is a very well placed foreigner.'

'I shall ask Jeanette Pottinger to come then and divert him.'

'I am sure she is less prejudiced than you, my dear. I think you very much misunderstand Mr Lambodar. I am told he is a very fine, cultivated young man.'

'You will see for yourself, he is not.'

'Now, what refreshments shall we have for him, Lucy? What would be nice?'

'Perhaps lotus root might put him to sleep?' she suggested darkly.

'Oh, for heaven's sake, Lucy, do cheer up. He was very pleasant when we met. And if you were to invite her, we have Jeanette to think of too.'

'Tomorrow is an ordeal I would gladly do without.'

'No, Lucy, no. You must not say such things. Each day we have is a blessing. Life otherwise is far too short. Now come, let us consider tea and what our Josephine can offer.'

Josephine had never been more than a kitchen assistant, despite the effusive French references she had in her small oilskin notebook, before Mrs Huyton taught her the small repertoire of English dishes she now practised. On her own she had tried to learn the art of home baking with very moderate success. Her madeleines were more like macaroons, her curled pastries could easily be mistaken for sea crabs if met with upon a beach and her Madeira cake, Lucy had teased, could change the building industry in Port Louis from timber to brick at a stroke.

But this was the one occasion when the dear old cook could do her hardest, Lucy thought, and it would only add to her pleasure.

'Come, Lucy, what do you think a gentleman from Ceylon might like?'

'A Bath bun might have some appeal.'

'An excellent idea,' Aunt Betty applauded, delighted at her niece's improved attitude. 'Do you think Josephine could rise to them?'

'I will instruct her. I used to help my mother make them.' Lucy saw her mother, misjudging the mixture, mistiming the heat. A dense unyielding dough. A masquerade of baked rocks.

'There, you see, Lucy. Sometimes if you are able to look forward to an event, the whole experience becomes a great deal more pleasant. I think you might find tomorrow much more to your liking than you expect.'

'Yes, Aunt Betty.' Lucy bit back a smile and went to find Josephine.

Communication was a challenge with the big warm cook who liked to wallow in a past no one else understood. She had no family that anyone knew of, and no life outside, but all the world seemed to drift in and out of her domain like so much flotsam. 'Is me and milk stool belong here longest, missie. Rest jus' come and go, jus' come and go ...' she would sing between English and French whenever something new was brought into the house.

When Lucy told her what cakes she wanted, Josephine wrung her apron, bewildered. 'Bath?'

'Yes, Josephine. Like the scones you made last month.'

'You wan' break teeth?'

'I would not mind if it were his jaw that cracked and if he could never use his mouth again, Josephine.'

'Missie, tha's wicked. Who this fellar you wan' so bad?'

When Don returned to the cottage, he found the Prince caressing a small red-chested fody in his hand. 'Poor thing.' The Prince stroked its feathers. 'Her wing is broken. A bird that cannot fly is in a very sad predicament. Can you imagine it? Unable to do what one is born to do.'

'We are all in much the same boat,' Don muttered.

'No, no, Don Lambodar. Do not confuse a little constraint with the crippling of one's natural gifts. In fact, my dear boy, we are rather more free here than we might be at home with all that rigmarole we had to put up with. I am very glad to be away from it all, and you, I can see, have some charming diversions here.'

'What do you mean?'

'There is a card for you.' He lifted it up and sniffed it. 'From an English lady, I believe.'

Don's heart dipped. How could she push so and pull at the same time?

Don opened it quickly, but it was from her aunt, not her. 'It is for tea, to discuss Narayena's case.'

'At your beautiful forbidden house?'

'The man is the Superintendent in charge. His wife perhaps will ensure he fixes things for us.'

'Us?'

'The Hindoos. There is no harm in charity.'

'I didn't say there was.' The Prince picked up the card. 'Very sharp, this writing. Their letters are like swords, don't you think?'

# Chapter 10

THE EVENING air was cool; darkness rolled across the lawn to lap at the house. Mrs Huyton lit a candle and hummed softly to herself.

'What is it?' Lucy asked her.

'When Don Lambodar comes tomorrow, I am afraid your uncle will have to attend however much he might remonstrate.' She pinched in her lips in the yellow light.

She told George of the impending visit while he was sipping his evening glass of wine on the verandah. He had mellowed enough to shrug at the prospect. 'Tea, is it? Well, I dare say the fellow doesn't take anything much stronger. Weak constitutions these Asiatics have. No stomach for anything more than warm water. As a matter of fact, I'd quite like to see how he handles his tea.' He swatted another flying dragon.

The wind coming up through the cane fields carried the sweet notes of a guitar, low voices stringing an anthem of nightfall from the village beyond. Drums started to beat. A monkey crashed through the trees.

'Boy,' George called out, raising his voice as if to push back the sounds of the night. 'Boy!'

Muru appeared at the doorway.

'More wine, boy.' George held out his glass, tipping it forward. 'Merlot.'

Muru came closer, wiping his hands on his white breeches. He reached out for the glass.

'Where is the tray, boy?'

'Sorry, sir. Inside.'

'Bring it, boy. Have you not learned to use a tray yet?' He laughed tipsily as Muru retreated into a spasm of shrinking shadows. 'That little sambo needs a good whacking, I think.'

Lucy flung down her book. 'That is horrible.'

The darkness swallowed her words; the clamour of night insects rose to fill the void. She turned to her aunt. 'How could you let him?'

Her aunt sank further into her cushion.

A few minutes later Muru returned with a wooden tray. He stretched his neck and looked about before collecting the glass. He took it away and came back with it refilled and placed in the centre of the tray.

'Good. That's better,' George nodded. He took a sip, smacking his lips. 'Much better. I shall christen you Merlot from now on, boy. What do you say, Betty? Merlot would suit the boy, yes?'

'What?' Lucy stared angrily at her uncle. 'What do you mean?'

Muru waited for a few moments longer, watching, trying to anticipate the next command. George Huyton settled back in his chair. Nothing more was forthcoming. Muru glanced at Mrs Huyton who signalled his dismissal; he receded slowly into the background.

George Huyton patted the arm of his chair. 'Come, sit down here, Lucy,' he said, slurring his voice with the warm rush of grapes and a memory masked by cane.

'You know, Uncle —' Lucy started, but he interrupted her.

'Betty, I was thinking, perhaps it is time for Lucy here to find . . .' He paused to clear his throat as if he needed to concentrate and locate the right nail for a coffin. 'Ahem.'

'Quite, George, quite. We know exactly what needs to be done,' his wife quickly chimed in. She glanced at Lucy. 'There is nothing to worry about.' Then she stood up. 'I am a little tired. I will go in.'

Before Lucy could say anything, Betty left.

'Good.' George took another noisy sip. 'Very good. I'm glad that's all in hand then. We must have you settled.' His eyes slid, barely kept in by the sagging lower lids. He clasped his glass with both hands, the backs of which, like his face, were speckled with brown dots as though the blood of Africa had been splattered once secretly in his genealogy and was rising to the surface of his skin. He rocked back in his chair.

Lucy looked at her uncle, foxed. The words would not come out of her mouth however much she tried, but they blazed in her mind. Her life was not for him to settle. He was an old man with a cold heart and a shrivelled tongue and no future of his own. An old man stuck in his chair, his terse blue eyes staring out at the trees, his short, fat fingers clenched, his head solidifying around the grim thought of his own eventual demise. No, not for her this slow doom of convenience married to convention that he and her aunt embodied. Never.

As she tried to control her anger, she saw how he would die one day. His skin change colour. The pink drain away like blood from a wound and his face, his hands, turn to parchment, yellow and grey where the bone had pushed out, or the flesh was pressed; the brown spots coalesce. She saw how the whole house would be still that day, the darkness deep and the sky low and close to catch the remnants of his uncomfortable soul as it is released from the tissue that has swaddled it for surely too long. The velvet coat that has always been a little unhappily tight around his middle and the starched collar that seems to hold his head in place, like a plinth, will then loosen; his knees splay a little more than usual; and his life, those hours and days and nights he spends away, his secret life in Flacq, in Pointe du Bambou, on the roads and inns of this whole island, like his life in England, his childhood, his boyhood, his youth, will disappear for ever. We will never know the truth about him, she realised, as there will be no opportunity for him to expose it. Only a rumour, perhaps fragments of a story, and occasional confusing evidence of his apparent misdeeds in a life of wanton meandering.

He startled her by taking another loud sip of wine. 'Yes, very good, Lucy. You do need to start thinking about your future. It has to be done. Do you understand? You must not leave it to happen by itself. Not with the way you are. Rather blossoming, I must say. Very pleasingly so.'

# PART III

# Chapter 11

Don lambodar checked his pocket watch. Four o'clock, on the dot. He was keen to be punctual and prove he was no lotus-eater.

'Good afternoon, Mrs Huyton.' He bowed, to a very particular and almost imperceptible degree. 'I trust I am not late.' How easily the words come when one lets go, he thought proudly.

Mrs Huyton, dressed in gracious white, with a pearl necklace and silver brooch, sparkled. Her nose fine, her mouth prim, her grey eyes unexpectedly benign.

'Not at all, Mr Lambodar,' she sang lightly. 'Your timing is perfect.' She sat serene and unmindful of the wrinkles that had gathered, like tidemarks on a beach, as her life receded. Picking up a little glass bell, she shook a few lavender tinkles. 'Please be seated. My husband will be here very shortly. He is deep in his papers and it is quite a struggle to get him out from under them.'

'I understand. Administration requires the best of one's efforts. An art in itself, ma'am, at the heart of government.'

She listened politely, although Don Lambodar suspected it would not have mattered what he said, in rhyme or prose. He took the seat to her left; the wicker squeaked as the chair listed to one side under his weight. The cushion was like a mat; the coir had turned to wood. He knew he was sailing into difficult waters. He had no map, no instruments, no talent for this business. He could not be a buccaneer. Nor a horticulturist, but he noticed the scent of mature fleshly geraniums that wafted out from under his hostess.

'I am sure you know more of these matters than I do, Mr Lambodar.'

'I am acquainted with the complications of colonial ventures.' From within and without, he was about to add when Lucy Gladwell appeared in a gown as sharp as a razor.

'There you are, my dear,' Mrs Huyton greeted her. 'Come and meet our visitor.'

'Good afternoon,' Lucy said icily, despite the fluster in her face. She pressed her fingers to her chest as if to stop herself from stepping any closer.

He stood up.

'Good afternoon, Miss Gladwell.' Don Lambodar inclined his head appropriately, but it seemed to have a mind of its own. Well, why shouldn't it? he supposed. At least his voice was steady and firm, unlike at the Botanic Gardens yesterday. Thankfully there was no sex to her scent today.

She took the farthest seat and sat at its edge with her hands now hooked together on her lap, ready to spring. Don sat down again, a little too fast; his buttocks hurt. Even the wicker in this house, he felt, was quite unforgiving, aided as it were by a wooden implement designed to add discomfort to the coccyx. He surreptitiously removed the protusion – a spool of black thread. At the end of the verandah, positioned above her head as seen from where he was sitting, hovered a small painted cage. It looked for a moment like a gigantic tiara, but the illusion was spoiled by the movement of the bird trapped in it. The yellow beak was pulling at something hanging inside. Don could not quite make out what it was: apple, peach, meat or whalebone. Perhaps a drifting cloud, pregnant with rain, or was it her hair being teased into a nest? Watch out, Miss Gladwell, he was about to shout. It is that bird again. A black bird.

Poppy seed should not be eaten, nor sap smoked, he knew, before such refined intercourse, but he had needed much fortifying.

'What is it? You should not stare so, Mr Lambodar.'

'I am sorry, it was not you, Miss Gladwell, but above you. The cage.' It was disconcerting, as was his seat. He slipped the cotton spool under his chair and hid it with his foot – so much easier than a double coconut. He winched his eyes away: up, down. To the sea wherever it may lie, lest he was moved to spew out his mind prematurely.

'Oh, Charlie,' Mrs Huyton laughed. Then she called out a little louder, 'Charlie!'

'Charlie,' echoed the bird in a voice that might be Mrs Huyton's, in time to come: crackly, hoarse and struggling with the notes of a tune that had lost coherence. 'Charlie-charlie. Char-lie.' It is a brown bird. Not black. Don's ears tingled.

'A mynah bird, is it not, Mrs Huyton? I am no aviarist, but . . .' He suppressed a nervous giggle.

'Yes, indeed, Mr Lambodar. Although many mistake it for a blackbird. I understand they were introduced here by a French Governor, Desforges-Boucher I believe – from the coast of Coromandel. You have them too, in your country?'

'Yes, we do have our own. Blackbirds, mynahs and also a species that is even more fluent at mimicking speech: the salaleena.' He did not think he could say Desforges-Boucher right now despite the facility he knew he had to match any blasted bird. 'It is distinguished by having more yellow on its head.'

'Oh, really. Perhaps we should have one of those to squawk out that silly babble they lapse into here.'

'A dandy linguist with egg on his head?' Lucy added, speaking fast and breathless as though she might be flinging knives.

'Dan-dy.' The bird echoed her this time.

Don ducked.

Her throat was bare and delicate, her face curiously open, her eyes bright and beguiling – *charmante*. Her hair tied back looked too taut for her youth. Altogether she was surely too taut for this climate. Too, too taut, he thought.

'Not a linguist,' Don replied. 'The creature has a talent for imitation. It can mimic only; it cannot be taught to speak. And, Miss Gladwell, it is the female of the species, is it not, that lays the egg?'

She coloured and pursed her lips.

'Tell us, Mr Lambodar, how did *you* learn English?' Mrs Huyton interrupted. 'I must say, your English is very good. Do you not think so, Lucy? Have you been to England, Mr Lambodar?'

Before he could reply, the clatter of a horse and carriage intruded from the side of the house, punctuated by the loud clucking of a coachman.

'That must be Jeanette,' Lucy announced with a degree of relief.

'Of course, I quite forgot.' Mrs Huyton craned her neck as if it would enable her to see around the corner of the house.

'I told her we shall have an answer for her today.'

'About what, my dear? The clematis?'

'The theatre. The play. She would like me to go with her and I said I would tell her today if I may.'

'A play?' Don enquired politely while observing the speed with which clouds collided above the Ambleside lawn.

'Yes, Mr Lambodar. The Garrison Players will be performing at the theatre on Saturday. Do you know our theatre?'

'No, madam. I have not had the leisure − forgive me, my pleasure, I mean *the* pleasure.'

'Well, you must go to it then, Mr Lambodar. You must.' She turned to Lucy. 'Which play is it, my dear? I quite forget what Miss Pottinger said.'

'*Othello*, I believe.'

'What an extraordinary choice. I wonder who decided on that. It is Shakespeare, Mr Lambodar. I think you might find it interesting. All about a Moor.'

'I am happy to take your advice and will endeavour to attend.' He could see that her niece was distinctly less happy. A small annoyance above her winged left eyebrow was threatening to flap into a frown.

'I do not think it would be to Mr Lambodar's benefit.'

A little presumptuous of her, he thought and was about to

say something topographical about his affinity to mountains, dales and open moors when he heard a familiar contemptuous squeak behind him.

'I am sorry to impose, Mrs Huyton, but I happened to be on the road when Miss Pottinger passed by so gaily and offered me a ride thus far.'

'What an unexpected pleasure. Do sit down, Mr Asoka. And Jeanette, please.'

'Thank you, ma'am.'

'I saw my compatriot's carriage at the front and I thought I might continue to our abode with him in due course.'

'Mr Lambodar is here for tea. He has some business with Mr Huyton. You are very welcome, Mr Asoka, to stay until he is done.'

Asoka waited for Jeanette Pottinger to sit and then took the seat next to Don, patting him on the shoulder as he settled down.

'Are you much in the habit of riding in the carriages of young ladies, Mr Asoka?'

'Only when the ladies are as irresistible as our present company, Miss Gladwell.'

Lucy laughed. 'You are too forward, Mr Asoka. Is he not, Jeanette?'

'Indeed.' But there were dimples in her restless cheeks.

'I am out of control almost, dear ladies. Mrs Huyton, I apologise for not having the forbearance, the calm placidity of my countryman, the honourable Don Lambodar, but, you see, I simply cannot resist the irresistible. Hai!' He leaned across and slapped Don lightly on the knee.

'Forbearance, I think, is not one of your traits. You speak

more freely than anyone here, Mr Asoka. Although I fear my dear aunt might regard these carriage rides as perhaps a little too daring.' Lucy's teeth were unclenched, Don noticed. She seemed to have no trouble speaking her words now.

'The freedom to speak is one thing we exiles still retain, Miss Gladwell.'

Muru appeared with a tray that dwarfed him. He placed it on the cane table and unloaded it, arranging the cups and saucers, the teapot, the coffee, the sugar bowl with neat military precision.

'Thank you, Muru, I shall pour.' Mrs Huyton touched the teapot to test its temperature. 'Bring the cakes and biscuits. Let the battle commence. We cannot wait any longer for Mr Huyton.'

Young Muru caught Don's eye and smiled sweetly before melting back into the house. Something about the boy stuck in Don's mind like a word he could not translate, glossed over but snagged between this and that: a quiet hunger deep behind the boyish smile. He resolved to give the boy a book and teach him to read, if he did not know how yet. Put learning into action; make a mark as on a blank page.

'Tea or coffee, Jeanette? Or would you prefer a juice? We have cane and pomegranate?'

'Tea please, Mrs Huyton.'

'And you, Mr Lambodar?'

He was startled out of his reverie of a future in education and blurted out, 'The same, if I may. Thank you.'

Asoka and Lucy expressed a preference for coffee.

They each took a ritualistic sip before the delicacies arrived.

'Now, Mr Lambodar, I think you were on the verge of telling us about your visit to England.'

'I have never been to England, ma'am,' Don confessed, unaccountably ashamed. He felt suddenly hot and his head itched but he refrained from scratching it. All he wanted to do was to run his hands through his hair and rake his scalp. 'I have only read –'

'Lucy is forever reading, are you not, my dear? That Irish thing, Larry O'Rourke is it?'

'You mean, *Lalla Rookh* by Mr Moore.'

'And your cockney apothecary, who died so young? He wrote a lot of stories about Greek gods and their goings-on . . .'

'John Keats was a poet, Aunt Betty.'

'Our Don Lambodar lived with an English family,' Asoka remarked with a smirk.

Mrs Huyton inclined her head. 'Is that so?'

Don had no wish to discuss his early life and tried to be brief. 'In Colombo there was a Mr Berwick we knew very well. An Englishman, not a whole family.'

'How intriguing, Mr Lambodar. Do tell us more.'

'I like to learn languages. We have many opportunities with the jetsam and . . .' He struggled to find something to cling to.

'You are very accomplished. And you too, Mr Asoka, I believe.'

Asoka raised his hands grandly. 'No, no. I am not like our Don here. I was taught only English. My father thought it might be useful and engaged a tutor in my eleventh year.'

'How very far-thinking of him.'

'It has been our habit, Mrs Huyton, to accommodate ourselves to visitors from far and wide. Don Lambodar's family, for example, first appeased the Portuguese, as you can tell from his name, before siding with the British. And I suppose the Hollanders were accommodated somewhere in between, no doubt. His father, I believe, was Hindoo.' He examined his companion for a reaction having spun the web.

'My father was a pragmatist,' Don said, rallying a bit after another sip of tea. 'He said our faith was in the efficacy of conversion and we practised it with gusto. Each generation moved us on: from Guebre to Moslem, to Hindoo, Buddhoo and Christian espousing both the Sinhala and the Tamil. But his ancestors were in fact from Basra.'

Lucy looked quite at sea. She touched her hair with her fingers. 'Like Sinbad?'

'Ah,' Asoka exclaimed, as though he now understood all his colleague's shortcomings.

'It is a very curious business, indeed.' Mrs Huyton covered the pots with elegantly embroidered cosies and the carafe of juice with a piece of brownish lace that had black beads sewn like pendants around the edge to weigh it down. Then Muru appeared and she brightened again. 'At last, the treats. Please serve our guests first. Jeanette, do have something.'

She took a ginger biscuit and the tray rumbled towards Don.

'Mr Lambodar, we have a very English speciality for you. You must have the bun.'

He lifted one of the yellow crusted boulders from its nest on to a small plate, but elegance failed him as he tried to bite it. Eventually he managed to chip a small piece. 'Very gratifying.'

'I am glad you like it.' Mrs Huyton avoided the buns and sought a biscuit like Jeanette. 'It is a recipe that Lucy furnished for the occasion.'

Lucy sank, much exercised in measuring a lump of sugar.

'I am indebted, Miss Gladwell.'

'My pleasure,' she said defensively. Her eyes sparked. The bird hopping above her head was also staring at Don, or so he believed, flashing its yellow beak in warning. Yellow. Yellow. Everywhere. 'Pleasure,' he heard it repeat. A mocking echo. He saw himself floating on a cloud confessing his misdeeds in a dream: I killed a mynah bird once. I had not meant to but it was sitting on the branch of a temple tree and I was in a rage. I had been banished from my class for not having learned my verses. I picked up a rock, about the size of the ones on the plate, and hurled it at the bird in a desire to make it – the missile – go where I wanted it to go even if my tongue would not. The rock turned as it flew, leaving a trace of dust and debris in the air. A bird's bones are small and thin and smash very easily. Feathers offer no real protection.

'A lovely colour,' Asoka said, inspecting the buns.

'Saffron has a very remarkable effect,' Mrs Huyton explained. 'More tea, Mr Lambodar?'

Don nodded, grateful for any small action of normality and the effect of hot liquid on crusted sand. Asoka prattled on. 'I was telling Miss Pottinger, as it happens, on our way over, that in our country the colour of saffron is sacred. You see it in temples, on the roads, in fields. Our monks' robes are dyed in the colour and they, the monks that is, are everywhere.'

Don saw a robe wound round and round and round; a corpse wrapped. The gurgling of prayer – *sangham saranam gachchami* – that goes round and round his head. Ten monks all in a line chanting, their mouths opening and closing, drowning, their shaven heads lolling, the pleats of their robes rising and falling. Why are they doing this to me? He bit hard and swallowed. Sand seemed to scrape his throat.

'What do Hindoo monks actually do?' Jeanette's eyes widened to take in all possibilities.

'These are not Hindoo, Miss Pottinger.'

'Buddhoise, are they not? I have read about the religion of the Bodhi – is it?' Lucy added tentatively.

'Yes, the Buddhoo monks are the ones in saffron. But we have other holy men too, as our dear Don would attest. Ascetics: Sufis, Hindoo sanyasees, fakirs.' Asoka placed his palm on his stomach with the modest suggestion that, despite his present appearance and the many rings that engorged his stubby fingers, he may have known something of asceticism himself once.

'Fakirs?' Jeanette lifted a hand to her mouth to suppress a giggle.

'You would be amazed, Miss Pottinger.' Asoka teased his loose, curly hair with his other hand. Don feared that he meant now to describe the naked torsos, the unclothed loins and serpentine hair of those lost lingams, simply to excite the carnal imaginations of his genteel audience. 'They rub ash on their –' he began but was fortunately interrupted by the master of the house.

'Good afternoon. I had no idea we would have so many here for tea.' George Huyton struck a fist into his palm purposefully behind his back. He made a small bow in the direction of Jeanette and then turned to Asoka and Don. 'Our visitors from Ceylon?'

'How do you do, Mr Huyton?' Asoka sprang up.

'Mr Don, you are here to discuss your letter?'

Asoka inclined his head. 'Your business, Mr Huyton, is with my compatriot, I believe, not me.'

Don rose more slowly, in reluctant deference.

'There's my bobbin.' Mrs Huyton, strangely exultant, pointed at his feet.

Her husband addressed Don. 'I have very little to say on the matter, Mr Don, but perhaps we should go to my study in a moment. First, however, I must have my beverage.'

'What would you like, my dear?'

'The usual, if you don't mind.'

'No Merlot, I am afraid, but the coffee might do you some good today.'

His eyes narrowed and his gaze fastened on the plate of buns. He reached out and took one. Don watched, fascinated, as he bit into it. 'Good grief, what have you done to these?'

'Lucy had a recipe. It is a very special –'

'This is a disaster, not a recipe. You would do well, Lucy, to steer clear of such fancies.' He chucked the bun back onto the plate, which very nearly cracked. He drank his coffee determinedly. 'Right. If that is all, let us repair, Mr Don, and deal with this infernal business of yours.'


'Now then, what is this all about?' He had both his hands in front of him and squeezed them into each other; his skin noisy and angry.

'You have read the letter?' Don saw it skewered on the desk, next to a pile of packets and papers. He had to marshal his thoughts.

'What is it these fellows really want? And why, in heaven's name, are you involved with such rabble? You should take care not to get into trouble here, young man. You have a very comfortable position at the moment, but it should not be tested.'

'I am only trying to help in a matter of justice, sir.'

'Justice? What on earth do you mean? This man Narayena, I know his kind. Trouble, that is what he is. He has made himself a leader of a bunch of ragamuffins who are here precisely because of justice. I have seen it before, the way a demagogue will manipulate the ignorant to gain a position for himself.'

'It is nothing but a shrine, sir. A small temple.'

'A carbuncle, you mean. Why on prime land? This fellow Narayena has been given his own allotment to foul. They all have one.'

'Not the convicts,' Don said, momentarily confusing Narayena with Khola.

'Of course not the criminals, but all the other Hindoos, just like the blacks. And if all these Indians are so keen to worship together, can they not share their own heathen plots?'

'I believe they thought the land was theirs.'

'You are being disingenuous, now. This site was chosen as a deliberate act of provocation. You, Mr Don, understand perfectly well the strategy of provocation, do you not? I understand that is precisely how you people operate in Ceylon.'

'I fail to see –'

'The Reverend Archibald Constantine has no church around here. Pamplemousses has only a Catholic church. But we do not go and build our Anglican church on someone's plantation simply because we need one and think it is an auspicious spot. Why should these people – a bunch of convicts and labourers, slaves – be allowed to do it? Dash it all. I tell you, Mr Don, you should not get involved with such scoundrels. It is a bad business and will come to no good. You have already, with this indiscretion, jeopardised your position.' He stroked the bridge of his nose; it had turned bluish along the edge. Then he yanked Don's letter off the spike and folded it, running a square thumbnail down the edge to flatten it. His desk facing the windows was large and harboured a dozen drawers; he considered them for a moment and then pulled the smallest one on the left and dropped the letter in. 'Advise your little man that it is not wise for him to be in breach of the law. His construction had better be moved or it will be broken up. And you, Mr Don, would do well to remain aloof from the petty squabbles of the likes of him. I recommend you keep your distance.'

George Huyton's study had the air of an executioner's chamber: orders for hangings, for floggings, for branding would have issued not so very long ago from the slave master standing by the stuffed chair, whip in hand. Don realised this was where the fate of poorer men, darker men, would have been decided within the limits of the Napoleonic *Code Noir*. He saw their ghosts in Huyton's shadow. Huyton was a mere tenant in a rented house, but somehow he seemed to gain additional gravitas from the boards that creaked to his tread.

'Do you not think, sir, that perhaps he and his people have some rights in this place? I do not mean the convicts but the others who wish only to worship as their custom. They are not all slaves. There are free men among them. All men are created equal, are they not?'

'You have not understood the situation, Mr Don. Do not confuse the issue with a lot of American nonsense. Rights are to do with the ownership of the land. Property. Capital. These people you speak of have no right to the land. Not even the allotments, or the places where for some unfathomable reason they have been allowed to squat on by the imbeciles who governed this island in the past. The borders of the estate do not belong to any passing fool who wishes to pray as he pisses.'

'Is not the world given to men in common?'

The sun brightened, and a ray of light coming through the window bathed the small shelf of books next to Don. The brown leather of the bindings seemed to soak the light in and release it again through the tiny gold slits spelling out the names of a small posse of authors slotted in the straight neat spines. He spied a Bentham there, and Malthus and Defoe besides the almanacs and company results.

George Huyton sucked in the gay motes floating in the beam between the two of them. The expanded chest, his powers and responsibilities in administering this fast-swelling empire, gave him stature and added to his girth. He hooked his thumbs into his belt and pulled as if to test his true size; he raised his heels to gain his greatest height and shook his legs to adjust his pinched pouch.

'Not in Mauritius, young man. Do not be so Whiggish.

There is no land here that *they* have a right to,' he said. 'They are Indians. Here to work for us. That is all.'

Don wanted to tell him that he was wrong, that all men have some freedoms guaranteed by compact or consent, but he did not know how to; had the man not read the arguments of his own books?

'It might be a mistake to ignore this request,' was all Don was able, at that moment, to say; although in his mind he was fumbling with an equation where labour adds value to all human produce.

George Huyton stared at him, his mouth set hard. 'Fear not. He will not be ignored. It is time this troublemaker was properly dealt with. That is all there is to it, do you understand? He will be hung by his bloody testicles, and I should avoid that fate if I were you.' He opened one of the shutters and waved Don out.

At the end of the verandah, Asoka was regaling the ladies; his head thrown back, burbling. Don felt rocky. This day, he thought, perhaps he had taken a grain or two too much.

'All settled?' Mrs Huyton asked her husband, clearly pleased with her arrangements. 'Mr Asoka has been most entertaining while you have been immersed in Mr Lambodar's affairs.'

'Nothing more to be said on the matter, my dear. Our visitor fully comprehends, I believe, the gravity of his position.'

'That sounds very serious indeed, Uncle,' Lucy laughed, still bright with the levity of her previous conversation. She looked at Don, mockingly he thought, while Jeanette threw another reckless glance at Asoka.

'It is indeed, Lucy. On an island such as this, it is all too easy to transgress boundaries that one should not.'

Asoka sniggered and reached for another biscuit. 'Oh, dear. What has our dear Don done?' His face stretched and his cheek ballooned out, shrinking his eye to a gleaming little ball.

Don felt as though everyone was looking at him; that he had done something he should not have and must make immediate reparations. His thoughts tumbled about in his head: I do not like the eyes of devious men. I do not like the eyes of women when they are filled with pity. I do not like the way the colour of their irises – blue, grey or brown – deepens to drown any light or hope one might have to protect oneself when they are fastened on their target. Even Mrs Huyton looks to me as though she is offering a tender clemency I do not require. I refuse.

'I have done nothing,' he muttered, 'except write a letter.'

A beak scraped a bark, a bone; a feather was ruffled in the lamentable air. If the wretched bird were to say the first word, he reckoned, he would twist off its head and eat it, feathers and all.

Fortunately Jeanette burst out, 'I have a letter to write too.' Her voice dropped dramatically, like that of a conspirator. 'But every time I pick up a nib, my thoughts fly in so many directions I cannot begin. Do you find that, Mr Lambodar? They just go everywhere except on to the sheet of paper in front of you.'

Don wanted to tell her that to write down her thoughts she must hold fast. Force the nib against the texture of the paper and move it by sheer will to shape the letters and inscribe the word that will carry the whole world upon it. It is a hard terrain, a rough, uneven surface that the nib must negotiate, but it must keep moving, otherwise the ink will blot and become as meaningless as the final night of a drowned life. But that was not what he said.

'Your thoughts are as free as a bird's, Miss Pottinger, but sometimes they may need a cage, like that mynah, to find the right words.'

'You will have her in a cage, Mr Lambodar? Is that how you see us? Little birds to be tamed?'

He spun to face this new attack. 'You misconstrue, Miss Gladwell. I mean only that for the language to flourish, it needs a structure – cage, if you will. Our thoughts are bound in one way or another to things greater than themselves.'

Mr Huyton snorted. 'You favour the cage, Mr Don? It must be the climate to which you are born, like these bloody convicts from India, that makes you so amenable to such constraints. They too, I notice, much prefer to be incarcerated – in jail – than to be out working in the open air.'

'It is no mystery, Mr Huyton,' Asoka butted in. 'It is perfectly rational for them to do so. Why should a man break his back working in the hot sun, being pushed around by brutish – I mean, British – overseers on horseback, getting hungry, tired and thirsty all day, when he has the choice of being left alone in a cell with a bed, served the same rations, if not more, and free to think as he pleases? As our Don says, there can indeed be more freedom inside than out.'

Mr Huyton looked at Don with even greater suspicion than before. 'Is that the case?'

His unblinking eyes were like chips of blue poisoned glass; his forehead shone and grew lopsided, one section of it bulging with enquiry. Don had an uncomfortable feeling that his face was in more than one place. He seemed to have seen it outside the gates of the Botanic Gardens, in the general store, at the crossroads of Pamplemousses, at Reduit guarding the entrance to the Governor's House, on Rue de Rampart in town, inside the foyer of Hôtel de Mars. Mr Huyton was everywhere; guarding, acquiring, protecting, taking, stealing. A thief. He had the eyes of a thief, the mouth of a thief; his cheeks the sails of a pirate galleon. Don found it difficult to hold his teacup; he knew if it fell it would break and Mrs Huyton would be disappointed. He put it down on the table cracking neither the cup nor the wood. He stared at the black cotton reel that had been mysteriously elevated onto the table from under his chair.

'What is the matter, Mr Lambodar?' Mrs Huyton asked while her husband fumed. 'Are you unwell?'

Lucy Gladwell picks up the cake knife and inserts it between his lowest two ribs. It cuts open his chest and goes in to prick his heart and make a crimson fountain out of it. Everyone is drowning. No, she does not. Not really, he told himself. But she wants to. I can see she wants to. I can feel her steel gown slice into my flesh: cold and hard and slowly turning me into the same. It is not a pain I feel, but a change in the vessel I leak in. I need a bandage. Black thread will not do. She has what I need in her hands. A saffron boulder is what I do not need.

'I am sorry, ma'am. Just some minor discomfort. Something I ate earlier in the day.'

'I do hope it is not the bun,' Lucy's face seemed to drift to and fro before him.

'No. I am sure it is not.'

Asoka patted him on the shoulder. 'You should be more careful, Don. You should not indulge –'

'Perhaps I should take my leave.' Don struggled to his feet with the garden, the house, the cups and pots still all in place, but only just. He managed a bow to Mrs Huyton without tipping over and banging his lapsed foreskin on the floor; he heard something hit something and caught his head in his hands.

'Is it wise to travel in a carriage just yet? Would you like to lie down for a while inside, Mr Lambodar?' Mrs Huyton's voice turned to honey.

I would like to lie down, he thought, but I know I must not. It would be the wrong thing to do and I will regret it, much as I like this house – the airy spaciousness of it, the sense of its constancy, the tall French windows and the scent of lavender in the room I walked through. The heady smell of geraniums wafting every time any of the ladies moves a ruffle. The gentility of their redolent lives. The eroticism of her perfume. Yes, I would like to stay, to lie in Lucy Gladwell's bed, to dream fervidly between her petals, but I will not. Her sheets are made of metal. I do not wish to live in regret for ever afterwards. Too much of that is already soaking me through.

'Thank you, but I must go. It is better I do so now.' No one looked particularly crestfallen. Jeanette, he noticed, was absorbed in the contemplation of the decorative stitches on Asoka's breeches; Lucy more enamoured of the clawed legs of the tea table. What is it that enthrals a young woman's heart? he wondered. As he stared at her, she seemed to steal a glance back at him. He suspected it was another trick of the light that played a smile between her teeth and eyes.

'Very well then, if you feel you must, you had better do so. Goodbye, Mr Lambodar. Do come again, with the Prince perhaps, next time.'

'Goodbye,' came a raspy echo from the end of the veranda. Don looked for the laughing bird and missed his footing on the steps. He would have been face down on the gravel if not for Muru who happened by and whose arm he managed to grab. Unfortunately, Muru had a tray balanced on his spray of fingers; it flew like a discus. In Greece he might have been a beautiful agile athlete, but here the jug of water splashed the garden and one, two, three, four, five, six glasses tumbled in the air making a juggler out of him and a clown of Don.

'Char-lie,' screeched the mynah again.

As the glasses rained down, catching as they turned a few of the higher flung diamantine drops, Don heard a yelp of protest from Muru and a cackle of laughter from the veran-dah – was it Asoka, or Mr Huyton? Or Lucy? Or the bloody bird? Or all of them?

'Oh dear, are you hurt, Mr Lambodar?' Mrs Huyton enquired from what he suddenly realised was a bed of ardently scrubbed geraniums.

Don mumbled his apologies, still on his feet but his legs were on the verge of collapsing; his thigh bones, his shins were turning gelatinous. He lifted an arm to push away a cloud that had escaped from the birdcage, and stumbled towards the stables.

Asoka waited a moment or two before breaking the awkward silence. 'Our Don has not been at his best,' he explained by way of apology and then, when Mr Huyton had also stomped off, suggested a diversion. 'Perhaps the three ladies would enjoy a walk by the river? I have found a most delightful excursion, particularly in this weather, which I am certain you will find very agreeable.'

Mrs Huyton kept a watchful eye on Muru as he collected the fallen glasses and took them back into the house. 'Will Mr Lambodar manage?'

'Do not worry, Mrs Huyton, I will help him home. At the bridge at ten o'clock tomorrow, then, if you charming ladies would care to join me?'

'Not tomorrow, Mr Asoka. We have the trousseau to air tomorrow. A busy day.'

'I do not wish to press the matter, but Friday then? I would be happy as a . . . nightingale, is it?'

'Alas, we have no true nightingales here, yet, Mr Asoka, only a whistling blackbird.'

'Then the lark, perhaps?' he said, undeterred. 'Meanwhile, for now, I had better go see about our poor Don.'

# Chapter 12

THE NEXT morning, out on the verandah, the Prince was hopping about, furious. 'That *buruwa*. Kick him out, kick the ass.' His Sinhala was always undignified under stress.

Don was heavy-headed, gravel-voiced. 'Why? What the hell has he done?' He too lost his carefully learned manners when the day began with bluster – questions, instructions and accusations – rather than a civil greeting of an *Ayubowan*, *Namaste*, or Good morning.

'Broke my cup. The stupid shrimp.' The old man stamped his bare narrow foot.

'Your teacup?'

'Yes. The Captain's gift. From Staffordshire, you remember? That pretty cup with gold around the rim?' His face was runkled like an overslept sheet, the bags under his eyes looked soiled. 'It gave the tea in this country some taste. Now, the moron has broken it.'

'It is only a cup.' Don's stomach tightened, remembering his own accident.

The Prince's white shawl sagged around his shoulders and

his head rocked as it sank; the heavy grey cheeks wobbled. 'Are you a vandal, Don Lambodar? Do you not see the significance?'

'We can get you another cup at the market today.'

'That is not the point. We have many cups. We have enough cups to serve a dozen guests. I insisted we were given proper china and cutlery. I will not be looked down upon. I will not allow that, but this was a very special cup. The Captain gave it to me in the middle of the ocean.'

'I know. The day we saw the whale.' He remembered the black flukes slipping down into the water. 'But what to do? If it is broken, you must use another.'

'It is very inauspicious for this to happen today. You ask Surangani. She understands these things, even if you do not. Speaking all these tongues has made you forget your heritage. You cannot understand anything any more. Neither the heritage of your mother, nor of your father. I tell you, that oaf will be the end of us. You must get rid of him.' He folded in his arms and hissed. 'We will be ruined if you don't. Completely ruined.'

The picture of serenity feeding birds was a sham, Don realised. This was a man for whom a broken cup, or the bickering of doves, heralded the end of civilisation. He could never have been a king.

The ipomoea flowers that curled along the hedge behind the well lay lazy on soft green lineny leaves, sucking the morning sun into their dewy delicate tubes and releasing faint undulating vapours like the music of some inaudible flute.

'What happened to the cup, Khola?' Don asked.

The culprit chewed a small twig stuck in his mouth, shifting it like a cheroot from side to side.

Don repeated the question.

'It broke.' Khola spat out some bits.

'Why did you break it?'

'It fell.' He looked at Don. 'Anything can fall. Break. Is that not so, sir? Did you not fall yesterday? Is nature. You let go, it falls. *Pa-tas*. Breaks.'

'It was not good, Khola. It was not good to break the Prince's cup.'

'Not good? Why, sir, how many cups did you break?' He tittered like a youngster who had lost control. 'Not good? That's nothing, sir. Nothing to what'll be coming soon. The boys plot a big plan, sir.'

'What boys?' Don frowned. Khola's partiality to opium sometimes led him very astray.

'Factory boys. A *masta* plan. You know the *Malacca* came on Tuesday? It brings Kishore here. You know Kishore, sir?'

'Should I?'

'Great leader, sir. The British cannot chain him for long. Led the Penang rebellion. Very famous, sir.'

'Penang? Famous?'

'Against a dragon.'

'So did our Prince.'

'The Prince fails, sir. But this Kishore they say *will* be a king.'

'I thought you said he came on the *Malacca*. He is a prisoner then.'

'The word is out. All we have to do is rise and he will lead us to victory. Starting in Belvédère. That bad foreman is one dead goat soon.'

'Your Kishore has come to an island of fantasy.'

Khola's fervour drained away leaving his face desolate; his large coddled eyes slid down. He chucked away his twig. 'Do not mock, sir. I have no fantasy.'

Perhaps not, Don pondered for a moment. For him it might not be a question of fantasy, but of hope. The ships that plied the Indian Ocean always carried secret cargo hidden among the bales of cotton, the coffee chests and the menageries of outposted naturalists: rumours of war and rebellions, tales of lusty sultans and brave souls, buried like weevils in grain, dormant until the ship berthed and the sacks were put out in the sun. Then suddenly they would appear like small quivers of excitement rippling under a warm skin. Don wished he could feel that excitement, that certitude of it, whatever *it* may be, finally arriving. To see this Kishore stand tall on the deck, see the chains falling off him as he raises his arms. His hair growing by the second. Possibly wings to waft him down on to the dock.

'An avatar, is he?' Don suggested.

'What's that?'

'Your Kishore, man. Is he like Rama, an incarnation of Vishnu, come to vanquish evil?'

Khola rubbed his eye but said nothing more.

At Miramont Don thought he would find the civilised answer to his teatime blunders: a flowering plant for Mrs Huyton. He went over while the Prince was out on his circuit, taking the high road, even though it was much longer, simply to clear his head.

He found the nurseryman sharpening his secateurs over a

heap of unhinged purple bougainvillea. 'Mr Pottinger, do you have something special for a lady, sir?'

'Good morning, Mr Don.' A thin smile cracked open one of the many lines creasing his face. 'Are you courting?'

'No, not at all. I mean it as a gift of thanks. For a married lady who has been most hospitable.'

'Hospitable? Aye, that is a very good sign, is it not?'

'What do you suggest, sir?'

'An aphrodisiac for the bedchamber?'

'She is an English lady,' Don replied. 'I would like a decorative plant.'

'For the house I would suggest an orchid, and for the garden, perhaps a Chinese tea rose. We have a new consignment.'

'Tea, under the circumstances, might be most appropriate.'

Mr Pottinger led him to a specimen he had on display. Perfect. Yellow as a burst of sunshine in the heart of a monsoon day. Don saw, to his surprise, between the clouds in his head, Lucy's face light up with a sudden beautiful radiance even though the intended recipient was her aunt.

'I'll take it. Can you put it in that red pot?'

He instructed Khola to deliver the gift to Mrs Huyton, and gave him a short note of thanks, apologies and doomed hopes to take with it. 'Go to the back, where the servant boy sits. Leave it there.' He kept the note short. Very short. His refuge was a sentence in English and a magic cloud where he could lose his footsteps, his cloak and shadow, and then the thickening shape of his innermost thoughts, the tangled threads that linked his past to his present, his hunger to his fault.

When he had been a clerk in Colombo it was very evident to him that the foreigners who had come there were all fugitives. Fidgety and footloose even when they sat in armchairs and drank gin. Inside their heads they were living in limbo. Anxious lest they be immobilised, yet wedded to the heaviest of possessions. They would burden themselves with things that made free and quick movement almost impossible, buying – where they could not pillage – everything they could lay their hands on but could barely lift: cavernous pots, giant statues, massive carvings, stone pillars, *contadors* and almirahs, chunky tables and overwrought chairs. Even their clothes were traps: every limb swathed, each wrist cuffed, the neck noosed. They ate copiously and grew big and heavy while congratulating themselves on their itchy feet. A self-defeating cycle of determined inertia coupled to an unquenchable restlessness.

His desires, he thought, were different: material objects held no appeal, nor did he wish for adventure, novelty or movement. He had no use for a life of exploits or acquisition. What would he do once it began to fade? To sit and remember was, to his mind, no great achievement. We all do it until we cannot do it any more. Is there any difference in quality between one slip of memory and another? Rapture and rupture? Pleasure and pain? It seemed to him all memory was made of the same sad tissue woven from a dream. What he was looking for was something more vital. He had seen it in the glances exchanged between men and women, men and other men, between women: a ray that fastens one to the other, and illuminates even as it bounces off like light on the surface of water. He could sense it in its absence. He wanted her to look at him, see beneath the folds, the buttons and threads of his coat. Recognize him for what he was, and not the trappings of his circumstances.

Don could feel her breath even now, in the current of the air that lifted the banana leaves in the yard and swept down to the Savanne in the south. It was her eye he wanted to meet with his, her hand to be locked to his.

At midday, he went over to Mr Amos's house. The old man was rocking on his chair outside. Don tipped his hat.

'I was not at the Gardens today. The Prince wanted to walk alone,' he explained.

Mr Amos shifted his head to one side in a slow tortoise-like movement. 'I was not there either. I have been looking for some help, but nobody is around. I need someone to move the pianoforte that Madame Renoir so kindly offered. You see, her people just left it in the hall. Singularly unhelpful.'

'A gift?'

'She has obtained a proper modern instrument from Europe and offered this to me in recompense for my help last year with her domestic tribulations. I was enchanted by its sound, and I believe it is not very damaged.'

'Perhaps I can assist you?'

'You see, my granddaughter is coming today. My Eulalie's daughter.' His eyes sank a little, pressed in by the tissue clouding them. 'I thought our luck might turn at last with this.' He had taught himself to read European notation and was determined to teach the little girl. 'I heard a composition of Mr Beethoven in Port Louis last year. Truly wonderful. Have you heard music played on a piano?'

'I have seen a piano,' Don admitted guardedly. He had glimpsed one in Colombo. A piece of polished furniture that looked like the surface of a mirror floating on four elegant curved legs braced for something ecstatic.

Mr Amos's apparatus was of a different nature altogether. Closer to a child's coffin: an oblong box with an indented side, inlaid with black and white keys. It was not big but too awkward for one pair of hands to carry.

'They left it right in the middle of the hall. Two big burly Wolofs. I asked them, very courteously, to please take it into the parlour, just through that door. I had the table by the window prepared. But these fellahs now are very inconsiderate.' His face slumped.

'Can you lift one end?'

'I worry about my back. You see, it gives way suddenly and then it is very difficult for me.' He patted his left hip.

Don spotted a small rug at the end of the hall. He brought it over and slipped it under one end of the piano. It was quite simple then to drag the box across the polished floorboards. Mr Amos followed chuckling happily.

Getting it on to the table, however, was a more difficult matter. Although it may have contained only strings, felt and small hammers, the instrument was not a light piece.

'You like some chicken? A glass of wine?' Mr Amos asked after Don had managed to lever it into place.

'I would be very glad of it.'

'Eulalie will be here with the child soon. You must meet them.' His eyes took on a new lustre; there was a fatherly pride there that Don had not seen before despite their bond.

'It would be my pleasure.'

'Not been an easy life for my Eulalie. I wish I could have done more, but she has her own, very strong views on what matters. Her mother, I suppose, might have been able to do more. Never mind, you will see she is a remarkable girl.' He dusted his hands and shuffled into the larder. 'I hope you like your chicken peppery?'

Mr Amos was a man of healthy appetite and his teeth were in good working order, as he explained. 'You see, I did not use the cane to clean my teeth like the other black boys used to do. Your Indians do it too, but that sugar cane brings nothing good to the body, or the soul. I leave it for the whites. Sweetness hides something very unwholesome. Very bad. It corrupts not only the flesh but the moral fibre as well, I am sure.'

Pink wine, however, was very drinkable in the afternoon with the sun lolling about between the fronds of sibilant palms. Delicious in fact, Don thought. Lovely shadows danced across his eyes. The sea did not need to be any closer to lend its balm to the air, nor birds to offer the humming of small wings. He settled back against the soft ropes of the chair and let the coir strands tickle his ears. Mr Amos started to talk about his wife who had died six years ago. 'She was a big woman with a big voice,' he said spreading out his hands. 'Strong as an ox. When she came back from market, she'd be singing with a pumpkin the size of a cartwheel dangling off her finger. She loved pumpkin. She made pumpkin soup, pumpkin pie, pumpkin bread. She could spit a pumpkin seed right across the yard.'

'This yard?' It was a good forty feet across.

'She did not live to see this house, my dear Don. She died from the cholera that was brought on the *Topaze* sailing, I am sorry to say, from your homeland.' He looked at his open crackled hands. 'She was so cold and clammy. So awfully wet. Her nails turned blue. You could hardly hear her in the end.' He stopped and stared out at the periwinkles in the garden. 'She never saw the house. We never saw it before but, you know, we both did dream of this place. Exactly this very same house. This garden as it is now with the hibiscus there and the peppers at the back.'

'You had not seen it?' Don was unsure where else to take the conversation. 'Surely you must have had your eye on it?'

'We were in Mahebourg in the south. I was working on the old Department of Justice building. Renovating the gallery. The wood smelled of blood, you see, from before. Black blood. We only dreamed of coming up here. You know how you dream, son. How you think of something and it stays in your mind. For years it sits there, like a friend. Reminding you. We didn't talk much, you know, my wife and I. We were very tired in those days. We knew each other's thoughts and took comfort in silence. We didn't need to say much to dream. Just a word or two . . .' He settled back in his chair and ran his tongue around his teeth teasing out the stray chicken threads lodged in between. 'Freedom. Verandah. Pamplemousses.' His bad eye winked and a mysteriously youthful grin split his mouth. 'But enough of these old dreams of goosing. What about you? What news of that young lady of yours?'

'She cannot see me for who I am, that is as plain as it is unalterable,' Don complained rubbing his brow. 'But the fault cannot be only mine.' He blamed a sour world where the innocent eye is curdled by sight, where the day is lit by malignant rays and the night sowed with the spores of a sorcerer's apprentice and a hundred other things.

'You do like your flights of fancy, don't you, son?'

'There is no point in panning for gold from piddle however brightly the sun may shine, is there?'

Mr Amos laughed. 'Quite true.'

'The disposition of a woman is a very curious thing; it follows no logic, as far as I can see. Why do they not see what is blindingly obvious to everyone else? The defects of a philanderer like Asoka are plain to any man – his scruples are so severely cauterised – and yet to these Englishwomen he appears endowed with such absurd appeal. Perhaps scruples are not what they admire, but what if not scruples do they seek in a man?'

Mr Amos poured him more wine. By the time Eulalie arrived with her child, the two men were both snoring on their chairs with the empty flask of wine on the floor. The child's voice woke Don from a luscious dream of fruit orchards and pink ink.

'Grandpapa, grandpapa.'

The little girl was much fairer than her mother, with strong sharp features.

'Nicole.' Mr Amos straightened in his chair and greeted her in gentle French. 'Nicole, my little princess, from where did you appear?'

'We came in a cart, Grandpapa. A funny *bonniquet*.' She giggled and skipped around mimicking animal, cart and ride.

'Very good, princess.' Mr Amos chuckled. 'Very good.'

Eulalie dropped her two bags to the ground. Don climbed out of his chair, unhappily late.

'This is my friend, Mr Don,' Mr Amos added. 'My daughter, Eulalie, and the princess Nicole.'

'Enchanted,' Don said.

The little girl laughed at his accent and ran to Mr Amos. She clung to his legs, hiding her face behind his knees.

Her mother gazed steadily at Don as though she was watching to see what else he could do. Her black eyes were unflinching. Don could not hold her gaze. She pulled at the sleeves of her clean white blouse.

He removed his hat from the chair next to him and offered her a seat. The child burst out laughing again.

'I will take the bags in,' Eulalie said in a low voice. She picked them up and stepped inside the house. Then she called the child. 'Nico, come and drink water. You need water.'

The child wrinkled up her face at Don and he smiled back fraudulently. Then she went in too.

'I am so glad to have them here,' Mr Amos switched back to English. 'She has been released from a château in Flacq.'

'She is free?'

He sighed. 'There are so many chains. We have to break them one by one. It is hard work. Very hard work.'

They heard a bucket being drawn from the well in the garden on the other side of the house. The clanking was like a broken bell. 'Will she live with you now? Or does she intend to find another position?'

'I would be happy for her to stay with me, I am alone here, but she has been called to the house of Mr Huyton and she is determined to go. The young must have their way and learn for themselves the tricks of life.' He nodded at the road. 'If not to Huyton, she says she will have to go to the mill.

Monsieur Champney takes women, but she does not want that.' His eyes shifted uneasily.

'I have written to Mr Huyton about another matter to do with Champney. A problem with a Hindoo shrine.'

'You know my views on heathenism.'

'There is trouble at Belvédère.'

'Always trouble there. The foreman plays everyone off against each other and ends up with trouble that is beyond his control.'

'Monsieur Brousse?'

'That is the one. But the deeper fault, in my opinion, is Monsieur Champney. He does not really understand how things work here. He relies too much on Brousse.'

'Belvédère is one of the biggest plantations, is it not? A most successful one. Surely he is a man who knows what he is doing, even if he is a little harsh?'

Mr Amos waved a hand slowly, patiently. 'No, he does not. He does not understand the land, nor does he understand us. He won the house and the western estate by gambling while he was in France. Montpellier, I believe. The original planta-tion was much smaller. He came and amalgamated his good luck with greed. Bought out his neighbours and replaced the coffee, cotton and clove with cane. The future is sugar for him. Nothing else. Belvédère, as a result, is a very big mistake for him and for us. And Monsieur Brousse will ensure that it remains so.' He drummed his temple with a bent finger. 'His brain is in brine, that Brousse. A stupid man, trapped in the wrong decade. Neither of them belongs to this time or this place.'

'Do we?' Don asked, intrigued.

He smiled. 'That is for you to find out, my dear son. You, not me.'

Eulalie came out. 'Is there no rice left?' she pouted, her mouth strong and full of unspoken hopes.

Mr Amos frowned. 'Rice? Yes, there is rice. A big pot full of rice in the back room. You know I always have rice, my dear. Also chicken. Two pieces of fried chicken for the two of you, and good thick pumpkin soup.'

'Excellent,' Don said more delicately. 'The pumpkin and the chicken are excellent.'

The daughter's expression seemed to mock him. She was, in her own way, as peculiar and as bold as Lucy Gladwell, he thought. Both of them in one house, even as large as Ambleside, could be catastrophic. They were much the same age and although there was a wealth of difference in their experience, they both had the same uncanny ability to rise out of their corsets and discomfit a man. Don felt he was making a fool of himself, every time, in front of Lucy whether he opened his mouth or not; Eulalie seemed to pose much the same challenge.

'I became a rice-eater after she was born,' Mr Amos explained to Don when she had gone back into the house. 'It kept well and kept us well. If we had rice with us, and pumpkin, I felt safe.'

Don realised it was time to leave him to the joys of his daughter and granddaughter. 'Thank you for your hospitality.' He retrieved his hat.

'I am the one who must thank you. You should come again and listen to the piano. It really makes a very lovely sound. You can eat rice, our way, and listen to the compositions of

Mr Beethoven when one of us has mastered the instrument. An exceedingly pleasant way to spend an evening.'

'I am sure it is.'

Before going, he looked into the house and called out goodbye. The little girl peeped out of the back and waved, but her mother was nowhere to be seen.

Narayena was winding a ribbon around the gatepost, bent in two, when Don arrived back at the cottage. Narayena never walked straight; he scuttled sideways like a beach crab: one shoulder jutting out, legs bowed, head lowered, looking out of the corners of his eyes. Before Don could blink he was right up next to him.

'How are you, sir?'

'Good enough,' Don replied. 'Why the ribbon on the gate?'

'For your good luck, sir.' He glanced furtively around. 'Things happening, sir. Serious things.'

'The temple?'

He rubbed his bony hands together in front of him as if to cleanse them in the damp air. 'What did the man say, your Mr Huyton?'

'His opinion is not −'

'Told you, sir. Not a good man. He will never listen. Will not take any notice, whatever you write.'

'I will write to his superior.'

'Too late, sir. Already the wall is broken. Trash everywhere. We must fight back. We have been pushed around long enough. Our people now find determination. That little shrine is hope, man. Like a fountain in our hearts.' He twisted around and looked back over his shoulder. Don noticed, for the first time, that he had two scars on his neck. 'You know what the *masta* done now?'

'Brousse?'

'Abuse all convict rations.'

'He cannot do that.'

'Their rations cut. Half of everything from Government Stores go straight to his black slaves.'

'But he is meant to provide for them himself, surely.'

'He wants them strong because he has them for ever. The food of our brothers goes for them. Malabar convicts are useless to him. They can go to hell because their time is limited. Not owning, not caring. When their sentence is done, they go into employment, or back home. So endurance is no good to him.'

'And you? All of you who are not convicts. Are you not the same as the Africans?'

'No more Indian slaves for him now, but Africans he can still smuggle in. So he wants to divide us and cut his expense. But the effect is that all us Indians now are one. Convict and slave. And we will be strong, man. We will be a nation.'

'What is it *you* want, Narayena?' Don asked. Could there not be a union of races, even if not continents?

A muscle near Narayena's mouth trembled. He seemed to be translating a wish as much as a plan into the words that foamed out of his lips. 'Like you, sir, to be recognised for what we are: true men, good and strong as any on this little bastard rock.'

# Chapter 13

NOT FAR away, at Ambleside, Lucy sat to supper that evening and studied the grooves of her mashed potatoes. Josephine's forked decorations suggested an erratic future, a dark world devoid of the conversation that Lucy had always imagined burbled around the adult world. Bridleton was never this lonely: the river was full of noise and London simmered twenty miles away. Ambleside, Pamplemousses, Mauritius, the Mascarenes were mere specks in the middle of a vast combed ocean. She had meant it when she had said to Don Lambodar at their first meeting that the island was full of poetry, but now it seemed every word was in a language she could not understand. Uncle George had disappeared again with that perturbing glint distilled in his eye that she had noticed he gained rapidly even from the shortest snort of liquor. Her aunt, across the table, demolished the last of the celery with the determination of a mantis. When she was done she realigned her cutlery and her glass thoughtfully. 'Shall we go, Lucy, on the walk tomorrow with Mr Asoka?'

'I dare say he will entertain us with some amusing conversation.'

'Yes, my dear, he does lift the melancholia some gentlemen seem to exude in company. Why the river, I wonder? I rather wish we had a good hill nearby as we did when we lived in Port Louis. You know, Lucy, at first we used to go up Le Pouce by palanquins. It was very jolly, ferried by those boys. We were not meant to be carried, of course, except by horses, but it was a very minor offence, and we were simply learning the customs. You could see the soldiers in Barrack Square – little toy men – and even hear the bugle from up there. It was quite lovely, the fresh air and all of the harbour before us.'

'Mr Asoka perhaps will offer us a more pastoral view.'

'He is hardly pastoral, though, is he, Lucy? I think the boudoir is more to his taste.'

'You do have a mind to go?'

'I can think of no reason not to.'

And so next morning, at ten o'clock, they were there, greeting Asoka at the bridge where he stood like a cherub who had lost his footing, hastily clad in borrowed outdoor clothing. He grinned when they alighted. 'Ladies, good morning. I am so glad you have accepted.' He whistled a little tune. 'Hai, you see, I am happy as the lark.'

'I am afraid it is only us, Mr Asoka. Miss Pottinger has not been able to come.' Mrs Huyton held out her hand and let it float in the warm air with the yellow pollen and the whirr of slow drones.

'I am sorry for that, but it is perhaps for the better for now I may divide my attention in two, rather than three.'

He had missed a button on his tunic and his belt was twisted in a couple of places; his breeches, although in a French cut, appeared oddly stuffed. He had the ruffled look of a man who thought he had more to offer than his packaging; but Lucy thought each disharmony was probably quite carefully conceived for a very precise bravura effect.

'Allow me to show you the way.' He descended awkwardly down the toeholds cut into the slope. 'It is only treacherous here, please understand. The path itself offers no obstacles.'

'I should hope not, Mr Asoka. Or else I shall be most disappointed in you,' Mrs Huyton laughed.

'I have no wish to disappoint, Mrs Huyton. Especially not you. I wish only to delight and give you occasion to smile.' He glanced at Lucy. 'And, perhaps, gladden Miss Gladwell if I can.'

The river was about thirty feet across at that point, and flowed lazily. The trees had been thinned on their side and framed a meadow of young grass for a hundred yards or so before the cane. Lucy put up her parasol and followed behind, content for the moment to have Asoka's attention diverted. 'It will be about half an hour's stroll to the spot I have in mind,' she heard him say to her aunt. 'I hope that is not too far?'

'We should have brought provisions, Mr Asoka. It will become very hot, will it not?'

'My dear Mrs Huyton, I would not make this little outing a matter of endurance. I have a man waiting for us who will provide our refreshments. Pastries and wine and sweetened lime galore, although nothing to match the delicacies of your high tea, Mrs Huyton.'

'How very kind of you, Mr Asoka.'

'Not at all. It was my invitation, and we in our position here, as you know, have to extend our hospitality outside our abode. The cottage we are installed in is not yet suitable for entertaining.'

'I am sorry to hear it.'

'If we were in my country, I would be so happy to show you, and Miss Gladwell, the manner in which we live.'

'I suppose it must be a palace. Quite different in fashion, as befits royalty.'

'Our ancestral home in Sabaragamuwa, our province, is a large traditional house, but it is not quite a palace, Mrs Huyton. Even the Prince, I am afraid, does not have a palace as such. Mine was built by my father and uses red tiles and some very intricate wooden latticework but it is not extravagant. However, at the front we do have four modest pillars with inscriptions that give details of the family history going back five centuries.'

'My goodness. In that case, should you not have five pillars?'

'There is also the garden. You would find the garden very enjoyable, Mrs Huyton. Unlike in the British or French fashion, it is full not only of flowers but also of animals and birds. The Prince, for example, would visit us simply for the birds. He is very fond of them. And yes, we do have true songbirds.' He looked knowingly at Lucy, the nearer eye growing a little larger, cocked in anticipation of some reciprocal response.

Lucy imagined him in a Ceylon garden of cassias and silken plantains, as Princess Lalla Rookh might see it, surrounded by parakeets and peacocks, lazing on some divan, feeding his colourful birds with coconut crumbs while being fanned by a heavy-tasselled punkah. A bevy of half-veiled brown nymphs pandering to his whims, soothing his feet and polishing his nails while spotted deer nibbled flowers in their hair. How he could have ended up as a danger to British rule defeats me, she mused. Mr Asoka was hardly the fighting cock of the East.

He paused and turned to look at Lucy as though he had divined her thoughts. 'Miss Gladwell, I cannot provide protection if you stay so far behind.'

'Protection from what, Mr Asoka? We have no savage beasts here, do we?'

'Perhaps no leopard or bear, but there is always danger for beauty when it ventures abroad.'

'You are a poet, Mr Asoka?'

'Only when I am in such inspiring company, Miss Gladwell.'

Ahead of them, the path curved to the right through a grove of tall fruit trees. The shade welcoming to the ladies as the air was still and the sun piercingly hot despite the valiance of their parasols. They moved forward as if on a barge, trying in vain not to break into ungracious perspiration. A kingfisher darted across the burning water, blue sleeves outstretched.

Lucy stared after it.

Asoka chuckled. 'I think the bend in the river provides the birds with a good feeding ground.' His voice had a pleasing lilt to it and made Lucy curiously glad. It has the quality of cheerfulness in itself, she thought, and therefore was cheering in its effect.

'You have kingfishers as well as kings no doubt on your serendipitous island?'

'No kings any more, alas, Miss Gladwell. Only the fishers.'

'Of course, I knew that. Forgive me.' Her bodice already showed too much damp and she regretted her inability to stem a further flush.

'No, you are not at fault. Our King brought his downfall upon himself. As the Prince would tell you, our history has been a story of misfortune and grievous errors, but as far as I am concerned there is nothing to regret. I consider myself extremely fortunate. The cottage leaves much to be desired, as I said, but other than that we have a great deal to be thankful for here.'

'More than in your country?'

'Not more, Mrs Huyton.' He widened that eye in her direction now. 'But a good match, and different.'

'You have a very enlightened approach, Mr Asoka.'

'Enlightenment is not a prerogative of Europe, Mrs Huyton. We too have a thirst for it.'

'I am sure you do.'

'Our land is known as the land of enlightenment, even if, I have to admit, we suffer from periodic bouts of very dismal darkness.' He laughed a little falsely.

'You do not mean British dominion, do you?'

'Dark deeds like dark thoughts are brought upon us by ourselves. But enough of these gloomy ruminations, Mrs Huyton, let us move out into the open air. We have much to enjoy here. One must always try to make the best of things, do you not agree?'

The path rose to a small plateau of about twenty feet in

elevation; the wide S of the river brought the cane fields of Monsieur Champney almost within one curl while holding the forest close to the other. In the distance, a splash of white extended a tapering brick chimney upwards, like a stinkhorn, blackened at the tip.

'What a very fine panorama, Mr Asoka.' Mrs Huyton shielded her eyes against the sun, her fingers stretched and elegantly curved. 'Is that the Belvédère mill over there?'

Lucy had not yet visited the interior of a mill, but she suspected the tranquil scene was as deceptive as the surface of the water. Muru had told her how thankful he was to have escaped the fate of a millhand. He said the slaves at Belvédère were whipped with a hundred lashes and their wounds rubbed with salt and pepper if they were not at work by four in the morning; he had seen one who was branded with a fleur-de-lis, and then had his arm cut off the second time he had tried to escape. When Lucy protested that there were rules governing the treatment of slaves, Muru had looked baffled: those are the rules, missie, he had said.

'The big river flows past the mill, but we will follow a tributary to a much wilder terrain.'

'Is that wise, Mr Asoka?'

'I speak in jest, Mrs Huyton. It is not a jungle we will be entering. Our destination is a very peaceful spot near a bathing pool.'

'Bathing? Surely ...'

'Fear not. What I mean is that sometimes the children from the nearby estates come there to paddle and play.'

'I am not sure I wish to see any coolie children prancing,

divested of their rags. It is not really very fitting for a ladies' excursion, Mr Asoka.'

'There will be no one to disturb the peace, Mrs Huyton. My man has instructions to clear the place. You will see nothing but the beauty of an oasis, unparalleled in these parts.'

'If it is as you say, I look forward to it. So, do we go down here?'

Asoka nodded and guided them. As he had said, the bridle path veered to the right and they followed a smaller stream into a stretch of rampant ferns and boggy earth. Surprisingly he did not seem as out of place as Lucy had expected him to be among the trees. Perhaps it was because he continued to talk as they progressed, enveloping them in his entertainment of sights seen here and those available in his native island, comparing one bush nearby to another in his memory, this wild flower to that, a pattern of rocks, a caterpillar or a lady-bird, to what might be found on the hillsides of his Ceylon; they were carried along as much by his stories as by the small eddies and currents of the water beside them. It was not so much what he said, or what he talked about, but the momentum of his voice; both ladies felt drawn into it and would interject, in tandem, to make their own comparisons and notes. They were an ensemble, making music rather than speech as they strolled. Lucy had no accurate recollection of the content of their dialogues but it made for a pleasant passing of time together. As the stream babbled, so did they. Asoka was very adept at maintaining the flow and Lucy was in much admiration of his abilities. Englishmen of her acquaintance were not so prone to the delights of inconsequential chat.

After picking their way between stone and moss, his ludicrous comparisons of honey bees and honey bears, they came to a glade that Lucy supposed must be their destination.

The grass was young, the banana drapes bright and fresh. Pink and yellow shrubs, periwinkles and lantana, flowered almost as she looked.

'How delightful, Mr Asoka,' Mrs Huyton exclaimed.

'You see, no little ragamuffins to disturb you, Mrs Huyton.'

They moved towards the edge of the water. 'How blue it is!' Lucy cried. The stream up to now had been like any English brook: clear as it tumbled over a rock, but brown as ale from its bed. The pool was as blue as the sea, although only fifteen yards or so across. A cascade of water fed it at one end.

'It is quite deep in the centre. I suppose during the heavy rains, the waterfall digs in. But on a day like this the water clears up and it is quite refreshing.'

'You have been in it, Mr Asoka? Are you able to swim?' Mrs Huyton smirked, glancing in her niece's direction.

'In our Lanka – Ceylon – we are brought up to love water.'

'Of course, you too are an island people. Lucy tells me propelling oneself through water is quite an art, although I have to say I am not at all sure I approve.'

Asoka raised his round little shoulders in surprise. 'You swim, Miss Gladwell?'

'My father was a Navy man who believed everyone should be able to swim. So, I taught myself.'

'But not in the sea, I trust. We have a serious fear of the sea.'

'Even the beautiful sea around this island?' Lucy's eyes sparkled. 'Are you not drawn to it, Mr Asoka? I cannot wait for the day I might jump in it.'

'Lucy, you must not. It is simply not done, my dear,' her aunt interjected. 'We do not have bathing machines and all that paraphernalia here.'

Asoka made a sweeping gesture. 'Rivers, lakes, streams are far more inviting. Fresh water is bliss for us.'

'It must be the poet in you, Mr Asoka. Have you read our Mr Wordsworth? He is a man very fond of lakes,' Lucy said.

'No, Miss Gladwell. I have not read as widely as I should like to have done. We have a great fondness for poetry. *Kavi*, we call it. Our poets have written our history in verse for thousands of years but not much on water.'

The idea amused her: words hopelessly sinking. 'Like the Persians? For wine, then?' she suggested.

Asoka laughed.

Lucy wondered whether he would see his native land ever again. She did not know the terms of his banishment, but supposed it may be for life. Perhaps it was wrong to broach the subject, but given the way he had talked, it seemed to her perfectly legitimate to ask him.

'Do you expect to return to your home one day, Mr Asoka?'

'That is not in my hands, Miss Gladwell. In fairness, I do not think I belong here. I was not part of the Prince's plot, but unfortunately our enemies had the ear of the British authorities. There is nothing I can do about it now, except to wait for the truth to emerge. I have to say, however, that I am very happy to be here for now. The company, as I said, is delightful and your compatriots in my country, I am afraid, are not nearly as charming.'

His jaw moved to prop back a smile. A ball slid down his

throat and bumped at the bottom. He took in a weightier breath; his chest swelled up and improved the balance of his figure. He grew a little taller and his mouth opened, but he did not utter anything more. He put his hand up to his breast and fingered his chest.

'Where is your boy?' Mrs Huyton asked. 'Has he brought us something to sit on?'

The mis-buttoned shirt seemed to upset him. 'He should be here.'

Mrs Huyton went over to a large boulder and perched herself upon it. 'Some of these boys can be a little lackadaisical. What is he?'

'He is from our country too. We have two Ceylon convicts assigned to us. A man and a woman.'

'Did they come with you?'

'They have been here for some years, I believe.'

'Transported for what crime, do you know? I suppose you are entitled to know, if they sleep at your house,' Mrs Huyton added drily.

'Their crimes are tattooed on their foreheads. Apparently they were involved in the murder of a child. Attempted murder, I should say.'

'Goodness me. Are they not dangerous then?'

'Well, we are not children and have none in the cottage, so I suppose it was considered an acceptable risk. They are actually very well suited to keeping a neat house. I cannot understand what could have happened to the fellow.'

'Perhaps he got lost. This place is quite remote.'

Asoka squirmed. 'No, he has been here before. In fact, it is not very far from the silk factory, if you come along the road.' He made an uncertain gesture in the direction of a lime bush.

'Surely he would not be hiding?' Lucy asked as he pulled at the leaves.

Asoka's face had lost some of its roundness; despite his cheerful disposition he was not a man who found it easy to deal with adversity. His eyes kept shifting and his head twitched like a puzzled night-owl's.

'Should you not call out?' Mrs Huyton suggested. 'Perhaps he is nearby and waiting to hear us. Or sleeping. As you might have noticed there is a great propensity for sleep in this country.'

'Wait here a moment, ladies. I will go to the top of the cascade there, and see if some explanation is to be found.'

'Do not go out of sight, Mr Asoka.'

He climbed up through the rocks, preoccupied more by his thoughts than his surroundings. Once at the top he stood, hands on hips, nonplussed.

'Perhaps it was rash of us to have come on this excursion,' Lucy whispered to her aunt. Uncle George certainly would not have approved. The foolishness of the idle female, he would jeer, to think that Mr Asoka could be regarded as reliable. To Uncle George anyone who did not belong to his club was a scoundrel and not to be trusted an inch. 'There is no difference between the coolie and the prince,' she had heard him say, 'except in their hats.'

'Did you say children come here to play, Mr Asoka?' She imagined a vulture, or some such disturbing creature, taking up its position nearby.

'Sometimes, yes.'

'And you asked him to rid the place of them?'

'Just while we enjoyed nature's harmony for an hour.'

'And you say his crime was in the persecution of a child?'

He made an odd sound that indicated as much surprise as realisation.

Lucy's own naivety frightened her more than the import of the conversation. 'Mr Asoka, do you not think you had better obtain some help?'

'Let us not alarm ourselves, Lucy.' Her aunt spoke with quiet reassurance from her perch. 'I am sure the servant will turn up. It is a rare thing for one of them to make serious mischief, you know. In their situation they do not have much regard for time, that is all.'

Lucy tried to shut her ears. Her aunt glossed over trouble much too easily. A pretence of normality was always preferable to her than to admit disharmony, or the disagreeable. She watched Betty Huyton open her silk fan as though their predicament was of no import even though this servant, a murderer at heart, might have run amok and killed a dozen children.

Asoka's hands had become very agitated; he clasped them together, switching his grip, as if trying to catch an invisible rake between his palms.

'Did you say that this path continues to a road? Is it too far for us to continue?' Lucy asked.

'It will take us another twenty minutes or so,' he replied. 'The route is less picturesque as we leave the stream here and go across the cane fields. I asked for our carriage to be kept up at the road to collect us.'

'Is your coachman more reliable?'

He gave a weak smile. 'Coachman?'

'In that case,' Mrs Huyton stood up, 'let us go on. We might as well. Lead the way, Mr Asoka.'

They set off once more, but as they took the first turn Asoka stopped short.

A lopsided brown man of alarming proportions confronted them in a state of complete nudity, dripping wet. He had his back against a tree and one foot on an upturned hamper; a couple of small cushions and various bits of cloth, including his garments, lay scattered around him along with items of food – biscuits, grapes, oranges – and bottles.

'Avert your eyes, Lucy, look away,' Aunt Betty hissed, but she did not and neither did Lucy. She had never seen anything quite so insolent in all her life.

She had, of course, studied the torsos of the ancient Greeks, and there was a replica of an almost complete David that she had once tried to draw during a visit to the Museum in London, but this was a figure of manhood startling in a way she had never quite imagined. He was a very dark glistening brown, unlike the marble nudes, and looked distinctly more uncomfortable for his protuberance than any model of the Italian, or indeed Greek, masters.

Asoka held them back with his arms out. 'Khola,' he cried, more in astonishment than challenge.

Lucy watched the man sway dangerously towards them.

Asoka shouted again but the man ignored him and began to come closer. His wet hands seemed enormous; a machete dangled in one, but he made no attempt to cover his flaring virility with the other as it swung blindly and looked at every inch more proud than ashamed. His rough tumescent features expressed, to Lucy, a frightening moral absence.

To his credit, and his foolhardiness, Asoka jumped forward: smaller, rounder and clearly ineffectual. His voice failed to match his bravado and squeaked out another unheeded command.

Mrs Huyton cried, 'Come back, Mr Asoka.'

Lucy lowered herself slowly and picked up the largest stone she could lay her hands on. She felt extraordinarily calm. He was a big man, but no more so than the poor wretches she had seen half naked in the fields, or shackled on the roads barely able to slake even their thirst. His glazed eyes turned towards Asoka rather than the ladies; Lucy could see his native animosity was addled by considerable confusion in his mind.

Asoka stamped his little foot and shouted once more; the man advanced further. He raised the machete, tarnished and bent, as though it might explode in his hand. Asoka retreated a step.

Lucy prepared herself, ready to throw the rock; it was heavier than she had thought. Would it carry far enough?

Then, before she could hurl it, the tall figure of Don Lambodar burst out of the trees. She saw him grab the naked man's hand and twist it until the knife dropped. Asoka scurried in and retrieved it. The man slipped free and swung his fist; Don Lambodar neatly avoided it and struck him a blow to the chin of such unexpected force that it felled him at once. He then stood over the whimpering huddle and berated him angrily. The man cowered as though Don Lambodar's words were lashes – there seemed some considerable violence in them, despite the roundness of the syllables. Slowly the man crawled over to the clothes lying by the hamper and wrapped one around his collapsed middle, spluttering out a plea.

Don Lambodar turned to the ladies, his surprising strength subdued and masked once more. 'Come, ladies, the carriage is not far.'

'What about him?' Mrs Huyton asked.

'He will find his way to his quarters.'

'Should he not be in chains?'

'He was temporarily distracted, Mrs Huyton. His head had been turned.'

'I think, Mr Lambodar, you are being too indulgent of him. He was, I hardly need to remind you, naked as a savage before two ladies brandishing his machete and heaven knows what, intent on the most horrific crime.'

'I understand, Mrs Huyton, it is a most upsetting encounter. But I assure you his intention was simply go back into the water. I doubt he was even aware of your presence, ma'am. He needed to quench the fire within him.'

Lucy watched the man struggle into a shirt and feebly collect the parcels and bottles strewn about. She felt some sympathy drawn out of her by Don Lambodar's explanation, but her aunt was less easily persuaded.

'Don't be ridiculous, Mr Lambodar. Is he some insane fire-worshipper? There was good reason for you to exert the force you did upon him, although perhaps you need not have struck him quite so brutally. His was not an ordinary thirst. His intent was obvious.'

'Not a thirst, no. But I know him to have a weakness that sometimes disorients him. When I came upon the carriage in disarray, on the road, I knew something was amiss.'

'What happened to the coachman?'

'He *is* the coachman.'

Mrs Huyton glanced at Asoka. 'Is that so?'

'I followed his trail as I thought he might be in some distress,' Don Lambodar continued.

'You followed your servant?'

'I know his habit, ma'am.'

Asoka, having regained his nerve and somewhat wayward humour, leaned forward. 'You mean at your farm?'

Lucy found it difficult to imagine Don Lambodar with hoe and spade; farming could not be one of his occupations even if he clearly could wield more than just a pen. Her aunt was also incredulous. 'A farm, Mr Lambodar?'

He glared at Asoka. 'Some of our people work at the silk factory.'

'Oh, I see. A mulberry farm?'

Asoka laughed. 'And a poppy farm, ma'am. The habit he speaks of so knowledgeably is that of the poppy.'

When they reached the carriage, a much relieved Mrs Huyton thanked Don Lambodar, huffing only a tiny bit. His head tipped down as though something inside had rolled forward. 'My pleasure, Mrs Huyton.'

The phrase was mere politeness, but to Lucy's ears, it seemed his voice had returned to that annoying tone of apparent conceit. Her rebuke was swift. 'Pleasure? At our predicament? You would have us in mortal danger for your pleasure? To prove your superiority?'

'No, Miss Gladwell. I meant duty. I misjudged the word.'

'Oh, duty is it? Was that man disordered by you then?'

'Lucy!' her aunt stopped her.

She did not know why she had lambasted him except that she wanted a more sincere reaction from him. He was too evasive, always hiding himself, his words no more than veils to her. Could he not meet her fair and square?

At Ambleside, the two men took their leave, altered both in manner and disposition. Lucy watched the carriage turn, Mr Lambodar flick the reins.

Mrs Huyton said she needed to rest for a while and that she would take some cold ham in her room. Lucy was in no mood to eat meat. She asked Muru to bring some water to the verandah.

In England, as a child, whenever she had felt unhappy or dissatisfied with her circumstances, Lucy would find recompense in the interior of a book. She had only to open the cover and feel the texture of the paper, the impression of a printed word, the tiny indentations where ink had collected and solidified to form the letters by which one discovers an ever expanding world, to feel herself righted. She would wonder, and still did, how it was that the markings of a nib, or the scratches of a stranger's sharpened quill, either by itself or through its reproduction in the more formal pressed letters on a page, could result so unerringly in a blue ribbon of sea, a strip of white sand, a red boat, or whatever imagined thing, in her mind as magically as a rose in a desert. It was not so much the content, although that had always provided its own special charm if it were poetry, or an imagined story, but the transportation by the word itself that delivered for her an extraordinary exhilaration. A few letters and some blank space were enough to remove her from whatever discomfort she might have felt, into a world in which nothing was impossible and everything was in some way hers, not only to behold but also to bring into being. Although her eye would move on in hunger for the novel, her mind would be held suspended by a single phrase, even a word, and she would feel that she was living there in that moment of delicious first apprehension for ever. Something in the shape of the letters in close proximity, the meaning coiled within their embrace, the sheer magnetic power would hold her and she would be overjoyed with the knowledge that this is precisely what she or he who first put these parts into one whole meant to create. Then, slowly, the rough wavy paper she held in her fingers, the weight of the volume balanced in her hand, its edges coloured in blue veins and smelling of mortality, would draw her back to the sensible earth and give her the means by which she could perceive her place in it.

She would seek that reparative now, except that he taunts her too much, like a creature of fancy who sips life – a little at a time – between the page and its figment in a reader's mind, and disappears.


'My mother would count the fingers of my hand. "One, two, three, four, five," as though it were a mystery that I had so many; that a hand could be so extravagant. I would think of how many hands there might be in the world and what they might be doing. I would look at my mother's hands and wonder whether mine would be like hers one day.' Lucy reached over and stroked her aunt's – the clutch of veins rising under the papery skin, twisting and turning. 'Sometimes it seemed to me that my hands were an unfinished part of my body; that somehow everything rushing inside had been stopped. My fingers had to be connected, otherwise I would be left stranded with broken links at the ends of my arms. Do you know what I mean?'

Betty Huyton nodded. 'We are unfinished animals, like those legendary creatures – Paul and Virginie.'

'I often see them passing behind the trees, hand in hand. I follow them and they follow me everywhere. I never catch their eyes. Sometimes the sun comes out and their bodies turn golden and shadowless.'

'What colour is his hair?'

'Do you not find the companionship of a figure of figment outweighs that of the breathing body? He, yes he, is yours as no mortal man sadly can ever be. The dream is all and lasts as long as you do.'

But even as she spoke, she recalled the physicality of the deranged servant, naked in the forest; his wide face hovered in her mind. Slowly she began to see that what marked him out was not the indigo tattoo on his forehead, not his sex, his race, his position or his colour, but rather his will – and the thoughts inside him. An attribute Don Lambodar shared with him, more crucial than all the physical ones they had in common however prominent they may seem.

'A husband, Lucy, is what you need. Not a fantasy.'

'A man is not what I need,' she replied. Then added, in a lower tone, 'What I need is to know my own mind.'

When Don Lambodar had burst into that perilous world and saved them, he seemed unlike any man she had ever seen or heard. Neither gentleman nor boor, but some other kind of being beyond the common frame. There was something in the charisma of his voice, the language she could not follow, the unflinching grip with which he held the servant, and the manner in which he made the naked man submit to his will that revealed to her a form of sinewy poetry she had never encountered before. She had felt she was seeing him – and the world – through a new eye. She had wanted to say something to him, to acknowledge the transformation, but she had not been able to then; her tongue had turned, despite her best intentions, to rebuke.

She wished there was a way in which she could make amends; establish some common ground. Start afresh.

Muru opened the door and tiptoed in. He had a note on a wooden tray. 'The Ceylon gentleman sent, missie, for you.'

'Did he bring it?'

'No, missie. Messenger come and go. No answer? Funny people. Don' know nothing. Nothing at all like normal manners.'

Lucy took the folded paper. The penmanship was distinctly less able than Don Lambodar's; the letters carefully formed, but from a nib that had been pushed and pulled like a cart drawn by a lame cow. Inside, Asoka had formulated an apology and a hope that he might have an opportunity to make some recompense, if they were to meet at the Playhouse tomorrow evening. He should have written to her aunt, of course, not Lucy; but then he would not know the finer points of English etiquette, she supposed. Although she had avoided a commitment to Jeanette, she now resolved to go. Don Lambodar would surely be there.

★ ★ ★

'I do not see why a man in his position cannot control his servants.' George Huyton wiped his mouth with the edge of his napkin. On the table in front of him he had a glass of beer and a plate of cold chicken. Next to it a small silver cup with minted toothpicks. He selected one and proceeded to clean his teeth. Between bouts he cocked an eye and added, 'He probably planned it, simply to frighten you.'

'No, George. That is ridiculous. Why would Mr Asoka want to do that?'

'Perhaps it was the other fellow. A devious plan to present himself as a hero rather than a villain. I would not put it past him.'

Betty Huyton dismissed her husband's fantasies. 'He is peculiar, but not ungallant.'

'You have to admit, both of them must be fascinated by the two of you. How often do you think they get to prance in the woods with the likes of English ladies?' He swilled more beer noisily down his throat. 'Pretty rarely, I dare say. Most women, English or not, would not stoop to it, however strong their curiosity might be.'

'You are quite wrong. It was not curiosity, but politeness. We were invited in a most courteous manner and it seemed quite the right thing to do.'

'An invitation by a convict?'

'They are not convicts as you very well know, George.'

'They are here, as all the other sepoys in the department, at His Majesty's pleasure.'

'So are we.'

'At any rate they have no business inviting you, and you

no business accepting. We surely have society enough without them.'

'He has apologised,' Lucy intervened.

'How?'

'He sent a note.'

'To you?' her aunt asked, surprised.

'You see what I mean about deviousness.'

'He will be at the Playhouse. If Uncle George is so suspicious, perhaps he too could join us.'

'No fear. I have better things to do than sit on those intolerable stools to watch grown men reciprocating poetry.'

'I am sure you do,' his wife said. 'Gadding about, then?'

'I have to see to some matters on the coast. I shall stay overnight tomorrow so you may do as you please, as long as you do not expect me to come to your rescue.'

'Is it Flacq again?'

'Near enough.'

'Well then, Lucy, let us to the Saturday theatre tomorrow night. At any rate I should like to see how Mr Asoka redeems himself. Pity the great correspondent, our rescuer, has not seen it fit to provide an apology too.'

# Chapter 14

L UCY LIKED being alone for breakfast. An empty verandah soothed her. She loved the clear yellow morning
light, the flights of full-throated birdsong vaulting and
tumbling around her. Her thoughts, freed from the uncon-
scious tugs of submerged need, leapt from note to note
like a child on stepping stones. This morning Uncle
George had gone on tour and Aunt Betty had declined to
eat, as was often the case on the first report of his absence.
She would ask not to be disturbed until noon and stay in
her room with her needlework.

Muru brought out a sliced grapefruit, toast, a selection of
jams in small white saucers, and stood in the doorway, pretending to study his feet.

Lucy cut the toast into four small triangles and put a
spoonful of different jam on three of them: guava, pineapple, marmalade. Unable to decide which she liked best, she
ate all three pieces, one after the other, and made a small
mound with the crumbs at the tip of the one remaining
on the plate. She would have liked some honey, but there

was none. It had not been known to run out before. A small knot tightened inside her; she could feel it sink and harden in her middle. A molten sleeve unrolled under her skin.

It occurred to her that Don Lambodar may well *not* come to the theatre with Mr Asoka. She had tried to dissuade him, after all, at the tea, and the two clearly did not get on well together. Perhaps it would be better to seek him out herself. If the bee does not move, then surely the flower must.

She bit the last piece of toast already softening in the humid air. Folding her napkin, she placed it next to her fork; the cotton felt limp.

The knot in her stomach made her nauseous. She felt something entering through her pores and filling her to the brim. Her clothes pressed in and everything inside pressed out. She had to do it.

'How far is it to the house of the Ceylonese, Muru?' She tried to keep her voice calm, although she was almost out of breath.

'Not far, missie.' He collected her empty plate guardedly. 'Horse and carriage has to pass Botany Gardens and by damn Presbytery.'

'Please, Muru, no bad words.' It was too much: to keep order and yet seek bliss. 'Have you finished your work?'

Muru nodded. 'Sorry, missie. *Masta's* word. Study all done very quick.'

'In that case, ask Denis to get the gig ready. We are going visiting.'

'Cannot, missie. Boy not here.'

'Where he go? I mean, where has he gone?'

'Donno, missie. Is nowhere.' His face hung in the air, a brown fold flapped around the mouth. 'But I fix up.'

Twenty minutes later, as the clock chimed the half-hour, Lucy was out on the road, Bonnie in harness, and with Muru as guide.

The cottage was prettier than she had expected. Shaded by the ubiquitous coconut and bedecked with small delicate flowers sprouting out of the sand that surrounded it, the little bungalow exuded an air of ramshackle tranquillity. Although beans and chillies bustled in the vegetable plot, they were neatly sectioned into a grid of squares. Someone had taken care to erect wooden frames and nets for support and protection, and put signs for each crop. Beyond the vegetables a couple of outhouses leaned into each other and a chicken coop rambled into the lime bushes. The shutters of the cottage were closed but the central door was open. Lucy was surprised at the sorry state of the verandah, but much of its chronic decrepitude was masked by a printed cotton sheet and a large dilapidated armchair.

She opened the front gate. Muru edged forward. 'I ask for Mr Asoka, missie?'

'See if Mr Lambodar is inside.'

She waited beside the gate while he went up the broken steps. He called out in Tamil and tapped a brass plate that was hanging on a string.

Lucy noticed the front yard had been brushed to make delicate fan-like patterns and the flowering creepers on the avocado tree had been twisted into intricate garlands. There was a sign fixed to a post that looked as though it might be a name board, but the script was indecipherable: the fastidious letters swung like a set of round pots with plumes and curls and dots steaming above and under them.

Muru retreated. She asked him if he could tell what language was used for the sign.

He shrugged. 'Maybe Prince's language?'

'Can you not read it?'

He lowered his head bashfully and studied the imprint his toes made in the sand. Then he said, 'Missie, I check back. Please be seated.' He gestured innocently towards the verandah.

She declined and hurried him on.

The small whitewashed cottage and its sand trap of hibiscus and bougainvillea, peppers and legumes and chickens, was another world from Ambleside. Lucy was not sure what she had expected to see, perhaps a scene out of *Lalla Rookh*: a garden of perfume, peacocks and Persian minstrels. As it turned out, the ordinariness of the island cottage was in some respects a revelation. She had not looked at one in this way before; with a fair consideration of its occupants and a vaguely guilty expectation of entry. The prospect was intriguing beyond anything incorrect.

A few minutes later, Muru appeared in the doorway with a small dark woman at his side. She wore a simple wrap of cloth and a tight frilly blouse more suited as an undergarment. Her face was plain but pleasant enough except for the scars on her forehead which, as Lucy drew closer, proved to be a tattoo of words and numbers. Her crime and punishment.

'Cook say nobody here, missie.'

The woman's lips peeled back to reveal a set of enormous teeth and wide pink gums. She made a whimpering sound that made her expression at once less alarming.

'Is Mr Lambodar expected back shortly?' Lucy asked her.

'Has no English, missie. I try Tamil. She understands only little.'

'Is that not her language either?'

Muru shook his head. 'Speaks same as Prince.'

With some difficulty and a few redundancies they established that the Prince and Mr Asoka had been summoned by the Governor, and that Mr Lambodar had disappeared with the other servant on an expedition elsewhere. It sounded most mysterious, but Lucy suspected the lacunae in Muru's linguistic skills may have contributed to this impression. Nevertheless, the attachment Mr Lambodar seemed to have formed to his impertinent servant, and his neglect of duties as interpreter, was to her mind becoming increasingly eccentric.

The cook woman, bowing and beseeching, insisted Lucy come inside the house. The armchair on the verandah was not suitable for a lady and therefore she entreated Lucy to follow her into the parlour. Lucy stepped past a small clay bowl with floating flowers by the door. The room itself was spartan. Lucy took the chair by the table: a simple seat without cushions or covers. The table stood as bare, made of unpolished wood. There were no paintings, no curtains, nothing but the washed walls, a coat stand, a dresser and the purely functional furniture required for dining. Not a single book in sight. The only reading matter seemed to be a few papers on a dresser, held down by a metal weight. The poverty of the interior seemed to her extraordinary even for a journeyman, let alone an oriental prince.

She was brought a cup of tea. A harsh bitter brew, but in a fine china cup. She smiled in appreciation of the vessel, if not the content, and the woman let forth a stream of fast-flowing words to Muru.

'Trouble,' he said in an admirably concise translation of her torrent. 'Much trouble. Mr Lambodar gonna fix it.'

'What kind of trouble?'

'Everything, missie. Peace, cup all broken. The Prince is not happy, but Mr Lambodar gonna make everything good. Pick up all the little pieces.'

'She has a lot of faith in him.'

'Yes, missie. With so many languages, man can talk to everyone.'

Or perhaps to no one, Lucy thought. She took a final perfunctory sip. 'What is your name?

Muru made vague signs and noises; the woman replied, slowly. 'Surangani.'

'A very pretty name,' Lucy said, marvelling again at the unexpected concurrence of poverty and charm. She was grateful for the glimpse of this foreign life, even if she had not succeeded in confronting the architect of her confusions. It struck her that in their everyday experience the Ceylonese exiles may, in truth, share more in common with Muru and his fellow subalterns than the nawabs cavorting in the fantasies of her extravagant poets.

On the way back, driving past the Gardens, she saw Asoka and the Prince under the cannonball tree. Don Lambodar was presumably close by.

She parked the carriage by the gate.

'I go now?' Muru asked.

'Yes, Bonnie will be fine here. You return to the house. I shall be back soon.'

She walked towards the lily ponds, the still air at odds with the increasing turbulence inside her. Crossing a small water-way, she turned by the cummerbund palms and slowed down; I must not show haste, she thought, nor art but arrive by happy chance.


'Miss Gladwell, good morning. What a pleasant surprise to see you gracing these Gardens.' Asoka bowed his head. The Prince standing behind him looked up at the trees with a bemused expression.

'Good morning.' She very nearly tripped on a small broken branch on the ground. 'Oh dear.' She kicked it aside. 'Thank you, Mr Asoka, for your note. We are looking forward to the theatre tonight.'

'I am too, Miss Gladwell. Very much indeed.'

'Do you like the Gardens, Mr Asoka? I find it much safer than the jungle, don't you?'

Hints of green addled his round cheeks, but he held his course. 'The Prince finds it comforting. We have some of our own trees here, you know.' He turned and translated the conversation for the benefit of the Prince who nodded sagely and said something curt in return.

'You mean the palmyra?' She had heard Madame Benoît say once that the seedlings had come from the island of Ceylon.

'Yes, indeed. And the talipot.' His eyes appeared smaller

than before; perhaps his cheeks were puffier. He made a gesture with his hand extending his podgy fingers into a spray of palm fronds. 'Jaffnapatam,' he said to the Prince.

Unlike his fellows, the Prince had no trouble looking Lucy straight in the eye. He did it almost as an imperative, a substitute for the language he did not command. He took a regal breath and spoke one terse word of English. 'Come,' he said and started walking at his stately pace.

Lucy followed with Asoka next to her. There was no sign of Don Lambodar. Asoka was chattering, slipping back into his usual effervescence. 'To have the opportunity to see you twice in one day, Miss Gladwell, is indeed a pleasure multiplied.'

She smiled politely and tried to contrive a question about their missing companion. 'Mr Asoka, where –'

'Miss Gladwell, our Prince would like to show you the gift he gave to the chief.'

'The chief?'

'We heard about these botanical gardens before we left our homeland. The Prince's dear friend, a Britisher like your good self, often spoke of establishing something very similar in our hill country. So when we came we brought with us a token of that idea: a box of seeds and saplings. The gift the Prince wants you to see is a flowering tree we plant around our temples.'

'I see. And what colour is the flower?' she asked inanely, wondering why it was that everyone wanted so much to transplant their seeds.

'White, sometimes red. Very nearly scarlet, but always with a yellow centre.'

They arrived at a promenade that had recently been made

with borders of African marigolds. The Prince stopped and stared at a pair of silver-grey branches stuck into the ground on either side of the walkway. A few small, thick leaves sprouted from the twigs like whiskers.

The Prince spoke; Asoka translated. 'The Prince would like you to imagine this promenade in five years' time. These two saplings will be propagated to make a line of trees on either side. The branches will be entwined and the flowers will be as numerous as the stars and as beautiful, shining by day as well as by night.'

'That would be very pretty,' Lucy replied.

The Prince smiled and gave another little speech for Asoka to convey.

'He says you must remember this sight because he will come with you in five years' time and remind you of our conversation. He says he is looking forward to it, as this is where fate has decided he should spend the rest of his days and he intends to make his surroundings as much like home as possible. You see the cinnamon over there?'

'A commendable attitude, as my aunt would say. Would you agree?'

'I am not so enamoured with the notion of fate, Miss Gladwell. There is much that can change in circumstance, and sometimes sooner than one might expect.' Asoka pressed his hands together, she noted, as men do on the brink of what they consider an important point.

'A change in what? The weather?'

'Most wittily done, Miss Gladwell, but I am afraid I mean something much more serious.'

She was intrigued. 'Indeed?'

'The authorities, your countrymen, Miss Gladwell, do not understand the grievances of their subjects. We were with the Governor for our breakfast as he wanted our advice, but I fear he does not hear what we say even though he asks us to speak. The intention to understand is there but, I fear, the capacity is not.'

'And what was the advice you offered?'

'A warning, Miss Gladwell. Discontent may soon lead to a call to arms on the plantations.'

'The Malagasy?'

'No. The Malabar. The Indians and, I dare say, our own fellows: the convicts. We suggested he meet their leaders and discuss their complaints.'

'Which are?'

'They do not wish to be maltreated in the way the Africans have been. The plantation owners, I understand, simply carry on as they always have. I only know what I translated for the Prince at the Residence. The Governor had a man from the *Malacca* there to be questioned whom he thought the Prince might understand.'

'Is it not Mr Lambodar who is the interpreter?' At last she thought she might discover his whereabouts.

'Ah.' He raised his eyes. 'Poor man was indisposed.'

'At your house?'

'His difficulties are quite surmountable, Miss Gladwell. I believe he is anxiously recuperating, even now, with his own medication in some den or the other. He means to attend the theatre tonight, although I wish he wouldn't.'

'Oh, but why?' She blushed, sure that he intended her to do so.

'Our Don and the Prince are both morose by nature and a little dampening, don't you find?'

'This man from the ship, what is he?' Lucy avoided the question.

'Kishore? He has a fervour in him that is charismatic and seems to burn brighter the more one stamps on it.'

'You mean he is a firebrand?'

'Certainly not a pragmatist, Miss Gladwell, that's for sure. This Kishore, although not much to look at now, is a man with a great thirst for anarchy. He harangued us all through a complicated circuit of translators.'

Lucy smothered a smile. 'I can hardly believe he harangued *you*, Mr Asoka. What did he say?'

'It would be of little interest to you, Miss Gladwell, but he has somehow had some connection made with the discontented elements among the Indian slaves here. He has taken their grievances for his mast, as it were, and speaks for them.'

'I should like to hear more of what he has to say.'

'I would not recommend it, Miss Gladwell. Politics is an unsavoury business.'

Kishore had been brought into the Governor's room in chains – handcuffs and leg irons – an emaciated, gaunt figure pinned with rags. At first he had stood silent, head down, with no indication of listening to the questions put to him. His lacerated fingers clenched together. Then, when the Governor had flung down his papers in exasperation, Kishore had begun in a voice that rose in volume and strength like the lapping of the tide; he spoke and paused for his interpreter, and then spoke again, raising his voice a notch higher. 'I was a man who only wanted rice, but I had none,' he said. 'I was a man who only wanted shelter, but I had none,' he added louder and shriller. 'I was a man who only wanted a chance, but I had none.' He worked himself up through a litany of wants that grew to encompass his whole community of hope and ended with a line that he chanted over and over: 'Freedom is the song of the heart that cannot be stopped.' His hands circled, his chains rattled. 'Freedom is the song of the heart that cannot be stopped.' He stamped and stomped and chanted, throwing off the guards who tried to restrain him.

'Freedom is the song of the heart that cannot be stopped,' Asoka said to Lucy. 'That is what he chanted, over and over again.'

The Prince, a little way off from them, was cooing; he extended an arm and sprinkled some breadcrumbs on the ground. 'Uh-ooh,' he imitated a wood pigeon.

Asoka followed her gaze. 'Not like him, a mere feeder of birds, or our Don, the chronicler of constraint.'

His words threw a new light on Don Lambodar. She saw he was a man ensnared; caught in a web of obligation and custom no less crippling than the strictures of a prison. Like her, he too had no true allies in this world. She saw the impoverished cottage again with the Prince out sowing feed, Mr Asoka dallying with the cook, and Don Lambodar slumped in that broken armchair without even a book to comfort him. She thought she had better leave quickly. If only the evening could be hurried.

'Well, good day to you both. I should leave you in peace to enjoy your exercise,' she said and made her excuses.

'Good day, Miss Gladwell. I look forward to the Playhouse.'

She felt a little dizzy, as though the centre of things had become unsteady with the song in *her* heart. When she reached the central peepul tree, she paused to regain her equilibrium. Between its elephantine branches she could see the crumpled summit of Pieter Both in the distance pointing for ever but never quite reaching heaven.

Outside the gates, near her carriage, a black man was sitting sucking a dry stalk of cane.

Bonnie had her head in the water trough, gurgling noisily. Lucy used the pump next to it and took a handful of water for herself, ignoring the man's small eyes – hardened lumps of muscovado – and the glazed look he hurled her way.

She shook her hands to dry them and climbed up to the driving seat, but before she could get Bonnie moving, a horseman came cantering down the road. He halted by her in a cloud of dust and commotion. Pulling off his hat, he shook his blond curls at her, much as his mare did. 'Mademoiselle Gladwell,' he cried.

'Good morning, Monsieur Champney. You are in unusual haste?'

'It is a bad day. Very bad.' He glared at the seated man and then turned back to Lucy. 'You must go home quickly and stay in the house.' He had lapsed into French, which flowed smoother than it had ever done before.

'Why? Is it a storm?'

'You are in danger, mademoiselle. I must escort you home immediately.' He rose in his stirrups, squeaking from boot to saddle, and reached for Bonnie's bridle. His corduroy knees were damp with the sweat of his horse.

'Really, Monsieur Champney. I can manage perfectly well on my own.'

He did not listen and they set off at a brisker trot than Lucy cared for. At the crossroads that usually had at least a handful of people milling about, there was no one to be seen. 'What has happened, Monsieur Champney?' she called out. 'Why are you behaving in this quite absurd manner?'

He was riding well, rising with manly control holding both his own horse's and Bonnie's reins. 'My foreman was attacked. The Malabars are in revolt. They have taken his two guns and escaped. About ten of them.'

'Is he hurt?'

'A broken arm. The rebellion may spread across the island. We are all in most serious danger.'

'Surely not all, Monsieur Champney? Is it not more likely that you will be in danger, not I? Their dispute is with the mill, is it not? Not with the population at large?'

He pushed back a few stray fritters of hair. 'I fear not. Their discontent has no such limits, and your uncle Monsieur Huyton is very possibly one of their targets.'

When they reached Ambleside, Lucy's uninvited escort dismounted and helped her alight.

'Mr Huyton must find out if your boys are here today.'

'He is out on his circuit.' Lucy frowned and called out for Muru.

'Is anybody missing from the house?' Antoine Champney demanded when Muru appeared.

'No, sir. Only Denis.'

He looked at Lucy. 'Who is Denis?'

'The coachman.'

'Black? Or Malabar?'

'I suppose you would say he is black.' She pushed back her hair, astounded. This was not the sensitive, stuttering young man she knew from before.

Antoine looked unconvinced. 'Are there any convicts quartered at Ambleside? What about the other servants?'

'Jacob and Tusa are not agitators.'

He stared at Muru and then addressed him again, his voice a little more in control. 'You, boy, when did this Denis disappear?'

'Gone this morning, sir. Missie knows. I look for him at breakfasting.'

'What do you know of what is going on?'

'Nothing, sir.'

'Has anybody come here from the plantation? Anybody at all?'

'No, sir.' Muru moved his head back as if he expected a blow. Lucy could sense the fear in him, despite the fact that this young man was as slight a figure as Muru. The authority Antoine carried now, so suddenly: where did it come from?

'I should like to speak to Mrs Huyton, if I may.'

'Yes, of course.' Lucy asked Muru to go and tell her aunt that Monsieur Champney was here.

'Would you like to sit out on the verandah while we wait?'

Antoine Champney with his nervous mouth and pale skin was a serious disappointment to his father, one of the ruddiest, rudest Frenchmen on the island, and that had been to the young man's credit. Lucy had heard that Champney, the elder, beat a slave to death for spoiling his revelry one night with the crying of a sick child. Antoine would never do that; he would have neither the inclination nor the strength to commit such malevolence. There was no Madame Champney; that is to say, the mother of Antoine was long dead. Poisoned, it was said, by a disaffected servant, who was subsequently hanged for the crime. Antoine had spent some years in England before being brought back to his father's plantation apparently unwillingly. Today, however, faced by crisis, he seemed to have been transformed.

'Why did they revolt? They must have a reason. Are they poorly treated?' Lucy settled herself on a large soft wicker chair.

'The convicts we have been allocated only want to escape. The slaves – the Indian slaves – ever since I let them dance at their heathen festival, think they can do as they like. Ungrateful idolaters. Now it seems they are all plotting together.'

'I have heard your foreman is a harsh man.'

'Monsieur Brousse is only trying to do the job he has been asked to do. Produce sugar at the required price for the English market. That is all.'

'Do your Indians not comply?'

'The man I trusted is a demagogue. He is the cause of this mischief.'

'But why would he lead them against us? Surely his interest – their interest – is best served by a working mill. This is not Demerara, full of fever and upheaval.'

Antoine Champney tried to straighten his frame. He tugged at his sleeves as his father might. 'They have learned,

I fear, from the abolitionists that rebellion might lead to freedom.'

'Is that wrong? Is not the desire for freedom natural?' She kicked off her shoes and stretched out. She was glad to hear of resistance although she did not quite admit it.

Antoine looked out at the garden; his large pale eyes seemed to congeal with the severity of his thoughts. 'These rebels include convicts, Miss Gladwell. Bad men serving their sentences. They are violent men who now wish to spread their anger among all the Malabars. Their feelings are running high and they possess firearms. Our lives are at risk, as no doubt Monsieur Huyton will appreciate.' Lucy had not heard him speak with such force before.

'What do you do, Monsieur Champney, at the mill?' she asked to divert him. The whole business was too murky. 'Monsieur Brousse, I can see, striding about the factory floor shouting at his men and getting them to do this, or that. But you, Monsieur Champney, what is it that you do there?'

He smiled, shunting aside for a moment the cataclysm he feared. 'I am there as the repository of responsibility. I watch our proceedings.'

'You sit at a window and watch?' She laughed. A house-wife's duty, as she had once thought.

'I sit at a desk and calculate what we produce, how much cane comes in, how much sugar we process. I write letters to merchants and try to get our system of production ready for the change we hope will come.'

'My uncle says that since the war, the French are unable to face the prospect of change.'

'We expect the duty on our sugar to be reduced in London so that we may compete on fair terms with the West Indies. We believe we may be able to sell to England a great deal more sugar than many here imagine.'

'Is that your father's plan?'

His lower lip shook a little. 'He can see enormous opportunities. All the other old French planters can imagine only the life of their youth.'

Before Lucy could ask another question, her aunt stepped out on to the verandah. 'Good afternoon, Monsieur Champney.'

He quickly rose to his feet. 'Good afternoon, Madame Huyton.'

'How nice to see you here. Have you had some refreshment? Tea?'

With all the excitement and the deepening conversation, Lucy had completely forgotten her manners, but Antoine very considerately said that he was not in want of anything. 'In fact I am here, very briefly, to warn you, madame, of the very serious situation that has developed in our district.'

'Something we can do for you?'

'Madame, I do not wish to alarm you, but there has been a revolt and a group of Malabars are running loose.'

'Nobody runs on this island, young man, least of all the Malabars.'

'These are men from our mill, I am afraid, unruly slaves and convicts. Not Monsieur Huyton's road workers, as far as we know, but villains, nevertheless. Therefore it would be wise not to leave the house. The district is unsafe. An evil alliance has been struck between the convicts and some discontented labour.'

217

'Surely they will sneak up to the hills, Monsieur Champney, as all fugitives do, until the cool weather drives them down.'

He looked lost for a moment. 'I found Miss Gladwell abroad and thought I should escort her back to the house. I understand some of the men here are also missing.'

'Really?'

'Only Denis, Aunt Betty. Muru could not find him anywhere this morning.'

'Not surprisingly, Lucy. He went to Port Louis to make arrangements for tonight. He should be back to take us to the theatre by half past two.'

'There will be no theatre tonight, madame. The curfew bell will ring at dusk in Port Louis. It is best you do not venture out at all, even into your beautiful garden. I will ensure an inspector from the police visits Ambleside this afternoon. In the house, you should be safe.'

After Antoine left, Mrs Huyton called for some tea.

'Of course, he is a Frenchman, after all, and a little prone to exaggeration,' she said.

'He certainly talked a lot today, but I don't believe we should worry.'

'Quite. You see, Lucy, in Jamaica there are settlements of runaways – maroons. They have a long history that they can draw strength from. It is not the same here. These people have no one to go to. I am sure one or two of them are returning to their homes at this very moment, back to their bean soup and bread. Domestic comfort has an uncanny ability to defuse discontent.'

'But not soon enough for the theatre tonight.'

'Yes, that is a disappointment, Lucy.'

'I had been so looking forward to the evening.' She felt everything had conspired against her.

'So it seems, my dear. But never mind. We must amuse ourselves.' Aunt Betty clapped her hands together briskly. 'Now, shall we consult my new catalogue from the Brompton Park nursery, Lucy? It arrived with the *Malacca*. I believe it has some species from Argentina. I would like to see a little more of the Americas here in Ambleside. Would you, Lucy? I truly believe you would benefit from some serious interest to occupy you, my dear. A proper passion.' Adversity, in her opinion, was best overcome by the discharge of practical household duties, or a campaign that marshalled a legion of hobbies.

Lucy could not think of gardening at such a time. Even in her calmer moments gardening was never a counterpoise.

'I have passion, proper or not; I feel I have more than I know what to do with.' She remembered how her mother used to say she was like her father: too curious about what lay on the other side and too passionate about things she could do nothing about.

Her father was abroad on one campaign or another all her childhood; at home only for a month or so at a time, once a year, sometimes not for two. A man's place, he claimed, was in the precincts of his destiny, not in the comfort of his home. Even in his last injured months, she felt he never quite let her close: as though he was worried she might say something that would upset the precarious balance of their separated lives. Unlike her grandfather, he had seemed afraid of her; afraid that somehow she would see something beneath the mettle that she should not. But he would approve, she believed, of her venturing forth as she had done, sailing the high seas, learning to swim like Lord Byron himself. He would be glad to know she had travelled and seen the world from such a southern latitude, although this Mauritius, she was sure, he would have found too tame a place to settle in. What campaign could there be here where ten men with two guns can cause such consternation?

After tea, Lucy wandered down to the garden hut. The pink dombeya was in flower, but nothing could fill the emptiness inside her now that her small design of possible redemption had been disrupted; the claw of some beast ahead had reached back and twisted the curtains of her prepared set. She sat drained of her vague vulnerable hopes.

A small grey-headed perruche landed on the stone statue by the steps to the lower garden. It looked about brightly, then swelled up into a song before taking to the air.

Lucy had been a solitary child, content with her own company and a world of make-believe; never conscious of the yearning that often marked childhood. Only now she began to wonder if a sibling or a friend might have made a difference, or whether we are always ultimately alone.

'Missie, missie.' Muru's soft, sweet voice called repeatedly. 'Missie, missie.'

Lucy peered out. He was by the birdbath, wringing his hands.

'What is it, Muru?'

'You must come to the house, missie. Officer here, asking. Inspector Maurice, missie.'

'How is he here so soon?'

'Donno, missie. But asking to see you. You must come, or else he be looking for you in there.'

Lucy reluctantly made her way back to the house. Inspector Maurice was standing on the verandah with his long, tapering head inclined towards Mrs Huyton, listening to her theory on runaways and the mistakes of the colonists in the West Indies.

'Good afternoon, Miss Gladwell.' He straightened up and tapped his thin chin back into place.

'There you are, Lucy. The Inspector would like a word.'

'I am sorry to trouble you, Miss, but perhaps we could step inside the house for a moment. I have a few questions.'

'About the runaways?'

'Not exactly.'

They went into the front room and she plumped down on the sofa; he remained standing, one loose trouser hem flapping unstitched.

'Miss Gladwell, I understand you went to the Botanic Gardens this morning.'

'Is that prohibited?'

'No, of course it is not prohibited, but we understand that you met Mr Asoka and the Prince there.'

'How did you know that?'

'You were seen, Miss Gladwell. It has been noticed that you keep company with the Ceylonese.'

'You must keep a close watch.'

'What we would like to know is whether anybody was with them. Or if you met somebody else in the Gardens.'

'You mean a secret assignation?'

Inspector Maurice twisted himself into an awkward tangle, clearly much embarrassed. He tucked in the loose hem and licked his lower lip. 'We are trying to ascertain the whereabouts of Mr Lambodar, and wondered if perhaps you might have seen him in the vicinity.'

'Could not Mr Asoka say where he is? Have you not asked him?'

He looked bashful. 'We are conducting an investigation.'

'Into what? Do you think Mr Lambodar has run away with those ragamuffins at Belvédère? Surely not, Inspector Maurice?'

'It appears that he is missing, Miss Gladwell. We thought you might be in communication with him.'

'I do not care for this French system we have inherited of young inspectors running around investigating matters.' Mrs Huyton wrinkled up her face in distaste. 'It is an excuse to poke their noses into things in which they have no business. All we need is a constable in each province, that is all. Preferably an Englishman.'

'What do you think is wrong with Mr Lambodar?' Lucy asked. 'Mr Asoka said he was a little muddled and taking some native medication.'

'He certainly was not at his best at tea the other day, was he?'

'No, but he appeared to be well enough when he saved us from . . .' She coloured a little at the recollection.

'Well, yes.' Her aunt nodded. 'Although I have to say that I think he may suffer from some misdirection.'

'What do you mean?'

'Your uncle believes he has been much misled by the local Hindoos, and I am inclined to believe that your uncle on this occasion might be right.'

'That is surprising, Aunt Betty. I do not recall you ever concurring with Uncle George on such matters before.'

'On troublemakers in this instance, my dear.'

'The escaped convicts are different, surely. Don Lambodar came with a letter on behalf of that man with the shrine, or temple, or whatever it is. He was not one of the prisoners at Belvédère, was he?'

'Not a prisoner, but that is the man who has instigated this ridiculous rebellion.'

'A rumour only, Aunt Betty.'

'No, my dear. The Inspector confirmed that violence most definitely has been committed.'

'Might they be rebelling because Uncle George did not follow Mr Lambodar's advice? If so, perhaps we are to blame and they will indeed come here to make us pay for their grievance.' Her voice edged up a little.

Her aunt puffed aside the idea. 'I do not see why your uncle should do as Don Lambodar suggests. The man is not a clairvoyant.'

'He does like to be mysterious.'

'He does not help himself by the mystery he offers.' Her face clouded and she squinted at some dust in the air. 'I must say I thought he would be more charming than he is. Not even an apology for the extraordinary behaviour at tea, never mind the business with his insolent servant. The problem may be that he overindulges, as his kind often do. Vanity and inebriation make an unreliable couple.'

'His kind?'

'Those with a little too much vanity.' She paused. 'Like your uncle, my dear.'

Lucy was taken aback. 'Do you really think they are alike?'

'That is not what I said.' Her tone became quite defensive. 'Only that they have something in common. It is not their most defining characteristic, but one that is recognisable, do you not think so?'

'No.' She did not see it. Of course, Don Lambodar had an element of vanity that was obvious in his grooming, if nothing else. But what had Uncle George to be vain about? His blustery paunch? His inept yellow cravats and frayed leather crops? If anything, surely he was the antithesis of Don Lambodar? 'Neither in vanity, nor in extravagance. They are both male, that is all. To be fair, I am not sure that Don Lambodar takes any wine at all, Aunt Betty. I believe the Ceylonese may all be abstemious.'

'The Prince, perhaps. But Mr Asoka is someone who clearly enjoys his tipple, Lucy. You cannot deny that.'

She waved a lazy hand.

Aunt Betty sniffed. 'Mr Lambodar is less frivolous, perhaps, but an inebriate he may very well be. Perhaps a rather more serious one.'

'You paint him very dark, Aunt Betty. I thought you had a better opinion of him.'

'I am undecided on him now, to be frank.'

'Is it because of the aspersions cast by Mr Asoka? He is very mischievous.'

'I had thought better of him, but the Inspector's words are not at all to his benefit.' She smoothed a fold at the side of her mouth. 'He has not altogether impressed me at close sight. There is, I suspect, a rather baleful undercurrent to Don Lambodar.' Then she chuckled. 'But he appears to have created quite the opposite effect on you, Lucy. How he has managed that is quite beyond me.'

Lucy blushed. 'He has had no effect on me. I am simply trying to remove my earlier prejudice.'

'And why, my dear? A young woman of intuition will do well to hold on to her prejudices. They are likely to be quite to the point.' She took out a small scented square of silk and dabbed the glistening creases about her throat.

'You cannot seriously believe that, Aunt Betty. A prejudice is surely never acceptable.' She was determined to take control of the conversation and her unruly emotions.

'Of course, you are quite right. But sometimes, if your prejudice is confirmed, then perhaps you are entitled to believe that it is warranted.'

'My intuition tells me we should invite Mr Lambodar to come to Ambleside this evening.'

'What in heaven's name for, Lucy?'

'To entertain us. Would you not like to hear the strange songs they are said to perform? Since the play will not be resuscitated for ages, with all the garrison so dispersed, we should have our own theatre.' Lucy's eyes gleamed.

'Mr Lambodar?'

'Why not?'

'He is missing, Lucy. The Inspector said so.'

'If we send word to the cottage, I am sure that servant of his will get it to him. He is missing only to the likes of the Inspector. I do not think he would be absent to us.' Her youth gave her confidence, but in truth it was only hope and a little hollow at that.

'No, I cannot agree. Not even if he is accompanied by the Prince. He is not of sufficiently stable character, Lucy.'

She changed her mind about an hour later when Muru sheepishly brought in Don Lambodar's note apologising for his behaviour on Wednesday afternoon. The potted rose he had sent with it was somewhat flaccid and downcast. 'Sorry, ma'am. Flowerpot hiding in the hullabaloo.'

'When did it arrive?' Aunt Betty demanded.

'Donno, ma'am. Was left with no word. No one notice, ma'am, until jus' now. Very sorry, ma'am.'

'Well, water it and put it by the side of the gazebo.' She stroked the container. 'And keep it in this pot. I like the red.'

She quickly sent the now thoroughly rehabilitated, courteous and gallant Don Lambodar an invitation for the evening, but Jacob returned empty-handed. He said there was no one at the cottage except the cook woman who understood neither French nor English. 'How inconvenient,' Aunt Betty sighed, gazing fondly at her slowly wilting niece.

Jacob brought no new reports of the rebellion, and no message came from George Huyton, although that did not particularly bother his wife.

The sky was luminous with a silver light; the roads like metalled rivers, every shadow flattened out. Dogs barked, agitated everywhere. Lucy tried to picture Don Lambodar: would he be alone, or with a band of armed runaways after all? Would he be in his finery, or in bandit clothes like his fellows?

The red blade broken in his hand
And the last arrow in his quiver.

It was too fanciful, her *Lalla Rookh*. But if he should somehow
come tonight, she wondered, what would she say or do?

And what would he do? Would he stand by that window
and stare, impotent? Or would he use the violence of that
gaze to break the barriers that separated them?

For a man of so many tongues, she thought, he was remarkably obtuse. What does he think? And in what language?
Why does the expression in his eyes, when he looks at her,
not move his tongue to speak of things she so wishes to hear?

Tonight, she thought, the poetry of the theatre might have
inspired him as voice begat voice and one word another.
Instead he will be shot before a syllable is uttered. She could
see it. Shot dead. A hole in his head. A mouth full of blood.
No longer able to speak to her, or on behalf of the poor and
the downtrodden.

The door squeaked as it opened. 'Missie, gentleman come
to see you.'

'Who is it, Muru?' she asked, but he had already scampered
back down the stairs.

The inside of her chest hurt but she followed him calm as
a queen. Her suitor was standing at the table, biting into a leg
of cold chicken.

'Henri, what on earth are you doing here?'

'Good evening, mademoiselle.' He quickly wiped his
fingers on a napkin and trotted forward for her hand, his lips
pink with grease.

'You should not be out on a night like this, Henri.'

'I was concerned as I heard Monsieur Huyton is away.'

'We are quite safe at Ambleside. You need not worry, but it is very sweet of you to do so.'

'They say that the runaways may be passing this way to collect more rebels. There is much agitation.'

'Who says so?'

Henri retreated a step and withdrew his head a little into his neck and shoulders. A swarm of flying ants thrashed about the lamps, shedding their incongruous transparent wings.

'It is common knowledge. I was at Monsieur Dupont's house earlier this afternoon. Many of us had gathered there. There was much concern at Monsieur Huyton's absence. Apparently his convicts are involved.'

Mrs Huyton appeared in the doorway opposite. 'Is that so? It is good to know our neighbours are so interested in my husband's duties, even if they misunderstand his responsibilities.' She advanced. 'Good evening, Henri, how kind of you to come.'

'Good evening, madame.'

'So what news do you bring us?'

'A dozen men, madame. Armed and rebellious. Their leader is the troublemaker from Belvédère.' He blinked. 'The Governor is considering a state of emergency.'

# PART IV

# Chapter 15

Earlier that Saturday, before Lucy Gladwell cut her toast in Ambleside, before she had any thought to visit the cottage, before the Prince would wake and be whisked away with Asoka to meet the Governor, before any glimmer of an Emergency, the sun parted the grey unlaundered dawn mist strewn about the garden and Khola crept into Don Lambodar's room to wake him. 'Sir,' he whispered, 'please come.'

He held a finger to his lips and withdrew. Don, bundled in hemp, followed him out into the back garden where dew lay in puddles.

Khola was a fisherman by birth, condemned to a spit of salt flanked by a crocodile-infested lagoon on one side and a shark-lined sea on the other. He had told Don once that if not for the charges brought against him, he would still be mending nets by day and bobbing in an ocean he feared every night, killing fish he hated to eat. 'So, you decided to kill a child instead?' Don had suggested. Khola had shrugged lazily. 'That is what they say, but why would I harm a child, sir, when even the fish I sometimes set free?'

This dawn there was urgency even to his words.

'We must go to the *kovil*.'

'Why, Khola? Why must *I* go to a Hindoo temple? Why me? Why this Saturday morning?'

His face dropped. 'Sir, I mean, only Nariya's little shrine.'

'Shrine or temple, why at this ungodly hour?'

Khola banged the back of his head with the heel of his palm in anguish. 'Please, sir, you must. Tea made, already.'

'I need to know what is going on.'

Placing his big ungainly hand on Don's elbow, Khola steered him between the gluey clusters of damp bougainvillea towards the garden table where a slow plume of steam rose from a mug. 'The big day, sir.'

'I know.' Don thought it was bigger for him. He intended to go to the Playhouse and confront Lucy Gladwell. Speak straight. But not until evening and twelve hours of rehearsals had strengthened his resolve.

'Kishore's day.'

'The rebel?'

'Nariya and all his men will come to the *kovil*. He says I must bring you to see Kishore there.'

'I thought Kishore was chained.'

'Mr Badani arranged the escape. He can do anything, sir.' His eyes slid about, briefly unmoored. 'Drink tea, sir, and let's go.'

The temple was smaller than Don had expected – not even the size of his cottage bedroom. The mud wall around the bare garden was crumpled and flattened in places. The building itself – a three-sided shell of scuttle and scrub – was already on the point of collapse.

Narayena sat on the only solid step, with a gun propped against what had struggled to be a doorway. He watched them approach but did not stand.

'We are taking things into our own hands, Mr Don. I warned you.'

Don looked around at the dry dust patch they were in. 'What is it you will take into your own hands?'

Narayena indicated the gun beside him. 'First weapons. Then freedom. Then land.'

It was a mantra that belonged in Badani's opium pipes, Don reckoned, or the feverish rants of a deluded peewit.

'Do you have any idea of what you are up against? It is not just Monsieur Champney, you know. This is a colony that is entirely organised to keep people like you in your place.' Don frowned. 'What is Badani up to?'

'We can fight, Mr Don. The British needed our boys to win this island from the Frenchman, but they have no gratitude.'

'Are the regiment's sepoys from Mahebourg joining you?'

'We are hungry. Our hunger is greater –'

'Than their chains? Their medals?' Don snorted. 'Narayena, you are only going to get yourself killed and all the poor fools who will follow you.'

Narayena picked up the musket and balanced it across his knees. He ran his crooked hand along the barrel. The lock was rusty. 'Write a serious letter for us, Mr Don. You will do that?'

'To the Governor?'

'Whoever, but not that Huyton. You, sir, are the letter writer. You said a letter is what they understand. So, let us see. Give notice: their life on this island is about to change. We will not be treated like before.' He cracked his knuckles.

'You have demands?' Don asked.

'Liberty.' The English syllables leapt high in his voice.

The mist in the fields behind the shrine had evaporated. Three Indians appeared, all convicts – branded. 'Two more are coming from Souhait. The message is out,' one of them mumbled to Narayena. The three men dropped down, on their haunches, a little apart, like sticks on which some dusty blue rags had snagged by an accident of wind; hardly the army of an island Tippu Sahib.

'You have just three men? Half-starved convicts?'

'They are the vanguard. I need men experienced with weapons. Others will join soon, when they hear how we dealt with the foreman.' Narayena's face hardened into a sallow mask streaked with grime and the shadows of his bone lines: the chameleon in him finally fixed on the colours of a tiger. The bones shifted to make his jaw stronger, his teeth more pointed. 'Across the whole rotten place, they will join us. Not only convicts, but all of us too long abused.'

The sky turned lighter; the rumpled clouds loosened from behind, thinned out. Don heard the bell of a stray cow down by the river. A cock finally crowing.

'You need to spell it out to me. What you want, who you want to do it, and when. And how.'

Narayena was not happy at that. 'You tell them. You spell it out. You write it. You are the writer. Tell them, things have to change. No more of this treatment. This bad, bad stuff.'

'At the mill?'

'They whip us. They cut off Johwaher's ears. Now we cut them up. Monsieur Brousse into little pieces. We'll burn the fields, all the fields, and houses, and the mill. You tell them that. We will burn everything, and cut that man, cut any man who comes, into little pieces. Chop, chop. Roast them like their pigs. We will do unto them what they have done to us.'

He wanted Don to write of Armageddon, nothing less. 'Do you know how many soldiers are in the garrison?' Don asked in exasperation.

'We have justice, right.' His eyes were hard as pebbles.

'Not if you butcher —'

'Revolution demands blood. I know, sir. I heard what happened in France. I am not a stupid man.' He spat out some aniseed.

'You have a family. A son. You should think of him.'

'I am thinking, Mr Don. Especially of him. That is why this cannot go on.' He mashed his fists together.

The argument was cut short by a distant volley of gunshots. Dogs barking. Khola stared at the ground. The grass was yellow by his feet. The three convicts stood up abruptly. The youngest trembling. 'Where do we go now?' His voice trailed away.

Narayena shut his eyes and scrunched his hair with both hands.

'No time to pray, Nariya. Let's go, let's go,' another urged leaning forward.

Don realised these were men whose lives were shaped entirely by what happened around them; whatever Narayena might say, they were not in control of anything: not their desires, not their destinies, not even their discontent. Another shot rang out. Closer. The yapping grew louder. The hunters were on the other side of the river.

A dark ripple moved across Narayena's face. 'Too late for writing, Mr Don.' He grabbed Khola. 'Must be Kishore they chase. Find out what is happening and tell Basu. He will find me.'

Then he left, scrabbling over the stones, followed by his confederates.

Don asked Khola how he intended to find out about Kishore.

'Don't know. Wait and see?'

'It is too risky.'

'Why, sir? In a shrine? I am here to worship.'

'You worship only the poppy. Even a donkey knows that. This Basu, who is he?'

'Works at Souhait. Nariya has many, many friends, you know.'

'When they are caught, as they undoubtedly will be, you also will be in big trouble. No one will be able to help you if they think you are linked to rebels.'

He nodded gloomily. 'I know.' His face collapsed. 'I only do what I am told, otherwise Mr Badani will kick me out. I cannot afford to go to Port Louis, sir. You know that. Scoundrels there sell it at two dollars a piece.' His hands and limbs and facial muscles ran hopelessly out of control. 'Sir, what to do?'

The barking drew much closer.

'Don't like dogs,' he muttered, alarmed at a thought growing in his head. 'I was bitten by a white dog once. Bad British dog.'

'Where would this Kishore go to be safe?'

Khola perked up. 'I know. This way, sir.'

After about half an hour, they came to a kaffir hamlet where two of Badani's labourers lived. Khola said he would go and find out what they knew of Kishore.

'Will they not be at work?'

He rolled his head and patted the side of his neck. 'Badani closed his factories for two days.'

There was more planning here than Don had expected. 'Are his kaffirs in it too?'

Khola paused for a moment. He might have been considering how much he could divulge, or he simply could not remember. 'He has other plans for them.'

While Khola went to the first of the small shacks in the line, Don found a vantage point where he could hide and yet have a good view of the place and its approaches. A few wisps of smoke drifted above the thatched roofs. Each dwelling had a small yard in which orange, pink, red and yellow flowers glistened with the drool of busy spiders. Around the nearest cottage a low hedge of hibiscus unfurled in quiet violet curls; a quiver in the leaves hinted at small flycatchers hopping about. There was little else happening. At one end of the hamlet, a patch of grass dawdled around a large flame tree from which a rope swung with a stick tied to the end of it for a child's seat. A couple of mongrels lay sleeping on the road and some hens pecked out patterns in the sand. If not for the yoke of forced labour around the neck of each of its poor inhabitants, Don thought, this could be a hamlet of some contentment.

When Khola came back he said that Kishore had not been seen. No one knew anything. 'Not fit,' he announced as though he had been testing their size rather than interrogating them in his half-cut pidgin. 'I think, Mr Don, we try the three arches bridge,' he added, suddenly seized with an almost ferocious determination.

'On the Curepipe road?'

'Mr Badani will be there at noon. It is the place we set, if the first plan failed.'

'Instead of the shrine?'

He nodded.

'Why did you not say so before? Surely that is where we should go immediately?'

'I forgot.' He grinned stupidly. 'Anyway, sir, no point no, before noon?'


Mr Badani always dressed neatly and simply. Despite the worms and looms that worked for him, spinning and weaving all day, he did not adorn himself with any of the silk they produced. He preferred plain linen, the colour of ash. He kept very separate the accounts of his business and the accounts of himself. The produce of his workers was neatly divided between the columns of cost and profit. Don appreciated that from his own training, but he did marvel at the man's discipline in not indulging in *any* of the surplus, never diluting his profit. No silk, no smoke, no blurring of the neat lines in his meticulous ledger.

'Good afternoon,' Don said as though he had happened upon the bridge entirely by chance.

'Mr Don, how nice to see you out here.' Badani's head tilted back. The curved sharkish smile hung low.

'I saw Narayena at his shrine a little while ago,' Don said cautiously, not sure how much of his involvement to reveal.

'A happy chance, no doubt, Mr Don. Our Nariya is a good man.'

Badani's irritating confidence clinched it. Don cut straight to the point. 'I am afraid I do not think this confrontation, this business with Kishore, bodes well. I understand you somehow had him freed, but by now I suspect he may well have been caught again.'

Badani coiled his fingers into a knot. 'He should have been there.'

'We heard dogs. They were after Kishore, Narayena said.'

'The fool.'

'I must confess your motives in this enterprise confound me. You have your concessions, your supplies and your customers. Is it not more profitable for you to keep things as they are? Do you want him to disrupt your trade?'

Badani examined Don with the patience of a physician who has had to treat the same malady time and again, and for whom the defects of the human mind, like that of the body, are unremarkable and ordinary. 'One has one's debts which cannot be ignored.'

'Of honour?'

He stretched back his head again; the teeth gleamed. 'You must always be clear about profit and loss, my friend, and exactly where honour falls between the two.'

'What are you planning?' Don paused but Badani did not answer. He was forced to continue. 'Narayena wanted me to write a letter of threat at first, then when we heard the dogs he decided it is of no use. He wants to act with greater speed and speaks of a ragtag rebellion. It is ridiculous. Can you not stop him?'

'Fear is a great motor to harness, Mr Don, like the thirst for freedom.' Badani pulled at the lobe of his ear thoughtfully. 'I will go and see the Inspector before things get out of hand.' He turned to Khola. 'Come with me. I may need you.'

After they had disappeared from sight, Don decided to make his way to the Botanic Gardens; he found Mr Amos at the Saint Géran water trough, towelling his mare's brown sweaty neck. Nicole lay asleep in the gig, chasing crabs and sea froth in her dreams.

'I took the child to the beach. She misses the sea.'

'Your daughter did not accompany you?'

Mr Amos frowned. 'She had some business. What about you, my son? You seem a little disturbed. Is something wrong?'

Mr Amos was what Don had always imagined a true father might be: patient, concerned, always there when needed. He listened as much as he spoke. He always wanted to know how Don saw the world.

'You know Narayena at Belvédère?'

Mr Amos moved his head slightly. 'The organiser at the mill?'

'He is in deep trouble now. I do not understand him. He has a child and he is putting himself in such danger.'

'One must do what one thinks is best.'

'Narayena wants chaos. He thinks a rebellion will bring deliverance for all the Indians here.' The words tumbled out of his mouth.

Mr Amos widened his lower lip, revealing a line of tender pink. 'I see. Just the Malabars?'

'A wedge has been driven between the African slaves and the Indians. Narayena wants the convicts and the Indian slaves to come together as one people. He is convinced the merchants and free Malabar will be behind them. He seems to have the support of Badani from the factory.'

'Badani? That is most unfortunate. Badani's interests, you can be sure, are never altruistic. He is a man who has designs on us all. He now owns a sugar factory as well, I believe.' Mr Amos moved his shoe to allow a small overburdened beetle to trundle slowly past. 'I am not a man of violence, my son, but perhaps this place does need some stirring up. Like Haiti, we need a Toussaint L'Ouverture. One who will bridge the races.'

'Haiti?' Don had read in the *Bulletin* that over thirty years ago, in Haiti, 100,000 Negro slaves had risen against their owners; that thousands of white people had been killed. He found the report difficult to believe. Slavery as he saw it practised was surely designed to prevent any such uprising? No Robespierre, or Danton, could get up from his knees if he is yoked day and night and whipped for moving his lips out of line. Who here could read *The Rights of Man*? The probability of truth suggested that the *Bulletin* was an organ of exaggeration, but Mr Amos was much animated.

'You know it? The rallying cry? "Liberty or death".'

'Brutality seemed the watchword, from what I read.'

'Toussaint fought, reluctantly, and for a just cause. A brilliant general, not a murderer. He believed our natural instincts were corrupt. He abhorred idleness, quite rightly. But he was magnanimous. He did not persecute whites. Instead he worked to banish slavery. That was his sole purpose. I have a great deal of respect for the man. I think we can learn much from his life – except for his foolish admiration of that scoundrel Napoleon.'

'So you think from the mayhem that Narayena plans, some good will come? Is this Kishore your Toussaint?'

Mr Amos shrugged. 'What do you think?'

Don was transported back into the kind of philosophical dialogue he enjoyed with Mr Amos.

'Authority is a phenomenon I have never properly understood. How is it derived?' he asked, as though the present predicament were a matter of mathematics. 'How does the one gain the compliance of the many and their subjugation?'

'It is the way things are. Most of us give in. Not only to kings, and invaders, but to thugs and bullies. Slave owners, merchants, fathers, husbands.' Mr Amos pointed his foot at the beetle retracing its steps. 'Little creatures have little room. We can only see what we see. Nothing beyond, unless we believe in what lies beyond.'

'So Narayena is right. Why should they be enslaved? He is right to look to someone like Kishore, is he?'

'The problem is leadership. Even if they succeed, will Kishore and Narayena become, like Badani, owners themselves in due course? Is it possible to become free without the manacles locking on another? I believe this authority we talk of has a life of its own within the great flux, manifesting itself in these instances of fear. It propagates itself. It moulds us, as nature does, to fit a pattern we cannot see but can only partly sense. Unless we are all brothers, there is no hope.'

A greenish heron flapped up into the air with a harsh cry.

'I must go.' Don suddenly felt sick. He was in the wrong place. Khola's torn body flashed through his mind, the dogs leaping at it; then Narayena mounting an assault against Ambleside, screaming, his puny fusillade meeting a greater one of cannon shot. Pamplemousses in flames. Lucy Gladwell in a burning house. The theatre on fire.

Khola was sitting on the steps of the cottage, waiting for him. He put his fists up to his head and banged it again, this time from side to side.

'What have you done?'

Khola moaned. 'He is dead, sir. They shot him.'

'Narayena?'

'Kishore, sir. The dogs found him. He tried to cross the river, but they trapped him. They had guns. Boom. Boom. They got him. First his legs, then they got hold of him and cut off his hands.'

'You saw him?'

'His body is hanging on a pole. Other bits have been cut off too. Like a carcass at the butcher. He is hanging by a hook. His penis is in his mouth. Narayena will go mad.' He said that he had managed to get the news to Basu. 'Fury, sir, is everywhere. These bastards do not know what they have started. Monsieur Champney has got his dogs after Nariya but Nariya now has every Indian on his side.'

'Is the Prince in his room?'

'He is not here, sir. Surangani says he and Mr Asoka are gone.'

'Where?'

'She says many, many visitors today. In the morning people come, they take the Prince. More come looking. In the afternoon they come back, then more visitors come. They go again. It is too much, she says.'

'Have they gone to Port Louis? The Playhouse?'

Khola shrugged. 'Crossroads talk is that no one will be allowed out on the streets of Port Louis until tomorrow daylight. Everyone shut in.'

# Chapter 16

A T AMBLESIDE there were no further reports of disturb-
ances. Lucy was convinced Don Lambodar would turn
up on the verandah, emboldened and brimming from his
adventures; but he never did. The whole of Sunday passed in
quiet looks and half-nods.

'Do you think Mr Lambodar might be in some difficulty?'
Lucy asked her aunt as they sat down to breakfast the following morning.

'I doubt it, Lucy. The Ceylonese are probably quite used
to intrigue.'

'Monsieur Champney was most discomposed, was he not?'
Lucy tried not to show her own anxiety.

'As I say, a propensity to panic, my dear, does not bode well
for the French. Dear Antoine, like Henri, suffers the complaint
most acutely. It is quite unnecessary to excite oneself to the
extent that they sometimes seem to do. Things get more out of
hand when one loses one's self-control, as I am sure you appreciate.' Aunt Betty smiled as though to confirm her presumption
as fact, by polite agreement, whatever the truth may be.

'Can one always control oneself?'

'*We* can, my dear. Indeed, an Englishwoman must.'

At mid-morning, Lucy had the two boys together on the back steps, as usual, to remind them of their duties for the week. Mrs Huyton insisted on regular supervision to enable her servants to develop suitable habits. 'We have to help them achieve their full potential,' she had explained to Lucy. 'To punish and exclude them from our society is not to anyone's ultimate benefit.' Cleanliness, neatness and regularity were the measures by which she judged their work, and Lucy always began the week by repeating the cosy refrain to Muru and Jacob.

This Monday morning, though, they both looked uneasy. Jacob appeared particularly downcast. Lucy asked him what was wrong.

'Everyone frettin', missie. All talk, no peace.' He had just come back from his village after his day off. 'Rubbishy, missie. Talkin' rubbishy all night.'

'What is it they say, Jacob? Are they for the Indians?'

'Not for, missie.' He glanced at Muru. 'No business, but plenty frettin' after *mastas* chop up the Chief.'

Lucy was horrified. 'Chop up?'

'They say, the *Malacca* man hang in pieces on Alderman crossing. Nobody like it. Bad times.' He clicked his tongue.

'Denis say barn at Revermont burn to seed,' Muru added.

'Who by?'

He swivelled his hands in the air. 'Don' know.'

Revermont belonged to Mr Willcox, who was not liked by anyone. If it was arson, the perpetrators could be any number of his many enemies, not necessarily the rebels. There was no profit, Lucy thought, in speculation. 'Well, at Ambleside at least, we shall not be disrupted. There is plenty for us to be getting on with. Today, Muru, what is the order?'

'First, Jacob sweep and tidy hall and stairs, missie. Clean and neat.'

'And you?'

'Market for oil and salt fish. In the afternoon, dust and clean. Polish the *masta*'s study. Also the parlour.'

'And the servants' quarters?'

'Jacob, missie. Second job.'

'Good. And tomorrow?'

'Dhobi day, missie, with naughty Adonis. I change bedding, Jacob cleans. All upstairs rooms.'

They went through the rest of the week's chores with Lucy testing and the boys vying with each other to please her.

After she set them to work, Lucy went down to the lake.

George Huyton came back from his excursion that afternoon at about half past five, flushed and beery.

'What is it, George? Is this misbehaviour serious?' Mrs Huyton enquired with a rather pointed look.

'What do you mean?' he snapped. 'Whose?'

'These rebellious Indians that people have excited themselves about.'

'The rascal was caught.'

Lucy felt uncomfortable as though the seams around her waist had tightened.

'The fellow that Mr Lambodar wrote about?' Mrs Huyton asked.

'No such bloody luck. Not him yet. No, they caught the other bugger, the one who was brought on the *Malacca*.'

'The servants say he was hacked to death,' Lucy interjected.

'Better dead than plotting on Robben Island like all those other vagabonds we herd together down there. Why transport them so far? I ask you. So damn expensive. A waste of time and money.'

'I think you are a little too fond of violent punishment, George. It is an ugly characteristic in a civilised man.' Betty's cheeks sagged a little.

'On the contrary, my dear. Swift action has a purgative effect that is both necessary and desirable. Justice demands it. If a man attacks the norms of our society, then he needs to be removed from it forthwith. It is very much a part of civilised conduct.' He frowned at the pitcher of water on the sideboard.

'Even if the norms you speak of might be immoral, George?'

'What on earth is the matter with you? Are you taking that wretched cut-throat's side?'

'I believe it is you, George, who is the more agitated by the matter. The sea air at Flacq appears to have had a rather unwholesome effect upon you.'

He shifted his gaze; his head settled firmly into his moist neck. He braced himself and spoke slowly with great deliberation like an admiral altering course. 'I have decided to employ a new housekeeper, Betty. That boy, Merlot, needs proper training. In any case, I think you would find it more soothing to devote more of your time to the garden. There is much to do there.'

His wife stared at him, her dismay turning to disbelief. 'Muru is a perfectly capable young lad. Lucy manages him very well. You are scarcely ever in the house, George. It does not need another servant.'

'I would be obliged, Betty, if you would let me be the judge of that. If you prefer you may consider it as charity towards yet another of these unfortunates in need of employment. She will come before the end of the month.'

'Are you not on circuit again this week?' she queried, seeking another tack.

'I will be daily at the office for now. I think the arrangement will suit us all. As a matter of fact, Betty, I have today negotiated the purchase of Ambleside. We shall no longer be tenants of a coloured man.'

'My goodness, George, have we come into some unexpected wealth?'

Her husband looked a little uneasy. 'This is a land of opportunity, Betty, as I have always maintained. Therefore one must seize the chance to invest when one can, using whatever one has at one's disposal.'

Aunt Betty was not a woman easily perturbed; her husband's usual errors she dismissed as the peccadilloes of a jaded colonist too much abroad, but these new acts of acquisition indicated a troubling enthusiasm. After he had withdrawn to his study, she took her embroidery and went out onto the verandah. Lucy joined her.

'Are you pleased about the purchase of Ambleside?' she asked, as that at least seemed favourable news.

No inner strain ever disrupted the composure of her aunt's face. 'I have been very happy here and ownership can only improve that contentment as long as it is not at the expense of something more dear.' She looked at Lucy, gauging the risk. 'I do hope he has not put any of our prospects in jeopardy.'

'What is it that he intends with this new arrangement?'

'He intends to make a fool of himself, my dear Lucy. It happens when a man's appetite outstrips his capacity and he is no longer able to judge what is best for himself. Your Uncle George is possibly suffering from a form of male myopia that is often concomitant with expanding opportunities of procurement.'

'His sight is deteriorating?'

'Morally, perhaps, more than visually.' She held up her needle against the evening light and slipped a pink cotton thread through the eye in one unerring movement, before dusk would render it impossible; her hands were remarkably steady. Her ability to appear unruffled and to maintain her composure in the most disagreeable of circumstances was impressive. It was more than self-control, Lucy thought. Her aunt had a deep belief in the fundamental goodness of the natural order, and her own place in it, that Lucy could not but admire.

'Is there nothing you can do to compensate?'

She made a soft clucking sound. 'For his failure to manage his affairs? No. But for one's own equilibrium, I would recommend engagement with the damask in whatever form you please.' Lifting the hoop of cloth she showed Lucy how far she had come with her needlework. 'If done with true feeling, like any art – within or without – it will divert the distress that may otherwise consume us.'

Lucy could not agree with her. Needlework did not, in her view, bear comparison to the art available to a brush or pen no matter how much one may wish it. Nor is it equal to the spade that shapes a bed of hollyhocks. No. It may be a means of diverting what is undesirable but that is surely not the purpose of a proper art? Lucy required more integrity. She did not say it; she could see her aunt had stemmed too much true feeling with her words even as she punctured the fabric. For her, George was more than a short-sighted blunderbuss. The years together had formed a bridge between them, shaky perhaps and somewhat unsound in purpose, but indisputably there. Lucy had seen her looking at him in the dining room after he has finished his repast, when his eyes would begin to thicken and his mouth droop. Her aunt never admonished him for his intemperance; her gaze instead seemed to revert back to the man he must have been once, at least in promise to her. It was a facility she had perfected – to conjure with the past for her solace – but Lucy was not convinced of its efficacy today.

'Fortitude,' Mrs Huyton claimed, 'is not only a virtue, my dear. It is our best defence.'

In that, Lucy thought, perhaps she was right, but from where does one obtain a dose of fortitude when in dire need? Lucy believed she, unlike her aunt, had no such inner resources. She supposed they came with age and incremental survival, harnessed and nurtured with the daily drift of tide, but in Lucy's case it seemed each day filled her to bursting with everything but fortitude.

In the evening, while her aunt turned to her correspondence, Lucy sat in the front room and tried to read. Outside, on the verandah, Muru stood as though on guard. Slowly she became aware of a light pattern of sound that was like the drip of water following a precise score. She went up to the window and saw it was the boy tapping out a tune on the balustrade with his fingers.

Later, in her bed, while the candle still had an inch to go, Lucy rested her eyes on a page of verse and let herself wander. She imagined walking through the cane, the light and shadow in it like the bars of a cage, listening to the swish and rustle of the leaves. She wanted to walk far beyond the fields, far from houses and cottages and all human habitation, and be close to the true nature of this outcrop of earth and sand. Talk of rebellion and danger only made her want the dark even more.

On the long voyage from England, she remembered going out alone on deck at night and contemplating the sea as it swelled and spread its starry shoals to sparkle. These were the very same lines she thought of then, from Lalla Rookh's 'Fire-worshippers':

> 'Tis moonlight over Oman's Sea:
> Her banks of pearl and palmy isles
> Bask in the night-beam beauteously,
> And her blue waters sleep in smiles.

Alone with the wind and the extraordinary illumination of a milky moon brimming in the sky, she marvelled at the phenomena about her: the rhythm of ceaseless motion, the smiling waves, the abundance of blue from midnight to noon. In Bridleton she had never seen such brilliant blue – the lapis lazuli of dreams – except in her mother's eyes, but on the ship everywhere one looked offered a different shade of this heavenly colour: *azure*, *azure*, as the poets sang. She did not feel lonely then. She was bound for an established place of some security. Aunt Betty had spoken of estates, cane, and the Gothic rocks that loomed out of the sea mist. A plantation house made of wood. She had pictured it: Ambleside – set among green hills, creaking in obeisance, waiting for her with her scent of heather and blackberries, her hair riddled with the brown hints of a northern autumn. She imagined her life as a trail across the ocean, a wake that subsided into the tentacles of a Portuguese man-of-war stretched over thousands of miles; its veiled head washed up on the shore of Grand Bay like a sleeping bride.

While Lucy quietly plaited her memories to her turbaned dreams, three miles south of Ambleside, two men broke into the Dupont house. Monsieur Dupont tried to repel them but was struck down. They trussed him up like a chicken and threw him out into the garden. His wife and two daughters were gagged and bound to the kitchen table. The men scoured the whole house ransacking every room: ripping open doors, tossing papers, emptying drawers, nuzzling through clothes, ferreting out jewels, searching for guns or swords.

Dupont was found the next day, stung, bitten and pecked about in the damp sand, squawking and cursing and vowing revenge.

Although his assailants had been masked, Dupont was convinced that the leader was the son of the dhobi. Several neighbours joined in a pack and they raced over to Adonis's home. The boy was not there. Nobody wanted their dhobi incapacitated but they wanted him to learn a lesson he could pass on. At first, pots and plates were broken and he was slapped around; then kicked and beaten with a stick. Denis the coachman told Lucy, the next day, the dhobi was lucky not have been whipped or have had his ears nicked.

Lucy was livid; she wanted to go to him immediately.

'No, you cannot, Lucy,' her aunt said. 'We cannot interfere in these matters.'

'But he needs help.'

'He has his own people, Lucy. Just as the Duponts do.'

'Denis says he is alone. His son must be hiding and his daughters are stuck in town. I am going, Aunt Betty. Please do not stop me.'

Adonis lived in a small wooden shack by the river where he did all the washing; the bushes in the garden were draped with clothes put out to dry. He lay crumpled in a rickety rocking chair under a canopy fashioned out of a torn sheet, nursing a bandaged head.

Lucy jumped down from the little gig and went over to him. 'Poor you. I have brought you some chicken broth. Josephine says it is the best restorative.'

'Miss Lucy?' He moved his swaddled head to an angle. One eye was swollen and blind.

'I am sorry, Adonis. Truly, I am so sorry this has happened. It is very wrong. They had no right ...'

'Not suitable, Miss Lucy. My home is very humble.'

'Have you sent word to your daughters?'

'It is no matter, Miss Lucy. Misunderstanding, tha's all. Madam Dupont's tablecloth is hanging right at the back. I iron it and take it tomorrow. Everything be all right then. Back to normal. Must not fret, Miss Lucy.'

'May I go inside and get a bowl for your soup?'

'My bowl is there.' He pointed at a small shelf attached to the side of the shack, under an awning made of dried palm leaves. 'Everything dries best outside,' he smiled lopsidedly.

Lucy stepped over a small thin gully cut for the sink water to flow away. She picked up the unglazed clay bowl and wiped away a few specks of sand that had settled on the rim. A line of tiny ants made their way along the shelf. Lucy poured the broth and looked around for a spoon. There were no cutlery drawers, but in two pockets of an apron hanging off the far beam she found some utensils. She picked the smaller of the two wooden spoons. 'Do you have a tray I can use?'

'No, Miss Gladwell. No tray. No Muru here, Miss, to carry trays.'

'Never mind.' She brought the bowl over and handed it to him. 'This will help you, I am sure.'

His open eye was like a piece of cracked porcelain in a muddy ruin, greying with age and tinged with old blood losing colour. 'No pain there,' he touched the bandage. 'Only here.' He jabbed his chest. 'Don' want my son to see. Boy boil too damn fast.'

He slurped a spoonful of the broth. In the tangle of trees behind the shack a dry palm branch crashed down. Lucy started, but Adonis waved a hand unperturbed. 'Dead fall all the time.'

She waited with him until he had finished the bowl, then took it back to the sink and washed it using a coconut shell to scoop some water from the large pitcher. There was no drying cloth to be seen but she knew better now than to ask for one. She placed the bowl on the shelf to dry.

When she turned round she found a band of five white men standing in the yard staring at her. Their clothes were streaked with red dust and sweat. She recognised two of them, a small pig-eyed man carrying a flintlock and Martin, a taller, burly man with a cutlass. Both neighbours of Monsieur Dupont.

'Mademoiselle, you should not be here,' the tall man said. 'You fraternise too much with these blacks.' He swung his cutlass over the tips of his boots.

'How dare you,' Lucy burst out. 'Put that thing away before you talk to a lady. Have you no manners at all? Why have you crept up here like thieves? Where are your horses?'

The man sheepishly sheathed the cutlass. 'We have business here, Miss Gladwell. It would be best if you would leave, please.'

'Business?' The word exploded in her mouth. She steadied herself, hands clenched. 'Have you brought your dirty laundry? Shirts? Sheets? Where? I can't see any business.'

'His son is a rebel,' one of the men yapped from behind. 'We must find him.'

'*Non*,' Adonis managed to croak.

'Even if true, that is no reason for this abomination.' Lucy's whole body shook, but anger gave her courage. 'I would like to know who thought it right to beat an innocent man who cleans their clothes.' She stepped closer to the leader, Martin. 'Do you know the brutes who did it?'

He shuffled back. 'No,' he mumbled.

'Well, I know you, Monsieur Martin. You find the villains who hurt Mr Adonis and I will get the Superintendent to deal with them.' She picked a towel off one of the bushes and violently shook the dry leaf crumbs off to hide her own tremors. The flap of the cloth was like the crack of a whip in the still quiet air. One of the men jumped and dropped his stick and the others shrank back. 'Go now, and don't you dare come back here unless you are carrying your laundry – or the names of those cowardly scoundrels, you understand?'

# Chapter 17

O<small>N HER</small> way back to Ambleside, she avoided the road where the Duponts lived; she was not sure whether she could be as brave again with another mob. Thank goodness, I do not always stop to think, she said to herself with a shudder. Where the courage came from, she did not know, but she thought perhaps one grows firmer each day one lives, or clearer about what matters. Perhaps that is how one comes of age.

Her route circled Miramont, but if she had turned left at the culvert, she would have passed Narayena's defunct shrine where Don Lambodar had come to see the noxious effects of colonial justice.

Three days had passed since Kishore, the prisoner, had been killed. Don did not think of the state in which the corpse might be, nor indeed what a pack of hounds and a vindictive blade might have done. The wretched piece of carrion that hung in a cage on the gibbet bore no resemblance to any man Don could have imagined. The air was thick with the stench of putrefaction.

There had not been much flesh to begin with, but now all that remained was a skeletal frame shrouded with ripped tissue and hardened skin. His hacked arms and legs were not much thicker than his ribs; the naked torso had been gnawed and the neck lacerated. The bearded face bloated: the cheeks gashed, the jaw loosened; the tongue cut out and strung to rot around his neck, his mouth stuffed with his mutilated genitals. The chest below had burst open. The pitiful rotting carcass, clotted with maddened flies, was pressed between thick black bars made into the shape of a head and body to keep the bits roughly in place.

Standing before the iron cage, Don could feel his own blood thump. The island was choked with metal traps – yokes of iron, spiked collars, leg chains and handcuffs, gibbet cages – but could these restrain the song that beat in so many human hearts?

At the crossroads, there were only four or five others – blacks, Indians – around. Don could see no proclamation in words. No sign, or banner, to serve as sentence or warning. Only the stink of the thing itself in the wind: a warning for the illiterate.

The intent may have been to induce fear, but the result evident among the small group around Don was to feed rage, as it always has in the past and always will in any unjust future.

Don slipped back into the Botanic Gardens, angry and ashamed.

Mr Amos was contemplating the lotus in the pond, seated at his usual place.

'Have you seen him hanging in that contraption?' Don's question rang out like an accusation.

Mr Amos did not reply immediately. His head too seemed misshapen, inanimate, maltreated in its own way.

'Do they not do it in your country, son?'

'What do you mean? Torturing?' He remembered stories of men split in half, ripped open by their legs, crushed by boulders. Pulped. All in the name of authority, the rule of law. Foreign or native.

Mr Amos looked at him patiently. His eyes crinkled and broken at the edges, fractured and chipped. 'The human mind is too susceptible to dreams, and the heart too weak to resist cruelty when faced with its own mortality,' he added. 'You see, when the unbeliever discovers his body is itself a cell for his incarceration, he goes mad and rips it – and all like it – to pieces.'

'That Kishore? Asoka says he scolded us, you know, for not doing more. "Freedom is the song of the heart," he chanted. It cannot be stopped.'

'We do too much wrong, because to do right is too difficult.'

'Is that an excuse? Surely you cannot be saying that the perpetrators of these acts are unable to help themselves? That the business of slavery is an understandable failing? Surely that is not what your Toussaint preached?'

'Slavery is not a purely European invention. The Nyamezi do it, the Yao, Africans in the South, Arabs. It is not endemic to one place only.'

His words, perhaps the tone of his voice, conjured up in Don a memory of his father. He could see him through a crack in a door. His father was seated on a cushion, talking to an English officer in a red coat who had come to the house. The Englishman nodded and then used a quill to sign a document Don's father had placed before him. They shook hands when he had finished and they both laughed. Don's mother then came in with two cups of sherbet and the two men drank to each other's health and the Great Expedition to the heart of the Kandyan kingdom. That was the first time Don had heard the word *kaffir*.

'You know, Mr Amos, I have only just understood something.'

'It is usually a matter of time.'

'I do not mean the barbarity here.'

'What then?'

'You are right. We have it too and the slaves are black men.'

'From Africa?'

'My father was a freighter who sold and transported anything to anyone. He did not think of right or wrong. One day, while the British were still stuck between the jungle belt and the coastal strip, his carts were ambushed; he died on the road to Trincomalee.'

'You mean, he was not killed by the British?'

'He had sold slaves to the British for their campaign.'

'The slaves rose up?' Mr Amos's eyes glittered briefly.

'Not the slaves. The Kandyan King's men. It must have been them. It changes everything.'

Mr Amos lowered his head, puzzled. 'I don't understand what you mean. Was he hung on a gibbet like this Kishore?'

Don closed his eyes and pressed the lids with his fingers. 'When my mother fled, with me, to Colombo, she had nothing: no money, no home. I thought her family had ostracised her for marrying outside her clan – my father was a Tamil-speaking Moor – but I think it was more to do with his slave-running for the British. I assumed it was bigotry, but we were on the wrong side of a war. Only her cousin, who already worked for Mr Berwick, came to her aid. He found her a place in Mr Berwick's kitchen. From there she was promoted to parlourmaid while I was still a small boy.'

'Your saviour was not your Mr Henderson, then?'

'It was a war. The British against the Kandyan kingdom. My father helped the British. That's why they supported me.'

Mr Amos patted his thighs and rubbed them, rocking back and forth as if preparing to stand up. 'So, despite war and slavery, it all turned out for the best, in the end, for you. You found a place where learning could erode your mental confinements.' He offered an extraordinary faith in the ultimate good of the world. 'Now you know there is more than one story to a person. More than one history to a country.'

Don was not listening. 'It must have been in my twelfth year that Mr Henderson came to talk to Mr Berwick about me.' Both men looked so different from Don so as to be very nearly of a different species, he thought, and yet they discussed his future as though he was the son of one or both of them. Don remembered his mother leaning against the doorway watching, for she had only the most rudimentary English, while his teacher praised his facility with language to his ... what was he? His owner? Was he like a slave too? A walking, talking, sentient piece of chattel? Was Mr Berwick no different from a slave owner, despite his liberal skin? Had he – the young Don – been traded by one failed father to another? 'To his credit, he allowed me to pursue my schooling as far as I could and then arranged for my apprenticeship.' It was a form of freedom he felt he was fortunate to enjoy, and certainly more liberating than anything poor wretches like Narayena could ever hope to see, even if they managed to earn their complete manumission.

'You should be grateful.'

'I am, but I know every single thing in this world has a price – that much I learned even before I was trained at the Company.'

'Learning the price of a thing, not the cost, is the difficulty. Your friend Narayena needs to understand that.' Mr Amos got up and tested his knees. 'Have you read Olaudah's account of his life?'

'Who was he?'

'Another slave who freed himself.'

'I have not heard of him.'

'But he wrote in English. It seems there is a great deal you have yet to read, son.'

On his way back from the Gardens, Don noticed ladies out on their own again, armed only with parasols and headscarves, servants carrying baskets of radishes and potatoes, and cane cutters wielding machetes in the fields. Several rosy children, in the care of a governess, passed by in a carriage. The Presbytery door was open. There were no armed guards at the sugar mill. Narayena might have been fomenting a full-scale rebellion, but there was not a sign of it that Don could see any more in Pamplemousses other than Kishore's caged remains and the occasional squad of soldiers on the move.

For now it seemed, here in his temporarily adopted island, polite high society had resumed its normal state of indifference as though the bloodletting of one coloured man would ease all tensions and drown the pain of all the enslaved. The horses and the cattle, the sparrows and the hawks were oblivious of the disorders. The wind blew the rotten air out; the flowers in hedges and riverbanks opened; birds flew. The earth slumbered, open-mouthed, in a reverie.

As a child Don had often marvelled at nature's capacity for regeneration. The way a gecko could replace its amputated tail. How swiftly the colours of the setting sun obliterated the harsh white heat of the day, and how even he could blot away a bubble of tears with a printed page out of Mr Berwick's bookcase. In the garden of Mr Berwick's house there was a hedge of lantana that was periodically cut down to waist level, but within weeks seemed to recover its full size and blossom into a hundred sunset rosettes as though it had never suffered from a pruning blade. Life, it seemed to him, was amazingly robust.

Or is it that barbarity soon disperses in a hot climate?

At the cottage he found Sergeant Murray waiting for him, drinking coconut water on the verandah. 'Mr Don, I have a proposal.'

'For me?'

'I understand that you are a customer of Mr Badani. Are you aware that after the recent hullabaloo there will be some new arrangements with regard to his trading?'

'I understand prices will rise. Mr Badani has many calls.'

'Prices will be hellish. The Governor has added a tax on local sales. Mr Badani is also now committed to supply his best-quality opium only for export.'

'Very good for him, no doubt.'

Sergeant Murray nodded. He picked at a loose thread dangling from one of his tunic buttons. 'You know, Mr Don, I can obtain a premium supply, direct from the export office. Mr Badani's very best, in fact.' He paused. 'In exchange, Mr Don, for a regular lesson in the language.'

'English?'

'No. There is a lady prisoner from your country at the Powder Mills. I want to learn to talk to her in her own tongue.'

# PART V

# Chapter 18

'MA'AM.' MURU trotted up holding out his tray. 'Letter from ship.'

Two ships had arrived and anchored in the bay since the killing of Kishore. The garrison had been redeployed; the planters emboldened. All the world, it seemed, saluted ruthless efficiency. Lucy had heard the apothecary, Dr Lawson, say that only on this golden island did people know how to deal with ugly troublemakers. 'A single bullet in the right place,' he had remarked, as though he were measuring a sleeping draught, 'is worth a hundred hours of dillydallying.'

Mrs Huyton picked up the envelope and opened it, snapping the seal neatly in two like a biscuit. 'How delightful. A letter of introduction from Mrs Trent. Do you remember her, Lucy? We met her with her daughter Vanessa at Meadowfield before we left England. Apparently a most charming historian, Mr Fry, is on board. An expert on Egyptian antiquities. She hopes we could entertain him. I think that would be splendid, don't you, Lucy?'

'Entertain him?'

'Indeed, let us have a soirée for Mr Fry,' she exclaimed brightly.

'Is this a time for it?'

'There is no better time, my dear. I believe his ship has to be in port for quite a few days.'

'You think this Mr Fry will be sufficiently sociable? Is he not likely to be one who prefers his own company? Is that not why he is travelling alone to India?'

'My dear, a man who travels must be well disposed to the company of others abroad, even if not in his homeland. At any rate in India he will still be among his own species. I am sure he will appreciate the introduction we can offer to the marvels of the East.'

'At a party?'

'I shall wear a turban with a peacock feather, Lucy. And perhaps you can get young Muru to organise some musicians?'

'I cannot imagine much enthusiasm for native sounds?'

'Not that dreadful village cacophony, my dear, but music from India. He will know how. He is quite a musician, our Muru. And I believe Mr Badani has two Indian cooks who can be commissioned for a splendid Eastern banquet. We will not need to rely on Josephine.'

'That would make a difference.'

'It would be wonderful. A mad midsummer revel for our exotic visitor. Or midwinter, I should say, in our topsy-turvy world here.'

Lucy wondered what Uncle George would think of it. He was not a man who liked to mingle so freely. She began to say something about him, but Mrs Huyton cut her short.

'Your Uncle George will see what Ambleside truly needs for its management and who is, and will be, most accomplished for the task. Let us invite everyone, Lucy. Your Ceylonese gentlemen will certainly come this time, I am sure.' She raised herself an inch or two. 'I shall deal with the caterers and leave you, Lucy, to organise the entertainment.'

Mr Huyton lurched in at about three o'clock looking decidedly unwell from his day in town. His face was swollen as though he had been over-exercised by his horse, or the unreliability of his umpteen subordinates.

'What is your aunt up to now?' he demanded.

Lucy said she was in the throes of organising a social function.

'A social bloody nuisance.' He tottered into his study and slammed the door. Once inside he bellowed, venting steam, as an engineer might in a pressure chamber. Poor man, thought Lucy, he probably finds social occasions a little trivial when set against the great Colonial Project and its snarled expression in little Mauritius. Lucy hoped he would be pleasantly surprised to find their guest of honour was a man of serious imperial vision. She was curious herself to see what this engine of progress looked like.

Over the next few days Ambleside became a hive where Lucy, her aunt, Josephine and the boys fussed and buzzed to prepare for what Mrs Huyton claimed would be the most dazzling gala night that Pamplemousses had ever known. The verandah had to be repainted, the gazebo renewed, the lawn clipped. Her collection of outdoor tables brought out of storage and cleaned, the chairs restrung. In a rush, tureens were polished, braziers blacked, livery laundered.

The prospect of providing music at the party made Muru break out in a huge grin. 'Can do, missie, but please talk to Mr Badani for extra musicians,' he hummed happily.

Mr Badani's town office was a small room in a tall, salty building where he spent the beginning and end of each week on paperwork. The other tenants were all traders and ships' brokers of one sort or another, mired in accounts that netted practically the whole globe. Mr Badani had one of the front rooms with a window that opened to a view of the port.

'Miss Gladwell, what an unexpected pleasure. Please sit down.' He hurried over to the visitor's chair and dusted it vigorously with a swatch of coloured silk. 'What can I do for you, Miss Gladwell? Anything would be my pleasure.'

'I am here on the advice of our boy, Muru,' she said. The windows, she noted, were encrusted with dust.

'How very remarkable, Miss Gladwell. Ambleside must indeed be a most favourable spot for young Muru to rise to such dizzy heights. An adviser, indeed. May I offer you some coffee? *Eau sucrée?*' He raised his head to show his low-cut smile.

'Thank you, Mr Badani, but no. I will not take up much time. My purpose –'

'Time is never wasted, Miss Gladwell, when one spends it in company. It has a curious propensity to expand, don't you find, as one accumulates experience?'

She looked around the room. The place was crowded

with statues and figurines and herds of different-sized carved elephants. 'I have to say I have not considered it in that way.'

'So, coffee then?'

'Thank you.'

He picked up a small wand and struck a brass bowl on his desk like a bell; a small brown boy peeked in from the doorway. Mr Badani called for coffee and then resumed his conversation. 'So, you are here with regard to music, no doubt.'

'How did you know?'

'Muru, you said. It is the grub of his heart and the thread of our connection, you might say.' He laughed, shakily, as a man practised in amusing himself more than others. 'You know, he was my houseboy here in Port Louis. When he was about ten, he found a music guru in a house just two doors down. Even when I put him in Ambleside with the predecessors of Mr Huyton, he continued his lessons in secret. A very resourceful boy.'

Two cups of coffee, already poured and sweetened, were brought in. Lucy stirred hers with an expensive spoon and took a sip. 'Lovely coffee, Mr Badani.'

'I do my best to get the best, Miss Gladwell. One has to try, as I am sure you would agree.'

'Indeed.'

'Muru is a prodigy, Miss Gladwell. I am very glad Mrs Huyton supported him with extra time when she found out about his passion. It gives the boy, despite being an orphan, a place in our community. And we are a respectable and growing community, you know. He is able to uplift us at our festivals and commemorative days and help us remember our heritage. It is very enlightened of your aunt, Miss Gladwell. She is a most remarkable lady.'

'I am very glad of it,' Lucy said. 'I had no idea of this aspect of our Muru's life, until she mentioned it the other day.'

'Ah, you see the wisdom of Mrs Huyton. She allows things to grow in their natural way.'

'The reason I have come, Mr Badani, is because we are having a soirée at which we would like to introduce young Muru and his music.'

'Indian music to high society?' He eased back to consider the proposition.

'It will be an evening with an oriental theme for Mr Fry, an orientalist, or one who aspires to be one, who has just arrived. Muru said that you might be able to help with some musicians to accompany him.'

'Of course, you have come exactly to the right place, Miss Gladwell. Consider it done.'

'You are very kind. I believe my aunt is also keen to discuss the catering with you.'

Mr Badani brought his hands together, pressing the fingertips one to the other, as if testing the tension of east and west. The omnivorous smile widened. 'It will be my pleasure to assist in any way I can. I may no longer be the landlord, but I am always here to serve.'

Two days before the party, while Lucy was painstakingly stitching in the last alteration to her evening gown, taking in and sharpening the waist, Muru peeped in. 'Missie, two black girls downstairs. Claim they belong here.'

'Two?' Her Uncle George had said a housekeeper would be arriving, not a family.

'One big, one small.'

'Have you told madam?'

'Not yet. Madam in bath.'

'I'll see them then.' She finished the stitch like a proper seamstress, and stabbed the green velvet pincushion. It was possible, she was beginning to realise, to live like a lady in limbo as much as in Pimlico.

The bigger girl, Lucy thought, might have been her own age; the other, her sister she supposed, was a child. They both had proud oval faces brimming with expectation. 'Did Mr Huyton call you here?' Lucy asked.

Eulalie, Mr Amos's daughter, nodded.

'With your mother?' Lucy had assumed that the housekeeper her uncle wanted would be a matron of some experience.

Eulalie, more defiant than shy, said nothing. Her shoulders sloped like fresh cane syrup; her dark lips, parted slightly in repose, showed a faint white line of recessed teeth. Her gaze was almost impertinent. The surprising lack of subservience made Lucy uneasy. Her uncle was not a man to tolerate such effrontery. Lucy repeated her question in French.

'He said come to the big house.' Eulalie spoke in clipped, sharp English.

Lucy instructed Muru to show them to the family room in the servants' quarters, and to inform her uncle when he returned. 'There is no need to bother madam,' she added, thinking it unwise to alert her straight away.

Lucy watched the elder girl walk with the confidence of one of the Creole ladies in town, her head held high, her chest thrust forward. Her dress, with its coloured rushes, was quite unsuitable for a working girl, and Lucy wondered if it had been purloined. Ignoble of her to think so, she realised, but the girl acted so unashamedly free.

Along with Mr Fry and fresh correspondence, the new ship had also brought the latest gardening catalogues, albeit printed six months earlier. Items of great excitement for Mrs Huyton and rather special interest to the Reverend, for reasons that escaped Lucy for he grew nothing that was cultivated in soil. Reverend Artichoke, as her aunt sometimes wickedly called him – making fun of his gasps at the illustrations of winged beans and eglantine – came over bringing with him a copy of the new magazine produced by the Society of Arts and Sciences. He raised it above his head like a flag. 'Miss Gladwell, your aunt will be very interested in this. A most fascinating article on the business of hybrids in the garden.'

'I should like to see it too, please,' Lucy said.

'Indeed, you too may find it quite stimulating. It is on the second page and written by a botanist in Edinburgh who spent three years in the colonies.' He explained that the scientist had visited Mauritius and maintained an enthusiastic correspondence with the Society in Port Louis.

'Are you a member of the Society?' Lucy asked. 'Is it permissible for a parson?'

He gave a soggy laugh. 'My dear Miss Gladwell, I believe we gain a greater appreciation of the work of the Almighty, the more we seek to understand it. The more we question, the more we discover, would you not agree?'

Lucy thought it remarkably enlightened of him. He never looked complacent, unlike most others of his vocation; he had none of the smugness one sees in those who believe they have a superior line of communication to the higher authority. Instead, the Reverend had a face of congested curiosity: somewhat frenetic, each fold and bulb constantly bullied by perplexity. For him there was only ever a partial resolution of any problem; faith, he kept in a separate compartment. His spirit of enquiry, Lucy admired, but his constant questioning sometimes made her want to grab his cassock and pin it to the floor, as comical as that might seem. A man of cloth, in her view, ought to be less wavering. He was not a young man and one would think the many years of sermonising – week in, week out – must have built up some inner certitude, but he was unable to speak outside the interrogative. Aunt Betty's opinion was that he had been relegated to Port Louis on this island because in the middle of the Indian Ocean he could pursue his scientific interests without causing too much embarrassment, or harm, to the Church at large; at any rate, the apparently formidable Bishop of Madras could keep an eye on him and sail to rescue the flock within a matter of weeks if it proved necessary. The Reverend had come late into the Church having misspent his youth, as he gigglingly put it, miscast on the London stage. He was often too loud, in Lucy's opinion, but her aunt suggested that perhaps his manner of speaking had been an asset in his various voca-tional pursuits. At any rate he was always diverting, even if not a source of spiritual solace.

'Do you go to the meetings in town? Are they very excit-ing?' Lucy asked him.

'We do have some excellent discussions. Mr Geoffroy, the founder, is a good speaker and quite provocative. He is a black man, you understand, but of a prodigious intellect.'

Lucy said she should very much like to attend one day.

Aunt Betty came out then. Her face bright and animated. 'We have a very extensive new catalogue, Reverend. I think you will be quite transported.'

'Indeed, Mrs Huyton, and in return I have an article for you to read at your leisure. That is if your niece would be good enough to part with it.'

They took their usual pews on the verandah. The Reverend liked to sit facing the pink azaleas.

'And how is the parish after all the kerkuffle, Reverend?'

He wiggled his head to free it from his tight white collar. 'The rebellion at Belvédère has been most distressing. I do not believe we are completely out of the woods, just yet.'

'Slaves of course will always wish to revolt.' Betty waved a hand.

'A natural enough desire, when one is unduly suppressed, surely?' Lucy added sharply.

'I am indeed with Wilberforce on this matter, but my parish is very conservative.'

'Do your parishioners not include the disadvantaged?'

'They do, Miss Gladwell, and what I hear from them worries me a great deal. Their hearts are heavy.' A spidery shadow spread across his face. 'There is a theory that suggests we all find it mutually advantageous to live competitively, but I find that difficult to fully accept, whatever the merits of political economy. How can we not know in our hearts the good that comes from the Samaritan?'

'I see no harm in sharing space,' Aunt Betty replied. 'In an island of such diversity, it is very good if we can accommodate each other. But will people here co-operate?'

'I am hoping to acquire the old abandoned salt house and turn it into a church of our own. It is a very strong structure and will offer good refuge even in a hurricane. We need proper pews, of course, and a pulpit which I believe we will be given by the Catholics, at a reasonable price, as they are replacing theirs with one more monumental. Rosewood is their preference and gold leaf. The steeple I have been promised by Mr Badani as a gift. A remarkably generous man.'

'Already a convert? That is most encouraging.' Aunt Betty turned to Lucy. 'My dear, would you be so good as to ask Muru to bring us the catalogue and some refreshments for the Reverend?'

Later, when the Reverend was leaving, Lucy walked with him to his gig. 'Aunt Betty has been a little upset,' she said.

'She seemed in very good spirits just now.'

'It is to do with my uncle.' Lucy paused, unsure once more of her ground, but she wanted his advice about the impending rearrangement in the household. Her Uncle George, she feared, may well be out of his depth. 'We have a new housekeeper coming – her two young girls are here already – because he believes my aunt needs more help. But she does not think so and, I have to say, neither do I. The girls are in the servants' quarters and I have not yet told my aunt of their arrival. I cannot think what she will do when she sees them. The elder is quite bold.'

The Reverend stopped; the crescent of his chin receded.

'It is good to be charitable, Miss Gladwell. For the moment, perhaps you should let things be. Your aunt is quite invigorated by the plans for Saturday's soirée and I dare say she will be glad of a few extra pairs of hands on the day. Produce them for her then, when they will appear as a solution rather than a problem. I will have a word with Mr Huyton when I see him next.'

'He is in his study now, although he tends to sink into a rather poor mood when he has been with his accounts.'

The Reverend glanced back at the house. His pale lips failed. 'I think it would be better to wait. Haste in these matters leads to regret. Saturday, with all its revelry, might be the more opportune moment.'

That night, George Huyton found his bed unyielding; the shot of dark rum he swallowed before he lay down did nothing to mitigate his sense of unease. Having crumpled his pillow and kicked off his sheet, he gave up any attempt to sleep and went down to the verandah to the comfort of his rocker. He lit a pipe and stared at the glowing bowl that lay like a bruised red moon in his fist.

Eulalie was not the first, but she had affected him in a way none of her predecessors had. Perhaps it was her freshness, the lack of servility in her relations with him. She treated him as a man, not a master, and though at first he had been affronted, later he begrudgingly began to admire her attitude. In the house in Flacq where he had installed her, she had become a mistress of considerable allure. When with her second pregnancy she had announced that she would like to be closer to her father, George had suggested she come to

Ambleside. He could not accept the idea of having her at her father's house – a black man's abode. There had been no conjugal relations with his childless Betty for many years. She was a fine companion and a pragmatic woman, and at this stage of their lives, he expected her not to be too concerned by his intrigues.

Betty Huyton lay awake listening to the slow deliberate rhythm of her husband rocking away from her. In the darkness of a cloudy night, she hoped she could retrieve some lost ground. She stole down to the verandah. In a whisper, she asked, 'George, do you know what you are doing?'

'At this moment, my dear, yes, I do know what I am doing.' He took another pinch of tobacco from his box.

'You will not bring us into ridicule, will you?'

'Time is marching, Betty. There is no sense pandering to appearances. You said you wanted to live out of the town circle of tittle-tattle. That is why we are here. We should live as we see fit. You do understand that, don't you, Betty?'

'No, George. I do not understand what you are saying.'

'Dear Betty, it is not a competition. The arrangement is for our mutual benefit.'

'I fail to see how it can be to my benefit. I do not think we can all live under one roof. I shall not allow it. We shall have some decent society here on Saturday and I trust the company will bring you back to your senses, George, for *our* mutual benefit.'

# Chapter 19

'From mrs Huyton to you,' Don announced, opening the invitation and enjoying the scent of bergamot that hovered around the flap.

The Prince was baffled. 'Me?'

'She is inviting you and your attendants, meaning us, to a soirée. The occasion is to honour the arrival of Mr Jeremy Fry from England.'

'Honour a Britisher?'

'I do not think this is a political issue, sire. Merely a party. Mrs Huyton is much impressed by you and is no doubt keen to show this Mr Fry the pre-eminence of her neighbours.'

'Will they have biscuits and cake?'

'Undoubtedly. Ginger nuts, rock cakes, baked boulders and many other English exotica appropriate for a road-builder's function. It will be an occasion to display the riches of a colonial palate seasoned by the produce of far-reaching trade and manic conquering. There is much confidence among them now after the killing of Kishore. You know how it is with the British when they have thrashed an enemy.'

'The bravado could be misplaced.' The Prince circled his half-open mouth with a finger, in preparation for a pearl of wisdom. 'I do not like their savouries. They have an unpleasant meaty smell.'

'I am certain there will be sweeteners in all the food. Sugar is one of their weaknesses, even in lard.'

'Reply then and say that we will come.'

'Asoka also?'

He bunched the side of his face into a gnarled shell. 'You can be sure he will not miss out on a whatever it is you called it.'

'Soirée.'

He grunted. 'Yes. *Soirée.*'

Don wrote a short reply in the affirmative, on behalf of the Prince, with nothing added, and sealed it with the royal Lankan crest. He resolved to be careful this time; not bolster his confidence with foolishness, as the Prince would say. Before he sent the reply, he did show the invitation to Asoka. Don wanted to see his reaction, to measure his own feelings against another's — things became much clearer, he had learned, when set against something else.

Asoka's eyes lit up. 'This is the chance, my dear Don, that I have been waiting for. An English bacchanal.' A grin wriggled across his face. 'Oh yes, my dear Don. Most definitely, yes.'

In the afternoon, Don went to see Mr Amos and told him about the invitation to Ambleside.

'That is very nice, son. You move in very excellent society.'

'An invitation has not been extended to you?'

Mr Amos laughed very slowly, a low rumble that barely troubled his lips. 'Even Mrs Huyton is not quite so liberal, my dear Don. You must understand.'

'What about the case of Mr Geoffroy, whom you admire. He is welcome in the most exclusive of houses, is he not?'

'Mr Jean Baptiste Lislet Geoffroy was never a slave, you see. He was born free. His father, a white man from Paris, freed his mother, before he married her, as was legal in those days. In any case, she was a genuine princess from Guinea before her capture. Designations, as you well know, make all the difference, even within the sad "aristocracy of skin" that has taken root in our world. The black can be surmounted, if one has but a touch of royal blue.'

'Have you never been to tea with the English? What about the French?'

This time his lips split and a laugh erupted. 'Would you like a drink? A glass of wine?'

'Perhaps a small one.' Don settled into one of the cane chairs on the verandah. The garden was neat with all its shrubs clipped into small bowed heads, the sand raked clean, straight and flat up to the small circle of pebbles around the red sorrel.

Mr Amos handed him a beaker. 'Although I will not be present on Saturday, you will see my Eulalie.'

'She is employed there already?' Don found the prospect of her working in Ambleside a little unnerving.

'She seems to think . . .' He inclined his head and appeared to measure some movement in his mind. 'In truth, I do not know what she thinks to do. I have made a good place for her here, but she is no longer a child. She sees things so differently now.'

At the cottage, Sergeant Murray presented the six yards of English cloth that he had bought from the newly arrived stock in the market. Surangani unfolded the length carefully and draped it across the table.

'So, there we are. *Hoddhai?*' Sergeant Murray announced, bridging the language gap with a Sinhala tag he had learned.

The Prince, returned from his gilded pissoir, cocked his head. 'Good,' he said. '*Hoddhai* good.' He always felt a little buoyed when a foreigner made the effort to learn his language.

Sergeant Murray's big face beamed with success. He turned to Surangani. '*Mageh adaraniya.*' He squeezed out the syllables with great concentration. Surangani burst out laughing, covering her large teeth with the back of her hand. Even the Prince smiled, despite his intention to remain suitably aloof.

Don Lambodar, who had arrived in time to hear this endearment, congratulated him. 'Very good, Sergeant. Very good. But perhaps you should not be addressing all Sinhala women you see as "my love". They may take it to heart.'

'I am practising, Mr Don, because I do want Soma to take it to heart.' He tried again, in a soft croon. '*Mageh adaraniya.*'

The Prince asked what was exciting the soldier this time; Don explained the Sergeant's scheme to win a Sinhala prisoner's affection.

'The man is as mad as you,' the Prince replied. 'What folly. I hope we don't find more of this nonsense at your soirée.'

# Chapter 20

Don's advice to the Prince was that they should arrive promptly at 6 p.m. as invited; Asoka's view was that they should be there no earlier than half past six. 'We must make an entrance.'

The Prince brushed some breadcrumbs into his sack. 'We do not need to impress these people with our status, Asoka. They know who we are. What I would like is for them to realise that we understand their conventions. It is a mark of respect and civilisation to take the trouble to discover the etiquette of one's host.'

'Their habits, I think, are somewhat befuddled here on this island.'

'In that case we shall arrive just a few minutes past six.'

They set off as the sun was beginning to melt into the trees. The crows took to the air like black heralds. The Prince, dressed in his traditional white with an orange sash from his last Kandyan office, and a maroon four-cornered hat that Don suspected he transformed into a crown in his own mind, waved a hand to his winged subjects and mumbled a small prayer. Asoka, also in traditional costume to show the nobility of his birth, if not his demeanour, looked at Don and shrugged with a little upward roll of the eyes which, Don supposed, was to draw him into his superior confidence.

The stone lions of Ambleside were surmounted by flaming beacons. Khola clicked his tongue and urged the old mare through the gates and the carriage trundled right up to the house. Don alighted first and held the door open for the Prince.

Muru appeared.

'This way, please.' He led them to the other side of the house. Don checked his pocket watch: it was ten minutes past six. He felt queasy and hot around the face. Half a dozen small tables, rigged with starched white linen and clusters of bawdy cane chairs, secured the lawn; a group of guests stood goggle-eyed around Mrs Huyton near the steps to the verandah where Don had been to tea previously. She noticed the new arrivals and launched herself towards them, majestic in a cambric robe and a mantle of Pomona green.

'How delightful to see you. So good of you to come.' She began to offer her hand, but then moved it upward to adjust the pale turban fluttering around her head. A tense smile broke across her face.

The Prince inclined his head, as did Don; his ears clouded alarmingly.

'Let me introduce you to our guest of honour.' Mrs Huyton led them towards the centre of the gathering.

Asoka stepped to one side; his face had that eager social brightness that he was able to bring on at will, as though all he had to do was breathe in and blow on an ember.

287

'Good evening,' he said happily to the small flock of frocks at the nearest table.

Don turned all his attention to Mrs Huyton. Quarter past six was not, to his mind, the best time to be meeting new people out of doors. The sun had given up; the sky was bruised and heaved with long purple welts. Torchlight in twilight lent a lurid colour to the most innocent of faces and one was in constant danger of stumbling in the wretched confluence of shadow and darkness.

Above the party, fruit bats had taken wing: dozens appeared, squealing, tugging black tufts of cloud.

'Bloody pests,' Mr Huyton exclaimed. 'Boy, Merlot, bring me my pistols. Quick.' When Muru brought them out – two, with engraved silver panels and round brown knobs – George Huyton took one in each hand and fired into the air. One or two of his guests jumped, taken unawares. The squealing became momentarily shriller and then the bats flapped away. 'Our mangoes never get a chance,' someone complained in the dark. The Prince muttered something about how the man should use a fowling piece if he must shoot innocents on the wing. 'John D'Oyly gave me a bird gun,' he added, 'in the days when I was bloodthirsty.'

'Bats are not birds,' Don corrected him and suffered the contempt of a peer towards a pedant in return.

Mrs Huyton touched Don's warm arm as they strolled across the grass. 'Mr Lambodar, I must congratulate you on your most elegant correspondence.'

He bowed, colouring. 'My hand is suited more to the pen than the pistol, ma'am.'

Her voice dropped to a note of near conspiracy. 'I fear

Mr Huyton is not very good with a gun. In fact, I should say, growing up in the West Indies, I am rather more expert. I could hit a bottle of rum at twenty paces. Does that shock you, Mr Lambodar?' She laughed lightly. 'Now, tell me, what will the Prince drink? I understand he abstains from wine.'

'Sugar-cane juice. The Prince is very fond of the *fragoulin* here.'

'Oh, he does enjoy a tipple then. That is very good news.' She smiled at the Prince, a little surprised.

Mrs Huyton called one of the boys, prettily done up in white, to bring some fermented cane juice. 'And you, Mr Lambodar, what can I offer you? I imagine you would prefer something a little stronger. Would you try the rum punch?'

'If you recommend it, Mrs Huyton.'

The punch, when it came, was both powerful and delicious. He drank it quickly.

A moment later they reached the visitor from England. He said something as they were introduced, but Don missed it; he found, that is to say, he caught sight of Lucy Gladwell who had just emerged from the house like an echo from the mountains of a dream.

'Lucy, my dear,' Mrs Huyton called out. 'Come here and meet Mr Fry, and indeed our good friends from Ceylon.'

Don picked up a second glass and hoped for numbness, if nothing else.

'Good evening,' Lucy said, bold and clear, and the company all reciprocated as best they could, at different pitch and speed. 'Mr Lambodar, I thought we might have seen you in Ambleside sooner than this,' she added with a warm smile. But was there a touch of tartness to her voice? he wondered.

His body tightened, belly up. Darkness, he was beginning to understand, was his soul's true mate. He stared dumbly at the sequins on her shoes. His feelings confounded him; his natural disposition was to run his emotions, like all his bodily functions, on habitual lines. He was a tall, suave man who liked to know what to expect. Young Lucy was playing havoc in his world, veering this way one day, that way the next, and sending him into a most deleterious spin. Surely the last time she had been ice. What did she mean? Sooner than six o'clock? What has happened to his voice?

'These troubles,' he mumbled, realising too late that vagueness was probably unbecoming in a man, even in his bluest silk.

'How do you like our island, Mr Fry?' She moved to address the guest of honour, and Don felt as though he and the Prince were the smallest of minnows, easily dispensed with in the presence of the great white whale.

'An exceedingly pleasant place, Miss Gladwell. I am amazed it had not been populated before the French arrived. You would think the seafarers of the ancient world would have settled here at first sight, but I understand there are no signs of any older civilisation.'

'You are the expert, I understand.'

'Mr Fry is from the Museum in London,' Mrs Huyton added, for the benefit of the Prince, through Don. 'He is travelling to India.'

'I have an interest in antiquities,' Mr Fry mentioned modestly.

When Don translated this, the Prince stiffened. The issue of the gilded throne from the Kandyan palace and its proper ownership had been a contentious matter, and the Museum had been quoted many times by the British in Colombo after the capitulation.

'I think Mr Lambodar would be most interested in the Museum's famous language stone. I read the article you wrote about it.' Lucy seemed to glow before him.

'The Rosetta?'

'Yes. A fascinating story. Mr Lambodar here is a very proficient translator himself. A most remarkable linguist. Do tell him about it, Mr Fry.'

Don was astonished: she had referred to him, twice; her sentences were both quite definitely and incredibly about him, the invisible undispensed – perhaps indispensable – tongue. *A most remarkable linguist.*

A moment later that phenomenon – Lucy extolling his virtues – was overtaken by Mr Fry's response.

'How very good to meet you, sir. You read Greek?'

Don found it extraordinarily delicious to hear a lofty Britisher call him 'sir'. For so much of his life he had had to say 'sir' and 'sire' where no respect was deserved: a Kandyan sir, a British sir, a Sabaragamuwa sire. He hesitated a fraction of a moment too long, savouring the moment. Where were the words? 'Not Greek, no.'

'Pity.'

The remorse he felt then was not to do with Greek, but how was Fry to know that? Lucy Gladwell had turned away to look at some frippery by the steps. Don had no chance to catch her eye, much as he wished. He was yet a boy; she a girl. Bravely, he did not follow her gaze; he tried to be steadfast, whatever Asoka may be up to. Her neck was exposed; a perfect milky line, flowing like the everlasting light of all the distilled stars in the sky. The black night kissed the white clouds, and heaven spun on a loose button.

'Is it five or six languages you speak, Mr Lambodar?' Mrs Huyton asked, anxious to encourage the flagging conversation. The Prince had stepped back and briefly shut his eyes, humming a little intemperately.

To speak a word you have to move your mouth; Don understood the requirement. With great effort he managed. 'Perhaps a dozen, ma'am, but none with true fluency. I distract myself in each case, with another –'

'But that is not true, Mr Lambodar. Not true at all,' Mrs Huyton objected with a nervous laugh.

'Miss Gladwell will certify, I am sure, if she cared to think on my ineptitude.'

Lucy Gladwell remained utterly distracted; he frowned, wondering if she had even heard him.

Mr Fry cocked his head, as though he had spied some unexpected fragment of Atlantis in the grass. 'Your languages are from Ceylon, are they, sir?'

Don tried to concentrate on this unexpected peer from England.

'The languages, other than English, are local to your island, sir?' Fry leaned forward, closer to his target, clarifying his question through modulated repetition as one versed in the instruction of languages tends to do.

'I am sorry,' Don said. He reeled off a few from Telegu to Farsi. 'And you, Mr Fry? Besides Greek?'

'Italian and French, of course, are the ones I am most fluent in, but my passion is now Asiatic. The Rosetta Stone from Egypt changed everything for me.'

'We had an ambassador in Egypt, El Hah Abu Uthman, at the start of the Mamelukes,' Don replied, keen to display at least some historical learning.

'Well, as a linguist and historian, I am sure you will appreciate its significance. You see, it has Greek inscriptions from which we have been able to understand the language of the ancients.'

'The Vedas? Sanskrit?'

'Hieroglyphs. The Greek provides a clue to deciphering the writing from the time of Ptolemy V Epiphanes, two centuries before the birth of Our Lord. The technique is remarkably simple. You see, one does it by using one part to illuminate the other. Do you follow? It can apply to virtually anything.'

'Is that so?' Don did not entirely understand. Not measure, but elucidate? Anything? Would it be the same between one civilisation and another? One story and another? One chamber and another? One heart and another? Why does she flit so? Hiero, thero.

'My father's cousin did the work of translation and I was able to join as an assistant. It fired my interest in other parts of the world.'

'India?'

'Egypt, first. Now India, as Alexander might have said.' Jeremy Fry's mouth widened in a haphazard smile of cluttered teeth.

Lucy, whose attention had returned to him as he spoke, now shifted her gaze. Don very nearly trapped her eyes this time, but she quickly said to Mr Fry, 'Would you excuse me?' A moment later, in a twirl of white satin, she was gone, zigzagging her way back to the house.

'Now what is she up to?' Mrs Huyton exclaimed. Then she noticed Mr Huyton welcoming a few more guests, late-comers, who were entering the garden from the side of the house. 'I should take you, Mr Fry, and introduce you to the Champneys.'

'Do feel free to greet them, Mrs Huyton, but let me continue my conversation with the gentlemen from Ceylon for a moment, please.'

Mrs Huyton's eyes shone. 'I am so glad you are enjoying the company of our distinguished friends. Do carry on. I shall bring the Champneys over in due course.'

'Thank you, Mrs Huyton. You are very kind.' Mr Fry turned to Don. 'I am afraid I am not very familiar with the situation of your homeland. Other than the obvious, that is. I know there was some trouble, but I understand it is now part and parcel of British India.'

'Not quite.' Don pulled himself back to matters of history. 'Why don't we sit over there and be comfortable?' he suggested, indicating some chairs that were set a little apart. There was no sign of her returning. Don hopscotched through the island's palimpsest past, mentioning how various foreigners had been invited to usurp each other, century by century, in the coastal areas, until the British decided to extend their regime to the heartland of the island. 'Direct rule, however. Not through India.'

'Ah, direct rule. It has long been our policy to sympathise and provide relief to oppressed people; to interfere, or rather *intervene*, when there is just cause, as we say, and support the general wish of the people who are in suffering. Quite enlightened, would you agree?'

'Policy, is it?' Or was it Lucy he let slip?

'You must investigate the Congress of Europe. Idea of Castlereagh. Complicated fellow: Foreign Secretary, Leader of the House of Commons, reviled by the poets. He went against the establishment on the Catholic question in Ireland, but the suspension of habeas corpus after the Peterloo Massacre was a serious error. Shelley, I believe, could be very educative.'

Don had noted the name on one of his early forays. 'The poet?' he asked.

'Most pertinent perhaps are the political pamphlets and poems on freedom and anarchy he apparently wrote in Italy; they are said to shake all our chains to earth. Sadly, however, publishing these days is in a parlous state under our laws of seditious libel and, I am afraid, economics. His widow has had printed what she can but the best, I understand, is only privately available.'

'Why in Italy? Was he exiled for believing in the brother-hood of men?'

'Not quite.' Mr Fry paused, unsure how much of a gulf there might be between them.

'This business of the hieroglyphs, you believe it is a language?' Don tried to move the conversation from poetry muddied by politics to sounder scientific philology. He wished his thoughts would not flit so swiftly.

'According to Monsieur Champollion, in Paris, there is a syllabic alphabet there,' Fry said with some relief. 'Although some of my colleagues would rather I did not look over the Channel, I think the Frenchman is right.'

'The French? Were they in the business too?' He craned his neck: was that her, opening the tall window?

'We have to thank Napoleon, as distasteful as that might be for some of us. If not for his vanity – his Egyptian Expedition – we would not have the Stone, and therefore would have no idea of the language of the ancients. Even Satan must have a purpose.'

'Language without sound is something I have difficulty with.' Also, Don added to himself, the inarticulateness that results when speech is lost in the weakness between loin and ankle. With Lucy Gladwell he wanted a stream of words.

Mr Fry grew animated, drawing Don back to their conversation. 'The sound you might say is trapped in the stone. In the material itself. When one deciphers the meaning, one is almost at the edge of breaking it open and releasing the sound like the pop of a cork from a bottle.' He snapped his fingers. 'We discovered that the hieroglyph for the sun might be pronounced *ra*, and that for birth is *mes*. This gave us the name Rameses and now the whole of the ancient world is beginning to sing to us again.' His voice grew as he emphasised each syllable. 'The scribe is like a magician, a maestro with a wand.'

Don, caught up in the excitement, imagined his pen pressing in, cutting the skin of vellum and filling it with the sound of ink, sealing the flight of meaning. 'Yes, I can appreciate that.'

A man is nothing but a nib chasing immortality, he thought. I should write to her. Write. Write. Write.

'I find it extraordinary,' Fry continued with enthusiasm, 'how even in antiquity, there was this powerful desire to put things in writing. To cast the story in stone. A premonition perhaps that the voice might not survive. That a people may wither away and all that would be left of their thoughts would be the scratches of some poor scribe trying to climb out of a cell.'

'Our history also has always been in writing,' Don said.

Fry struggled with his breath. 'In India, I hope to find an oriental equivalent of the Rosetta Stone that will open the door to a time we cannot otherwise reach.' His eyes wavered between hope and desire.

So did Don's. He wanted to reveal to this stranger from London his deepest longing. Jeremy Fry seemed to him a kindred spirit that confounded what had seemed the imposed order of the world around him. If it was possible with him, why not with her?

Before he could say anything more, a neighbour of Champney, stick in hand, came punting across the lawn towards them.

'I say, Fry, how do you do? My name is Willcox. What is the news in London?'

Both Don and Jeremy Fry stood up.

'In London?'

'Yes, man. What are they saying about the sugar tax? We heard those blasted West Indians are lobbying hard to keep their special status and condemn us to utterly exorbitant duties. What do they say in London?'

'I am afraid I do not know, sir.'

'You do not know?' Willcox banged down his walking

stick in disbelief. 'You set sail for the Mauritius without knowing what they are saying about the future for our sugar?'

'Sugar is very popular, sir.'

'You are damn right, my man. Next year we will double our production for England, if only those damn coolies stay in line.' He glared at Don.

'Your workers?' Don suggested quietly.

'What?'

'You mean your Indian plantation workers,' Don repeated, feeling a need to give voice in some sense to someone – Narayena, at least.

'Workers, slaves, prisoners, I do not care what you call them, but lately they have been getting bloody uppity. They are too indulged these days, far too much.'

'Is that dismembered Kishore, hanging on a pole, to redress the balance?'

'Exactly. We are a tolerant island, but we cannot tolerate rebellion.' He spoke at some point midway between them as though he did not wish to sully his words by establishing a direct link with a dark man.

'Narayena will not be so easily frightened,' Don replied. He felt an urge to defend the man and defy his adversary, although he did not see what poor Narayena could really achieve.

'You are the fellow who has been writing to Huyton about him. Is that right? What business is it of yours? The man is a pest. You had better stay out of it or you too will reap the consequences, you understand?' He wagged his finger.

Jeremy Fry tried to intervene. 'Dismembered? Who was he?'

Don wanted to make Willcox stub his finger. 'I do not understand,' he replied. 'I am employed to provide the means of efficient communication. I write as I am required to write. Perhaps, Mr Willcox, you have some need of my services?'

'You may write an elegy for your friend, for he will soon keep that other vermin company. They will both hang like gutted bloody bats for the rest of you to learn your lesson.' He turned back to Fry. 'I told the Governor, you have to keep up discipline. You cannot simply replace rotten apples any more. There has to be a thorough flogging every Sunday. Once a month you pick one and thrash him to pieces. All the way until the mutt is dead. A serious cost I admit, but the investment is worth it. One flayed dark skin will keep a hundred others quiet. You will never have these problems then. The French never did, you know.'

Mr Fry blanched.

'Is that how it is done in Europe, Mr Fry?' Don asked.

Fry swallowed hard. 'Well, if you mean crime . . . I suppose you do see the corpses of criminals. Capital punishment apparently requires a certain display to be effective.'

'Most definitely so. The beast in such creatures must be whipped into line, or they turn criminal. And crime,' Willcox wagged his flaming finger again, 'as you very well know, must be punished.'

Don dug his fists into his crossed arms. He exchanged a glance with Fry and tried to keep a steady voice. 'I am not here because of any crime on my part, Mr Willcox. Are you?'

Willcox quivered, but before he could utter another word George Huyton came up and clasped him. 'I say, could we have a word?' He gave Don a nod and made a gruff sound to

Fry before steering Willcox away. Don heard George Huyton mention the name 'Amos' as they moved along.

Jeremy Fry leaned close. 'I thought the planters here were all French.'

Don looked at him. The Englishman's eyes softened. Don shrugged. 'French and English. They have two societies whose common interest is in cruelty and control.'

'I thought we, the British I mean, simply administered the colony.' He adjusted his coat, brushing away some jessamine petals that had settled on him; his thin face lengthened. 'I know there is the suggestion that our laws against the slave trade may have had some unforeseen consequences – even Mr Wilberforce concedes that – but this flogging to death, is it true? Is it done now? I thought the whip and cane had been banned by the House of Commons. He is speaking of slaves, if I am not mistaken?'

'There are both slaves and prisoners here: black and brown. The usefulness of the prisoner is limited by his sentence, Mr Fry, that of the slave by his master's sadism. This is an island that the French emancipation failed to reach and the English abolitionists have yet to discover. Cruelty comes easily to the alienated soul and injustice is its anchorage.'

'But is this Willcox speaking of what has taken place, or what he wishes?'

'The example is the case of the rebel prisoner Kishore who escaped and was caught. He has been butchered and hung on a gibbet for us all to see. But apparently even in the most enlightened of plantations there have been incidents where slaves have been severely mutilated by their masters. I have heard that women have had their breasts cut, men castrated, their noses chopped off. Amputation was a legal punishment under the French. I am told it is now even worse, under the British, as it is done without a trial.'

'Surely not?'

'The previous British Governor allowed a certain flouting of the law in order to keep the peace with the French slave owners, and a blind eye to one law allows all to be ignored, I suppose. The British are in a difficult position here, for the natives they rule are French. "Family", as the Prince says, unlike in our country or India. They try to accommodate each other at the expense of the rest of the world. But I fear, Mr Fry, that they forget that the greater number here are dark men enslaved. With the recent ghastly example, there may be repercussions soon that will be very disturbing.'

A small group of other guests began some boisterous cheering.

Jeremy Fry suggested to Don that they move somewhere quieter. They walked towards the front of the house in thoughtful silence. 'There is some agitation in London for a commission to come and examine the situation here,' Fry eventually said. 'I can see there may well be a need for it.'

'I do not understand what drives your countrymen, Mr Fry. Or indeed the French. Why are they here? Or India? Or the British, the Portuguese and the Hollanders in Ceylon? Is it really for a peck of pepper? A few sticks of cinnamon? Cardamom pods? You, Mr Fry, are travelling thousands of miles to feast on the prospect of new knowledge, to reach the far recesses of human history, as I understand it. But why? Is life so poor in England?'

'Mr Lambodar, I wish I could escort you to our Museum. You would see then how much the spirit is stirred in the presence of histories we do not fully understand. The colonial adventure is only an inducement – we need some baser instincts to get things done. If you could see the marble Lord Elgin brought us from Athens, or the Barberini vase from Rome, or Belzoni's Egyptian statues, you would understand. There is much power in the fragments of great civilisations. The project is much greater than the mere acquisitiveness of a single nation. Knowledge is a boundless and unimaginable joy, sir. And it is but human nature to seek out what we do not know.'

Don considered the idea. Surely we seek the comfort of what we know, rather than the unease of uncertainty – the unknown? But there was a doubt in his mind. He recognised the compulsions in his own behaviour which were not in the normal interests of his comfort. We go, sometimes, where we are not wanted; to places which perhaps we would do better to avoid; we go despite what we believe we should do. He could not explain it. Was it a form of magnetism, that force which Mr Amos was so excited about?

When they reached the house, Don saw Lucy again, framed in a window; lit by chandeliers. Her face high with excitement; her eyes catching the light like glass twisting behind glass. He stared at the window.

Jeremy Fry, who had spotted the Prince sitting alone, suggested they join him again.

Don saw a shadow move, in supplication towards Lucy. Then Lucy was gone.

Inside the house, Muru was close to tears; Lucy held him still with both hands and asked what was wrong.

'No sarod,' he snuffled into his sleeve. 'Gopal disappear.'

'Where has he gone? Mr Badani assured us he would be here.'

'Run away, missie. Everyone wants to run away.'

'Nonsense.' Ambleside was not a place to run away from, whatever may happen elsewhere on the island. 'Let us consult Mrs Huyton, she will know what to do.'

Earlier she had introduced the new black girls and her aunt, unperturbed, had immediately put them to work in the kitchen.

On their way, they came upon Asoka in animated conversation with two ladies who arranged the flowers at the church. Lucy hesitated, an idea forming. 'Forgive my intrusion, Mr Asoka, could I speak with you a moment?'

'Of course, Miss Gladwell.' He excused himself from the others and ushered her into the next room.

'Mr Asoka, I understand you have a distinctive musical talent.'

He smiled coyly. 'I am fond of music, yes.'

'Good. We have a little recital this evening. I wondered whether perhaps you might agree to play the accompaniment. Could you by any chance play the sarod to our Muru's tabla?'

Asoka's surprise turned to dismay. He looked at the servant boy. 'Alas, these instruments are not within my repertoire, although I would gladly sing for you, Miss Gladwell, after the drumming. Perhaps you could get one of your other boys to pluck a few strings for Muru. I doubt if anyone in the audience would notice the difference.'

'I dare say you are right, Mr Asoka. We are not connoisseurs.'

She asked Muru who he thought might be able to do it. He shrugged, somewhat unenthusiastically. 'Garden boy Tusa plays guitar.'


'Mr Lambodar, will you introduce us, please?' Jeanette Pottinger shimmered up in an emerald dress cut low, exuding a powerful scent of nascent *pachcha*. Her shoulders were bare and she had garnets on her bosom and her wrists. She ignored the Prince, who stood in his habitual pre-victual trance, and waggled her jewels at Mr Fry.

'Good evening, Miss Pottinger,' Don said. 'Mr Jeremy Fry, may I present Miss Pottinger from Miramont.'

He clicked his heels and stuttered a compliment midway between French and English. She smiled dazzlingly in return.

'I thought, Miss Pottinger, that Mr Asoka was with you?' Don said.

'Mr Asoka? Why, yes he was, but then Mrs Huyton requested his assistance.' She turned back to Jeremy Fry. 'I believe, sir, you live in London. I would love to see London. I am told it is so *resplendent*. Is it truly wonderful?'

At a loss before her attentions, he wavered. 'Well, you know . . . '

On the other side of the lawn, a torch on a garden stand ignited, and then another, illuminating a line of tables. A moment later several servants arrived bearing large silver tureens; they proceeded to place these on metal racks. The servants were all in pristine livery, which might have made them uniform and indistinguishable, except that each was of such a peculiar shape: one round, one square, another gawky, a fourth hunched and so on. Muru, unmistakably lithe even in the shadows, darted from tureen to tureen with a taper, lighting the wicks below the racks. At the end, a small barrow of hot coals was rolled out with a spit on which several birds were roasting. The evening air, already rich with the fragrance of Mrs Huyton's musky roses, became corpulent, laced with singed meat, curried mutton, grilled crustaceans and garlicky fruits of the sea. When all the dishes were in place, three of the servants lined themselves behind the tables with spoons in their hands. Mrs Huyton made her way over.

'Mr Fry, do come and have something to eat. We mix the old with the new here, so we have food that is warm as well as cold, oriental and occidental. We stand on no formality at Ambleside.'

Her guest of honour was visibly impressed. 'What an extraordinary array, Mrs Huyton. A feast to rival the splendours of Carlton House.'

'We are at the cusp, Mr Fry, of the East and the West.' She happily floated away to entice her other guests.

Jeremy Fry turned to Jeanette. 'Would you care to partake? There is much on offer this evening, it seems, Miss Pottinger.'

She nodded vigorously. 'Oh, yes, Mr Fry. Yes, very much indeed. Very much.' She held out her daintily curved hand breathlessly.

Don let them trip together towards the tables and went to collect the Prince.

'They have rice, and some nice curries.'

The Prince's eyes widened and filled with tears at the sight of the rotisserie. 'Chicken and *wild* duck?'

Don moved him towards the vegetables. 'Brinjal and okra.'

'Have the Muslim cooks here got the better of the English?'

'Mrs Huyton is a very enlightened lady.'

The Prince held his plate tightly while he was served.

'This is quite good,' he said grudgingly after a couple of mouthfuls. 'Surangani should find out how they do this channa and spinach. She needs to extend her range. Every day she makes the same sad mess.'

'Channa?' A modest enough ambition in our circumstances, Don thought. The days of overthrowing tyranny and resisting imperial designs belonged to another world.

Then he saw Lucy emerge from the house alone. She looked anxiously about, like a swan at a water's edge, before descending the steps to the lawn with her skirt held up a couple of inches off the ground; the tips of her shoes sparkled like tumbled stars.

'I'll be back,' Don said to the Prince and left him to his tempered chickpeas and quiet fizzles. He did not know what he would say, but he felt he had to do something.

'Eat first, then go,' the Prince advised, but Don had lost his appetite. She had started towards the gazebo on the other side of the lawn where someone was moving about with a lantern.

He quickened his steps, but before he could reach her, a tall, thin figure uncoiled from a chair and stopped her. Don shrank back.

'Antoine?' he heard her exclaim.

'Yes, it is . . . I am, I mean.'

'Why are you sitting here all alone? Have you eaten?' She looked at the gazebo again. 'I am sorry but I have to attend to something. Will you excuse me?'

'Can I be of service?'

'Not at the moment. Everything is in hand. Do enjoy the food, please. It is quite special and, I am sure, exactly the nourishment that you need.' The tone of her voice made Don withdraw. The fervour he had felt before, ebbed away.

She hurried on, but Don did not follow her. Instead, he returned to the Prince, only to find him floundering in his first unmediated conversation on the island with someone who was not a fellow countryman. He and Jeremy Fry had discovered they had some rudimentary Sanskrit in common. Enough to name the moon, the night, the bitter, sweet and fiery taste of curried vegetables and laugh at each other's incompetence. Miss Pottinger was nowhere to be seen.

'Ah, Don, is it not? If I may call you by your Christian name now that we are better acquainted, do help us elevate our conversation.' He turned to the Prince and said, '*Akase*.' He raised his hands heavenwards to indicate the lofty heights they might now interact at. 'Sky.'

'Tell him,' the Prince responded by grabbing Don's arm, 'tell him we are kings, noble in our own land. Not criminals.'

'He knows you are a prince. Mrs Huyton introduced you.'

He tightened his grip as a falcon might on a gloved arm. *Fragoulin*, although only mildly alcoholic, seemed to have stirred a desperate desire in him to be more elevated.

Jeremy Fry leaned forward. 'Is there a problem?'

Don looked around but Lucy had not reappeared. 'You see, Mr Fry, the Prince would like you to know that to begin with he was England's greatest friend. He helped the English conquer the kingdom of Kandy, but then –'

'Why? Why did he do that?' He looked at the Prince with surprise.

'Many reasons, Mr Fry. Very many. Firstly, our Kandyan King was not much liked. He was doing unpopular things, at least that is what we are told. He was also poisoned, I mean his feelings for the Prince were poisoned, and he therefore suspected him of various plots.'

'This was *before* he plotted with us against the King?'

'Yes. The suspicion brought about the greater consequence. The King applied the harshest punishment for this apparent disloyalty: he killed the Prince's whole family.'

'Poor man.' The Englishman's eyes filled with compassion as he looked at the Prince.

'It was most gruesome, Mr Fry. You see, the King had the Prince's children beheaded and made the mother, the Prince's wife, pound their heads to pulp with a pestle and mortar.'

'Good grief. Can that be true?'

'It was proclaimed in Governor Brownrigg's *Official Declaration of the Settlement of the Kandyan Provinces*.'

He nodded solemnly. 'I suppose we are quite adept at slandering our enemies. It is useful to demonise those you wish to destroy.'

'We have been told of many monstrous misdeeds, but this was the worst. She had to pound her children as other women pound grain to make flour.' Don made a fist with his hand. 'So, you see, the Prince wanted to lead the British against the demonic King and rid the land of his tyrannical rule. And he did it with the help, as I now comprehend from you, of your Mr Castlereagh's foreign policy.'

Mr Fry looked at the Prince as though he was trying to place him in some pantheon of heroes. 'I can see he had good reason then, if that is what had happened. But then why did he turn against us?'

'No, Mr Fry. He did not turn. He expected to be given the throne in due course by his allies. He was wearing the royal robes the night the British marched into Kandy. But his expectations were not met. Although the British said their interest was commerce not conquest, the issue of sovereignty came in and the status of the English Crown. The Prince was not allowed to take the title of King, which he so desired. And, I am afraid, some of your compatriots thought the Prince might therefore inspire another revolt, this time against them. That is why they imprisoned him and then decided to banish him. The Prince would like you to appreciate the fact that he is not here because of a crime he committed – as you know, a large proportion of the people on this island are – but because of the justice he might demand if he was still in his own home. The difference is important.'

'I understand.' Fry nodded sympathetically.

The Prince pulled Don's sleeve. 'Does he see the full picture?'

'I have told him about King Rajasinha, and the fear of the British,' Don said. 'Enough?'

The Prince snorted. 'King?' He scraped up a last spoonful of channa.

309

'Is it the Portuguese who first came to Ceylon?' Jeremy Fry asked, grasping for some academic line of enquiry to pursue in the wake of such personal catastrophe.

'Why is he interested in the Portuguese?' The Prince frowned, recognising the word.

'He studies the history of foreign countries,' Don explained. To Jeremy Fry he offered a choice. 'Would you like me to ask the Prince, or shall I answer?'

'What?'

'I am not merely a dictionary.'

Don prepared to launch into a disquisition, but a gong boomed. Lucy appeared on the verandah. 'Ladies and gentlemen,' she called out, 'your attention, please. Ladies and gentlemen ...' The chattering and the clatter of cutlery slowly died. 'We are pleased to present our special entertainment for the evening. As our guest of honour, Mr Fry, is en route to India we thought it would be fitting for him to be introduced not only to some of the culinary novelties he will find there, but also to some of its artistic culture. So now, we give you a sample of the fabulous music of India. *Voilà.*' She pointed to the gazebo. As she did so, a tarpaulin that had been hung over it fell to reveal two musicians on a stage lined with dozens of tiny bird-like oil lamps. The one with the sarod Don did not recognise, but the tabla player was the ubiquitous Muru. Next to him, Don saw the potted rose he had sent Mrs Huyton. The small yellow flames bickered and Muru began.

> Thakita thakita tha tha tha da,
> Thakita da tha tha, thakita da ...

As the sounds tripped out of his mouth as fast as a tongue could flit, his fingers tapped the tabla and began a cycle of beats that followed, responded and led first his own voice, then the notes of the sarod.

'Extraordinary.' Mr Fry made a mild chirping sound. 'What is the chap saying? Is it a song? A poem?'

'He is speaking the language of the tabla. That is the name of the drum, derived, I believe, from the Arabic.' Don watched Lucy go towards the gazebo.

'He speaks with it?'

'Yes. Not as in using it, but as in talking to it. It is a language that cannot be translated.'

'Not yet translated.'

'No, Mr Fry. It is not like your hieroglyphs. It *cannot* be translated.'

Fry's pale brows knitted together and his lips parted as his tongue tried to follow the unfamiliar sounds.

Thakita thakita, thakita thakita, tha tha tha . . .

Muru's hands were a blur. The sound entered Don's body slipping between the beats of his quickened pulse. His heart pumped to match the tremor in his ear, Muru's fingers on the skin of the drum, the reverberations that filled his head. He wanted to touch Lucy with his eyes at least, like light on light. He left Jeremy Fry and edged his way around the crowd to the path that led to the area behind the gazebo. But by the star flowers he had to stop. Mr Huyton and Willcox were talking to each other, blocking the way.

'Too loud, if you ask me. Too confoundedly loud,' Mr Huyton puffed out to Mr Willcox. 'Trouble is women these days have such notions.'

Willcox grunted. 'Sheer folly, Huyton. You should not allow her to encourage the coloureds this way.'

'What can I do? While I was battling with the bloody Committee for an English turnpike, they plotted this bizarre gathering.' He allowed himself a small furtive smile. 'But I suppose a little celebration was in order. I have just bought the damn place, Willcox. Ambleside is mine now.'

'Bought it?'

'A spot of luck with a little investment I was mucking about with, you know.'

'So, a lucky gambler and now a man of property? Well, all the more reason for you to put a stop to it, Huyton. The blacks are surly, the Malabars disgruntled. One rotten corpse is not enough now. That makebate Narayena still out on the loose, no doubt whipping up villainy up and down the country, and here we are pretending bloody India is a land of culture. It is not music, man, it is the abominable sound of the pariah bugle to them. I fear it will excite them to set to with their damn daggers and torches. With wimps like Captain Gates forever in the infirmary, the buggers will run riot. That young niece of yours —'

George Huyton's expression changed. 'No, Willcox, no. It is not the girl's fault. She is quite headstrong, I admit, and sometimes speaks too soon for her own good, but she always does as Mrs Huyton suggests. I am afraid this is the fault of my wife. She has lost her head and cannot seem to see nonsense even when it is served up to her at the breakfast table.'

'But the girl looks positively thrilled.'

'I believe she has been talking to your neighbour's son.

Champney. She is very well disposed towards him. I have high hopes. She needs a good match.'

Willcox looked incredulously at Huyton. 'Antoine Champney? That spineless scamp?'

'She needs a man with a decent income. Poor thing was left nothing at all by the father.' The small lie slipped easily out of his mouth in the wake of all the others.

Don backed away. The music from the gazebo had settled into a less flamboyant rhythm. Conversations had resumed between mouthfuls of chicken and chickpeas; the clinking of glass, the rattle of ivory-handled forks and the syncopated talk conjured up a symphony of sorts. Don crossed the lawn to find another route to the back of the gazebo.

He came to a table set apart, lined with bottles of gin and rum, red wine and bubbly white, and pious jugs of holy water temporarily unmoored. The centre of the table was dominated by a huge crystal bowl engraved with scenes of bacchanalia, full of lust, liquor and juice. Slices of apples, pineapples, limes, segments of orange and grapefruit, floated carefree and concupiscent. The prospect of Champney and Lucy together, reinforced again by George Huyton, had shaken him. His courage failed him. His hand wavered before another glass of punch.

'Monsieur Don?' a hesitant female voice whispered.

He could not make out who was standing in the shadows; for one irrational moment he wondered whether this might be a messenger from Narayena, drawn by the drum.

'I am Eulalie. You remember?'

'Yes, of course,' he said, relieved but puzzled by the diffidence in her voice. 'Your father said you would be here.'

'I cannot stay. George, Mr Huyton, does not understand. I

313

have to talk to the Reverend Constantine. Have you seen him?'

'He is somewhere here with Mrs Huyton.'

She trembled. 'I must see him.'

'Does he know you?'

The twitching of a torch made the shadows jump around her. She stepped out and he could see her face: full and urgent as though something inside her was about to burst. Her lips trembled. Her eyes searched the scene behind him. 'It is very important,' she whispered as though it were a matter of life and death. 'Please tell him.'

Then she vanished.

The musicians were still playing; near the front Don spotted Asoka squeezed into a bench, close up against a bundle of jaconet muslin and French sarsenet erupting in small moon-sprung convulsions.

Don traversed the crowd in a mixture of solicitude and dread. One pink lady he had not seen before smiled effusively, eyeing his silk jacket; he bowed, drawing in the last vestiges of his precious sangfroid. Then, behind a couple of engineers, he found the Reverend distracted by a passing punch and champagne tray.

'Mr Amos's daughter wishes to speak to you,' he said. 'She is at the back with the servants.'

The Reverend jerked back. 'Eulalie?'

There was a pause in the music. Some small applause from the guests near the gazebo. Don craned forward to see if Lucy might have stepped onto the stage to make another announcement, but it was Asoka preening, full of amatory glint. 'Where can she be?' Don muttered.

'Eulalie?' the Reverend repeated.

'I am looking for Miss Gladwell.'

'I saw Lucy going down to the hut,' the Reverend said, before slipping away towards the servants' quarters.

Beyond the torches, where the lawn ended and stone steps descended, Don breathed easier. The hubbub of the party faded as he stared out at the swollen star-pricked sky.

He made his way down the steps, slowly, carefully, and went towards the wooden hut perched at the edge. He paused but could not see her. He watched the fireflies blinking around the hazards of the terrain below like small beacons failing down the coast of Madagascar, the horn of Africa, the broken tip of India. The stones of the terrace were riven; cracked chips had been swept up against the wall. The path dropped a few feet lower; he felt a ripple of fear in the dark.

Only when he stepped onto the deck did he see her outline, sunk in a chair. She started at his tread. 'Who is that?'

He said his name: the syllables tumbled into nothing.

'What are you doing here?' she asked nervously.

'I was following the fireflies.' He hesitated. 'Why have you left the party?'

'I wanted to think.'

A desire he could understand. She could not see him nod, so he added in a soft solemn voice, 'To think?'

'Yes,' she retorted, defiance mixing with mischief in her voice. 'Do you find that such an impossible notion, Mr Lambodar? Is it your opinion that a woman is not capable of it?'

'I thought you might be with the musicians.'

'Evidently not,' she said coyly.

'So I see, as it were. It is not sufficiently melodious, perhaps?'

'The percussion is sublime.' The words seemed to clot her breath. 'I am here because I am in need of some solitude.'

'I am too,' he admitted quickly and immediately regretted his words.

'Well, I am sorry to disappoint you then.'

'I did not mean that I wish to be alone now.' A faint yellowish scythe revealed itself as a cloud thinned far above them. They looked at each other in the weak light. He eased down next to her, a joint cracking in the process.

'Oh,' she winced. 'That must have hurt.'

'Only my knee.'

If the beat of a drum can reach a human heart, surely there must be words in the English language he could use, he thought. 'The music stirs much that is inside,' he ventured hopefully.

She sighed, letting go. The air lifted in a light breeze and the leaves around them lisped as they lilted. 'Yes, it is the sound of my dreams. Muru is a talented boy. He plays the vina too.'

From below, beyond the cane fields, another drumbeat started as the goatskins of the ravanes in the African lines were heated by their campfires.

'The drum is the spring of life,' he said in a voice of rare tenderness. She looked at him as though he had spoken the poetry of her heart and that the words had steadied the world; perhaps the boat would no longer rock.

'Whenever I close my ears with my fingers, I hear the ocean. A roar of water churning: it is in me as well as outside me. Everywhere like a song unheard that I must sing.' She moved her hand in the air between them. Her face floated dreamily.

'Yes,' he said, for want of anything better. 'I know what you mean.'

From their fingertips the land dropped away and the night sky seemed a vaulted dome stretching out to heaven.

A thick band in the sky moved: a slow stream of stars swirling between the clouds. 'Oil lamps floating on a river,' she whispered, looking up at them.

'The stars, they say here, are children who hide in daylight.' The words came unbidden.

'Perhaps they are the sparks of the Divine that will be made into souls, each a world of his own.' Her voice was secretive, as though she might be speaking to herself.

'Like us?' he asked, to draw her closer into the space they inhabited. He envied not only the distance that beckoned her, but her self-containment. The bubble that seemed to protect her as the globe's own breath protects its life. Is there no way for me to pierce through that diaphanous integument? He thumbed the dictionary in his head.

'Do you feel in a world of your own? Liberated?'

'I don't know. Sometimes. But then suddenly I find such wickedness.'

'The man on the gibbet?'

'I have not seen him.' Lucy drew up her knees and clasped them. 'I was thinking of Adonis – our dhobi. He was beaten so awfully and unjustifiably by Monsieur Dupont's bullies.'

Don lowered his head. 'Power breeds cruelty.'

'Why?'

'Perhaps because some mistake it for order.'

'But violence is surely the disorder?' Lucy turned and examined his face; hers had turned silver.

He felt her gaze as it moved over him tearing the veils of a lifetime. He had never felt the need to speak from the heart more than he did at that moment. To move his lips to hers. Utter the syllables that would bring them together like the earth and the sky.

But all he managed was, 'It is the fault.' He saw the muscles in her face move, a quickness there, a glow; then a shift of the silver clouds.

'Only here at Ambleside do I really feel safe. It is as my aunt said – a refuge. The songbirds never cease.'

'But the masters of this house have been as harsh as any.'

'It belonged to Mr Badani.'

'Colour is not the factor that causes cruelty.'

The moonlight lessened. The native electricity that had coursed through his veins towards her, seeking some inner polarity, suddenly ebbed away. His arms grew heavy and he sank back in the dark against the wooden side of the hut. The spent sparks like burnt-out flies scattered about him.

'I am sorry you did not get the opportunity to see the play last week.' She spoke quietly, but the words seemed to unfurl and flap and separate them again.

'I am sorry too. I would have liked to have experienced it.'

'I understood you were unwell on the day. I am glad to see you are recovered.' Her voice was regaining some of its vigour.

'Unwell?'

'I happened upon Mr Asoka in the Gardens, before all the commotion, and he said you were taken ill.'

'I have been perfectly well, except . . .' He wavered. If he was in pain ever, it was now. He touched his chest. 'My heart aches . . .'

Lucy stiffened at the words; the air became tense. Then the shadow of a night bird, or a large moth, flitted across her face and she released her breath. ' "And a drowsy numbness pains my sense," ' she murmured with a slight pause before the last two words. She turned up the wick of a small lantern. 'You know John Keats's ode? Is it not truly wonderful?'

The dark melted. Her face bloomed in a circle of light. The soft lines of her mouth seeking the reassurance of his.

He wanted more than anything else this moment to last. He cupped his hands and held the moon-thaw like water.

A voice from the lawn called, 'Missie, missie.' A note forlorn.

A strand of her hair had come undone. Her neck shone and a small rivulet of moisture glistened as it streamed down to the dip below her collarbone. The whole surface of her skin changed colour in the wash of lantern light.

'Missie, missie . . .' the servant called again.

'They are looking for you,' Don said.

Her fingers trembled and the lamplight dipped and dimmed near to death. He reached to secure her hand.

'Yes.' She let him touch it. Her skin was damp; her fingers light and soft as petals. He thought she must have used laven-der on her neck as the scent enveloped him as he leaned closer. She smiled in utter ineffable radiance. The little garden hut was incandescent like a newborn star.

'Yes,' he echoed her as though her syllable must dance with his. He felt a surge within himself and her, quickening her pulse, colouring the seams of her hands.

A torch came into view and bobbed closer.

'I should go.'

'No, wait.' He circled her wrist with his fingers. The bones in her arm were like those of a small bird. He did not want to let go, fearful that she would not stay. He cannot let go. He cannot. She must know, he cannot lose her. He tightened his grip. Her bones felt thin.

'Let me go.' She freed her hand and picked up the lantern.

In the yellow light, he felt frightened of everything: the moment that had passed, the two of them together in the hut, the future to come. His hand had strayed too far, too fast. Too hard. Too unsure. He should not have touched her yet. The air between them swelled like a sea in which each of their thoughts swam trapped in its own current.

'Madam is looking everywhere for you,' the voice complained.

'I am coming, Jacob,' she replied.

'Wait.' He grasped for the words to form a line.

She glanced back and caught his eye. White scraps of light flashed falling from a shattered constellation. 'Not now.' Was that a rebuff or a promise?

'Stay,' he implored.

She hesitated, but a moment later she was gone, leaving him in darkness again, misjudged, longing for a lungful of hope, his thoughts jostling for words they could not hold.

The discrepancy between his feelings and his words was as great as between a seed and its flower; one full of promise, the other of uncertainty. He climbed back up to the main lawn, each step heavier than the last. From there the house looked like a palace in a dream: bejewelled by chandeliers. Magical and magisterial but a palace where a young girl's hopes and desires were baffled by shutters, doors, thick warped panes of courtly design. Lucy Gladwell, despite all her dash and verve, spark and zeal, could not cut free. He watched her being drawn back past the gazebo, to vanish into the shoal of guests. Dark bloated clouds rolled over the house. He felt a sorrow he had never felt before, a tremor inside him as though a harbinger of some alarming proportions had crossed his path. The air was thick, dank, hard to breathe.

He returned slowly to the Prince who was still in conversation with Fry stumbling over their Sanskrit as if in a game of *chaturanga*. Mr Fry looked up with great happiness. 'My dear Don, I find this most enlightening. Conversing with His Highness in a language that I thought only existed in books.' He seemed quite over his fascination with Miss Pottinger.

Don left them to continue on their own.

Asoka came up and placed his hand on Don's arm. 'So, Don, how have you got on this evening? I noticed a certain young lady rushing back from the far end, with you in hot pursuit. Is that a conquest, hai?'

'It is not what you think.'

'This house is a grand place for a chase. The trouble is that dear Jeanette has the nicest inclination but no conversation to speak of, whereas that Lucy has rather too much, I fear.'

321

'You have been in conversation?'

'Too much so, as I say. Do you think she might be quieter making love in the dark?' He swayed on his feet looking at Don with a loose gag sliding about his fattened face.

Don resisted temptation and kept his hands hooked to each other. One of the servants passed by with a platter of fruit. 'You should try the pineapple,' he said instead.

'Really? Does it work? You also have tried the pineapple, have you?' He broke into an exaggerated laugh and clutched at his capsizing middle with both hands. 'You are too much, dear Don, too much,' he guffawed, wheeling away.

'Where is the lady?' Don asked the servant. 'Miss Lucy?'

He said she was in the yellow room.

Don hurried up to the house, and slipped in through the double doors. There was a small group sitting and talking by the window. He heard mention of the Belvédère revolt. Then peals of laughter before they noticed him and stopped their conversation.

'Excuse me,' he said. The chance of coming upon her, in solitude and silence, anywhere on this island ever again, he knew, was so remote as to be non-existent. He might as well hope to see her in England.

Then he recognised Mrs Huyton's voice in the next room. 'Yes, of course, I will come with Lucy. I think Maharoun is a very pleasant spot. The lake is lovely there.'

The door going through to the yellow room was open, but by the time he entered Mrs Huyton's companion had left. She was there on her own, lightly fanning herself and staring out at her guests on the lawn. 'Poor Vanessa Trent,' she said to herself.

'Mrs Huyton.' He steadied himself against the wing of a chair.

She turned and smiled. 'Mr Lambodar. I hope you have been enjoying your evening.'

'An excellent evening, ma'am. Ambleside is a magnificent house.'

'I am so glad. It is a house that I would like to fill with happiness. I thought we should use the natural talents we have in our servants, rather than bend them to a purely English taste as our friends tend to do.' She gave a merry little laugh. 'But I insisted they cook the tomatoes. Most disagreeable otherwise.'

'The tomatoes were delicious.' He cleared his throat as discreetly as he could. 'I thought I might find Miss Gladwell in here.'

'She was here a moment ago, but then stepped outside again. Dear Lucy appears to be very much in demand this evening.'

'Outside?' His thoughts were racing but to no effect.

'And the Prince? Do you think he might be persuaded to take the stage too?'

'He is engaged with Mr Fry.'

'How delightful. That is most gratifying.'

'I should get back to him.'

'You had better be quick if you wish to find her in the garden, Mr Lambodar.'

Mrs Huyton's face had fallen into an expression of weariness. She was looking out at another couple at the very edge of the garden. He followed her gaze and made out Mr Huyton as one of the two figures. Further on, he spotted Lucy in the middle of a group of young officers toasting the success of the musical entertainment. Before he could get close to her, she was gone.

# Chapter 21

EMPTIED OF lingering conversations, Ambleside slowly subsided. As soon as the day was light, Muru began the process of returning the house to its normal state: the tables and chairs had to be put back in storage, the catering equipment carted out, the china shelved, the cutlery sheathed back in green felt, the gazebo divested of its theatrical accoutrements. Eulalie had taken her daughter and gone to the Reverend. Mrs Huyton, content again, was happy to potter about the garden. Lucy made a couple of forays into supervision but found she was not needed.

When she eventually retreated to her hut, Don's appearance the previous evening filled her mind: she could feel again his hand encircle her wrist. His fingers so warm she thought her skin would burn. She had wanted to tell him what she felt, but the heat evaporated the words. His face had been close: his eyes and his dark lips. His curled cupped ear. Is he another figment of my imagination? she thought. No less fanciful than the vales of Cashmeer, or the coral gardens of Taprobane?

★　★　★

Towards evening, Mrs Huyton suggested a walk down to the pond where she liked to watch the sun gild the ripples of water spiders, tint the clouds with soft blushes and ink the bluish air. Where the warm light fades as the heron appears; where the sounds of fish turning in the water, perhaps even the song of a star, or its reflection, might be heard.

'Did you enjoy the party, Lucy?' she asked.

Lucy pulled a couple of lime leaves off a bush. 'Muru did very well, and the food was delicious.'

'What did you make of Mr Fry?'

'Not what I expected. Quite shy.'

'He seemed to get on very well with the Ceylonese.'

'Did he?'

'And our Miss Jeanette Pottinger. Altogether, I thought it went off rather well. The meeting of East and West.' She laughed lightly. 'Simply not available when I was young.'

'I am glad we can intermingle here.'

'Nevertheless, I think you might be a little more discreet.'

'Me?'

'With our dear Don. Mrs B was most upset at your flirting.'

'That is ridiculous.'

'You were seen, my dear, hurrying back from the little hut with him trailing behind. Not surprisingly, I might add.'

'Mrs Benoît is a beast.'

'I am afraid in some respects this island is no different from any other. Full of beasts.'

'Black and white?'

'Quite,' Betty nodded. She gazed wistfully at the water. Her face was long and had rather more folds than before tucked under her chin, holding back the swell of time. 'I have some very happy memories of my early years. Do you, Lucy?'

'Of my grandfather and his books, yes. But beyond that, I do not like to think about it much,' Lucy said.

Her aunt smoothed down the edge of her blouse. Her fingers are lovely, Lucy thought, and I would like mine to be like hers when I am her age.

'In July, the trade winds used to blow and the rain was never far away. A lovely warm rain. Jamaica is a very green island.'

'Does it not all become overwhelming? Living here, there, England? To travel so much, so quickly.'

'It is not all at the same time, my dear. We go from one season to another.' She peered at the other side of the pond. 'I do believe that is a kestrel on that branch. Do you see it?'

She craned her neck until the cords running up to her ear stood out. Wrinkles spread out of the corner of her eye like the rigging of a sail.

The sharp brown bird raised its wings as if to give its audience a blessing and then took to the air.

'Do you see it, Lucy? Look how marvellously it flies.'

Despite the two months she had been on the island, Lucy felt she was still a stranger in a dreamland: I know so little of the shape of things, she thought. Where are the boundaries? I have been to Port Louis; I have been to see the sea; but that is like making a picture of England by going from Bath to Brighton, or on the long ferry from Gravesend to the City. Hardly sufficient. The kestrel in the air has seen more of this island than I have even conjured with. On those wings it would have floated over the Three Mamelles, the Mare des

Yaquas, the Isle of Amber. It sees my situation better than I do.

'Shall we sit for a moment, Lucy?'

They perched close to each other on the viewing bench. The late mellow sunlight gave everything a glow as though surviving another day in itself merited serenity.

'I could sit here for ever,' Lucy murmured.

'You know, Lucy, I have been married to your Uncle George for nearly thirty years now.'

'Were you my age when you met him?'

'I had turned twenty.'

'Did you know you loved him straight away?'

'That would be a rare thing, my dear. I am not sure if it mattered.'

'Then why did you marry? Surely it was not necessary, even in those days?'

'I did not have an inheritance due.' She smiled.

'But you could have chosen whatever suited you best out there, could you not?'

'A woman, even in the colonies, cannot live without an income. My father, like yours, made no provision and my grandfather, unlike yours, was a clergyman. He expected the good Lord to provide.'

'What did Uncle George offer?'

'Peace and security.' Aunt Betty paused. 'That is what I like about this spot. That is why the kestrel comes here, I am sure. It knows nothing will harm it here. There are no native predators on this island.'

Lucy waited for her to return to Uncle George. When it was evident she would not, Lucy tried to re-engage her.

'The kestrel is a predator, is it not?'

'I suspect it was imported.'

'Like us, you mean?'

'How very astute of you, my dear. Yes, I suppose we are. When I was a little girl I used to follow my father when he went hunting. He was an excellent shot. I think he wished I had been a son. Like any good father, he wanted most of all to teach his child what he knew. It was not easy for him, not having a boy.'

'And your mother?'

'He would have liked you, Lucy. A strong girl.' She looked at her niece, her gaze like a net of kinship gently securing Lucy and pressing her into the fold. 'And you would have liked him. He would have taken you on a real adventure.'

'Would you have liked to have had a child?'

Betty put her two steady hands together and clasped them tight. 'One must learn to overlook one's circumstances and make good of the imperfections one suffers.'

'Did Uncle George not want one?' How does such a marriage survive? Lucy wondered. Or why, for that matter? They seem to prefer distance to proximity, adjustment to ardour, childlessness to parenthood.

'Your Uncle George comes from a family of six siblings, therefore his urge to procreate is powerful.' Aunt Betty placed her hands over her abdomen. 'But not every woman can oblige.'

Lucy felt something in her throat thicken. Sometimes she could sense an animal appetite in the air when he entered a room; it would reek with the sharp stink of a fox that almost made her gag. 'I do not entirely understand what I feel.'

'After last night?'

She let the memory of the evening redress the present moment. 'Sometimes perfection seems so very close. But is it truly an impossibility?'

'We do not live in a perfect world, Lucy.'

'I do not like constraint, Aunt Betty. I do not wish it upon myself.'

'You, my dear, do not have to marry –'

Lucy interrupted her. 'But, Aunt Betty, you never stop urging me.'

'Except for love.'

'Surely love does not need to be bound. Is it not a free gift we offer?'

'Is that what you understand from your books, Lucy?' Aunt Betty's eyes clouded as the sunlight sank in the lake. 'I do not believe love is a human possession. We have no right to it; no more a right than we have to pluck a flower in a jungle, or a feather from a bird. We can do it. We can pick it, but we cannot wear it and say it is ours. If it blooms, it blooms despite our faults, neither to mend nor to commend, but simply because it is in its nature to bloom.'

'What are you trying to tell me, Aunt Betty? You cannot tell me both to resist and to persist.'

Don had hardly slept since the soirée. When they had returned to the cottage that night, he had quickly slipped into his room. The sega music of the ravane, the bobre, the maravane wafted over in waves from the village, pricking his senses and plucking his nerves. He lay on his bed tense, legs drawn up, cupped in the empty curve of untouched desire, his mind racing. He had not been able to speak to her again. The farewell line he had joined led to the Huytons only; Lucy was on the other side presenting her hand to a queue of fair-haired drunks in gilded uniforms. She did glance his way once; then the moon fell out of the sky.

He went over each moment of the evening in forensic detail, looking for some gap where he might imagine an alternative that would shift everything and transform what had happened to what might have happened. Our lives are surely not writ in stone, he thought, whatever Fry may say. Why had he spoken so much to the Englishman when Lucy was there, waiting?

He took a candle and went to his desk. The yellow flame flickering like a heart tossed aside to reduce, drip by drip, with every passing moment the flesh that gave it life. He felt he was shrinking too, clutching at shadows. The strains of music rose; he tried to focus his thoughts only on her.

He found his paper, his pen, his ink and started to write her a letter. The first stroke stuttered and a spray of ink dotted the paper. He crumpled the sheet and tried again. The marks he made looked wrong; the script jumbled and ugly, stupidly short of what he felt inside. He wanted to make something flow more true and real, but he could not decide even how to begin. Dare he write *Dearest*, or *My love*? Should it be a poem? A sonnet or a *kavi*, or something that linked the two, mirroring their own two lives?

When the music in the wind finally faded and the night sounds of snores and coughs and insects spluttering in the dark filled the air, he began to write. But every line he wrote, he scratched out a few minutes later.

At daylight, he stole into the Botanic Gardens hoping he might find her there, or at least the lines that would draw her near. He examined every spot where he had seen her before, looking for traces out of which he might weave a token of love. Sometimes a place does indeed have the heat of longing, he thought, that Narayena mistook for devotion and he a trespassing shadow.

He went through the cinnamon grove to the Ceylon ink tree where the black sap flows from a whitish trunk to mirror its roots in a tangle of lines written on the surface of the ground. 'Inscribing the history of its presence here on this island,' Mr Amos had once said. 'The black, as always, working deep for the white.'

He wrote and rewrote in its shade until finally, about the time that Lucy went down to the pond at Ambleside with her aunt, he had a poem. Each line translated from language to language until the English bled.

# Chapter 22

A T THE cottage that evening, he found Asoka had gone to the crossroads inn with Sergeant Murray, and the Prince had retired early apparently feeling unwell. Don sat alone and read the lines he had written, testing the weight of each word; its position, the sense, sound and look; balancing every aspect to a point that might pierce both satin and velvet.

He considered taking it to Lucy, but baulked at the prospect. He could not risk facing her without an invitation and decided Khola should deliver it, in secret, the next day.

'Give it to that Muru and make sure he understands it is from me to Miss Lucy this time,' he instructed the servant in the morning. 'Tell him you will wait for an answer, if she has one, but do not show yourself to her. You must not frighten the ladies again.'

Khola put the envelope in his satchel and sauntered away as if on wings of lead, giving Don more cause to fret.

While he was staring out at the road, wondering whether he was right to have trusted such a lackadaisical man, the Prince came out into the front garden. He was still in his pyjama shirt but had a shawl around his throat. 'You know, that Mr Fry the other night proved a very interesting fellow. Observing him is an excellent way of understanding our adversaries in Colombo.'

'Our adversaries?'

'I can see how North and D'Oyly started out. Those men who came out of England to our land. It is a very curious thing, you know, to go somewhere new and make it your own.'

'As you have also done,' Don suggested. The exiled near-monarch looked to him quite at home, despite the croak in his voice. 'Are you feeling better?'

The Prince broke into a cough. 'Not with this damp air.' He brushed his hand over an okra plant and removed a spider's web, lifting it carefully like a gossamer veil, away from the buds and leaves. 'These, however, are all looking very fine.' He released the web on a turmeric patch, where it could do no harm. The sun blinked as a cloud swept overhead. There were more, moving fast across the sky, to gather like troops on an enemy hillside. 'Look at the leaves of the clove. The plants in this garden may be more functional than Mrs Huyton's, but they do have a beauty all their own, don't you think?'

'The capsicum is in flower.'

'Even the manioc will, if only that Khola would do as he is told. Where is the fellow? I want him to dig a new bed today.'

'I sent him on an errand.'

'A wonder if he can manage any errand.' The Prince coughed again, leaving Don to harbour another ripple of anxiety.

★   ★   ★

The day turned sultry as the air overheated. From time to time, Don would look out for his errant emissary but there was no sign of him. The goat lay dozing by the guava tree, the pariah dog that had adopted the cottage floated flat on the sand. None of the usual birds were to be seen.

He resisted the temptation to go in search of messenger and message and tried to distract himself with a page of French conjugations.

At about four o'clock, he checked the back again to see if Khola had sneaked into his hammock, but found only Surangani. She was at the clothes line pulling at the bedclothes and towels as she teetered between the drooping aubergines and the creeping cucumber.

'Khola back?' he asked.

'That puff-head?' She shot out a mouthful of crimson betel juice. 'You won't see him until someone plucks his finger out of his butty.'

She was always grumpy with the washing and often railed at the injustice of a prince not having a dhobi, while the Malabar shopkeeper at the crossroads, and even a former slave like Mr Amos, could afford one. This time, she frowned as though something more than the washing was troubling her.

She was about to make another complaint, when the sun dimmed as if the afternoon had dissolved into twilight in an instant. The yellow light of the day soused by a sudden blue-grey wash. The last towel on the line was whipped out of her hands and flew into the bougainvillea.

A powerful gust of wind blew around the house. Don heard one of the cottage doors bang and the sound of a star-tled horse on the road. Grit scraped his eye. Then a voice reached him, calling out from the road. He made his way to the front. Mr Amos, at the gate, lurched forward evidently in some pain.

'What happened?' Don went to help him.

'Thrown from my darn horse. Got the jitters and bolted.' A bump had formed on his temple and his English seemed to have been bashed about.

Mr Amos clung to his arm as Don guided him to the verandah. 'You have a swelling on your forehead.'

'Jus' need breath, man . . .'

'Does it hurt?'

'Only my ankle. Have you a cloth, please?'

Don seated Mr Amos and fetched him a basket of rags. 'I'll get the gig and drive you home.'

Mr Amos tied a strip around his ankle. 'Not enough time, son.' Looking about him, he added, 'You better fasten the windows and the shutters. Bring every rickety thing inside the house. Quickly.'

'Inside?'

'Within the half-hour, it will be here. Devastation.' His face turned grim. 'We are in for a hurricane. Do you know what a hurricane is? At this time of the year, it is often at its worst.'

The Prince, dressed for his afternoon stroll, shuffled out of the parlour.

'He must not go out,' Mr Amos cautioned.

Don translated the warning for the Prince: a great wind was coming; he would have to forgo his walk.

The Prince jutted out his chin. 'This wind? But it is exactly what I need to clear my chest.'

'He says it will be a big storm.'

'We must pray our homes will not be blown away,' Mr Amos added.

'What about your house?' Don asked.

'My daughter is due to visit me today. She should be there by now. She will know what to do. We have been through many hurricanes. There is nothing for it now, in any case, except to take shelter with you, if I may?' He had regained some of his composure issuing instructions. 'We are in God's hands.' He tested his foot; the ankle was sore but not twisted.

'What about Asoka?' the Prince asked.

'I have not seen him all day.' Don turned to Mr Amos. 'Did you pass our compatriot, Mr Asoka, on your way? He and our servant are both out.'

'I hope they have not gone far. The wind will come fast.' Mr Amos dipped a rag in the bowl of floating jessamine by the door and pressed the wet cloth to his forehead.

Don was not sure what to make of the warning. Tropical storms were familiar occurrences to him and, although fierce, were not to be feared. Monsoon was something one prepared for. He assumed this was something similar. He called out to Surangani and asked her to get the chickens into the henhouse. She grumbled that it was Khola's responsibility.

'All right. You do the windows then. Get the chairs in and stay with the Prince. I'll deal with the animals.' The chickens were already huddled up close to the wall and only needed one *shoo* to get them inside. Don lodged an old barn door at the front of the shed to block it. Then he pulled the mare into the stable. The goat was already in there.

Working as fast as he could, he collected the broom and

various pots and boxes dotted about the garden and put them all in the shed.

As he approached the verandah, another gust buffeted him. A branch snapped off the guava tree and flew up in the air. The door mat was flung out into the garden. He heard the bucket rattle down the well.

'Is everything in?' he asked Surangani.

She whimpered, 'Khola is not here. What to do?'

Then the sky turned black. A distant low roar grew louder as though the surf of the ocean was bearing down on them from the north coast. A shrill squall rocked the garden.

'The rain is on its way, but it's the wind that is fearsome,' Mr Amos warned from the verandah. 'You will see, it has no mercy,' he added. 'It comes to rid us of our wickedness.'

Don looked at the ashen face; the swelling thankfully had gone down. He wondered if Mr Amos was challenging him again in some way. Trying to make him see something he had missed. He urged him indoors.

'What is our wickedness?'

'Human disobedience.' Mr Amos hobbled in with Don. 'The hurricane is both a punishment and a lesson.' Don fastened the door behind him, but the wind was whistling through the cracks. They heard carriages of fruit crashing in the banana grove; papayas and breadfruit thudding to the ground. The mare in the barn whinnied and stamped and banged against the sides.

A lascar had once explained to Don the different words for 'storm' that he had discovered on his voyages around the world. *Hurikan*, he had said, was an angry god in the Caribbean who destroyed the innocent with his breath. This was surely

338

wickedness personified, Don had thought. He started to say so to Mr Amos when the small parlour split in a white fissure; the cottage shook as a cloud exploded. The plates on the dresser tumbled and smashed to smithereens. The Prince glanced up at the ceiling, doubt knotting his brow. 'My poor pink pigeon and those finches.'

A river burst out of the sky. Daylight was doused. The whole world sank into a cavern of wailing and drowning. The Prince, Mr Amos, Surangani huddled around the dining table. Don hurried from room to room, peering out; he imagined the Prince's menagerie pulverised by a hail of sharp rain pellets, the debris of the dead whirling through the air.

In a flash of lightning, he saw the huge tamarind out on the road being pulled upwards by the wind: the leaves and branches turned inside out as if in shock. Bits of fencing and roofing, bushes, logs wafted up in the air. Ambleside, at least, he thought would be secure; it was a solid house, built to resist adversity. Lucy would be safe in its steady light, unfolding his note, shielded from the tumult outside.

Mr Amos stood next to Don making odd shucking sounds. 'Tight. Everything has to be tight against the banshee. Flood and chaos is before us. I hope your compatriots have found shelter.'

Asoka no doubt would have, but Don felt sick at the thought of what might have happened to Khola. He probably would have stopped for a moment of buoyancy by the mulberries on his way back and lain down there, to dream as he often did with his mouth wide open. Don imagined him drowning. Would the factory have burst open? Don had a chilling vision of small piles of measured grains flying like bullets and clouds of poppy seeds peppering the sky. Badani's silk torn into a million ribbons. Lucy's reply in shreds.

Another blast flattened the potting shed and tore off half the roof of the chicken hut.

'*Ammé*,' Surangani wailed.

At about midnight the rain and the wind died down. Mr Amos warned that it was only a temporary lull. The Prince asked for a hot drink, but Surangani was too frightened to go out to the kitchen alone. The air was dense with silences. Within the hour, the storm was back: heaving, pushing, shoving the cottage. When the wind eventually moved on, the rain fell in torrents.

The sun, the next morning, was pale and watery. The barn, though listing, was secure but the door of the shed built against it had splintered open. Khola kept his garden tools in there and some packing crates; the wind had snatched everything. The Prince followed Don out and was crestfallen: his vegetable plot had been ruined; the line of papaya trees were all down, twisted like the fingers of a mangled hand. A giant rake had pulled all the bushes apart.

While Don brought the animals out of the barn, Mr Amos and the Prince helped Surangani clear the front of the house.

A little later Asoka stumbled in. His hair had been pressed down about his ears and some of the plumpness of his cheeks, the roundness of his shoulders, his girth, seemed to have been washed away.

'Where were you?' Don asked.

'He is cold,' Mr Amos said. 'He needs a blanket.'

The Prince, who was some distance away, must have understood something from the tone if not the words uttered. He came over and offered Asoka his shawl.

'Have you seen Khola anywhere?' Don asked.

Asoka looked charily out of the corner of his eye.

Mr Amos patted Don's arm and suggested softly that he let Asoka rest. 'The fellow is in a daze.'

The road outside the gate was strewn with fallen trees and boulders. As the gig would not go on it, Don offered Mr Amos the mare to ride. 'I'll walk you home and bring her back,' he said.

Near the Botanic Gardens, they met one of Mr Telfair's assistants who had ridden over from Port Louis. He claimed that many of the buildings by the sea had been demolished and two bridges on the main road had collapsed. Monsieur Dupont, who was also out, looking for his grey donkey, said the nursery had been destroyed and that Mr Pottinger and his daughter were sheltering in his house.

The railings of the Garden gates were clogged up with driftwood – a legacy of the tide of rain that had swept through. The air was damp.

Outside the Presbytery, they saw three Indian men lugging a body. Don recognised the dead man. Narayena had been sheltering in the church grounds and been killed by a falling tree. 'We have to hide him,' one of the men said, 'otherwise he will be strung up.'

'After all this carnage?' Don asked.

'The wind does not redeem,' Mr Amos said.

The men continued on their way. They crossed the road and turned into the fields. Don stared after them. Narayena deserved better, he thought. His wife and son deserved better. This was not how it should be.

Mr Amos clicked his tongue and got the horse moving.

When they reached his house, they found it had escaped the onslaught and showed hardly any damage except at one edge of the roof. Relief spread across Mr Amos's face as he dismounted.

Don let Mr Amos hobble to the house on his own. He watched him open the front door with a big iron key and go in. Don waited by the gate not wanting to intrude on the family. His thoughts were of Ambleside. He wanted to see Lucy. Speak to her. Hear her.

After about five minutes, he thought perhaps he should leave, but as he mounted the horse, Mr Amos appeared.

'They are not here.'

'What?'

'Eulalie has not been in.'

Don tried to reassure him. 'Then they must be still at Ambleside.'

Mr Amos laboured with his breath. 'I don't like it. I don't like her in that house.'

Don shook the reins. 'I am going there,' he said. 'If she is not already on her way, I'll tell her that you are safe at home.'

The pillars of the gates stood solid as ever, the stone lions impervious, but the trees along the avenue were bedraggled and the bushes had been beaten down.

Don left his horse by the coach house, which had lost its roof, and walked down. The mass of bushes that usually screened the kitchen wall had been shredded; the canopy that connected the kitchen to the house had been torn away and with it a section of the outer building that housed the servants. The scarlet mucuna that had adorned the pergola had been stripped off. The wooden posts along the walkway knocked down as though hit by a cannonball. Nobody was around. Much of the gravel was covered with blown leaves. Except for the largest, the blue and green pots that used to guard the front verandah were all broken. A few had smashed against the wall, the others had toppled into the beds below. None of the lovely maidenhair he had noticed on his first visit had survived.

The shutters of all the windows were still closed but the double doors to the hall were open. He climbed the steps and peered inside. The big table in the centre was bare. He called out.

There was no response.

He went through the deserted hall to the other doors opening out on to the veranda and the grand lawn. The flower beds on the edges were in shambles; the arches of blue and purple liana leading to the side gardens had been ripped to pieces; the gazebo had lost its decorative turret and the tulip tree behind it had come crashing down. The crowds of the other evening swam across the soft slow streams in his eyes. The garden had been bubbling with so much life – talk, music, food – but now looked as though it had been desolate for years. Then he noticed some movement inside the gazebo.

Muru was sifting through the rubbish piled up in the corner. He was crouched down by a couple of broken calebasse instruments and clay pots, pulling at scraps of paper and

343

bits of charred string; when he heard Don, he looked back over his shoulder.

'Where is the lady?' Don asked.

Something in the Muru's face gave way. 'Lady?'

'Yes. Where is she?'

He jerked his head towards the bottom of the garden. 'In the hut.'

Don remembered her there and the words that had failed him on the night of the soirée. The shame he felt then was still in him. It was a stain that coloured everything. He would counter it. This time he felt he was ready. He tried not to run, but took the steps down two at a time.

The woman who lay spangled on a wicker chair was in complete disarray; silvery hair loose and wild, a bare knee jutting out of an embroidered rumpled pelisse, a paisley quilt muddled around her feet. A muscle or two at her sharp mouth twitched in small discomforting spasms. She struggled to sit up, but seemed to find the weight of the robe too much and she slid further back down the chair.

'Mrs Huyton.' He hesitated, unsure of what to say next.

'Stop it. I hate that name,' she hissed out. 'Do not say it. Do not. Do not.' She pushed at the web of shadows around her.

'Calm yourself, Betty.' The Revd Archibald Constantine slipped past Don and knelt by her side. 'I found you some roses, Betty.' He paused. 'They are not all gone.' He had three half-open yellow buds in his hand. She looked suspiciously at them for a moment before snatching them and eagerly sniffing at the petals. The Reverend turned to Don, his face screwed up like an old wrinkled sheet. 'The rest have all disappeared.'

Don looked down at the devastated lower gardens. It was as though the wind had taken a blade and slashed open the ground itself.

'You see what is left of the lemon and orange orchard over there,' the Reverend added in a whisper. 'Even the rarabe has fallen.' His fingers seemed to grapple for the comfort of prayer.

'The house has been spared,' Don said.

'From the hurricane, yes. It skirted the building and this little hut, but the gardens below are ravaged.' He stilled his hands. 'What has happened further down, I dare not think.'

Mrs Huyton let go of the flowers. 'What has happened, what has happened,' she repeated. The words snagged inside. She looked at Don. 'Where were you?'

The Reverend took a small phial of laudanum from his pocket and administered it to her. She craned her neck and sucked at the bottle as an orphan lamb might.

'That will do,' he said and prised it from her lips. She tried to pull his hand back, but did not have the strength. Slowly she sank back in her chair. Her mouth remained slightly open, her eyes clouded over, the pupils blurring at the edges. One arm hung down the side, the other was stuck between the struts of her chair.

The Reverend said, 'The shock has been too much for her, you understand?'

'She loved her garden. It must be heartbreaking.'

'The storm was bad enough, but you see, Mr Lambodar, sometimes even greater damage is done by the misdemeanours of misguided men.' His hand shook as he corked the small bottle. 'This time Mr Huyton went too far and has paid the ultimate price.'

'He is dead?' He knew it somehow. George Huyton was dead, but Lucy was not.

'The beast inside us can be very savage, Mr Lambodar, if unleashed.' He looked pityingly at his wrecked charge.

'What happened?'

'A tragedy, Mr Lambodar. A tragedy.' The Reverend yanked his collar off. His lips were flecked with white as though each breath bubbled with increasing difficulty. 'He died last night, shot in the head and chest.'

'The rebels came here?'

'These are troubled times, Mr Lambodar.' The Reverend's round face clouded. 'Despite appearances, everyone is walking on the edge.'

'Poor Mrs Huyton,' Don said. She had slumped into a heap.

'Mrs Huyton, as you know, is a lady of considerable self-control.'

Don looked at her glazed, rocky eyes. 'And Miss Gladwell? Where is she?'

'God willing, she is safe with Madame Benoît. I sent her in a sedan this morning.'

'Should she not be here with her aunt? They are very close, are they not?' He was conscious that the priest was swiftly closing many doors.

'She needs rest. It has been a great shock for them both. All the servants here have fled, except for the boy. They always do when there is a death to be accounted for.'

'The girl Eulalie must be here. She is not at her father's house.'

'She is gone.'

'But she and her daughter would not have run away.'

'Mr Don, she is a fiery unstable creature who has sown calamity. She and her daughter could not remain here. I have seen to it that she will be safe despite this terrible misfortune. Mr Amos can rest assured. And you, Mr Don, should not concern yourself any more. These are matters for us to deal with, not you and not Mr Asoka, I should add.'

'Was he here too?'

Mr Amos was waiting for Don out on his verandah.

'Are they hurt?' he asked, scrabbling to his feet.

'They are safe,' Don said. 'Reverend Constantine is looking after them.'

'Why? What has happened to them?'

'They are safe, but there has been a shooting. Huyton is dead.'

Mr Amos covered his eyes with his hand. 'Another killing? I must speak to the Reverend. I want them back here.'

'He will call on you soon.' Don wondered what the Reverend intended to do, but for the moment his urgent need was to find Khola. Lucy must have sent a message.

When Don returned to the cottage, he found the servant sprawled on a mat outside the kitchen, oblivious of the world around him. Don prodded him awake.

'Sir?' He opened a bleary eye and moaned. 'The storm, sir, I was caught.'

'They saw you?'

'No, sir.'

'What about the letter?'

'I have it, sir.' He fumbled about for his satchel. 'I have it. I have not lost it.'

'You have a reply?' His heart leapt.

Khola screwed up his eyes. 'No, sir. I have *your* letter. That boy was not at the house when I got there and you said not to give it to anybody else.'

'Was she not there yesterday?'

He scratched his head and shifted uncomfortably. 'I don't know, sir. You said I must not be seen by the lady.'

'You went straight to Ambleside with the letter? Directly?'

'Yes, sir.' He looked away at the collapsed shed at the side. 'No, sir. I stopped by Mr Badani. He wanted –'

'Badani?'

'Sir, I just had to have some strengthening.' He emptied the satchel on the mat and shook the folds of his chequered sarong.

Don saw the letter and picked it up. The seal was unbroken. His chest hurt. But it was not too late. It is never too late. We live our lives at our own speed, he knew that. 'I should break your neck, Khola,' he said. He felt he could very easily have done so with his bare hands, but he also knew the fault lay with him as much as with the servant. He should have gone to her himself.

'Sir, I am going to fix the shed. Surangani said I must.'

Don glared at him, but there was nothing more he could say.

Back in the cottage, he found Asoka was talking with the Prince. The conversation stopped when he entered. Asoka had changed into fresh clothes; he had shaved and bathed and looked nearly his usual self, although still somewhat diminished.

'I went to Ambleside,' Don said.

'So you know.' Asoka looked at him with soft, uncertain eyes. His gaze wavered.

'Yes. Mrs Huyton is very distressed.'

'Poor soul,' the Prince said. 'She is a good woman, but the good never have it easy. Sometimes life is too short, sometimes too long.'

Don wondered whether he was thinking about Betty Huyton, or one of his own unfortunate wives who had suffered from his actions more than he had ever done himself.

Through the window behind him Don noticed a couple of chickens emerge cautiously from the battered henhouse, craning their necks this way and that as though expecting something else to come hurtling at them.

Asoka's head sank slowly as though he was falling asleep, but then he let out a sob.

'What happened to you?' Don asked.

He snuffled loudly and tried to pull himself together. 'It was my fault. The stupidity.'

'What was your fault?' An epiphany seemed unlikely.

'If I had been less sure of winning I would not have lost, and *he* would not have been so exultant. He wanted to gloat over us all. He thought he could do anything. Now everyone is ruined.'

The Prince leaned forward. 'Karma. It is our fate. We cannot escape our fate.' He coughed noisily.

'No, you are wrong,' Asoka snapped. 'It is not fate. It was a mistake, not fate. We are here because of a mistake. You lost because of a misjudgement you made about your Britishers, not because of some heavenly decree, some divine law. I lost because I was stupid.'

349

'Karma,' the Prince repeated, coughing again. A harsh, guttural cough.

'What happened?' Don asked. 'What have you done?'

Asoka began gulping in air as if he needed to puff himself up to his former dimensions, before launching out. 'At the soirée we planned a picnic down at Maharoun, by the lake. Antoine Champney, myself, Lucy, Jeanette and Mr Fry. I went to Ambleside to meet them after their breakfast yesterday. Mrs Huyton was to be our chaperone, but she said she had an urgent affair to deal with and told us we could go on our own. It was so calm in the morning, you remember? Just yesterday, but it seems like . . .' He paused. Don thought of his letter, folded, sealed. The day before yesterday he had thought he could bring the whole world into that tiny square, and yesterday he thought he had.

Asoka wrung his hands together. 'At the lake, we were all happy. The lunch was very fine: baguettes, cheese, cold meats. They like their vegetables raw, as you know, so we had green salads, grated carrots, cucumber vinaigrette and a delicious wine.' For a moment he looked inebriated by the memory, his eyes red and watery. 'We returned to Ambleside in the afternoon suspecting nothing. We were going to have a cup of tea, some titbits leftover from the soirée, and then part company, but Mr Fry took his leave and left with Jeanette in the Pottinger gig almost immediately. When Mrs Huyton returned, with the Reverend, the skies turned very dark. The wind started up. She was flustered. She said it was the hurricane and got us inside and battened down everything. There was no chance for me to get back then.'

Don tried to imagine what it would be like trapped in the

house with Lucy, the wind churning, beating at the shutters to be let in. 'You and the Reverend have been there since last night?'

Asoka nodded. 'He suggested we play whist. It seemed a good diversion from the havoc outside. Then Mr Huyton barged in, drunk and angry. He was very rude to Mrs Huyton. Something about the bloody servants' room bursting open. He said it was all her fault. He sneered at our game and made a disparaging remark about high stakes for little Ceylon vagabonds.

'The rain was thundering down by then. Antoine was edging closer to Lucy. I was furious with Huyton and his boorish manners and wanted to teach him a lesson. He is not a nice man and Mrs Huyton looked most hurt by his remarks. I challenged him to an hour in the storm – no mere bagatelle – on a cut of the cards. If I could usurp him there, cast him out of his own house, he might be chastened, I thought. I can cut a deck of cards to my advantage, as you know.' He turned over his puffy hands. 'Except this time, I did not. I lost to a jack of clubs. How it happened I do not know. George Huyton was jubilant. His win over my measly five of hearts made him cock-a-hoop. "Go to your ducking, boy," he crowed. He shoved me out and shouted for the servants. Antoine said something about bad luck, but Lucy was the one who mentioned fate. She said it was all written in the Book of Fate. Out on the verandah, it was hell. The wind screaming. Plants flapping, sand and gravel and a sea of water in the air, things crashing about behind the house. The noise was frightening and growing louder by the minute. When I looked back inside I could see George Huyton swaggering about holding forth with a bottle in his hand. The rain came in waves. I sheltered by the cushion cupboard at the end of the verandah until Huyton went upstairs. By the time I got back in, Mrs Huyton and the Reverend had left the room. Lucy and Antoine were on their own. She had been crying. He had his hand on her.'

Don closed his eyes and let Asoka turn the world upside down.

'Then we heard shots from somewhere at the top of the house. I told Antoine to wait with Lucy and ran up the main stairs. I had an awful feeling about Mrs Huyton. When I got to the landing I could see the door to the last bedroom was open. The Reverend was on his knees, pulling a bed sheet over a man lying on the floor. I saw George Huyton's face squashed down sideways. The back of his head was all bloody. The sheet was soaking up blood from another wound. Mrs Huyton was behind the door. There were two pistols on the floor. I went to her and took her by the shoulders. Only then did I notice the others. A black girl in a corner of the room, and a half-naked child.'

'And Lucy?'

'She would not wait downstairs. She came up with Antoine and that Muru boy. We were all so shocked. She took her aunt from me and led her to another room without a word. The Reverend asked Muru to bring some brandy and laudanum. Then he took the servant girl and the child down the back stairs. He said he would get them to Badani as soon as the storm was over. He said he did not wish to see anyone hanged.' Asoka paused, staring at the ground. His eyes were large and full. 'Huyton was bleeding like a pig.'

# Chapter 23

FROM THE turret window of Madame Benoît's château, Lucy could see the sheen on the surface of the sea change with every tiny movement of the earth, but hardly a frill was made in the long flat silk of gently merging colours. There was no wind in the bay; not even enough to fill a handkerchief. The hurricane had not touched this area; it looked as though it had been undisturbed for centuries. The sea air flowing into the room was pure.

'I wish no human breath could pollute it,' Lucy whispered to herself. She imagined this black rock of an island slowly becoming a sanctuary for the birds and the smallest creatures of the Ark after the Flood retreated; sea plants and anemones, starfish and sea urchins each finding a foothold at its edges. 'The island is not meant for sinners and murderers, slaves or slavers. None of us should be here.'

The green thread of the palm trees laced the water: blue, green, blue.

One solitary seabird circled high above the wooden pier, crying out. A bent wing making it dip and turn. It did not swoop to fish. It did not deviate from its circuit. It did not vary its cry. There was no mate for it in the sky. Nothing but the blue air and the consolation of its own echo.

Lucy watched it and waited for something to reveal itself like the shadow of a dream.

Madame Benoît brought a cup of tea, with a slice of lemon, notched at each end, placed on the white saucer. She had asked no questions and for that Lucy was immensely grateful. The tea was light; Lucy could barely catch its scent. She sipped it for warmth, and the sensation of moisture. She was thirsty. Where does it come from, she wondered: the tea and the thirst?

Lucy thanked her in French. Madame Benoît replied in English.

'We have some honey cake. Henri can bring you a piece.'

'I cannot eat. The tea is quite sufficient.'

'Perhaps later, then. He will not disturb you.'

She closed the door and Lucy breathed a little easier. What good is cake?

When she shut her eyes, she saw her Uncle George, spurred by his success over Asoka, blustering loudly about smacking the heathen all into line. She heard his drunken laugh swirling as he clambered up to his room. The wind wailing, and his shouting for his new housekeeper. 'He claims they are all useless, but he cannot be without them at his beck and call,' Lucy had said to Aunt Betty. Her aunt had given Lucy a hard, cold look. 'Perhaps a penchant for that runs in the family,' she had said before leaving the room. Lucy tried to push away the images, the questions, and when she did, Revd

Constantine drifted in, whispering, urging, placing his hand on her forehead, smoothing down her eyelids. He had arranged for her to leave Ambleside in the morning, as soon as he could find two bearers to carry the palanquin. No carriages could come on the broken road. He had not allowed her to speak to her aunt again. 'She needs her sleep more than you, my dear,' he had said and blessed Lucy with his fingers. 'Madame Benoît will look after you. I have already sent word to say you are on your way.'

'I do not need looking after,' she had protested. Not by her, nor by anyone else. 'I know what I want. I am not a child.'

The Reverend had bundled her towards the covered chair. 'You must go,' he had insisted. 'Go now.'

The words that pulse in her head are those of the Angel at the Gates of Light: the same words with which she had tried to comfort Asoka, when he had lost his bet.

> One hope is thine,
> 'Tis written in the Book of Fate.

To her the lines mean that there is always a chance to escape, even the fall of the cards, for malevolence may only be a cloak of temporary disguise.

A small tear forms in the raw red hollow at the corner of her eye. When it falls, it falls on a piece of paper she has placed on the writing box. She picks up a pen and dips it in the tear. The drop turns black like a moon eclipsed.

★  ★  ★

How I wish with Lalla Rookh for a Feramorz now to keep me enthralled. A Crishna of poetry 'breathing music from his very eyes'. I will be veiled then, as he would be finally unveiled. And when he is consumed by the spirit of fire, I would be a sea-flower in a garden of coral waiting for the elements to be transformed. A story within a story, a life within a page.

She can see from one end of the lagoon to the other without hindrance; the turret has been built for this purpose. There are four windows set in a semicircle and in each a serene segment of blue sea is framed like a dab of paint. The wood panelling is black, the walls white, the chair upholstered in grey velvet. She drums her fingers on the sill, but the glass does not rattle. The bubbles and imperfections trapped within it are immovable. The silver patterns engraved on these shutters are like laurel leaves entwined for ever, notes on a staff in perpetual harmony signifying unheard melodies that would never end, the prints of a hart always fleeing to permanent safety. Nothing can happen that has not happened. With her fingers she can touch the shapes but cannot render them out of their position. Ambleside was ravaged, she remembers, the gardens gutted, the placid pond pummelled and poisoned; her serenity severed and sepulchred in sods of sorrow; but here the water is calm, the palm trees and the haronga pose no threat, and she can hear the tread of normal life continuing in the rooms behind. She can hear French as well as English words, butterflies and moths. She can hear Henri talking to his mother. Somehow things appear utterly ordinary, although she knows she cannot ever live an ordinary life. She remembers the phrase, 'my solitude is sublime', and wonders if she, like her dear Endymion poet of immortal love, for ever young, would not live in this world but in a thousand other worlds of imagination, freed of time.

In the graveyard of the church in Bridleton the grass was brighter than on the common or the field. As a child she would sometimes slip in through the heavy wooden gate – lifting it clear of the dewy tufts – to read the inscriptions of longer, more beloved lives than hers. The church was old with headstones dating from medieval times. She was always most beguiled by the three grey mottled slabs, framed in furred lichen and mouldy moss, sinking askew by a waist-high wall of earth and stone pitched against the bracken, where the writing had all but worn away. She could only make out the faint indentation of the one word '*die*' as though time had corrected the engraver's tense to remind any passing soul of the temporality of a bag of bones. She would run her finger along its grooves, scraping little flakes off her skin. No one will ever know who lies under the turf there, or what they did when they breathed above. No one will ever know who lies beneath the stones of any of us, she supposes, if that is all that remains.

Henri's knock was tentative. She asked him to enter, as this was the third time he had come up the stairs. He crept in gingerly, holding a plate with a slice of dark brown cake on it.

'My mother says the honey is strengthening.' He placed the plate on the little side table.

'Perhaps you should have some then, Henri,' she replied, putting away her page of writing.

He faltered. 'I have taken part.' His small chubby fingers twisted into each other. 'Or partaken, I think. Is it a word?'

His confusion disarmed her. With a warm smile, she patted the seat next to her. 'Come, sit down. I am sorry I have not been more amenable.'

'It is understandable.'

'You are too kind, Henri. But as my aunt would say ...' She paused. 'As she used to say, there can be no excuse for rudeness. I have been thinking, and that is something I should not indulge in. It does a lady no good at all.'

'On the contrary,' Henri protested. 'Your thoughts, dear Lucy, are of paramount importance. They are indeed the very substance of your soul. Who can you be without your extraordinary thoughts?'

'They are very sombre of late, Henri. I see things a little differently.'

There was more anguish in Henri's face than she had thought he was capable of feeling. His bulging eyes seemed too moist to stay safe. She looked away and out and saw his mother amble across the front garden, carrying a basket of parsley and mint, like a woman who had lost her way early in life. Beyond her, the beach shone in white light. The blue of the sea hovered like a mirage.

'Would you care to walk out by the water? The morning air is very refreshing.' Henri made an uncertain gesture indicating the world outside.

'The sea breeze?'

'Yes, the sea breeze.'

'Perhaps on this side of the island it is beneficial.'

'Most certainly. The sea is good here.'

'I will go, Henri. I will go out and walk to the pier, but if you do not mind, I would like to go alone.'

Clearly dismayed, he nodded in a reluctant stutter. 'Of course, if it pleases you. I will find you a parasol.'

'No, Henri. No parasol. I have a hat. That is sufficient. Nothing more.'

'Is there nothing I can do for you?'

Lucy looked around the room. The bottle of medication that the Reverend had given her splintered the sunlight by the window into bands of colours. Annoyed by his presumptions, she had emptied its contents into the pot of basil that stood next to it. The spectrum slipped; in the glass she could see Henri's hand reach across the counter to meet the plain fingers of the apothecary's daughter Dorothy as she passes over a parcel.

'Perhaps, there is something, Henri.' She hesitated a moment, anxious to make some amends. 'Could you renew my medicine?'

'From the apothecary?'

'I am sorry it is a long journey.'

'Think nothing of it. I will go.'

'Dorothy, his daughter, will know what to do.'

'Will she? Should I leave now?'

'Yes, Henri. If you don't mind. Then you will be back before dark.' She ushered him to the door.

Her sense of guilt about poor Henri, about her uncle, about her aunt, about the girls she had let into Ambleside to such awful consequence, spread from the middle of her body to the furthest recesses of her mind. Slowly burning her from inside.

After he left, she went back to the writing box. The metal nib of the pen sparkled like the spur of a broken star. She pulled out a new blank page from the drawer underneath. All her books were at Ambleside, in a small bookcase by her bed, breathing in the tainted air. She felt alone in a way she had not felt before. Then the cold that comes once a summer is completely gone.

Can truth ever be conveyed by words? What is it we apprehend beyond the vessel they travel in: the thin hull of papyrus, leather, onionskin or paper on which they float, in search of a conversation of feeling – emotion and intellect – like us in our fragile unspoken bodies?

As a flower opens, so should our understanding of the beauty of the world and our place in it, if we but let it. Like the poet who waits for the right word to emerge out of the mists of sleep and addled time, we need patience and the natural idleness of an unbusy mind to discover the delicate pulse of life in our thoughts.

Our first breath fills our lungs, the second establishes life; the third begins the rhythm that fills the soul with poetry. I breathe in and out and try to remember how one rows a boat across the great divide.

I want love and I want to live free.

# Chapter 24

A T THE first cries of the birds ousted from their nests, Don slipped out. The air was cool; the sky grave with red contusions. Dawn mist wreathed the garden in long wisps of bullied cotton, soaking the dew. He completed his ablutions behind the stable and quickly dressed in his nankeen breeches and riding boots. He saddled the mare, muffling the metal bits, and led her out. He wanted to be on his way before the Prince awoke and curtailed his movements, before the road filled with goatherds and chain gangs, the clangs and clatter of a battered island coming back to life.

He used the back gate into the fields and picked his way through a wrecked banana grove.

He saw a feral cat tossed on the bridle path, then a crumpled sambar deer and two cows belly up in a clogged creek. Broken cartwheels and pieces of furniture – tables, chairs, cupboard doors – hung from the buckled branches overhead.

He dug his heels hard into the flanks of his horse.

Beyond Mont Pitou, he found an inn that had survived. A couple of dazed field hands said the Belvédère sugar factory had been completely ruined. Their families had been saved by a banyan tree. A dozen others in the village had died; all their *cazes* had collapsed. They said they had heard Port Louis had been hit worst. The two tall ships had been demasted and several boats were missing; scores of bloated bodies – sailors and slaves – had been washed ashore.

The clearest route to his destination, he was told, lay through a jungle of black wood. The storm, like a scythe, had turned at Rivière du Rempart in a sharply defined sweep. From there, they said, the journey should become easier.

When he came to the river, Don stopped again and watched the thick muddy water swirl.

As a boy he would skim flat stones across the surface of slow water and count the skips as though he were flying across the flow of time like some immortal from heaven; now he felt like the river itself, a tangle of twists and eddies, following nature's curve to its inevitable conclusion: the primeval ocean where all waters meet.

The Benoîts' small grey château, with its distinctive twin turrets, faced a wide bay stretched like blue linen between the arms of a supine sandy lover, a protector of coral, molluscs and shore-bound sea life.

The carriageway ran like a ribbon along the seafront right up to it. He tethered his horse to a post and banged the iron knocker on the door.

Madame Benoît opened it herself, concealing her surprise with a quick sharp voice. 'Monsieur Don, you are travelling on your own?'

'Madame.' He bowed handsomely. 'It is most heartening to find you safe.'

Her face eased. 'How kind –'

Before she could complete her sentence, he blurted out, 'I believe Miss Gladwell is here with you?'

An inner vexation coloured her taut cheeks. 'She is indeed here for some respite after the storm.'

He steadied himself. The spider's web in the alcove sported the remains of a dozen brown gnats. 'May I see her, please?'

Madame Benoît frowned, pinching the thin gold cross that hung from her neck. 'I am not sure that you should, monsieur.'

'I can wait, if she is resting. I would like to speak to her.'

'Resting? If only she would,' Madame Benoît exclaimed. 'She was in such a state when she arrived, and yet she will not take any proper rest. When she is in her room, she paces about, dragging her chair from side to side. Now she has sent Henri all the way to Dr Lawson, the apothecary, and taken some bread and ham and gone out to the water.' She sank back, relieved to have given vent to her frustration.

'On a boat?'

'No, Monsieur Don, the pier. I have warned her not to go out on the water alone. The barrier is broken in the middle.' A jagged line of white surf on the distant reef shielding the bay marked the barrier she meant. 'The water can be dangerous, pulling around and around.' She churned the air with her hand. 'The fishermen call it Ouragan Point.'

'I must speak to her,' he persisted. 'Where do I find the pier?'

She wavered and then gave in. 'You will see it, if you go through the coconut grove there to the beach. I will come with you.'

'Please do not trouble yourself, Madame Benoît,' he said politely but firmly. He bowed again.

A few quick strides away from the house and across the carriageway brought him to the start of the soft white sand. Sea creepers popped underfoot and whalebones cracked as he made his way between the palm trees leaning towards the blue water. Underneath the grey trunks, the long green fronds sipped at the light strains of the sea breeze; between them he could see the water was calm and bright as if lit from beneath by the innocence of the sun sucked in, day after day, since the earth began. If only our lives were as calm and sustained, he thought, coupling his hands. His boots sank deeper in the powdery white mounds until he reached the firmer, wetter, darker sand at the water's edge.

The sea at his feet was as clear as glass; its thin lips curled up the beach and flattened with barely a sound. A tiny starfish turned over and tumbled as the shallow current pushed and pulled it. Frail and unanchored, there was nothing it could do against the muted undertow. He moved forward and his footprints were quickly erased. A thin bleached finger of wood hovered over the water about fifty yards away. A small red boat bobbed by its side.

Lucy was sitting right at the end of the pier with her feet dangling. He watched her raise a hand to her eyes and squint at the waves breaking in the distance. The breeze gently lifted the brim of her pale cream hat and ruffled the lines of her white dress.

Above her a seabird circled. A lapwing called and flew over the coiled trees of the headland. She did not notice Don's approach until he was at the steps. Lucy tucked a stray lock of hair back into her hat and watched him climb up.

The pier swayed to his stride, grating in the warm salty air. When he reached her he stopped with his heels smartly together and his hands clasped in front, as though he had arrived in a foreign country.

She turned away from him and murmured, 'Is the sea not beautiful?'

He had all the words he wanted to say to her, but his throat was a column of crushed pebbles. He followed her gaze and observed the horizon, a line of ink writing their fate in sentences they could not read. After a minute or so of silence, he lowered himself stiffly and sat down beside her. The weight of his body shifted the balance of the whole wooden structure.

She pushed the small parcel of ham towards him. 'Would you like some?'

'I am afraid I don't eat it.' For a moment it seemed that was all he could say.

'Some bread?'

'No. Nothing.'

She shrugged and wrapped up the food, brushing the crumbs into the water. Her face seemed strained; her eyes subdued.

He waited in uncertainty. Slowly the morning ride, the events of the day before, and the day before that, everything that had happened in the past began to ebb away. He undid one of the tight covered buttons of his coat.

She looked back at him, head lowered sideways. A faint echo from their first encounter loosened a smile. 'By the sea you *can* be free.'

Encouraged and glad, he smiled back.

'I was told you were recuperating,' he said at last. 'I thought you would be confined indoors.'

Taking a deep breath, she leaned back and stretched out her pale ivory feet, pointing her toes so that her two limbs formed one straight line. 'If you had never seen the sea, could you imagine it? Imagine jumping in it?'

He had not seen an Englishwoman's bare feet before. They looked vulnerable, stranded in mid-air. Her toes were dainty and close together, but the nails of her big toes were corrugated across with shallow ridges, as though she had stubbed them at the edge of the sea repeatedly.

She could see he was fascinated. 'Do they offend you?'

'On the contrary, they are very fair.'

'In that case, to be fair, and in the name of equality, I think you should remove those silly French boots and compare yours to mine.' She laughed in a fresh, warm supple burst and swung her legs back and forth, shaking away all the hazy ills borne in the air.

'My boots are not French,' he protested. Then pulling them off, he dangled his brown feet not far from hers. The colour of the water seeped into hers and his as they stretched and dipped their toes in. The sun burnished the rings they made on the surface and a shoal of tiny striped fish swerved beneath their shadows stitching them seamlessly together.

They sat in silence until the flash of a passing fin caused a small sandstorm on the seabed.

She shrank back, hunching her shoulders with a shiver. 'All those rules of decorum. What is the point when they are broken so hideously?'

'Rules are not natural laws.'

She wound a thread from the lace fringe of her sleeve around her fingers. 'Our societies are prisons for my sex, and your race. Traps for conscience and grace.' She spoke the lines as though she were reciting them.

'Rules are made only by Man. You can change them.' Don found he too was repeating what he had heard before from Mr Amos. He had always urged Don to do what he thought was right, claiming that one can gain redemption through action as well as through belief.

'But you could not change my Uncle George's attitudes, could you? And look what happened.'

Don ran his finger along a dry fissure in the grey wood. A miniscule fault that would inevitably widen, cracking open the beam and wrecking the narrow little pier one day. 'I know he is dead. I have been to Ambleside.'

'I never understood him, I never did,' she complained, raising her voice. She bunched her hand and struck the wood violently with the heel of her palm. 'And I don't understand her. What was she thinking?'

'I saw your aunt yesterday, and the Reverend. And Asoka has told me what happened.' The words came fast, short, shallow.

'How is she now?'

'Somewhat troubled,' he said, unable to tear the tissue

hanging between them that compromised emotion so insufficiently to language.

A fish jumped, breaking the water and making a splash. The rest of her words tumbled out. 'She was standing with the pistols at her feet. That child clinging to the bigger black girl, with blood all over her bare back, was crying and crying.' She put a hand to her ear. 'I felt I had to take Aunt Betty away from there. She was like those zombies she talked about. I took her to her room and wiped the burnt powder from her fingers and put my arm around her but she would not speak to me.' Lucy shook her head baffled. 'The last words she said to me were down in the drawing room. Before the shots. Her voice was so cold and cruel.'

Don tried to picture the scene, fitting her words to all the others he had heard. 'The Reverend said the girls are gone.'

'I should have told her when they first came. I was so foolish to think that Uncle George would resolve it. I should have just told her. She would have sent them home straight away. None of this would have happened then. No shooting, no killing. Maybe no storm. None of this destruction.'

'It may have been a more complicated situation,' Don said. 'Your aunt might not have known what to do.'

Lucy stared at the dazzling water. 'My father loved the sea,' she said quietly. 'I have always longed to go into it. I learned to swim so that I might, but no one ever goes into the sea here. At least, none of us.'

The whole bay was empty, except for a couple of pirogues pulled up onto dry sand. Nothing interrupted the calm curve of the sea meeting the land.

'Maybe we could walk in it from the beach,' Don suggested.

She looked at him; he did not look away. The rare unerring beam of light by which one human heart steers another from beat to beat was incandescent between them. A gentle breeze blew her soft sheer dress against her legs. She held her hat to keep it from flying off.

They climbed down onto the beach and he followed her footprints, stepping from one receding memory to another. She lifted her hemline midway to her knees and splashed into the water. Broken limey shells prickled his soles but they did not seem to bother her. The sun blazed. Blinded for a moment by the bright sand and the sparkling sea, he blinked and was bereft. But then, when he blinked again, there she was in a sea-dance all her own.

Further up the beach, she drew a circle in the sand with her toe. Softly, almost to herself, she said, 'I wish we could go away. Somewhere far away.'

He tried to draw the same, bending his toe. 'Is this island not far enough away from England?'

She pulled one of the pale rose gossamer ribbons trailing from her hat and slung it around her neck. 'When I first came here, I thought this was a place from a dream.' She clung to the ends as though they were straps from a pair of wings and whirled around. When she stopped, her voice changed its tone. 'But now I can see that what has been made here amplifies all the faults and prejudices which should have been left behind. It is not right, is it?'

'For whom?'

'For us.' The strip of thin crêpe tore and came apart in her hands. She looked at the pieces nonplussed. Then her face slowly became radiant. She stepped back into the water, up to her ankles. 'We should swim all the way to Arabia, to Taprobane. Somewhere that lives in the cadence of poetry.'

His fingers felt for the poem in his breast pocket, still sealed. Unread. It would not do now, nor bear comparison to the lines of true poets she knew by heart and which so consumed her imagination. 'I can't swim,' he said in mock dejection.

'Let's take a boat then. Let's pretend we are sailing to your Ceylon.'

'Another dreamland?'

'Is it not your home?'

His face broadened in a slow smile. He clapped his chest. 'That remains always inside.'

She pressed her finger to his sternum and pushed him. 'We can become an island for a day then.' Her eyes were bright with the promise of dreams.

They strolled back to the pier and untethered the little red boat. She climbed in first, and gave him an oar. 'One each is only fair.' They started to row, in unison, each stroke marking the swing of a single pendulum bringing their tangential lives into one arc.

Small clouds sailed in a parade of swans and lions and elephants, growing like desire in a pattern to circle the globe. He regarded it a good omen: a decorated moonstone at the entrance to their own secret paradise. He wanted to tell her how time evens all disruptions. Where the shades of green and blue water mingled to turquoise, beyond the last small isles of the bay, they stopped rowing and floated free. There were only the two of them in the world.

She tipped her hat forward to cover her face down to her mouth.

'Are you hiding?' he asked, watching her lips.

'It is so hot,' she said. Her breath lifted her chest like the gentle swell rising in the sea.

He pulled in the oars. The light caught the wet blades and turned them silver. The wooden hull creaked like a fragile frame barely holding the line between heat and moisture. 'Do you not like it?'

'Everything I have wanted is within my reach,' she said and scooped up a handful of seawater. She let it drop. 'But the world is so corrupted I sometimes feel I cannot endure it.' Tilting her head, she looked directly at him. 'We can't go anywhere better, really, can we? To be free? Not your island, not mine. There is nowhere we can go, is there, that is untainted?'

'We do not need to. We are together here.' Don undid the black wiry bracelet he had on his wrist. 'Will you take this? My mother gave it to me for good luck. It's made from an elephant's hair.'

Lucy felt it. 'I think it is better that you keep it.' She seemed to him to hide a sadder unspoken thought. She closed her eyes, the veined lids barely able to curtain one world from another with their thin membranes. He watched something fill her to the brim again and light her from within. 'You are right,' she said. 'We are lucky to be here. And now, floating here, I *am* free.'

Then one of the drifting clouds veiled the sun to the hollow shape of a spent coin. She pulled off her hat and flung it into the sea.

This time when he reaches for her hands, she does not pull away; she grips his arms instead. Her lips open: soft and giving, the skin warm, pulsing, plucked by longing. She lets his tongue touch hers as though the sounds they will make are theirs and only theirs, the sea theirs and only theirs, the sky theirs and only theirs. She takes each of his fingers in turn to her lips as he caresses her chin, the clean straight line of her jaw, her warm cheek, her tender earlobe like the velvety peel of an orchid. In her mouth, her tongue, her lips, her teeth, he finds the true shape of the world; she feels it slowly dissolve. They cling close and kiss again, fusing the moment of their first engagement to the incandescence that had glowed between them on the pier. When Lucy releases herself from him, she lightly strokes her face, tracing the imprint of his lips. She searches his for her own indentations, and the space between them melds. From the hawthorn frosted lanes of her childhood to the ripened rainbows of this startling island, nothing has prepared her for the elation that engulfs her, and yet she is sure that everything from every line she has read to every songbird she has heard has been moulding her for it. Here at last, it seems to her, anything is truly possible.

The wind picks up. Small white caps dance around them. Spray mists the boat. 'I want to immerse myself in this blue sea,' she whispers, mesmerised.

'And leave me here?' He holds both her hands. 'Do you not love me?'

'I will live with you for ever.'

'Here?'

'My love is like the sun in heaven. Always there,' she replies softly.

He places her hands on his warm chest. 'But it must be kindled *here*, in this our physical world.'

She looks intently at him. 'What? Do you mean in our bodies?'

She peels off her flimsy sleeves and loosens the drawstrings of her muslin dress.

'Wait.'

'Come in with me.'

The smiling wavelets clap and swirl. She swings her legs over, tilting the boat, and plunges into the water, immediately sinking out of his sight. When she emerges again, her face is shining, her hair clinging to her neck, her dress spread like a translucent cupola. She shakes her head and a sparkling net of mineral drops fly out around her.

'Stay close,' he calls out to her, his fingers gripping the edge of the boat.

She moves with an agility he has never imagined, propelling herself in the water. Her toes curve as her feet come together; she pulls them up and scissors her legs again and again under the web of billowing clear muslin, while her arms sweep out and in at the same time. Her hair streams behind and her face has a transient light. Effortlessly, she dives under the boat. Don turns to look for her on the other side and sees with a shock that the breakers on the reef are close. The water is dark, heavy and dense. The surf spray shoots up from the half-submerged line of rocks and stony coral. The sea roars. He calls out to her, but she dips her head under a surge from the deep. When she rises to the surface again, she has been pulled closer to the dark blue swollen centre of the break in the reef. Madame Benoît's warning echoes in his

373

head. 'Come back into the boat,' he shouts, but she goes under again; this time when she comes up her young eyes are open wider than he has ever seen before. A sharp gust of sea wind tugs the lines around her mouth. She cries out but a big, thick wave pushes the boat back, while another, crossing over, pulls her away. Her arm lifts out of the water and then falls back. He puts out the oars and rows towards her, but swell after bloated swell works to separate him from her further and faster. In desperation, he throws out a rope. The sea surges; she disappears.

He plunges the oars in, digging at the water, parting it, pulling it. He throws out more ropes, cork bolsters, the keg of water, something for her to grab. He glimpses her, snatched up and trapped behind an opaque swirling wall. He shouts again but the sea only grows bigger. The boat heaves, caught in another current, and is rapidly pulled through the breach. The waves crash on both sides as it begins to spin.

He rows until the muscles in his arms burst and the rowlocks split: then a rolling wave lifts the boat and smashes it against the razor edge of the black barrier reef.

When Madame Benoît had noticed the boat drifting towards the danger point, she had used Henri's spyglass to take a closer look. She saw Don alone, much agitated, and had quickly raised the alarm, but by the time the fishing pirogues had started out the rowing boat had disappeared from sight. The fishermen had had to sail out of the bay, to the other side of the ridge, to reach the wreckage. They found Don clinging to the broken hull. He was brought back to the shore comatose; his left leg had been gashed severely below the knee. Madame Benoît had him carried back into the château where she bandaged the wound and put him in the same room where Lucy had stayed.

The seabird was still circling, dipping and dropping, but it was calling no more. All down the coast the ocean's slaps reverberated, one wave after another.

Late in the afternoon he came to, roused by the clamour of a horse outside. His body ached, but between the spasms, he saw again Lucy being swept away, the boat splintering, the ropes and oars of his rescuers. When he realised where he was, he dragged himself to the window and opened the shutter hoping that she too had somehow been brought back. But all he could see was a low red sun on the rim of the sea, bruised by its fall.

He imagined the lilies and the lotus in the Botanic Gardens, like flowers everywhere, dropping too, their heads down low; the scent of the roses and of the jessamine sinking into the earth, the leaves of the acacia and the mango, the palms in the sand, falling. The cane withering in all the fields of the island and lying forlorn.

Slowly, he became aware of a figure standing in the doorway behind him.

'What did you do to her?' Henri's thin voice floundered between anger and despair.

His mother took the small apothecary's parcel from his hand and placed it on the table by the bed. 'It was for her, but I think you will need it now, monsieur,' Madame Benoît said, hunching her shoulders.

Don stared at her and then at her son. He had not seen Henri since that day at the racecourse when Lucy had been so ruffled.

'Why did you take her?' Henri demanded. 'Why?'

The yellow tinge in the room faded as the sun was sucked into the ocean's blue sepulchre.

Don felt something turn in his stomach. At every step, he felt, he had stumbled except for that brief moment in the safe yoke of their boat, before she left it.

'I saw her palomino today.' Henri's face darkened. 'On the beach, running free.'

Don squeezed his eyes shut. *Free* was a word he could trust no more.

# Chapter 25

ALL NIGHT Don struggled in a delirium, sinking and drowning. When he finally awoke he found Madame Benoît huddled by his bedside, watching him with her little gold cross in her hands.

'The medicine would have helped you sleep more easily,' she said.

He rubbed his swollen eyes, easing the sea marks around them. The air in the room seemed turbid. 'Where is she?' he asked.

'The boys have walked the length of the beach. She is nowhere to be found.'

'I must search for her.'

'There is nothing you can do now, Monsieur Don.' She helped him sit up, plumping up the pillows on the bed and folding back the heavy linen counterpane. 'I shall change the dressing on your wound. Then we must arrange for you to be taken back to your cottage.'

'She is a swimmer, you know. She could have reached one of those small isles.'

'Henri went out with our two boats. They have searched all of them in the bay.' She spread out her hands. 'Nothing.'

'If she is not stranded, then she must have gone through into the open sea.'

Madame Benoît folded back the shutters, chastened. Then she started moving around the room picking up Lucy's beaded purse from the window seat, her ivory comb and fan from the dressing table, a pearl silk garment hanging on a chair. She put them all in a leather valise embossed with the name of a Captain Gladwell. 'The boats will go out again with the next tide and search everywhere they can. I will send word to you immediately, if there is any news. But I regret you cannot stay, Monsieur Don. Henri says he cannot have you here. I am sorry.' She stopped and gazed out of the window at the silver edge of the empty horizon. 'Perhaps she was picked up further out by some ship sailing by, on its way to India or beyond.'

At the cottage, Surangani helped Don to his room, reproving him for his injury and infirmity. She told him that the Prince had developed a fever and started to cough up blood the previous day; Asoka had sent for the Medical Officer, who had recommended Sergeant Murray take the Prince to the hospital in Grand River immediately.

Then, later in the day, Asoka had been summoned to help oversee the other Ceylonese prisoners, including Khola, as they worked to clear Port Louis of hurricane damage. 'They needed someone to do the talking, but we didn't know where you were,' she complained, while he rummaged around for his box of blue grains.

In the evening, she fussed around him, settling him; she made him a brew of Ayurvedic roots with which he tried to rinse his mouth of the sea. Afterwards, he sat by the window and waited for the stars to sprinkle heaven's hidden light on the mantle that had descended over them all.

When Mr Amos came to see him the next day, Don was propped up in the long cane armchair on the verandah. Mr Amos slowly climbed up the steps, a little out of breath.

He sat on a stool and rested his arms on his narrow knees. 'I heard you were saved from the sea, my son.'

Don stared at him blankly. 'But she was taken.'

Mr Amos could see blood seeping through the bandage on Don's leg. He touched it. 'I think I had better take a look at that.'

He unwrapped the bandage and found the gash was still open. He asked for some water and a needle and thread.

Surangani fetched her straw sewing pouch and a chipped bowl of water.

Mr Amos cleaned the wound and sutured it.

When he finished, he pulled out a wad of tobacco and offered some to his patient. Don declined. Mr Amos took a pinch for himself and chewed it in silence.

After a while, he said quietly, 'You know, my Eulalie sent me a message from the docks. She and little Nicole are on their way to Madagascar. From there they will sail to the Cape.' His eyes welled up. 'I will never see them again.'

'You might, one day. At least they are both safe.' Don tried to sound encouraging, but his voice was hollow. He pictured the sea lanes beyond the reef; the clippers, the schooners, the dhows that plied their trade across the world.

'My Eulalie should have been a princess. As a child she

dreamed of palaces and fine horses. You could feel her little heart throb like Nicole's now.' The memory seemed to unsettle him. 'The girl cannot fire a pistol. But how can the innocent prove their innocence here?' Mr Amos spat out his tobacco. 'God is the only *true* witness on this island.' He rocked from side to side, no longer the steady surgeon. 'I should have forbidden it. She did not need to step into that infernal house.' For a moment, he looked at Don as though the young man's attraction to Ambleside and its occupants were to blame, as though it had somehow infected his daughter.

'But do you know what *she* felt she needed?' Don asked his failing mentor. She would have had her own complicated wishes – far beyond a father's comprehension. He remembered how the first time he saw her he had thought she had something of Lucy's spirit in her. Ambleside and all its occupants mingled in his mind: their brief sojourns, that décolleté night of floating words, the bruised flowers, the remnants of dreams.

Mr Amos's face tightened. 'She is too young to know anything. Just like your Miss Lucy.' He paused to consider yet another young girl's plight. 'Do you think your Miss Lucy knew what she wanted? Why did she come here? To a place like this?'

Don wanted to say, *it was for me*, but instead he said, 'Maybe she wanted to escape. England was a place of the past. I suppose she wanted to find a different future.' He pressed his fingers against the broken rattan of his chair. 'Is that not what we all try to do?'

'But how can we, my son?' Mr Amos lowered his fragile head.

'Surely you of all people must believe we can? Did you not once say, "We live on the wings of the imagination"?'

'To imagine is to embrace, not to escape.' Mr Amos pulled out a handkerchief and wiped his face. 'We cannot forget those we love. They shape our lives for ever, by their absence as much as by their presence.'

In the days that followed, Don spent hour upon hour at his desk, pen in hand, pitting memory against oblivion, embracing the past. When he was not writing, he found solace in talking to Surangani, speaking to her of Lucy, of Betty Huyton, of his mother who had died – for the cook woman too had known pain and loss beyond her just allotment.

Sometimes he would stop and remember the ride out to the château, the rhythm of the saddle that had filled his whole being that morning. Then – going to Lucy – he knew he was doing what he should be doing and the conjunction of rider and the ride, on the nexus of past and future, had been a moment full of purpose.

'Now, I feel I am floating in water, but for no reason,' he said, trying to explain his disquiet to Surangani.

The next day, Sergeant Murray came with their regular crate of provisions. He said that Asoka was proving a surprising asset with the work gangs and would not be back for some time.

'How is the Prince?' Don asked, sensing a shadow behind his demeanour.

'I am afraid he is very ill and cannot be moved.'

'Can we visit him? He must need me.'

'I will arrange for you to go as soon as your leg is healed. It is too long a ride for you just yet.' Sergeant Murray looked at Don's pile of papers on the table. 'Why don't you write to him?'

Grief hung in the uneasy wind and flowed in the rivers and swirled in the swell of the sea, yet Don noticed signs of the garden reviving: the ragged bushes springing into early red flower and the barbets and green finches spilling the dew from the pearled hedges and singing louder, day by day. Beyond the gate, between the branches of the fallen shade trees, patches of broken cane blades glistened brighter. Sometimes in the damp morning mist he could envisage, as if in a quickening dream, how the sugar fields would turn to mild meadows one day, the small shabby shacks grow into solid houses, shrines become schools, seedlings flare into blossom forests.

He could see Asoka becoming a convert, helping the Reverend and Betty Huyton renovate the old salt house into a church; Jeanette and Jeremy Fry marrying at the new altar; Surangani binding Khola, hand to hand. The future back in its old grooves.

One morning, sitting at his desk, he heard the gate creak open. He steeled himself. He had received no further word about Lucy and good news, he thought, would not come in stealth. He put his pen down, and weighted the paper he was writing on with a Chennai slave bangle. He buttoned his shirt and, picking up the Prince's stick, made his way out to the front.

Don did not see him at first because he was on the floor at the far end of the verandah, his knees pulled up to his chest, his arms wrapped around them. He was biting his nails, staring at the guava tree still stripped of its leaves.

'What are you doing here, Muru?'

Without a word, Muru slowly rose to his feet. There was a quiet power in his unfolding. He was wearing new black trousers, which he smoothed down with quick anxious strokes. He seemed taller. His delicate face stronger. On the floor lay an envelope. Muru picked it up and brought it over. Don saw in his stride how the future might be improved, if one had the strength to grasp it. He remembered Lucy praising Muru's eager talents. Perhaps this island could become more than one of cane and hurricanes sooner than he had imagined. Perhaps, he could yet effect a change and shift the balance in favour of what is right, not wrong, in the world. Do something that both Lucy and Mr Amos, despite his present dejection, would approve and applaud. Don had never given Muru a book as once he had intended to do, but he could help him now. Perhaps not just Muru, but others younger than him too. He thought of Narayena's infant son. If he could teach the child to wield a pen, he might help him one day find the filament of words that forms the soul under every skin, whatever its colour, and brightens the blood to give each of us the liberty of an individual life. Perhaps he could stem the flow of sorrow, at least a little, in this vale of swift oblivion.

Muru held out the letter in his slender hand.

'Who is it from?' Don asked.

Muru's eyes were clear and brave. 'Madam says, missie write it for you.'

The thick flecked paper with brown whorls and loose watermarks was discoloured at the edges. Don's fingers trembled as he broke the brittle red seal. 'Miss Lucy?'

'I find it in missie's writing box they send back. I took it to

Madam Huyton. She cry a lot, sir. She says, it is for you. Crying she says, everything is for you. Says, you take anything you want from Ambleside. House itself, sir, is yours, if you want it. She can't stay there, no? Reverend has put her in a room in his place.' He gave a nervous laugh. 'I am the only one now in Ambleside.'

Don tried to keep calm. His heart was loud. He slipped his finger under the flap of the letter. The paper tore a little, and his skin. He unfolded the letter.

'Today I also find missie's book, sir, in her room.'

'What book?'

'Not a proper book, sir. You know, I cannot read. But I can see. Is not printed. Just many, many pages in Miss Lucy's writing, like that one. She has made it like a book.' He hesitated. 'Mr Don, is true missie went in a sailing boat? Is that how she die?'

Don looked back up at Muru. The smooth brown boyish face had puckered, his mouth dented by the last word.

'No, Muru. She was swimming in the sea.' He blinked, uncertain of what else he could tell the boy. He had a fleeting image of her on a deep-sea dhow with its triangular lateen sail full, set on a fathomless journey to the island that was theirs and only theirs. 'A sailing boat might have saved her.'

Muru's screwed up his eyes.

Don held the paper close and turned away. He did not want to read it like this, with Muru watching him. 'You wait here,' he told him and limped back to his room.

He wanted to read it alone. He wanted the words to rise through the wells and indentations, the ink marks and shadows floating on the surface of oyster light, and seep into him alone. The late-afternoon sun streamed in through the open window, yellowing the paper before him. He could feel her hand pressing on the other side. He knew his sustenance would grow from the words she was writing on his bonded heart, but he could not bear to read more than the first line for now. A line from a poem she loved on immortal love.

*A hope beyond the shadow of a dream.*

# ACKNOWLEDGEMENTS

In June 1825, Ehelopola, the former Maha Nilame (Prime Minister) of the Kandyan Kingdom of Sri Lanka was exiled to Mauritius by the British. He joined a contingent of about twenty-five other prisoners from Ceylon, and spent the last four years of his life in Pamplemousses, Mauritius. Details of his life there, and that of his interpreter, are sparse.

This novel, set a few weeks earlier, is not an account of them, although much is owed to their presence on the island. Similarities between the characters of these pages and historical figures and events are largely serendipitous.

I am indebted to a number of books and studies for helping me locate the period and place in which this novel is set, i.e. Mauritius after the abolition of the slave trade, but before the advent of indentured labour from India. A time when Britain, having gained control, was shipping convicts from other parts of the empire to work on the island. Chief among these publications are:

*Recollections of Seven Years Residence in the Mauritius, or Isle of France, By a Lady*, Mrs Bartrum, James Cawthron, London,

1830; *Paul et Virginie*, Bernardin de Saint-Pierre, 1787; *Convicts in the Indian Ocean: Transportation from South Asia to Mauritius 1815–53*, Clare Anderson, Macmillan Press, 2000; *The History of Mauritius or the Isle of France and the Neighbouring Islands from their First Discovery to the Present Time*, Charles Grant, 1801; *History of Indians in Mauritius*, K. Hazareesingh, Macmillan Education, 1975; *The Muslims of Sri Lanka under the British Rule*, M. N. K. Kamil Asad, Navrang, New Delhi, 1993; *A Biographical Sketch of Ehelepola*, Abeykoon Chandrasekera, 1934; *A Narrative of Events which have recently occurred in the island of Ceylon written by a gentleman on the spot*, William Tolfrey, London, 1815; *Indian Slaves in Mauritius 1729–1834*, Marina Carter, *Indian Historical Review* Vol XV; *The Inscrutable Englishman*, Brendan Gooneratne & Yasmine Gooneratne, Cassell, 1999; *Betwixt Isles*, R. C. Bandaranayake, Vijitha Yapa, 2006; *Journal of a residence of two years and a half in Great Britain*, Jehangeer Nowrojee & Hirjeebhoy Merwanjee, 1841; *Slavery and Anti-Slavery in Mauritius*, Anthony Barker, Macmillan, 1996; *Ayahs, Lascars and Princes*, Rozina Visram, Pluto Press, 1986; *Some Account of the State of Slavery since the British Occupation, in 1810; in refutation of anonymous charges promulgated against Government and that colony*, Charles Telfair, 1830; *Lalla Rookh*, Thomas Moore, 1817; *The Letters of John Keats*, ed. Maurice Buxton Forman, 1952; *The Collected Writings of Thomas De Quincey*, David Masson, 1890; *Samuel Taylor Coleridge, A Bondage of Opium*, Molly Lefebure, Quartet, 1977; *The Rosetta Stone and the Rebirth of Ancient Egypt*, John Ray, Profile Books, 2007; *Tri Sinhala The Last Phase, 1796–1815*, P. E. Pieris, The Colombo Apothecaries, 1939; *A Sketch of the constitution of the Kandyan kingdom*, Sir

John D'Oyly, 1832; and finally the booklet *Prisoners in Paradise*, Sheila Ward, Editions Le Printemps, 1995, which gave first wind of a story here and launched me on my way. I am especially grateful for her irresistible title, which has spawned mine.

Thanks to Bill Hamilton and Alexandra Pringle for guidance. Also Gillian Stern. The team at Bloomsbury.

Helen, as ever, for keeping the pulse and testing each word.

Thanks also to Somerset House for a Writer's Residency, the Scottish Book Trust and Isle of Jura Distillery for a Writers' Retreat, the Hills of Armitage Hill for a very special place and many other friends in Mauritius, Sri Lanka and the small isles of the world.

## A NOTE ON THE AUTHOR

Romesh Gunesekera is the author of four novels: *Reef*, which was shortlisted for both the Booker Prize and the *Guardian* Fiction Prize, *The Sandglass*, winner of the inaugural BBC Asia Award, *Heaven's Edge*, shortlisted for a Commonwealth Writers Prize and a *New York Times* Notable Book, and *The Match*. He has also written two collections of short stories: his acclaimed debut *Monkfish Moon* and a bilingual limited edition book *O Colleccionador de Especiarias*. He grew up in Sri Lanka and the Philippines and now lives in London. He first visited Mauritius in 1998 where he discovered the beginnings of this novel.

## A NOTE ON THE TYPE

The text of this book is set in Bembo. This type was first used in 1495 by the Venetian printer Aldus Manutius for Cardinal Bembo's *De Aetna*, and was cut for Manutius by Francesco Griffo. It was one of the types used by Claude Garamond (1480–1561) as a model for his Romain de L'Université, and so it was the forerunner of what became standard European type for the following two centuries. Its modern form follows the original types and was designed for Monotype in 1929.